BELLINGHAM MYSTERIES

Volume 2

NICOLE KIMBERLING

BELLINGHAM MYSTERIES

Volume 2

NICOLE KIMBERLING

Bellingham Mysteries
Volume 2
By Nicole Kimberling

Published by:
ONE BLOCK EMPIRE
an imprint of
Blind Eye Books
1141 Grant Street
Bellingham WA 98225
blindeyebooks.com

Edited by Judith David
Cover Art by Amber Whitney
unicornempire.com

This book is a work of fiction. All characters, situations and places represented are fictional. Any resemblances to actual people or events are coincidental.

First print edition July 2019
Copyright© 2019 Nicole Kimberling

Print ISBN:978-935560-60-9
Digital ISBN:978-935560-61-6

Printed in the United States

One Man's
Treasure

Chapter One

From the Turgid and Tempestuous Chronicles of the Castle at Wildcat Cove: On a stormy Friday evening in April, in the year of our Lord 2011, Evangeline Conklin (sometime found-object artist and all-time best friend of Peter Fontaine) approached the cliffside residence that Fontaine shared with artist Nick Olson.

Evangeline's long curling hair, plaited with dozens of ribbons of astonishing variety, now hung bedraggled by rain and wind and dripped water on the entry mat as she exclaimed, "Thank God you're home. I really need a favor!"

Ever willing to sacrifice for his BFF, Fontaine stepped up immediately with a cry of "How can I help?" only to be rebuffed by Evangeline's reply.

"Actually, I was hoping for Nick."

To which Nick, chivalrous to a fault, replied, "It depends on what you want."

Witnessing Nick's pragmatism in the face of a distressed damsel deflated Peter's gothic reimagining of the situation. Which was just as well because Evangeline was serious in her anxiety.

Over ten minutes of solid monologue, Evangeline's tale of woe unfolded. Stymied by the art world's insistent criticism and overall failure to buy any of her pieces, she had turned to food preparation as a means of personal financial survival. With her boyfriend, Tommy, she had won a coveted food table at the farmer's market. They sold gourmet *gyoza* with fillings both traditional and experimental, three for three dollars.

Why this lady thought she would or even should personally know all farmers in greater Whatcom County, Peter had no idea. But he'd been prepped for this eventuality as well.

"Green Goddess is a women-centered farming collective. They lease land out in Everson. A portion of their proceeds goes to the women and children's shelter here in town."

"I see." The customer—or potential customer, Peter amended, realizing that he still hadn't managed to sell her a three-dollar dumpling plate and was therefore failing in his role as front man and puller—nodded. Her gaze wandered the chalkboard menu.

"The spinach gyoza are also vegan and come with a gluten-free dipping sauce," Peter said. "They're my favorite."

"I think I'll try your banana-Nutella dessert gyoza with caramel sauce," she said sweetly.

"Do you want those steamed or deep-fried?"

"Oh, deep-fried please," the customer answered with audible excitement. "Three dollars, right?" She handed over three wooden discs—farmer's market scrip—and dropped a fourth disc into the tip jar. It plunked down insubstantially.

First transaction completed, Peter looked over his shoulder and said, "One dessert."

"One dessert," Evangeline echoed.

Evangeline dropped the gyoza into the tiny, propane deep-fryer. Beside Evangeline Nick, upon whom the job of stuffing and intricately folding the dumplings fell, continued his painstaking work.

Nick seemed to be right in his element. Many local artists and craftspeople had stalls at the market during the summer so it was, in a way, like an open-air version of Nick's former studio space, the Vitamilk Building. The Spinnin' Wimmin were there, across the corridor, selling yarn and demonstrating the lost art of spinning clumps of colored wool into thread. Luna sat at the wheel working the treadle like a hot, hipster Cinderella, attracting an odd crowd of onlookers comprised equally of curious grandmothers and young male gawkers.

Next to the Spinnin' Wimmin', Roger Hager sold ceramics. Roger was an original hippie from Berkeley who had migrated slowly north as California had succumbed to commercialism and sprawl. Nick adored Roger's style of glazing so much that he'd commissioned an entire twelve-piece dining set from the man. Peter ate off them every day and liked them, but would have been hard-pressed to explain what Nick found so special about them.

According to Evangeline, Roger spent a great deal of his time away from his stall, not wanting to tacitly pressure his customers by actually being present while they browsed. Roger had ambled over early and spent most of the morning hanging around in front of their table, chatting with Nick and nursing a mug of tea the size of a beer stein.

Beyond Roger's stall a skinny, pinched woman simply called Beekeeper Jackie sold local honey, honeycomb, and blocks of beeswax.

A couple of minutes later, Evangeline handed up a paper boat of crispy confections drizzled with caramel and doused with powdered sugar, which Peter passed along to the customer with a cheerful, "Happy Earth Day."

"Happy Earth Day to you too." Peter's first customer left, completely unscathed by any sort of sassing.

He turned back to Evangeline beaming with triumph.

Evangeline said, "I told you the candy sells. Didn't I say that, Nick?" Without looking up, Nick nodded. His pale blue eyes remained fixed on the circle of dough that he so expertly manipulated into a beautiful bite-sized purse of deliciousness. How Nick could craft such tiny origami-like structures with such big hands mystified Peter. His own efforts, made with skinnier fingers, had yielded nothing but ugly wads of sticky dough unfit for human consumption.

Peter turned away, vexed. And, as was his habit when faced with boredom or vexation or any combination of the two, returned to the calming production of internal prose.

A steady drizzle of rain slithers down from the bone-colored sky. Chill winds blow off the cold celadon waters of Bellingham Bay, rush up Cornwall Street, pause briefly to take a right at Chestnut and then gaily bluster through the miserable vendors assembled at the Bellingham farmer's market. Farmers, crafters and food vendors hunch against the cruel breeze. They stamp against the numbing cold radiating up from the parking lot pavement. The wind laughs, whips through the tables, blowing up their vinyl tablecloths and toppling carefully balanced sandwich boards. The vendors moan, jam their hands into their pockets and curse the weather.

And then some jerk starts to play a hurdy-gurdy.

Peter fixed the busker with a scowl, hoping to shatter his instrument with thesheer force of his scorn, but it didn't work. Go-Go-Gyoza sat dead in the center of the food vendors' row. To their left, three soft-voiced and exceptionally healthy looking women sold soup and highly elaborate salads with catchy and ironic names such as "Honky in the Andes" and "Red, White, Black, and Blue." On their right was a smoothie stand, which Peter found annoying for a variety of reasons. First, he disliked smoothies. Second, the proprietor had rigged up his blenders to be powered by stationary bicycles that the customers pedaled themselves. It was gimmicky, borderline pretentious, and loud, but Peter had to admit that the customers loved it.

Between the corridors of stalls and tables, buskers—organized by market administration because of a vicious pitch war that had erupted several years prior—sang, juggled, played instruments, and performed sleight-of-hand magic at thirty-foot intervals.

Hence the man playing the hurdy-gurdy six feet in front of him. The dreary drone of it matched the depressing weather too well.

Peter sidled back to his companions, whispering, "I'm not sure I can take listening to that all day."

"Don't worry. The buskers rotate through the pitches. At eleven we'll have somebody else." Evangeline kept folding her little rounds of dough.

"Neither he nor his hurdy-gurdy will survive if he's still here after eleven." Peter cracked his knuckles in the manner of Bruce Lee.

That won a smile from both Evangeline and Roger, who was still avoiding his own stall by loitering at theirs.

"At least you don't have a hangover," she said. "Speaking of hangovers, what's wrong with Jackie?"

Roger glanced across the aisle to his neighbor's table and shook his head. "One of her colonies collapsed. Then her dog finally died. I don't think she's having the best week."

As far as Peter could tell, the other one hundred and forty-six vendors at the market were all, in some way, not having the best week. Something about agriculture seemed to reward pessimism, and it showed on the faces of the farmers.

Fearsome minutes packed full of hurdy-gurdy tunes ticked by. Then the rain thinned to a drizzle before finally subsiding. Peter sold three orders of spinach gyoza. Roger returned briefly to his own stall to get a stool that he situated near Nick. They chatted about the local ceramics scene. The sun broke through the blanket of clouds just as the hurdy-gurdy man packed up his instrument and moved down to the next pitch.

He was replaced by a man who immediately launched into an a cappella version of "Amazing Grace." Over at the Spinnin' Wimmin stall Luna stopped her treadle and snipped the thread. Peter turned his attention back to the busker belting out his hymn.

"I'm not sure this is better," Peter remarked.

Nick smirked. "I dare you to ask him if he knows 'Somewhere Over the Rainbow.'"

"I was thinking more of 'Mack the Knife,'" Peter said. Roger began to chuckle, then to laugh, and then to cough, as seemed to happen to so many older guys. Acid reflux, that's what Peter's dad always told him. He glanced away, not wanting to embarrass Roger by calling attention to it.

But Roger kept coughing. He doubled over, hands on his knees, face reddening.

Evangeline abandoned her work and went to him. "Are you okay?"

Roger shook his head, seemingly unable to catch his breath.

Nick shouldered his way past Peter. "Roger? Can you breathe?"

Roger nodded his head, then suddenly vomited at Nick's feet. Peter heard a loud exclamation of, "My word!" from one of the fit women next door. Beekeeper Jackie rushed across the aisle, holding onto her sunhat to keep it from blowing away. "Is he all right?"

"Call an ambulance!" Nick commanded.

"I'm already on it." Peter pressed his phone to his ear. As he talked to the dispatcher, a crowd gathered around Roger. Farmer's market security forced their way through only to be repelled by Nick, who had plainly decided the situation was his to control. At last, uniformed EMTs arrived. Nick relinquished Roger's shuddering form to them.

The drama complete, the crowd began to disperse. Custodians arrived with a mop bucket and in minutes erased the evidence of Roger's illness. Invigorated by sunshine, people poured into the market so that soon the wide avenues between stalls were thick with people.

Nick washed his hands and then stood regarding Roger's now unattended pottery stall.

"Should one of us go over there?" Peter asked. He had no idea what the etiquette was in a situation like this.

"It looks like someone from market administration is taking care of it," Evangeline said.

Then a guy who'd plainly just arrived at the market ordered gyoza. He ordered it as though nothing had just happened, which from his perspective was accurate.

For a moment, Peter didn't know what to do. They'd just seen an old guy of their acquaintance collapse. He could be dead for all they knew. The reporter in him wanted to chase after that ambulance and find out the rest of the story. But that wasn't what he was supposed to be doing today.

Nick had already resumed his position at the Go-Go-Gyoza prep table with a concerned dedication that no mere snack merited. But that's what Nick was like—reliably calm and diligent. He kept high standards, always. It's why Evangeline had wanted him in the first place. Well, two can have high standards, Peter thought. Oblivious to both Peter's internal monologue and recent events, the customer said, "Beautiful weather for Earth Day, isn't it?"

Peter put on his brightest smile and said, "It sure is."

By the time Spunky the Squirrel got kidnapped two hours later, Roger Hager was far from Peter's mind.

Chapter Two

In addition to being the city's most alternative, free week-ly paper, *The Bellinghamster*, usually referred to as just the *Hamster*, supplied Peter Fontaine with most of his income. Though nowadays he often freelanced for national markets, he felt for Bellingham a strange devotion. He had decided that he could—nay—*would* make a lifelong project of chronicling the fundamental strangeness in the City of Subdued Excitement.

He would make a portrait of a particular city in a particular time. He would be the first to immortalize a Pacific Northwest town for something other than fictitious vampiric habitation, grunge, or software. His work would make a great monument of drizzle-fed conifers and ferns and moss. It would chronicle whole weeks of winter fog.

It would put a hoodie on the back of every right-thinking human being as well as some smaller, less cold-hardy dogs. Be-cause of his lofty artistic goal, Peter felt justified engaging in a level of nosiness that would have been otherwise indefensible in polite society. He felt that everything that transpired within the Bellingham city limits—in addition to greater Whatcom county—could plausibly be his business.

It was that freedom from shame that allowed him to rise on Sunday morning and immediately phone St. Joseph's Hospital with the purpose of trying to pry details about Roger Hager's condition from the legally sealed lips of the receptionist.

This morning she surprised him by saying, "I'm sorry. Roger Hager passed away yesterday."

"He's dead?" Peter glanced toward the bathroom door. He could hear the shower running. Hager hadn't really been Nick's close friend, but Nick's emotional reactions could be surprisingly intense.

"Yes, Mr. Hager passed last night."

"Can you tell me what he died of?" Peter asked.

"I'm sorry, no."

"It's just that I was there with him at the farmer's market when it happened—" Peter prepared to launch into a sympathy-inducing speech, but the receptionist was a professional and cut him short.

"I'm afraid all I can tell you is that Mr. Hager's funeral arrangements are being handled through Lopkin-Mole," the receptionist said. "Do you need their number?"

Peter said he did not, thanked her, and ended the call. After he'd completed another brief interview with Lopkin-Mole, he headed for the kitchen to make breakfast.

He figured that if he had to tell Nick that his art friend was dead, he might as well do it over a cup of coffee.

The kitchen of their home was a large, open space whose windows faced out over the cliffside patio. Peter hadn't designed it—the whole house had been laid out by Nick's former lover, Walter—but of all the rooms in their house, it was the only one he hadn't redecorated. And why would he? The kitchen was a masculine dream of granite and brushed steel with high-end appliances that, except for the refrigerator, Peter rarely used. The last time he'd been required to ignite the convection oven, for example, he'd had to consult the Internet for instructions.

But his limited cooking skills thankfully included the ability to make coffee and toast, and so that's what he did. As he laid out a couple of small, round plates he found himself really looking at them for the first time.

Since they were handmade, each plate was different, though they clearly comprised a matching set. They were heavy stoneware covered in a glossy rust-colored glaze. The interesting things about them were the circular blooms of steel-gray crystals that interrupted the rich oxide red. Sometimes the crystals formed an arc around the edge. Other times they sat in the center as though they were the main course.

Laid out on the granite slab that served as their counter/ bar/breakfast nook, the plates seemed like organic extensions of the rock.

Peter felt suddenly sad that he'd never bothered to mindfully observe the plates before Roger was dead. He would have liked to compliment him on them.

When Nick emerged from the shower, towel around his neck and clad in the ragged old jeans he painted in, Peter had still not managed to get toast onto the plate.

He slid a couple of slices into their ridiculously complex toaster, depressed the lever and went to fish a couple of cartons of yogurt from the refrigerator.

Nick poured himself a cup of coffee, sat down, and said, "I suppose Roger's passed away?"

Peter handed Nick one carton of locally produced touch-of-honey cream-top plain, and said, "How could you tell?"

"I couldn't think of any other reason you'd be looking at a plate that hard." Nick peeled the foil from the top of his yogurt, then paused, running a finger along the rim of his empty plate. "Roger really was a master of crystalline glaze technique."

"Is it difficult?"

"Extremely. Hardly any clay is mixed into the glaze. That's what allows the crystals to form."

"So he had no idea where the crystals would end up when he fired these?"

"Yes and no," Nick said. "He knew the crystals would appear where the crystalline glaze had been laid—that's everything that isn't the rust colored glaze—but he didn't know how they would look. There is such a thing as an ugly crystal, you know."

"I guess so." Peter went to retrieve the toast and divided it between Nick and himself.

"The hard part about it is that to create really dynamic crystal formations you've got to get the kiln up to cone ten really fast then bring it back down to a lower temperature for several hours. It requires a lot of experimentation and patience to get it right. In the olden days when kilns didn't have digital thermometers or accurate controls, the crystals were tiny and often seen as a flaw."

Nick reached for the butter while Peter unscrewed the lid of the jam. It was raspberry-rhubarb. The previous day he'd traded another market vendor a couple of orders of gyoza for it.

Gigi, their diminutive black cat, chose that moment to leap up onto Nick's lap, seeking a handout. Nick obliged, letting her lick the yogurt off his discarded foil lid.

Peter found watching her do this simultaneously darling and disgusting. The jam was good though, which brought his thoughts back to the market, to Roger's death and pottery in general.

"Somehow I don't think a career as an olden days ceramic artist would have suited me," Peter remarked.

"Not at all," Nick replied. He spooned a tiny bit more yogurt out for the cat, who lapped it up greedily.

It irked Peter somewhat that the cat he had rescued should have chosen Nick as her favorite. Then again, she sat with him all day in the studio, perched on Nick's big shoulder as if she were a parrot.

Also, Nick constantly fed her table scraps, which Peter was unwilling to do.

Nick munched his toast for a few moments, then asked, "So I suppose you know when the funeral is scheduled."

"No funeral, but there's a memorial service being held the day after tomorrow at Fired-Up Pottery Collective in Fairhaven. It starts at two," Peter said. "Apparently Roger had a registered domestic partner named Margaret Bear. She's the one overseeing all his arrangements."

"I've never met her, but Roger talked about her often. Did you find out what he died of, by the way?"

Peter found it charming that Nick would immediately (and accurately) assume that he had tried to find out Roger's cause of death.

"The hospital wouldn't tell me," Peter said. "But the kid at the funeral home said he thought it was food poisoning."

"Food poisoning?" Nick seemed thoughtful, as if he were searching his mind for the symptoms of all known food poisoning and comparing them to the ones Roger presented one by one.

"I thought it sounded strange too," Peter said.

"I'd like to go to Roger's service. Do you want to come with me?"

"Who *doesn't* want to go to a funeral?" Peter quipped. Then, at Nick's slightly reproachful look. he took a more respectful tone. "I mean, sure, of course I'll go."

"Thank you," Nick said, nodding. "It might make for a good article anyway."

"You don't happen to have a photo of Margaret Bear, do you?"

"Probably," Nick said. "We've been at a lot of the same events over the years. Why?"

"I just like to know who the bereaved is when I'm going to a funeral. It helps me keep my foot out of my mouth," Peter said, then, because he could not resist he added, "which is sometimes really difficult. You know how I love the taste of shoe leather."

For a moment, Nick appeared to be on the verge of acknowledging Peter's sleazy innuendo, then he seemed to reconsider rewarding bad behavior and merely said, "I'll see what I've got on my laptop and email you if I find a recent image."

Peter finished his coffee and rinsed the few dishes clean, geared up and started on his commute into town. Peter preferred to cycle. Though Nick, seeing him pedaling along the narrow, winding road into town always seemed always to worry.

This morning the air was crisp and fresh and perfect for cardio-vascular musculoskeletal exertion. He rolled up his right pant leg and headed out onto the blacktop. Cedars towered on either side of the road. Dappled morning light filtered through their branches, mottling the road with patches of sun and shadow. Birds sang.

The rushing air felt good on his face and in his lungs. He leaned heavily into the hairpin turns, delighting in the speed.

He might be on the wrong side of thirty now, but he could still go fast. So invigorated was he by his ride, that he decided to swing by the Bellingham Police Department and see what they had to say about Roger's death. Specifically, he wondered if they knew where and what Roger had eaten that morning. Had he given himself food poisoning, or had someone else done it? A restaurant perhaps? Not that Peter enjoyed destroying the reputations of Bellingham's eateries, but if one of them had killed a guy, he felt the public had the right to know.

Usually this newshound-on-the-case strategy yielded unprintably dull results or "no comment" statements. This morning was different.

This morning, he was shown to the desk of one Detective Larry Mills, homicide.

Not that it said that anywhere on Mills's desk. Peter just happened to know from reporting on previous crimes, that in between investigating the staggering level of property crime, Mills handled most of the city's extremely infrequent homicide cases.

And what did that mean? Could it be that the so-called food poisoning had been deliberate? His reporter senses tingled. Mills was stout, red-faced and thick-fingered. He wore a sport jacket that had probably fit him better in 1987 and had a pair of reading glasses perched atop his bald head.

"Mr. Fontaine." Mills glanced down at a piece of paper in his hand. "Would that be Mr. Peter Fontaine, who resides at 22975 Chuckanut Drive?"

"Yes, sir." It unnerved Peter to think that Mills had been reading a piece of paper with his name and address on it. "I'm a reporter with *The Bellinghamster*. I was wondering if the police were ready to release any information about Roger Hager's death. I was there when he collapsed."

"So your interest in this is…what? Personal?"

"No, I had heard the cause of death was food poisoning, so I wanted to know if you knew where he'd eaten," Peter said. He gave his most callous smile and said, "This kind of thing sells papers, you know."

"Insofar as I know, *The Bellinghamster* is free," Mills remarked dryly.

"Well, it sells ad space," Peter amended. "It amounts to the same thing."

Over Mills's shoulder he could see his two favorite Bellingham patrol cops, Officers Patton and Clarkson, walking together. The pair was always immediately recognizable. The combination of Patton's dykey haircut and Clarkson's cartoonishly retro moustache was easy to pick out, even from several yards away. Peter wondered if they were just arriving or just leaving. Patton caught Peter's eye for a moment, and then she turned back to her conversation.

"I'm afraid I don't have any information for you at this time," Mills was saying. "But it is convenient that you've come by. You were present when Hager collapsed?"

"Yes. Roger started choking, and Nick went to administer first aid."

"That is Nick Olson, who also resides at 22975 Chuckanut Drive?" Mills asked.

"Yes, he's my boyfriend," Peter answered. Usually he adhered to the adage that one should never volunteer more information to cops than required. But since he knew Mills's next question would be *What is your relationship with Mr. Olson?* he thought he should just expedite the process. Even if in doing so he was forced to use a term so inappropriately juvenile as *boyfriend* to describe his forty-two-year-old lover of three years.

Mills didn't bat en eye, which meant that either he'd already known Nick and he were gay or Peter somehow looked irrefutably queer today. He didn't think that having one pant leg rolled up qualified as homosexual-level fashion-forward attire, but what did he know? He wasn't that kind of reporter.

Mills blandly asked him to recount his version of events, which he did trying to be as boring as possible, as he knew that cops disliked dramatic story embellishments or any demonstration of flair. At the end of it, Mills inquired about Nick's whereabouts this afternoon, which Peter provided.

Finally, Mills said, "I think that just about covers it."

All through the conversation, Peter had resisted the urge to ask the obvious question: why was Mills asking him questions about Roger's death at all? Upon being dismissed, though, he went ahead and asked.

"Does your involvement mean that there is reason to think that Roger Hager's death is somehow suspicious?"

Mills smiled slightly and said, "I'm afraid I have no comment at this time."

When he arrived at the *Hamster* office, Peter found Officer Erica Patton leaning against his desk, waiting for him. At somewhere near forty, Patton was Bellingham's oldest policewoman. She had short, dark hair, thick arms and no real sense of humor as far as Peter could tell. But because of frequent interactions between them, Peter had grown quite comfortable with her over the years.

"Officer Patton, you should have called," Peter said. "If I'd known you'd be waiting here, I would have brought you a mocha."

Patton flashed a tight smile and said, "Thank you, Mr. Fontaine, but I've already had my quad shot today. I'm good."

"To what do I owe the pleasure?" Peter glanced over at the desk of his editor, Doug. But Doug was nowhere to be seen. In fact, the entire office was completely empty which was unusual for ten thirty in the morning. His coworkers had cleared out, no doubt, once the law arrived. Peter wondered briefly if Patton ever felt left out being a cop—if it ever hurt her feelings that people fled when she approached.

"I thought I'd deliver this personally." Patton handed him a sheet of paper.

"Why thank you. I didn't know you cared." Peter glued himself to the paper. It turned out to be a press release about Roger Hager's death. But why had Patton brought it to him personally? Excitement grew within him. Could this finally be an exclusive tip? He'd always known his relentless friendliness to cops would pay off someday. "So Roger Hager's death has been declared a homicide?

"That is correct. The medical examiner has concluded he was poisoned," she said. She took a notebook and pen from her pocket. "I understand that you were present when Hager collapsed?"

Peter stopped feeling sorry for her. Of course she hadn't come to give him a scoop. That would be an act of camaraderie, and they were not comrades.

But they weren't exactly enemies either.

"I just went over this with Detective Mills," Peter said.

"Humor me," Patton replied.

Patton questioned him rigorously, but her demeanor seemed different than it had during previous investigations. She'd either spoken with or questioned him a number of times, and although her eyes were still hard as lonsdaleite, her tone was much more conversational than on any occasion that Peter could recall.

He told her about the morning and about Roger's collapse. He described Nick's response and what he could remember about the onlookers.

Finally she asked, "So, you won't be returning to the farmer's market?"

"Nick and I were only helping Evangeline out for the day," Peter said.

"That's too bad," Patton said. "You're very observant. You could be a real asset to the investigation."

Peter took a moment to digest this statement and also to mentally edit his next words before they emerged from his lips.

"Are you suggesting that I become an informant?"

"No," Patton said. "I wasn't planning to offer you cash."

"But you were planning to offer me something, weren't you?" Suddenly Peter wondered if the empty office was completely an accident.

"I might have been willing to offer you certain relevant information if you would keep your ears open."

"What information might that have been?" Peter couldn't stop himself from leaning forward. Information was not only his stock and trade, but his crack cocaine as well.

"The agent used to poison Mr. Hager, for a start."

"Why would you approach me?"

"The farmer's market is a very closed and very tight community. Uniformed officers asking questions will only result in a closing of ranks among the vendors."

"Whereas a nosy reporter asking questions will result in them being unusually forthcoming?" Peter raised a skeptical brow at her.

"Spouting off to a nosy reporter results in free advertising, and they know it."

Patton glanced sharply up as the *Hamster* office's door opened.

Doug stood in the doorway for one second, then said, "Dammit, left something in the car!" and skedaddled back down the stairs.

"That was pathetic," Peter murmured.

This, at least, drew a laugh from Patton. She said, "So do we have a deal or not?"

"I don't even know if I can get Evangeline to let me help at the gyoza stand again. She's worried I'll sass the customers," Peter said. "Do I seem sassy to you?"

Patton looked at him as though he were hopelessly clueless. Finally she said, "I wasn't at the scene, so I couldn't comment on your customer-service skills. All I'm asking is that you try to find out if anyone there remembers anything. And that you let me know what you find out before you go to press."

Inside Peter an epic battle ensued. On the one hand, he did not, under any circumstance, want to become or be known as a police snitch. On the other hand, Patton was offering him a scoop. Maybe she'd offer more in the future if he played ball now.

And were they really working at cross-purposes? Now that he knew that Roger Hager had been murdered, didn't he want the killer to be discovered?

"Okay," Peter said. "I'm assuming that whatever killed Roger is going to be something you think the people at the farmer's market have access to. What is it? Destroying angel mushroom?"

"Are you going to share your information or not, Mr. Fontaine?" She leveled her cop gaze at him. Peter felt the cold of outer space reaching down to freeze him solid.

"Yes, fine, I'll let you know anything I discover. What was it?"

"What were they," Patton corrected.

"There was more than one?" What was Roger—some kind of Rasputin-like superhuman?

"Because his symptoms suggested poisoning, Hager's stomach contents were analyzed when he was brought to the hospital. The first of the toxic agents was grayanotoxin. It comes from the *Azalea pontica* which you might know as the rhododendron. That was ingested Saturday morning," Patton said. "But the other toxin derived from *Zigadenus species*—commonly known as death camus—was eaten by the victim on Friday night."

"I've never heard of death camus," Peter admitted.

"Look it up. That's what I did."

"Do you know how the poison was delivered?"

"The death camus was easy. It was present in his stomach. Chewed, but recognizable," Patton said. "The origin of grayanotoxin is a special kind of honey used as a homeopathic erectile dysfunction remedy. It's imported from Turkey. A jar was found in Roger's booth at the farmer's market."

"And that's all?"

"That's all."

Peter paused for a long moment, regarding Patton before saying, "I don't want to seem ungrateful, but why are you asking me to help you, really?"

"For exactly the reason I said. Poisonings are very problematic. First of all, they're hardly ever detected. When they are, they're difficult to prosecute."

"Okay, then, what made you decide that Roger's death was an intentional poisoning rather than accidental?" Peter asked.

"Intuition," she said.

"You've got to be kidding."

"I wish I was." With that she tipped her hat and headed out the door.

There ended the longest sustained display of personality that Peter had ever encountered in any police officer, especially Patton, who had previously evaded all Peter's overtures of chumminess. He considered phoning Nick and telling him all about it, but he held back. He didn't know how the other man would react to the news that Peter had decided to become an unpaid informant, but he could guess that displeasure would rank high in the list of Nick's probable emotional responses.

Instead he phoned Evangeline and wheedled his way into the Go-Go-Gyoza stall by uttering the magic words, "I'll work for free."

He was then free to research. He started with death camus.

It turned out to be an important native plant whose existence Peter had missed on account of having no interest whatsoever in gardening. Death camus was the poisonous cousin of *Camassia quamash*, a starchy staple food of the regional indigenous tribes.

It was a member of the lily family that displayed small white flowers when blooming.

When dug up, it resembled an onion bulb.

Although there was a Lummi reservation right across the bay, Peter didn't give much credit to the idea that some member of the tribe had ferried across the water to poison Roger with a highly symbolic food. Not that he could rule it out, of course, but since no fewer than five stalls at the farmer's market sold native plants, he thought he'd devote his research time to those individuals. By the time his editor came back, Peter had written a memorial for Roger in addition to penning a three-hundred-word filler piece in which he encouraged people to celebrate Earth Day all year round by landscaping with sustainable native bulbs.

Regardless of Peter's unusual early morning efficiency, Doug still wanted to know why the cops had been at the *Hamster* offices. He eyed Peter warily as Peter explained that it had been routine questioning.

"Officer Patton just wanted to talk to me because I have good powers of observation," Peter said.

"Good powers of observation, my ass. She's buttering you up. You know you can't trust cops, right?" Doug asked this while reaching into his pocket to retrieve a small, well-used ceramic pipe.

"I don't trust them or distrust them any more than I trust or distrust the mayor." Peter spoke blithely, waving his hand in a floating motion. He prayed Doug would take the bait and begin to rant about local politics.

"Now the mayor's a guy nobody should ever trust." Doug loaded the small bowl of his pipe with marijuana—probably his own homegrown—and fished a lighter from his pocket. He took a long pull at the pipe, then offered it to Peter, who demurred. Pot made him paranoid.

"I heard the city council—"

"Don't try to sideline me by talking about those yahoos." Doug squeaked his words out without actually having to exhale. "What else did the cop want?"

"Nothing." Peter kept his tone firm.

Doug finally let his breath out.

"You know, you're not that good a liar," he remarked.

Peter sighed and sagged into the chair in front of Doug's desk. If they were going to have this conversation, it had to happen now before anyone came into the office.

"She wanted to trade me an exclusive scoop for information."

"What's the scoop?"

"Exact poison used to kill Roger Hager."

"And what information did you trade?" Doug's eyes flicked down to the pipe in his hand. Suddenly Peter realized that Doug, in his unrelenting suspicion, always thought everything was a conspiracy to shut down the *Hamster*.

"Nothing yet," Peter said. "I told her I'd let her know anything relevant to the murder that I uncovered while snooping around the farmer's market next Saturday."

"Did she ask about me?"

"Not at all."

Doug relaxed back into his chair. Finally he said, "I don't like you getting cozy with the cops."

"But you like the scoop, right?"

"Yeah, I do like that." Doug screwed the lid onto his pipe and stashed it back in his pocket. "Just promise me you won't make the mistake of thinking that cop is your friend."

Peter placed his hand over his heart. "I swear, Doug, I won't forget my allegiance lies in fairly reporting the truth."

Doug looked at him levelly, then said, "Yeah, that's what worries me about you sometimes."

Chapter Three

Fashion experts are remarkably lacking in printed, or even digital, opinion about what one should wear to a Pacific Northwest hippie funeral. On the one hand, there is black, which is understood to be the appropriate garment color for funerals. It also provides the funeral-goer with a reason to break out the fine attire one normally reserves for award ceremonies and formal weddings. Sporting a black suit, though, has broad implications of being aligned with authority, power and The Man, which could insult the memory of the deceased as well as drawing acrimonious looks from survivors.

An additional concern surfaces when one discovers the purpose of the memorial is to bake a deceased and cremated artist into a series of clay vessels that the mourners are encouraged to take home with them.

Needless to say, when this reporter discovered the planned activity, he traded his Dolce & Gabbana for Carhartt.

Peter put his mental narration on hold the moment he and Nick pulled up to the curb alongside Fired-Up Pottery Collective.

The building differed from the rest of the small, historic Fairhaven neighborhood in that it was the only one of the early twentieth-century brick facades to have been painted hunter orange. The vibrant color stood out from the sedate, historically-influenced towers of newly built condos like a jester's cap in an annual shareholder's meeting.

The lettering of the sign had been assembled, mosaic-style, from broken tiles. Like the best works of architectural design, the exterior of Fired-Up perfectly transmitted what was inside—in this case, hippie artists who had taken up residence long before the Fairhaven neighborhood's adoption of bourgeois design standards.

Unlovely European cars, mostly old Volvos or Volkswagens, crowded the narrow streets and jammed the alley. From these beater chariots emerged gray-haired women in, loose shimmery dresses. Denim-clad older gentlemen accompanied them, the scraggly ponytails dangling down their backs serving as badges of authenticity.

"It's really interesting," Peter said.

"What is?" Nick asked.

"That any one of these people walking by could be a cold-blooded murderer."

"Do you mean of Roger, or just a murderer in general?" Nick asked.

"I was thinking of Roger, but I guess you've got a point. There are plenty of unsolved crimes out there. You know, I never have asked, but I guess you might have solved murders while you were in the military intelligence, right?" Peter asked this offhandedly

Nick's mouth curled up at the edges slightly. His eyes sparkled faintly, which was what happened to him when he suppressed what would have been robust laughter.

Finally, Nick said, "I was a linguist."

"So you didn't solve any crimes?"

"Not until I met you," Nick said. His degree of mirth had decreased sharply. "Anyway, we shouldn't keep sitting out here in the car."

"Yeah, people will think we have weed and start knocking on the windows, hitting us up for a toke to take the edge off the rheumatism."

Inside Fired-Up, students—Roger's students as it turned out—were already mixing their teacher's ashes with clay.

Though most of the front of the studio had been cleared, a small table had been set up to display the memorabilia of Roger's life. There was a framed newspaper clipping, a few beautiful vases, and a recent photograph of Roger and Margaret Bear standing among long rows of massive cabbages on some sort of farm.

Nicole Kimberling

Margaret herself sat in a folding chair near the table, accepting the condolences from Roger's friends. A portable oxygen tank rested on the floor next to her. The thin tubing of a nasal cannula rose up from that, delivering supplemental oxygen. Margaret looked older than her sixty-seven years and seemed as pale and fragile as a cracked china cup.

Nick introduced Peter to Margaret and conveyed their condolences. Then Nick went immediately to join the students who worked the clay, saying, "I'm not a skilled potter by any means but I can do this part and leave the craft to you," leaving Peter to fend for himself socially, which suited him fine as he had nosy questions to ask.

Most of the mourners were older people who appeared to be either in the art or craft industries. But a small group caught Peter's eye. Standing together, drinking beer from plastic cups were three farmers from the market. And one of them, Arthur Newman was on Peter's list of native plant growers. Peter recognized Newman from extensive photographs on his farm Web site. Jenn Jones, the co-owner of Green Goddess Farm, stood next to him as well as a third man whose name Peter did not recall.

The question was, how to approach them. He couldn't directly play the reporter card at a funeral, no matter how informal and nontraditional. Asking questions about Roger's death would focus attention too much on death itself in a gathering that had been plainly meant to be more of a celebration of his life.

So he did the casual thing. He went to the keg and poured himself a beer. Then he ambled past the farmers and simply stood near them. He didn't face them. Instead, he just perused some pottery and waited for the right moment to interject himself into their conversation. Their talk did not initially delight him. They spoke at some length about how they would ship their new tractor from Spokane. When the conversation moved to some random guy's stash of homemade applejack, Peter was almost interested. But the production of homebrew was neither illegal nor compelling when overheard in textbook-level detail.

Just as he was beginning to despair, Jenn said, "I'm really surprised Margaret's daughter showed up."

Arthur replied, "She's the good one of the four. I'm not surprised that she's here supporting her mom."

"I guess so," Jenn said. "I just think it's a little hypocritical, that's all. She never had anything good to say about him when he was alive."

The third farmer said, "You didn't have a lot of good to say about Roger either recently, and you're here."

"He's got a point," Arthur said.

"That's different." Jenn's distress sounded in her voice. "I thought he didn't know how to run a farm, which is true. She called him a mooch and a sponger and threw a drink in his face."

"Did she?" the third farmer said. "It's probably better that she didn't drink it anyway, if that's the kind of drunk she is. Speaking of drinks, I think we should get a refill while there's still something left in the keg."

Arthur and the other man went to get refills, which left Jenn on her own. Peter seized that window of opportunity to introduce himself. Jenn asked him if he was there on his own and Peter said that he wasn't.

He pointed to Nick. "I'm with that big guy."

At the sight of Nick, recognition lit in her eyes.

"You two were the ones who were talking to Roger last week when it happened," Jenn said. "You're working for Evangeline, right? Go-Go-Gyoza."

"We just help out from time to time," Peter clarified.

"I love that banana-Nutella thing she makes."

"So how did you know Roger?"

"Through Margaret. I lease farmland from her." Jenn gazed over at Margaret. "I think she's being incredibly brave, considering."

"Is she ill?" Peter couldn't think of a more casual way to ask about the oxygen tank.

"She's been diagnosed with colon cancer. She doesn't have very long according to the doctor." Peter heard Jenn's voice crack and saw her eyes redden. "It's so sad that she has to deal with this at the end of her life."

Peter gave her a sympathetic nod.

Jenn sniffed loudly and said, "I guess you just never know when your number is up."

Arthur and the other man, who turned out to be named Skuter, rejoined them, and conversation circled gently around the topic of farmer's market food vendors. Peter tried to introduce the topic of Roger, via talking about his own dishes, but the farmers didn't seem to be able to run with it.

As he surveyed the pastel-draped landscape of assembled sexagenarians, he did catch sight of Margaret again. She was in Roger's studio-proper, a space approximately ten by ten off the main gallery. The studio contained a large, clay-covered kick wheel as well as a wide variety of wooden tools, jars full of glaze and bits of glazed pottery. The studio door hung open but had been blocked with a DO NOT ENTER sign hung from a rope. Margaret was inside on a stepladder in front of a set of high, clay-dust coated shelves, carefully pushing a couple of very attractive vases back behind a couple of unglazed forms.

It was an odd and awkward thing to be doing while toting a portable oxygen tank.

Peter wondered why she'd felt compelled to move those pieces right that moment. Did she think they'd be stolen? Who pinched artwork at a funeral?

Margaret descended the ladder and returned to the main room. She raised one very delicate hand and a hush began to emanate from around her as the crowd fell respectfully silent.

She began to speak. Her voice quavered slightly, but she held her head high as she addressed them. She thanked them all for coming, and told them how Roger would have loved to see them in all their finery. She encouraged them to have a last look at his pieces before they went to auction and to remember Roger's amazing talent.

Polite applause ensued.

Margaret continued, "When I first started seeing Roger, my friends and family thought I had gone senile early. They wondered what someone like me, who had been a banker for forty years, could see in this long-haired old draft dodger who had never held an honest job for more than a couple of days in his whole life. And I have to say that some days I wondered what the attraction was myself." She paused while a sad but genuine chuckle rolled over the assembly. Then she continued. "But then I found the answer. I didn't love him because of anything he did or didn't do. I didn't love him for his artistic accomplishments or his charm. I loved him simply for being Roger. And as his friends, I think you know what I mean. I wish he and I had had more time together on this Earth, but I suppose I'll be seeing him soon enough. So please let's raise our glasses for Roger."

Peter lifted his plastic cup along with the rest of them. After the eulogy, people began to drift away. Soon only Margaret, Margaret's daughter, and the pottery students were left, finishing the simple clay vases and setting them on shelves to dry. The sun was setting.

It was time to go.

Chapter Four

The next day was a miserable day for cycling, so Peter elected to cybercommute rather than go into town. Without bothering to change out of his pj's, Peter shuffled across the hall to his office, which occupied one of the three bedrooms of their house.

The room was spacious, though architecturally perfunctory. Its main feature was a couple of broad south-facing windows that let in the day's meager blue-tinted daylight.

Rain beat against the glass, sheeting down in rivulets. Through a latticing of cedar branches he could see the celadon waters of the San Juan channel. Whitecaps topped the choppy waves. Beyond, the obscuring haze muted the outline of the San Juan Islands to faint humps that emerged from the water only to lose their tops in low-lying cloud.

On days like this Peter couldn't help but wonder why any sensible pioneer had ever stayed in the Pacific Northwest at all. Then again, many of them had originated in Norwegian fjords, and so would not have been easily dismayed by endless rain so long as an adequate supply of salmon existed.

And it was beautiful, even on a day like this. Peter had claimed this somewhat bland room for his own largely because of this ever-changing view of the islands.

Most of the room's interior was taken up with a large antique Georgian partner's desk that Peter had inherited from his bachelor uncle years before. This was supplemented by a couple of heavy bookcases that had once been solely populated with Peter's cherished personal library. Now a few dozen massive art books shared space on the shelves, their expensive hardcover bindings making Peter's old paperbacks look tatty by comparison.

Most of the time if Peter worked from home, Nick eschewed painting in his downstairs studio in favor of Peter's company. Today was no exception.

He sat opposite Peter, sketching, while Gigi perched on his shoulder. The cat's mood seemed to oscillate between intense desire to attack Nick's nubby graphite stick and abject comalike boredom.

And that was exactly what Peter was feeling about his own work as well—boredom. He'd started off reading about rhododendron honey and found that poisonous honeys were, in fact, not unusual or new. King Mithridates had once successfully deployed poison honey to bring Pompey the Great's Roman forces to a standstill. Modern East European naturopaths had taken to prescribing rhododendron honey as a Viagra substitute, as Patton had said, but not many and not often.

Peter tried to go back to death camus, but researching plants, even plants that were used to kill people, fell into the realm of activities that elicited within him a deadly level of tedium.

So instead he'd devoted the last half an hour to taking an online quiz about his relationship. He justified this as research by convincing himself that he needed to understand relationships in general (from a woman's point of view) in order to parse Margaret's eulogy in search of secret information and hidden meaning.

The truth was, her heartfelt words had both moved and confused him.

How was it possible to not be able to articulate exactly why you loved a man? His own list of aspects he found attractive in Nick would have required a whole steno book to list—in double columns, even.

But he'd only been able to fill out half the questionnaire because he was only one of the two partners involved.

"Why would you say you loved me?" Peter asked.

"Because you're just so good at fishing for compliments," Nick replied.

"I'm serious, though. Why do you think you love me?"

"Why does anybody love anybody? Nick shrugged. "Why are you asking? Are you filling out some kind of quiz again?"

"No." Peter closed the yoursoulmate.com window. "I'm just curious."

"Why do you love *me*?"

"I asked you first." Peter crossed his arms over his chest.

"Baby, I'm not going to answer online quiz questions to prove I love you. I completed enough personality assessments when I was in the army." Nick continued sketching, making sweeping, loose marks across the paper. Gigi followed his motions with intense feline interest. "If you want, though, I'd be willing to drive to Canada to prove that, for reasons of my own, I do love you."

"How are you going to do that?"

"By marrying you. What else?"

"Right now?"

"Sure. We could be at the border in twenty minutes and reach Vancouver in an hour. It's only nine thirty. If there isn't a long line at the Vital Statistics Agency we could get a license before lunch." Nick glanced over at him, the challenge in his eyes plain.

Nick obviously expected him to back down, say he had a dentist appointment and duck out of this the same way Nick ducked out of answering his perfectly legitimate online quiz questions.

Peter had never been one to cower from a game of chicken. "And what about this lunch? Can we get sushi?"

The level of surprise on Nick's face was not as high as Peter had expected it to be.

Nick said, "We can absolutely have sushi. We might have to stay overnight to round up a marriage commissioner on short notice anyway."

"You seem suspiciously knowledgeable about the exact procedures necessary to wed in Canada."

Nick merely smiled. "Or, if you haven't got the entire day,

we could go to the Washington State dot gov Web site and download the Declaration of Domestic Partnership forms. Ten minutes at the notary and we'd be legally entangled American-style, though not quite married."

"What would be the point of that?" Peter knew damn well what the point of that would be, but said it anyway because he couldn't think of a snappier comeback. His heart hammered in his chest. He had the very distinct feeling that in trying to get Nick's attention, he'd gotten into a much deeper conversation than he'd been planning for.

"Some rights are granted. If I died you'd get the Castle and all my worldly goods and rights to my artistic estate. And I'd have hospital visitation rights for you," Nick said, glancing up. "Which I would like, since you are prone to getting yourself into trouble with men who're holding guns."

"But you're always there to rescue me." Peter batted his lashes.

"I might not always be available," Nick said. "Plus you're a cyclist. It's just a matter of time before you get knocked down."

"Fucking inattentive drivers," Peter muttered.

Silence settled between them. Nick returned to painting.

Peter attempted to complete his online quiz but found he couldn't.

Quite suddenly, he realized that Nick had for all intents and purposes asked him to marry him.

He had to answer. For one moment, ambivalence surged in him. But unlike previous bouts of ambivalence, this one seemed to have no origin apart from his having become habituated to ambivalence.

Peter realized that he had no doubts—none of any real substance anyway. He experienced the normal fear of unknowable future events that always asserted itself when he imagined something as ambiguous and vague as *the rest of his life*, certainly.

About Nick, though, he felt no hesitation.

And that feeling was unique in all his life.

"So do you already have those forms downloaded, or do you want me to do it?" Peter asked.

Nick smiled very slightly and said, "You can do it after you get dressed. I've got to put my art stuff away so Gigi doesn't destroy it."

Peter did as he was bidden and headed to the car, pausing only briefly to phone Evangeline and tell her the good news.

Bellingham Credit Union was right in the center of downtown, a ten-minute drivefrom their place on Chuckanut Drive. So to save time, they filled out the forms in the car.

The forms weren't complex. The purpose of the domestic partnership bill was to establish some legal rights for unmarried, but established couples who were either of the same sex and therefore had no legal right to marry or who were of the opposite sex but were seniors who would lose the right to claim things like pensions from a deceased spouse if they remarried.

The forms had slots for the usual details: name, date of birth, place of birth, gender. Then, just above the signature line came these words:

We declare that we meet the requirement for registration of a domestic partnership pursuant to Chapter 26.60 RCW, and that: We share a common residence; We are both at least eighteen (18) years of age; Neither partner is married to anyone else, or in a state registered domestic partnership with any other person; We are both capable of consenting to this domestic partnership; We are not any relation to each other nearer than second cousin and neither partner is a sibling, child, grandchild, aunt, uncle, niece, or nephew to the other; **We are both of the same sex, or One of us is at least 62 years of age**

Peter had no idea why bold text had been necessary for the last two declarations. He would have thought if anything would be so strange as to require bold text it would have been the "I am not going to end up being my own grandpa" declaration. But what did he know?

And even though the forms themselves were dull, ugly and full of legalese, Peter still felt his eyes misting a little as he scratched out the letters of Nick's whole legal name. Nicolas Zimmer Olson. By the time they'd reached the bank, Peter had managed to fill in the forms. They waited in formed-plastic chairs alongside other, sadder-looking people. Their weird giddiness seemed totally incongruous and inappropriate, even to Peter. But then, the other customers waited for loan officers and mortgage brokers.

Only one other couple waited for the notary and those men appeared to be warily discussing the sale of a car.

Peter jumped when the notary, a woman with tufty blonde hair and an angular, birdlike face called his name.

His palms were sweating as he presented the papers. His voice shook slightly when he said, "We'd like to get this notarized, please."

The notary took the papers, glanced at them and smiled nervously. Peter couldn't tell if she was happy or disgusted to be performing this service. He glanced to Nick, who sat wearing a smug little smile that Peter had never seen grace Nick's face before.

The notary asked to see their identification, checked it, smiled again, and asked them to sign on the line. She then applied her signature and seal and handed the forms back to them. In a shy, flustered voice she said, "Congratulations."

"Thank you," Nick said. He gathered the papers and headed out the door.

And just like that, they were fake married.

Nearly married?

As good as married?

Everything but married?

Peter stared down at the papers in Nick's hand and felt an undertow of sadness moving beneath his giddy euphoria. The papers, he realized, were necessary. He wanted to stay with Nick, and Nick wanted to stay with him. They were most important to each other, most qualified to make decisions about one another.

These papers were the evidence with which he could force others to accept that. The papers weren't romantic, but they were pragmatic.

That was the source of his fleeting sadness—that he should need them at all to fight disapproving strangers who would separate them, given the opportunity.

But then the melancholy vanished as he saw Evangeline's run-down Subaru whip into the credit union parking lot. She leaped from the car, arms full of flowers, a beatific smile on her face. She was trailed by her lover, Tommy, who looked stoned but generally in good spirits.

"Is it done already?" she called, disappointment coursing through her voice.

"Signed and sealed," Peter said. "Not quite delivered yet. But close."

"I wanted to get a picture of you kissing," Evangeline said. "I brought my camera and everything."

"You didn't miss anything. We didn't kiss," Peter said, though now that she'd mentioned it, he felt bad that he hadn't even thought of it.

"How could you not kiss?"

"We were in a bank cubicle," Peter said.

"We could kiss now," Nick offered.

"Wait till I get my camera out." Evangeline fished a small silver box out of her purse and raised it in front of her face. "Okay, go!"

Peter glanced to Nick, suddenly awkward. A bank parking lot was not significantly more romantic than a cubicle inside. Traffic whizzed by as Nick drew close and very gently kissed him on the lips.

Evangeline whooped. Tommy clapped and offered to take them for drinks.

It was ten thirty in the morning. So they went to the nicest breakfast place in town and ordered mimosas.

Because it seemed to have become an impromptu party, Nick phoned his cousin, who came downtown right away.

Insofar as Peter knew, Kjell Olson was the only other member of the extended Olson clan who had any artistic leanings. He was a plein air painter who looked like the love child of a lumberjack and Sasquatch. He wore shorts in all weather, no matter how inclement. He slid into the booth next to Evangeline and after a round of congratulatory handshakes and toasts asked "Are you two going to throw a big shindig to celebrate?"

"Sometime," Nick said. "We haven't figured it out yet. This was kind of spur-of-the-moment."

"I know how that goes," Kjell remarked. It was hard for Peter to imagine that Nick's cousin had any kind of insight into spontaneity, but then he realized that although Kjell, like Nick, suffered from incurable stoicism, he must grasp immediacy on some level. He was a plein air painter, after all.

Peter said, "Maybe we'll have a great big to-do with a band and cake and everything. I think we should have two grooms' cakes with big images of our Washington State Registered Domestic Partner cards airbrushed on the top."

Kjell blinked and then laughed. "Like you would have a card."

"Apparently they're going to send me one in two to six weeks," Nick said. "Peter too."

Kjell's smile faded and then turned to puzzlement.

"They're really going to send you a card?"

"It's so we can prove that we've got the right to visit each other in the hospital and things like that," Peter said. He'd only mentioned the cards as a joke. Now the discomfort of having to explain and therefore highlight their inequity as homosexuals made him squirm.

"But," Kjell continued, his brow still crumpled in confusion, "am I supposed to have card?"

It was Peter's turn to blink in confusion. "For what?"

"To prove my wife and I are married," he said, as though the relationships were completely equivalent. "If she goes into the hospital or something?"

"No, I don't think they issue Official Husband cards. I'm pretty sure if you went to the hospital and said you were Carrie's husband, they would just believe you." Nick fielded that one.

"You've got matching rings," Peter pointed out.

"Right," Kjell said, glancing down at his hand. "I imagine the cards are supposed to protect you two."

"Mostly," Nick agreed.

"It's kind of depressing," Kjell remarked. "Not that you two are hitched up now. Just that you would need cards to prove it. I'm glad you're going to have them, though. We still have a way to go, I suppose."

Kjell's blunt, genuine delivery somehow managed to circumvent every callus and defense that Peter had ever acquired or erected. His sincere kindness brought tears to Peter's eyes. He wanted to throw his arms around Kjell and thank him for noticing the strangeness and precariousness of their situation—to thank him for caring.

But regardless of the fact that he'd just become Peter's new straight-guy hero, he was still Kjell Olson. Peter kept his gushy feelings to himself.

Apparently unaware of the tumult occurring inside Peter, Kjell kept ambling along the conversational trail.

"You know I think the farmer's market building might be a nice place to have a summer party. I hear it's pretty cheap to rent," Kjell remarked.

"Bad acoustics though," Tommy remarked.

"I can't imagine having a party in a space that…tall," Peter said. "Or that big. How many people do you think are going to be coming to eat our cheap cake?"

"Well there's the Olsons—that's probably about twenty guests right there. Then there's Nick's artist friends and your friends and the people from the *Hamster*." Kjell was ticking off subsets of people on his fingers as he continued to speak. "And then there's your family—I don't know how many that is—and there are probably a few groups I've left out."

"My army buddies," Nick put in.

"Your *what*?" Peter whipped his head around. Nick did not appear to be joking.

"You've never mentioned your army buddies."

"Sure I have. Shamus, Dale, Shantee. We e-mail. Shantee's still in uniform—stationed not too far away at Fort Irwin. I'm sure she'd want to come, at least."

"Where the hell is Fort Irwin?"

"California," Kjell said.

"I didn't realize they were your army buddies. I guess I didn't think you stayed in contact with anyone from that time," Peter said.

"I'm good at keeping relationships that I value intact," Nick said, deadpan. Peter didn't know if it was the effect of early-morning mimosa, but he felt a sudden sense of vertigo at the idea of all these disparate groups of people mingling in the same room. No, not vertigo. Vertigo was merely a symptom of his real affliction: complete panic.

And what would happen to this mishmash of guests when he and Nick doused them all with alcohol? How could they possibly all make it out of that party alive?

Unbidden a headline swam up in his mind's eye.

MASS SPONTANEOUS COMBUSTION KILLS DOZENS AT GAY NOT-QUITE-MARRIAGE RECEPTION

Bellingham, WA.

Firefighters from across Whatcom County were summoned to Bellingham late Saturday evening to battle a massive inferno ignited by the friction between guests at the Fontaine/Olson reception. The grooms, an almost-but-not-quite-married gay couple from very different backgrounds, survived but just barely. They were having a conversation in the restroom when the tension between their many and varied guests escalated to ignition level.

"Nick and I were hiding out in the handicapped bathroom stall when we felt the detonation wave," said Peter Fontaine (age 32), award-winning journalist and first-time groom. "It was all over in seconds. We rushed out into the parking lot but all we could see was a pillar of flame two hundred feet high."

Volunteer fire departments from all over the county were mustered, but failed to impact the blaze.

"I've never seen such a social disaster," a firefighter from Acme reported. "It was worse in there than a meth-lab TV party."

Air tankers dispatched by the Department of Natural Resources finally managed to quell the massive blaze early Sunday morning.

Fontaine and Olson could not be reached for further comment.

"—and you could probably borrow tables from the vendors if you didn't want to rent them," Evangeline was saying. "That's what they did for the Local Eats dinner on Friday night. It was BYOT—bring your own table." Her voice snapped Peter out of his apocalyptic vision.

"When did you say that dinner was?"

"The day before Roger died. I went over and made an appearance after I went to the Castle to see you two," she said.

"And was Roger there?"

"He and Margaret were both there. Margaret is one of the organizers of the dinner. She has been for years. I think that Roger took over most of her duties this year though. He emceed and ran the auction. Somebody took over wearing the Spunky suit for her as well. Beekeeper Jackie I think."

"So what was the menu?" Peter leaned forward keenly, already searching his pocket for his notebook.

"Salmon, camus, some kind of fern shoots, bumbleberry pie. You know, local native foods... I don't remember everything. I didn't stay." Evangeline turned to Tommy. "Do you remember what they served?"

"I mostly ate pie," Tommy replied. "I can tell you one thing though. Whoever was wearing that Spunky suit the previous night needed a fucking shower. I thought I was going to get jock itch on my face from that thing when I put it on the next day."

Kjell and Nick both snorted with laughter. Evangeline just rolled her eyes and said, "Sometimes I miss not being treated like one of the guys."

"You love it," Tommy said. He took a swig of mimosa.

"That's right you were Spunky the next day, weren't you?" Peter asked.

"Yeah, I kept it together for the kids but the whole time I was just thinking about getting home and taking a shower," Tommy said. "It was foul. There were even little pieces of food, like onions or something inside one of the feet. Who the hell eats inside a squirrel suit?"

"I think I need to text someone really quick." Peter fumbled for his phone, wanting to get this information to Patton before he forgot. Quite suddenly, Nick put an arm over his shoulders, pulled him close and kissed him on the neck.

Public displays of affection had never loomed large in Nick's repertoire, and it shocked Peter enough that he felt his cheeks start to redden. The hooting and whooping and continuous photograph snapping of Evangeline was not helping at all. Other diners—the late breakfast/early lunch crowd—were starting to stare. He heard one of the waiters say, "Those guys just got married," to a nearby table by way of explaining both their rowdiness and prior-to-noon levels of inebriation.

Very gently, Nick pulled the phone from Peter hand. He whispered, "Let's leave work alone for now."

"But Roger—"

"If he were here, he'd want us to celebrate," Nick murmured in his ear. "He'd say something like *I'll still be dead tomorrow.*"

Peter conceded that this was probably true.

Evangeline ordered another round of mimosas. Soon after that their food arrived.

In lieu of wedding cake, Peter and Nick fed each other forkfuls of French toast. The indulgent waiter overserved them, then Evangeline phoned a cab to shuttle them back out to the Castle for a carbohydrate-induced snooze.

At two o'clock that afternoon Peter was asleep, snuggled up next to Nick, and he realized that this almost-married thing felt just like any day lying in bed his lover. Only, something small had changed. Small, yet truly significant.

Nick sleepily pulled off Peter's trousers, then slowly unbuttoned Peter's shirt.

Peter was trying to put his finger on what the difference was, now that they were officially a couple.

"Are you writing something inside your head?" Nick asked, helping Peter shuck his way out of his underwear.

"No, just thinking," Peter replied.

"There's a difference?"

"Sometimes," Peter said, laughing. He realized he'd somehow been relieved of all his garments while Nick remained fully clothed, so he helped him undress as well. Full as they were on French toast and liquor, Peter doubted any screwing around would be record breaking in the slightest, but that didn't seem to deter Nick from making this noble effort to consummate their document-signing immediately.

He set a sleepy pace, kissing the side of Peter's mouth and then using his tongue slowly, as if coaxing a timid virgin into the mood. Peter rolled over and straddled Nick, drawn to his body heat and the feel of him between his legs. He sat up and glanced down at the sight of their two cocks, both heavy and hard now. He wrapped his fingers around them both and started a lazy rhythm, the kind usually reserved for hungover Saturday wanks.

Nick encircled the base of their cocks, with his hands and together they pumped themselves and each other in a languid, slowly-building movement.

Nick made eye contact and smiled, and that's when Peter realized what was different now. This wasn't just him giving and getting a handjob from some guy or even from a boyfriend. This was his de facto *husband*.

Now everyone knew or could know—or, for some, be forced against their will to know. Somewhere in some office in Olympia, there would always be a clear and unambiguous record of their connection to one another. Two hundred years from now, historians would have no reason to speculate about why they might have slept in the same bed. No one would be able to argue that their love had never existed. From now on, they were officially linked. And even their two bodies braced together, hands working in tandem to increase the power of each other's pleasure, one feeling stroked to a growing, ecstatic conclusion, and he knew he'd never had sex like this before, and might never have it like this again.

They didn't break eye contact. Nick sped the rhythm and Peter followed, and when Nick's ejaculation spilled over Peter's fingers and his own cock, Peter's orgasm shuddered out of him. Neither of them moved their hands. Peter glanced down at the sticky mingling of fluids, and couldn't help but grin—the idea of immortalizing this particular second filling him with a sense of childish delight at the vulgarity of it.

Nick reached up with his clean hand and cupped Peter's face and said, "Do you believe I love you now?"

"I'd believe anything you told me now."

"Just remember to keep believing it when you're sober," Nick murmured, snuggling deeper into his pillow.

By the time Peter returned from the bathroom Nick was already napping, sprawled across the bed. Gigi had arrived from parts unknown to claim sovereignty of Peter's pillow.

An urge to wake Nick and tell him everything he'd realized about this incredible day came and went.

He'd just wonder why Peter thought any historian would be researching either of them in the first place. Nick was practical that way. Peter squeezed between him and the cat and let himself doze, envisioning with fondness that far-off scholar on the tenure track at Lunar University. Standing, silhouetted by the Milky Way and dressed in shining silver lame, and protected from meteor strikes by a clear, geodesic dome he would bravely face a vast jury of skeptical peers. He would hold aloft the ancient, tattered papers Nick and Peter had just signed and pronounce *In conclusion, this document, unearthed at great personal peril from the mutant-riddled ruins of the Washington State Department of Vital Statistics, proves that there can be no doubt that Olson and Fontaine were lovers!*

Peter fell asleep smiling, listening to the thundering applause of the audience.

Chapter Five

By the time they woke up, exchanged frisky handjobs and had a snack, the shadows were beginning to lengthen.

Time to go back to work. Texting Patton about the Local Eats dinner was first on his list. He had no idea whether any of that information would turn out to be relevant, but if Roger had worn the Spunky suit maybe somehow he might have left some clue about what happened to him.

Peter knew he shouldn't be thinking of Roger on this special day, but once a question had lodged itself in his mind he had a hard time getting it out, special day or not.

Finally, the fourth time Peter sighed dramatically, Nick asked, "Something on your mind?"

"Roger's death. It's obviously not an accident, but I can't figure out why anybody would want to kill him."

"Is that your job now?"

"Officer Patton's stated plainly that the death was definitely a murder, but why? What could anybody possibly gain from killing Roger Hager?"

"I don't know," Nick muttered. "What?"

"That's just it. He didn't have anything. Maybe the culprit isn't at the farmer's market at all," Peter said.

"Go on." As usual, Nick did not look up from his drawing.

"Well, though they never married, Roger had recently entered into a registered domestic partnership with Margaret Mills," Peter said. "That's how she was able to oversee Roger's funeral arrangements even though he left no will."

"And you know this because…?"

"I asked at the funeral home, like I said."

"I see. And so?" Nick asked.

"So Margaret was and still is loaded. And I found out from one of her tenant farmers that she is also undergoing treatment for colon cancer. If she died before Roger, which before last Saturday seemed certain, Roger would have had a claim on Margaret's money." Peter shook a portion of kibble into Gigi's bowl. The cat regarded the kibble with clear disdain, ate one bite then walked over to Nick and mewed pathetically.

Nick gave Gigi's head a gentle but thorough scratch. "So you think that one of Margaret's heirs might be angry about Roger?"

"One or more," Peter said. "She's got four children. None of them liked Roger apparently. And at least one of them openly called him a sponger and a mooch."

"It's normal for children to reject a stepparent," Nick said. "Especially one whose lifestyle they don't understand. It doesn't mean they ganged up and killed him. Where is your proof?"

"I haven't got any yet," Peter admitted. "And then there's the matter of the vases."

"Which vases? The ones Roger had himself baked into?"

"No, the ones Margaret was hiding from everyone at the memorial." Peter briefly explained what he'd seen the previous day. "I really want to get into that studio and have a look at what Margaret was trying to hide."

Nick ceased his cat-directed ministrations. He folded his arms and made the kind of unnervingly hard and direct eye contact that had clearly been recycled from his time in the army.

"Are you trying to tell me that you plan to break into Fired-Up?" Nick asked. "Because I'm telling you, that is not going to go over well with the police."

"I was thinking of finding someone who could let me into his studio space."

"How are you going to do that?"

"By asking you to ask your friend who owns it to let me in?" Peter gave his best sheepish smile.

"First, Adele isn't my friend. She's just someone I know from Whatcom Artist Alliance. Second, what reason am I supposed to give for rummaging through Roger's stuff?"

"Maybe Roger owed you some ceramics?"

"He didn't."

"But you could say that he did," Peter said. "It's called fibbing."

"I think it might be called getting into a crime scene under false pretenses."

"The studio isn't a crime scene," Peter pointed out. "At worst we'd be trespassing, but not if Adele let you in," Peter said.

"You have a suspicious knowledge of the minutiae of our state's trespassing laws. You know that, right?"

"I've always thought it was best to know the laws of the land," Peter said.

Nick uncrossed his arms and sighed. Gigi immediately began scaling his bicep, attempting to summit Nick's shoulder. Peter felt a glimmer of hope. Though his lover's emotions were by no means obvious, over the last couple of years Peter found he could divine the other man more easily.

Nick had the body language of an android—and not an android that had been programmed for social interaction. Peter had originally supposed that Nick's years in the army were responsible for his taciturn nature. But now that he'd become better acquainted with a few members of Nick's family, Peter realized that Nick had simply been reared by Scandinavians. Nick's family was Swedish-American to be precise. To Peter, these descendants of Lutheran pioneers certainly qualified as the most relentlessly stoic of all the Nordic blonds inhabiting the North American continent.

Peter's own great-grandparents hailed from the Azores, spoke Portuguese, adored the Virgin Mary, and had no trouble expressing their feelings about anything. Though the Catholicism of his departed ancestors had faded—his own parents had briefly been Unitarians before slipping into secularism once that fad wore off—the Fontaine family culture of heated arguments and extended grudges had filtered down to the present day.

These arguments generally included so many gesticulations that they could be understood without specific cognition of the vocabulary being bellowed by the speaker. As a sullen teen, Peter himself sometimes wondered why he'd bothered to learn to speak at all.

With Nick, though, a simple uncrossing of the arms could mean everything. And right now it meant that Peter knew he was close to convincing Nick to go along with him on the Let's-Check-Out-Roger's-Studio plan.

Finally, Nick said, "Why don't we just ask Margaret to open the studio for us instead? It's hers right, isn't it? The items in there are her property now."

"Because…" Peter blinked. It hadn't occurred to him to just ask Margaret. He didn't know if she'd comply. It seemed too simple. "I guess we could ask Margaret, but she's the one who hid the vases."

"They were legally hers to hide and she might have had a lot of reasons other than murder for doing that."

"Maybe so," Peter conceded.

"Look, if we ask Margaret to let us into the studio we wouldn't be dragging Adele into some questionable activity of yours."

"I don't think she would get into trouble," Peter said. "And what if Margaret says no? What if she's the killer and she doesn't want us investigating?"

"So now you admit you are actively investigating?"

"I—" Peter realized he'd been caught. "Yes, but that's what newshounds do."

"Peter, I am willing to do a lot to satisfy your curiosity because nothing in the world makes you happier than snooping around and digging up other people's secrets. But I feel like I need to remind you that it's rude to yank unrelated people into your adventures." Nick made this pronouncement with no accusation in his tone but simply as a statement of fact.

Peter hated it when Nick played this reasonableness card. He had no defense against it. Then again, Nick was giving him what he wanted so why shouldn't he give in to Nick's one stipulation.

"Does that mean that you'll come with me to the studio?"

"With the amount of trouble you get into, you'd have a hard time stopping me," Nick remarked.

Peter rolled his eyes. "I won't get into trouble."

"That's what you always think. Then you end up in the dark in the middle of nowhere facing down some lunatic," Nick said, shaking his head. "You have no common sense."

"I do so have common sense. It's just that sometimes it gets wrestled to the ground by my sense of curiosity." Peter sidled toward Nick, snuggling himself against the shoulder not currently occupied by their diminutive but extremely territorial cat. "And anyway you love my sense of curiosity. And my sense of adventure."

"To be honest, I think I could live without them some days," Nick replied gruffly.

"You could, but you wouldn't want to." Peter slid his hand beneath Nick's sweater. "Otherwise there would be no more slutty nurses in your foreseeable future."

Strangely this statement seemed to annoy Nick. He carefully plucked Gigi off his shoulder and turned his full attention to Peter. "Let me make one thing clear. I do not love you because you think it's fun to dress up like a slutty nurse on Halloween."

"You don't seem to mind it though, either," Peter remarked.

"No, what idiot would?"

Peter thought of pointing out that plenty of idiots would have—and indeed had—rejected his various sexy dress-up ideas, but he stilled his tongue. He didn't want to jinx a good thing. Instead, he said, "So why do you love me?"

"Back to this again…"

"You were the one who brought it up." Peter could hear an edge of sour insecurity in his own voice.

Apparently so did Nick. He said, "I love that you're smart and funny and brave. I do not love that the by-products of being smart and funny and brave are being arrogant, snarky, and reckless. But I've made peace with that."

Peter didn't know whether to be irritated by the inherent truth of his recitation about Peter's fundamental faults or touched by Nick's admission of love. One path would lead to an hours-long fight and the other would wind its way to inevitable orgasm.

Momma Fontaine didn't raise no fool.

Peter flung his arms around Nick's waist, burying his face in the other man's heavily-sweatered chest.

"You *do* love me!" he burbled, being overly dramatic to downplay his own surge of emotion.

Peter felt Nick sigh, felt himself enveloped by strong arms, felt Nick press a kiss into his hair.

"I wouldn't have married you if I didn't love you," Nick said, reasonable as ever.

"I don't know. You might have."

"For what? Your tiny bank account? Your overly aggressive cat?"

"I don't know why I doubt your feelings," Peter said, "except that occasionally I can't find any evidence of their existence. Some days I wouldn't even know that you liked Gigi except that you literally let her walk all over you."

"That's not evidence?"

"You never let me walk all over you."

"Are we talking about another one of your weird costume fantasies?" Nick asked.

Peter chuckled and shook his head against Nick's chest.

Nick continued, "Anyway, it's better that I'm not an open book to you. If you could figure out everything I was thinking, you'd get bored and go find a more interesting puzzle."

"So being enigmatic is some kind of master plan of yours?"

"No, it just means we're a good match." Nick ran his warm hands down Peter's back. "So are you going to call Margaret?"

"Nine thirty seems late to call a sexagenarian who's battling cancer," Peter said. "I'll wait until morning. What are your plans for the evening?"

"Going to bed early," Nick said. His soft mouth rose in a suggestive curl. "What are yours?"

"Following you."

Some days when he headed for the bedroom, Peter felt like he and Nick were in some sort of race to see who could get naked faster. And then there were nights like this when shedding their clothes, showering, and sliding beneath the duvet seemed an activity that not only could, but should, take as long as possible.

Nick seemed to be making successive attempts at setting the record for the longest, slowest, deepest kiss ever performed.

Normally Peter would have been more aggressive, wanting to go faster and up a sharper incline toward the dizzying summit of passion before leaping off the precipice and free-falling into ecstasy.

In contrast, Nick had always favored endurance sports, and it really showed. All through the shower, he gave only the most teasing of caresses, driving Peter almost crazy with thwarted attempts to ramp up the game. More than once he prevented Peter from just dropping down to the tile and giving him head—which Peter considered egregious. But Nick seemed to be having fun.

"You're going to call the all the shots here, aren't you?" Peter said.

"You said you were following my lead."

Not exactly. But Peter didn't have the will to fight it. Or rather, he had the will but no motivation. He let himself be toweled dry and led to the bedroom.

They didn't fall upon the mattress grunting like animals.

Nonetheless, Gigi leaped off the bed when they climbed gracefully in, apparently having learned from experience that no good would come to her from two men engaged in kissing. She gave them one last, vexed look before adjourning to some other, more stable locale.

Continuing from his teasing in the shower, Nick moved slowly, kissing his way down Peter's torso. Peter felt his body respond to each caress of Nick's lips with fiery, demanding need, and had to stifle his desire to thrust upward and get things moving faster.

Nick's hands slowly pushed Peter's thighs open, and Peter enthusiastically opened himself up, liking where this was going. But Nick's glacial pace didn't alter. His fingers caressed Peter's scrotum and his kisses dipped down Peter's belly. Still, nothing was being done to address the urgency between them, sticking upward, waving a flag, hoping to attract some attention.

Unable to take it any longer, Peter reached down to stroke his own dick.

Immediately Nick intervened, removing Peter's hand.

"No touching."

"But—"

"Have a little patience." Nick had a devilish curl to his grin.

Peter moaned, but did as he was told, letting go and leaning back to give Nick free access. Nick fondled his balls and kissed him more until at last his tongue ran along the length of Peter's rigid cock.

It amazed Peter how Nick's touch could electrify him and feel so exciting, after so many years of fucking. Nick had sucked his cock more times than he could remember and yet every time still sent a shiver of disbelief down Peter's spine, a sense of wonder that any man as beautiful and remarkable as Nick would do this for him.

He wanted to make it last long enough for Nick to be satisfied, but had no idea how long that might take.

Peter tried to develop a narrative in his mind, to slow his response and revel in the feeling, but his intellect betrayed him. All he could generate were pornographic descriptions of the pornographic actions being performed on him, sportscaster-style.

Blow-by-blow.

Up at bat now it's veteran pitcher Olson. And there he goes driving hard down on the shaft. Olson's a real pro down there...

He giggled a little, causing Nick to raise an eyebrow at him.

It was no good, Peter thought. He couldn't concentrate. He could barely think, but then, why would he want to?

Peter resolved to flatly refuse to think and allowed himself to devolve into a whimpering thing, thrusting into the licking heat of Nick's mouth.

Nick's efforts grew more fervent, and he pulled Peter deeper...and then everything began to become more desperate and fumbling as Nick himself at last succumbed to a loss of control. Peter spread himself wider in invitation and Nick—never one to groan aloud—simply inhaled deeply and reached for the lube.

Peter expected Nick to take it nice and slow, given the way they'd started, but instead Nick immediately drilled into him, and Peter cried out in surprise. He groped Nick's back for purchase as Nick grabbed hold of his knees and filled his insides, fucking him hungrily.

For a moment it was almost too much. Then Nick began to pump Peter's cock with each powerful thrust, and Peter's body trembled with the overwhelming ecstasy of his lover around his cock and inside him at the same time.

Peter's orgasm spiraled from the base of his spine, flashing through him, deep and powerful. For several seconds, he lost all sense of the world outside of Nick's embrace.

When he came back to himself, he opened his eyes and took in the sight of Nick pounding into him, eyes closed in concentration, sweat beading his brow. The sight filled Peter with pleasure.

Nick shuddered, then collapsed over Peter, spent as a marathon runner at last reaching the finish line at Olympic Stadium.

"You're pretty good for an old kinda-married guy," Peter breathed, feeling congratulations were in order.

Nick didn't lift his head off Peter's shoulder, but Peter could feel his smile.

Chapter Six

Margaret met them at Roger's studio at Fired-Up at ten the next morning. As she unlocked the door, Peter couldn't help but note the painful slowness of her movements, but he couldn't tell whether that stemmed from her illness or spirits. He supposed that whether her discomfort was physical or spiritual didn't matter very much. He wondered what she thought about Roger's death being ruled a murder, but couldn't bring himself to ask. In the face of such clear sorrow, his usual audacity had abandoned him.

Fortunately, Margaret brought the subject up for him.

"I suppose being a newsman, you've already heard what the police have to say about Roger's death." She made the remark without really meeting Peter's gaze.

"Yes, ma'am, I have."

"I don't know what to think of that," Margaret said. "I think they might be wrong."

"Wrong?" Peter cocked his head. He'd heard of people not wanting to acknowledge that a loved one died of natural or accidental causes, but he'd never encountered anyone who chose the opposite tack.

"The lady police officer seemed to be the only one who thought it was murder. I think she's got her own agenda. And I'm not the only one." Margaret sank down into a chair.

Peter glanced to Nick. His expression was unreadable.

"I guess I don't understand what other agenda a police officer would have," Peter said.

"One of the detectives is retiring this year. That lady has applied for his job. I have a friend who works as a dispatcher who told me he thinks she's trying to use the investigation of Roger's death to get the job." Margaret adjusted her oxygen hose. "It makes me sick to think that someone would try and profit from a death like that. But I guess that's what you're doing too, right?"

"Me?" Peter felt himself flush. "I am not trying to profit from Roger's death, ma'am."

"Isn't that why you called me out here?" Margaret turned her watery eyes from Peter to Nick. "I don't believe that you're looking for some pottery that Roger was making for you. He always told me what he was doing, and he never mentioned anything about replacing any of your dishes to me."

Nick straightened himself and said, "You're right, Margaret, I didn't come here to look for replacement dishes."

"It's all right. You just want to help your boyfriend get some kind of story so he can get in all the national papers again."

"That's really not what—" Peter began to protest, but Margaret cut him off.

"All right. Maybe you're not just doing it for the story. That was uncalled for. I'm sorry." She directed her attention to Nick. "You're here because you think I don't know about Roger's naughty side, right?"

"Naughty side?" Peter blurted out. Immediately the honey sprang to mind. What if Roger really was having an affair? But how could revelation of an affair get him into national papers. It didn't make any sense.

Margaret gave him a long, steady gaze. Then a tiny spark lit in her eyes.

"So you don't know, huh, Peter? Well, Nick, I know exactly what you're looking for, but since you lied to me, I'm going to make you find it yourself." Margaret closed her eyes. "I'll give you half an hour."

Peter wanted to argue with her—to explain that he was on a mission—but their half hour was draining away, so he turned toward the still life of Roger's once-busy studio.

The vases he'd seen Margaret moving were, of course, gone. And with them went Peter's direction.

He had no idea what he was searching for. This was a terrible idea. Now Margaret thought he was some sort of ambulance-chasing glory hound and…really, was she that wrong? What had he been thinking getting a dying woman to let him into her dead lover's studio just to satisfy his curiosity?

If Nick suffered from the same guilt he didn't show it. He gave Margaret a stiff, "Thank you," and began to search. Because Peter had no idea what, if anything he was looking for, he found himself watching Nick.

Nick pivoted very slowly, taking in the entire room. Then he went to Roger's tools, lifting them, examining them. He read the backs of jars.

Minutes ticked away. Nick turned his attention to a small set of drawers that contained what looked like more tools, stamps that would be used to press a pattern into clay.

Nick seemed to find these of great interest. He laid them out one by one, examining them very closely.

Peter drifted up beside him.

"What is it?" he asked.

"Do you remember what I told you about the crystalline glazes that Roger used to make our dishes?"

"Not everything, but the basics." Peter surreptitiously glanced over his shoulder at Margaret, who still sat on the chair, eyes closed, expression drawn with pain.

"One company that made the technique famous was a place called Fulper. They started out making ceramic drainpipes in New Jersey."

"There is such a thing as ceramic drainpipes?"

"This was in the early nineteenth century. Anyway, one of the potters, Fulper, bought the company from the boss and started making pottery—things like decorated whisky jugs and then water dispensers. Eventually the company started making art ceramics. Those go for three to four hundred dollars nowadays. They frequently used crystalline glazes. One of the ways that they're identified is by the stamp at the bottom. It's like a signature that's pressed into the wet clay." Nick held up the raised stamp for Peter to inspect. "The Fulper stamp looks very much like this one."

"And so what are you trying to say?" Peter kept his voice low.

"He's trying to tell you that Roger was a forger." Margaret's voice rose behind them. "He told me once that if he died before me I should reveal his forgeries. I just haven't gotten around to it. I've been very tired. When did Roger tell you?"

Nick just gave a noncommittal shrug.

Peter's mind raced. Maybe this wasn't about food or art or inheritance at all. Maybe Roger had sold a forgery to the wrong person. Except for one small detail.

"Why would Roger forge antique pottery that was worth less than his own pottery?" Peter asked.

"Just to prove he could, I think," Margaret said. A wan smile curved her lips. "Roger could be feisty that way."

"But wouldn't his reputation as an artist have been ruined if anyone found out?" Peter felt this was an obvious question, but one that should be asked nonetheless.

Nick answered him. "Not necessarily. Several forgers have made their careers after having been discovered to have successfully placed copies of the old masters in major museums. The Chinese painter, Chang Dai-chien, is practically a folk hero for his skill at forgery while being an extremely famous painter in his own right."

"Which is why Roger would like his forgeries to be revealed?" Peter asked. "For that extra burst of posthumous promotion?"

"Honestly," Margaret said, sighing, "I think he just wanted to have a more interesting biography. He told me that when he first started making the bogus Fulpers in art school, it was when he genuinely did need the money. After that he would only make one if he was depressed. Passing them off as real then always cheered him up, apparently."

"So you want me to leave this stamp here, I suppose?" Nick asked.

Margaret shook her head. "No, take it with you. The only reason I let you in here was so you could break the story wide open…make sure you get it in that all those pretentious art magazines. It would have made Roger happy. I've got the last couple of Fulpers he made in the trunk of my car. You can take them with you too."

Nick thanked Margaret, then seemed at a loss for what more to say.

Peter finally found his voice, "I'm sorry to have troubled you, ma'am."

Margaret turned to him and said, "Just make the story big."

Nick drove back to the Castle to work and from there Peter cycled into town to make an appearance at the *Hamster* office. Doug was so deeply absorbed in writing—most likely his weekly column of rants and conspiracy theories—that he barely glanced up when Peter came in.

Peter sorted through the assorted notes and messages on his desk. He had to pound out a couple of articles, but neither would take very long, so he returned to his own personal mission.

This time though, rather than focusing on Roger or any of the suspects, he decided it was time to find out a little more about Officer Patton and see if Margaret's theory could hold any water.

Normally Peter was not the sort of person to be easily influenced by the opinions of others, but he found Margaret's comments about his new cop friend disturbing.

Was Patton just using him to get information?

Well, of course she is. That's what informants are for.

He wondered why the idea that Patton would be solving a crime sheerly for the purpose of getting a promotion bothered him. He supposed he really didn't know that much about her.

Peter had always found that Facebook, when properly used, was a most excellent tool for any stalker. Unfortunately Patton wasn't his friend—not in the digital sense, at least, and maybe not in any sense.

Police officers had official biographies, though and it was this that Peter first engaged. Patton was a Washington native. Born and educated in Sequim, she had attended the University of Washington before returning to her hometown for her first assignment—in traffic. She'd moved northward from there to Mount Vernon and finally to Bellingham. As far as Peter could tell her career had been dull—in cop terms anyway.

Though Patton was not married, Peter had a hunch that he could find her name on the title of a piece of real estate in town. And when he did, he found that she was co-owner of one of the long lots in the Birchwood neighborhood.

The other owner's name was Sharon Rodriquez-Patton.

For reasons he felt embarrassed to admit to, the discovery that his dykey cop friend truly was a lesbian thrilled him and filled him with a restored sense of trust. He knew that this was completely irrational. Homosexual cops had just as much capacity for corruption as any other category of cops.

And yet he'd never met a lesbian who screwed him over. He'd met plenty of women-loving women whom he didn't like, but never one whom he wouldn't trust with his credit card. Something about all that muff-diving seemed to encourage integrity.

It even changed his opinion of Margaret's comments. So what if Patton wanted a promotion? Who didn't? And what made Margaret's dispatcher friend such a reliable source of information about Patton's personal motivations anyway?

One thing was certain: there was a lot more to this whole crime than was meeting his theoretically objective but plainly biased eye.

Chapter Seven

Saturday turned out to be hot and the people of Bellingham rejoiced by flooding outdoors. Their pale, skinny bodies adorned lawns and stretched out on benches in the city's many parks. And inevitably, giddy from the sudden infusion of vitamin D, a thousand or so thronged the farmer's market. And standing behind the cheap cash register at Go-Go-Gyoza, Peter was ready for them.

Patton had been absolutely correct when she'd assumed that Peter could get the vendors at the farmer's market to talk. In fact, Peter found that it was harder to get them to stop talking than to start.

But not about the murder.

They'd talk about anything and everything else. Crackpot nutritional theories, government conspiracies, rants against the health department, rants against the FDA, heartfelt gardening advice, and straight-up gossip were easy to come by. Somehow the murder was off-limits, as if they'd all agreed in advance to not speak of it.

And maybe they had.

For a moment, Peter had a vision of all hundred and forty vendors making a pact to slay Roger, then ward off the police investigation with a wall of stony silence. But Peter couldn't credit that at all. A group that couldn't agree on whether free-standing umbrellas were acceptable could never group-murder anybody.

Usually, in a situation like this, Peter liked to ask leading questions, to try to keep the speaker on topic. But without being really obvious, he didn't know what questions to ask.

Peter's problem was that although he could generate a wide variety of theories as to the events leading up to Roger's death, none of them seemed viable. What he'd discovered about Roger Hager was that the man had only one secret: the forged Fulpers. But that seemed like a dead end. The pottery wasn't valuable enough to kill for and revealing that Roger had been a forger would only elevate his posthumous reputation.

Inheritance was a possibility.

He gazed across the way at Roger's stand. Market administration had set up a table in the space where his stall would have stood. The framed photograph from the Fired-Up memorial seemed to have migrated there. A few bunches of flowers, mostly tulips, sat in vases. A dozen or so votive candles burned. These seemed to be mostly provided by Beekeeper Jackie.

She sold honey, and honey had killed Roger, but that seemed way too obvious. Patton would certainly have gone straight to her first.

Besides the poison honey had been imported from Turkey. Jackie would have no reason to import any kind of honey.

The fact that Roger had been taking homeopathic impotence remedies was strange in itself. His lover was almost certainly too ill to require bronco-like sexual services.

Might there be some other woman? Might this mystery woman provide the key to understanding why Roger Hager had to die?

Peter introduced the question as subtly as he could to a variety of vendors, but no one seemed to be able to even speculate as to the existence of another woman, let alone her identity.

The only person who seemed even willing to acknowledge that Roger might have been engaging in activity that might have ultimately contributed to his death were Go-Go-Gyoza's neighbors, the fit female salad sellers. The owner, Skye, thought Roger's murder must be the result of fate.

"So Roger was up to no good somehow?" Peter asked. "He must have been," the curly-haired woman remarked. Apparently, Skye was a second-generation treehugger who believed emphatically in the healing power of micronutrients. Assembling and selling salad was, for her, a mission that would save lives. She'd expounded upon this for nearly fifteen minutes before Peter had been able to turn the conversation toward murder. "People don't get murdered for no reason," Skye pronounced.

"Don't you mean that people don't commit murder for no reason?" Peter asked.

"I mean in a karmic sense," Skye said, putting the finishing touches on a big bowl of salad. "Maybe he did something in a previous life."

Peter nearly asked her if she meant that literally, then decided that she almost certainly did.

"But you haven't heard of him doing anything in this particular life that would result in murder, have you?" Peter asked. An inspiration burst forth in his mind. "Like, do you think he might have been cheating on Margaret, for example?"

Skye, at last, seemed to grow suspicious. "Why are you so interested in Roger?"

To Peter's surprise, Evangeline stepped in. "Oh, I don't know, maybe it's because he died right in front of our table last week." She gave Skye an arch look. "Seriously, Skye, don't you wonder what happened to him?"

Skye shook her head. "I refuse to. Dwelling on negative events like that will only impair your inner calm. And it's not my business anyway."

Her answer stunned Peter into silence. Never mind that he was a career reporter for whom the idea of not discovering and subsequently revealing information was inconceivable; he couldn't understand it from a sheerly personal level. A man of his acquaintance had died. To deliberately refrain from even wondering what events led up to another human's demise seemed counter to basic survival.

Hadn't Skye ever heard of an object lesson? And what about basic human empathy? The search for justice?

And yet as Peter made his way through the market, chatting, making small purchases, doing his best to seem like just another vendor shooting the shit on a sunny Saturday afternoon, he found Skye's attitude echoed over and over.

Roger's death was sad, but essentially none of their business. They had other things to worry about: the late spring, the possibility of the Nooksack River flooding, the high price of seed. Their lives went on. And while most of them agreed that someone should be looking into Roger's death, no one felt as though it was their business to make sure justice was served.

In addition to that, nobody thought Roger was cheating on Margaret. That didn't mean he wasn't, but in a place as gossipy as this, consensus being against him dimmed Peter's enthusiasm for his primary theory.

And then there were a few who seemed to Peter to be putting it on a bit.

Beekeeper Jackie, for instance, had a sign on her front table that read, "Ten percent of all proceeds to be donated to the family of Roger Hager."

And she was doing a brisk trade in the votive candles that were being lit in the makeshift shrine next door, as far as Peter could tell. Peter couldn't tell if it was capitalism or capitalizing. Either way, he found it tacky, and that gave him incentive to subtly question the apiarist.

"Sad about Roger," Peter remarked, looking down at the lines of votives.

"I know. It really is. It's such a shock." Jackie adjusted her wide, straw-brimmed sunhat. "Did you hear that it's been declared a murder?"

"Yeah, I did."

"It's good that he wasn't shot," Jackie said.

Peter blinked at the sudden left-turn in the conversation, but he managed to say, "Oh?"

Jackie leaned forward, whispering, "Jenn once shot a man, you know."

"Jenn from Green Goddess Farm?"

Jackie nodded. "She shot her brother-in-law. She was arrested for manslaughter."

"That's not really the same thing," Peter said.

"Oh, I know. Her brother-in-law was seriously abusing Jenn's sister. Nobody thinks it was really an accident."

Again, Peter thought that wasn't really the same, but then again it did cast a certain suspicion over Jenn, in that she'd apparently already killed at least one man. He wondered if Patton knew about this and thought that she must. He really should go down and spend some quality time with police records to find out what else Patton wasn't telling him.

"I had a good friend who was murdered, you know, back in the eighties. The trauma of it awakened my awareness of my past lives. I had been murdered as well, once. I kept having these visions of my own death. I was in the court of the Borgias. I was just a servant, and we had all gone to the countryside to have a picnic. I drank from the wrong cup. I can still see the olive grove where I died. There were yellow daffodils."

It took all the strength Peter could muster not to roll his eyes. Why, he thought, do tragedies like this bring out the attention-seeking weirdos?

Aloud he said, "It must have been quite a shock for you."

"It was. I moved to Bellingham right after that. I just didn't feel safe in Port Townsend anymore."

Whether she didn't feel safe because of her friend's murder or the threat of continued discovery of her painful past lives, Peter had no idea. He didn't feel like asking, either.

Instead he picked up one of the votives. "How much for one of these?"

"Four dollars," she said. She swept her long, wavy hair over her shoulder.

So, forty cents to the grieving not-quite-a-widow. Peter chastised himself for his bad grace. He bought one anyway, lit it and added it to the shrine.

He turned to go and found Jackie watching him, head put

to one side, sad smile on her face. He supposed he shouldn't be so hard on the flaky old kook. She'd lost a bee colony, a dog and her market neighbor all in the same week. And she didn't seem like the sort of person who had a lot of friends, whether insectile, canine or human. Probably she was just lonely.

"By the way, I'm sorry to hear about your dog," Peter said.

Jackie looked up at him, at first uncomprehending, and then sadness rippled across her fine-boned face. Peter had the sudden awareness that he'd awkwardly blundered into what, for Jackie, might be a greater tragedy than the death of her market neighbor. He said, "Roger mentioned it last week."

Jackie nodded and folded her hands into the pockets of her apron. "Celestia was a beautiful dog. She had an AKC pedigree."

"Oh, what sort of dog was she?"

"She was a purebred Alsatian. I got her from a rescue. She had belonged to drug dealers before me. When they went to prison, she went to the pound. I was volunteering there. She put her paw on my hand. Sometimes I think she was the only person who really understood my needs."

Peter nodded and sidled slowly back into the thinning crowd. It was two thirty, and the market would close in half an hour. He ambled back over to the Green Goddess stand. Farmer Jenn was not there.

"I'm just really interested in writing about your farm," Peter said to the lank, skinny woman running the Green Goddess table. "Do you know when she'll be back?"

"She had an appointment this afternoon, so she won't be back, but I can schedule a farm tour if you like. Jenn does them on Sundays." The woman looked especially hopeful. Peter wondered if she got a commission for every farm tour scheduled.

"That would be great," Peter said. He thought it was a good idea to have a look at Margaret's property anyway.

The tour was scheduled for three o'clock the next day, which was apparently quite late in farmer time—the last tour of the day.

When Nick came to give him a ride home Peter had three grocery bags full of beautiful produce, bought more or less at random while conducting his interviews.

"Decided to become a vegetarian?" Nick asked.

"I've decided to embrace the healing power of micronutrients," Peter replied sourly.

"Did you hear anything interesting about Roger's death?"

"What makes you think I was fishing around for information about that?"

"Why else would you be here?" Nick shrugged his big shoulders. "Plus Officer Patton called the house. She wants you to call her when you get home."

Curse you landline, thought Peter bitterly. Aloud he said, "I wonder what she wants?"

Apparently, his delivery was unconvincing because Nick said, "So, are you working with the police officially or unofficially?"

"Why would I be working with the police at all?"

"Well, you said Officer Patton came to see you at the *Hamster* office, and then later you said that you had insider knowledge about the substance used to poison Roger. Who else would be your insider?" Nick glanced over at him and flashed a crooked smile. "You're not the only one who can play this sleuth game, you know."

"I had no idea that you would ever want to." And he hadn't. Nick's interest in the trials and tribulations of most other human beings was limited at best.

"I like to know what my registered domestic partner is up to."

In spite of himself—in spite of being busted snooping like this—Peter smiled.

"Okay, yes I am trying to get information for Officer Patton, but today I struck out. Nobody has any big ideas about who would want to kill Roger. Most of them saw him at the big dinner on Friday night. Those that did said he looked fine, argued with no one and seemed in good spirits. He had no enemies that anybody can remember."

"So you had a pretty frustrating day then?" Nick observed.

"Yes, it was a waste of time and I've got nothing to tell Patton." Peter shoved his toe against the paper bag of vegetables. Dark, crenulated leaves of black kale protruded from the top. He had no idea how one might transform bunches of leafy greens like these into food.

"What if I told you that I made my own discovery?" Nick asked. He did so casually, not even glancing over at Peter.

"And did you?"

"I did."

"Tell me," Peter demanded.

"Tell me what you're planning to do with all these vegetables first," Nick said.

"I was going to take them to the food bank."

"Not make me a delicious meal of kale, cabbage and garlic scapes?"

"I could make you a meal, but I guarantee it wouldn't be delicious," Peter said. "Now come on, spill it."

"Well, I went by the studio to go pick up my vase today—"

"The one that has Roger's ashes fired into it?"

"Right. It's beautiful. The crystals bloomed in this coral-like way." Nick paused and glanced slyly over at Peter.

He was enjoying this, Peter realized. He said, "Nick if you're going to torture me, I'd prefer it if you let me dress up in my slutty medieval heretic costume first."

"You don't have a slutty medieval heretic costume."

"I'll buy one and put it on if you stop tormenting me."

"All right, I'm sorry. While I was at the studio I ran into a few other people who'd been at the memorial with us. In particular, Jenn from Green Goddess Farm. She and another farmer were talking about improvements that she was going to make to her farm property," Nick said.

Nicole Kimberling

"Her farm..." All at once, understanding bloomed in Peter's mind. "Don't tell me. Jenn inherits the property from Margaret now that Roger's out of the way."

"Correct," Nick said.

"That is very interesting to me," Peter said. He explained what he'd heard about Jenn's former conviction from Jackie. Nick's eyebrows shot up.

"Do you think that's true?" he asked.

"It would be easy enough to find out," Peter said. "But about the inheritance—certainly the police have looked into that angle."

"I'm not sure they have. There aren't any formal documents drawn up. From what I could tell, a long time ago Margaret had made a verbal agreement to give the land to Jenn. Apparently, Margaret's decided to make good on this," Nick said. "What do you think? Do I deserve that dinner?"

"You deserve something. Pull over behind this building."

Nick eyed him in a sidelong and suspicious manner, and drawled, "Why would I want to do that?"

"I promise I'll make it worth your while if you do," Peter coaxed.

Nick remained unmoved. He drove down Cornwall Street, past the rows of warehouse parking lots—mostly empty because it was Saturday—as if he had no idea that Peter was offering to give him head.

Or maybe he didn't?

"When I say I'll make it worth your while what I mean is that I want to suck your cock right now," Peter stated in what he felt was both a reasonable and convincing fashion that would result in Nick immediately slamming on the breaks.

"Yeah, I got that." Nick turned up onto up a steep, winding road and ascended the slope to State Street. Boulevard Park would be on their right, but there would be dozens of people there on a nice day.

"Don't you think that would be nice?" Peter asked.

"Oh yes, I do."

"Then if you'd just pull over someplace somewhat secluded I'd be happy to do just that."

"What's in it for you, though," Nick said. They'd reached Fairhaven now, wended their way through its historic buildings and dull condos and were heading toward the Rose Garden.

"What do you mean, what's in it for me? I like your cock a lot."

"Yeah, we've got that in common. I like yours too." Nick gave Peter another sidelong look. "How's he doing?"

Peter didn't know whether this was an invitation to whip it out while driving, but decided that it must be and did so.

"He's doing okay, but he's sleepy from being locked up in the pants all day."

This seemed to amuse Nick, who said, "Looks like you're helping him stand up pretty well."

Peter felt his cheeks get hot. *So this is how it's going to be, eh, Mr. Olson?*

Peter reclined his seat and pulled his shirt up slightly. Keeping his eyes on Nick he slowly worked his hand down the shaft. It felt weird to make such a spectacle, but also very, very hot.

Nick seemed to think so too, since he abruptly jerked his eyes back to the road.

Peter felt the balance of power shifting back toward himself, which was where he liked it.

"Having a hard time keeping your eyes on the road?" Peter asked. He writhed obtrusively.

A truck whizzed by, going the opposite direction. Had the driver seen him? There was no way to be sure. The thought of it sent a rush of taboo pleasure through Peter.

His dick throbbed in his hand.

But he definitely had to tone it down if there was going to be anything left of him by the time they got home, which was clearly Nick's intended destination.

Still Peter couldn't help taunting the big guy.

"Does he look okay now?" Peter asked.

"He looks great," Nick said and stepped on the accelerator, blasting down the road as fast as the hairpin turns of the cliffside road would allow. Peter couldn't help laughing as the g-forces rolled him from side to side. His pants had worked down to his knees now.

He recognized the trees surrounding the private road that led to their house and propped himself up on one elbow. Nick skidded to a halt on the gravel alongside their house.

They were at the top of the bluff. Yellow late-afternoon sun sparkled over the glittering, emerald water. Out in the channel, sailboats slid past, skating the sea between them and the gentle mounds of the San Juan Islands.

Nick switched on the stereo. Deep, lazy summer drumbeats rolled through the car's perfectly matched speakers. He unbuckled his seat belt, pushed the seat back, and said, "I like this view better."

Peter wasted no time. Heedless of the e-brake pushing into his stomach, he bent to free Nick's already straining cock from the cruel bondage of jeans and boxer-briefs.

He took the head into his mouth. The music swelled and so did Nick. His hand rested on the back of Peter's neck.

Nick's hips jerked forward in enthusiasm, and Peter opened his throat wider to accommodate Nick's hearty entry.

It had been a while since Peter had given anyone head in a car, and it wasn't comfortable. But by stroking his own dick to the same rhythm he sucked, he managed to drown out the ache in his back and focus on the delicious sensations running through his body and the sight of Nick sitting there in the driver's seat, cock glistening with his sweat, balls tightening with each bob of Peter's head.

Peter changed up the rhythm, and Nick gave a quiet murmur of approval, his fingers massaging Peter's neck with increased distraction. Peter licked at Nick's slit and the fingers tightened further.

Peter pulled from Nick's cock to ask, "Better than my crappy cooking yet?"

"Oh yes," Nick whispered, his hand urging Peter's mouth back down to where he clearly felt it belonged. Peter took him deeper and sped up the action, reading the thrusts of Nick's hips for timing. Nick's hand clenched the back of his neck painfully, and he released, filling Peter's mouth with repeated spurts.

Peter waited until he was certain he'd gotten the last of Nick's orgasm, then pulled back to swallow. Nick kissed him sloppily, eyes looking a little glazed. His hand joined Peter's on Peter's cock, and within moments Peter gasped and came, shooting into his own palm.

He slumped there, breathing against Nick's neck. Then he caught a glimmer of motion from the corner of his eye. A navy-blue sedan festooned with far too many radio antennae to be a private citizen's vehicle prowled up the driveway.

"Shit! Cops!" Peter jerked away from Nick. He grappled with his pants, trying to hoist them back into socially acceptable position.

Nick glanced over his shoulder in a casual and relaxed way that Peter felt was completely unwarranted. He sighed and zipped himself up.

"We're on private property, you know," Nick told him.

"I know that." Peter dragged the back of his hand across his mouth. "It's just that if it's Patton, I want to look professional."

"Why would she be driving an unmarked car?" Nick asked.

"I don't know. But that is definitely a cop car."

Nick offered a handkerchief, and Peter finished cleaning off his face and fingers just as the sedan crunched to a halt.

Peter smoothed his pants, turned, and saw no dykey hairdo. Through the windshield he saw the cue-ball head of Detective Mills.

He wanted a private word with Peter. Though visibly reluctant, Nick excused himself and went inside.

"I've just had a conversation with Officer Patton, and she says you're working with her on this investigation of Roger Hager's death," Mills said.

"I've agreed to share information, yes," Peter replied. He crossed his arms over his skinny chest. He was having a hard time coming up to speed, having had sex mere minutes before. A haze of endorphins hung over his brain like an anesthetizing cloud.

"I've just spoken with Ms. Bear. She's not happy that we're continuing our investigation." Mills looked cagey, as if he were revealing information that he shouldn't.

"Yes, she told Nick and me that when we were at Roger's studio the other day," Peter said. "She thinks that Officer Patton is fabricating a case to solve so she can get that promotion. Some friend in the department told her as much."

Anger flashed over Mills's face. "Which friend?"

"All she said was that some dispatcher friend of hers told her."

"Bear specifically told you that an unnamed dispatcher thinks Officer Patton is...what...falsifying reports to construct a case?"

"I don't know. All Margaret said was that somebody in the department told her it would be convenient for Patton to have a murder case to solve," Peter said. "So, is it true?"

For one moment, Peter thought Mills would strike him out of sheer affronted rage. Belatedly he realized that by even voicing Margaret's concern, he cast aspersions on a fellow officer. Of course Mills would be angered by that—but how angry? Peter glanced around for any sign of Nick. If he was going to get beat up by a cop, he at least wanted a witness. But just as suddenly as Mills's temper flared, his cop self-restraint training appeared to kick in and he said, "That's not what I came here to speak with you about."

"So what can I do for you, then?" Peter leaned back against Nick's car. He found it strangely comforting, like leaning back against Nick himself.

"I came here to ask you not to contact Ms. Bear again. We don't want to antagonize her into filing a complaint. She's been cooperative so far, in spite of what she allegedly thinks."

"Did she say I was harassing her?" Peter had thought his interaction with Margaret had gone fairly well, considering what she thought of both him and the police.

"No, but if you keep questioning her, it's just a matter of time before she grows weary of interrogation," Mills said.

"Noted. I appreciate your coming out here. I won't contact Margaret again." As Peter shook Mills's hand, he forced himself to suppress all thoughts of what he'd just been doing with that hand and how Mills might feel about shaking it if he knew.

Mills started to go, but after a couple steps turned back. He said, "Make sure to let me know if you ever find out the name of Margaret's dispatcher friend."

"I will," Peter said.

In fact, he thought, he'd like to know that himself. As he watched Mills perform a perfect three-point turn with his sedan, he wondered whether it had been a good idea to reveal that anyone who worked for the police had been talking out of turn.

In fact, he got the distinct feeling that someone was about to lose their job.

Chapter Eight

On Sunday around noon, Peter phoned Officer Patton's private number. When she answered the phone, her voice was flat and noncommittal as usual, just louder. Quite loud, actually. And even then her high-decibel, "This is Patton," barely registered above a series of high-pitched shrieking giggles, childish music, and barking dogs.

It was, in fact the sound of children—quite a few children. And at least two dogs.

"It's Peter, I've got some news."

"Right, just let me get outside."

A few seconds passed while the sound of maniacally happy children receded. He heard a screen door creak open and then close, then the sound of nothing but traffic noise.

"Okay then, what do you have for me?" she asked.

Peter related the information as he'd heard it. Officer Patton interjected occasionally to ask for clarification. Interestingly enough, unlike Mills, she did not ask for the name of Margaret's dispatcher friend, which to Peter implied that she must already know. Finally she said, "You seem to have focused pretty exclusively on interviewing the women."

"I read that virtually all poisoners are female," Peter admitted.

"Just remember that the operative word there is *virtually*," she remarked.

"Anything else?"

"I couldn't find anybody who thought Roger was having an affair. Not one single person."

"What made you think he might be?" Her voice was cool, but there was something in the tone that told Peter he'd been following the right instinct.

"The honey," Peter said firmly. "If he really was taking it on purpose as a kind of homeopathic Viagra, then who was he supposed to be having sex with? Margaret is on oxygen, in pain, doped up, and dying. Roger was pretty healthy for an old guy. I can't imagine that Margaret would be so hot to trot that Roger would need more and longer-lasting boners."

"Not the way I would have put it, but a similar thought crossed my mind," Patton said. "And what was your feeling about Jackie Chambers?"

"Beekeeper Jackie? Harmless fruitcake," Peter pronounced. "I think that whoever poisoned Roger used honey to cast suspicion on her."

"And you didn't find the fact that she claims that a friend of hers has been murdered suspicious?" Patton asked.

"I...not really, no," Peter admitted. "Did you already know that?"

"This is the first I've heard of it. Jackie Chambers was questioned in a drowning death in Port Townsend, but the deceased was not her friend. It was her daughter. I find it interesting that she would tell you the daughter had been murdered."

"She also told me it triggered memories of her own past lives. Do you think that having her daughter die pushed her over the edge?"

"Possibly," Patton said. "What's your feeling on Jenn Jones?"

"She seems friendly but all these farmers are a little bit...I don't know...cold, I guess. I'm going to go out to Margaret's property this afternoon to meet Jenn for a farm tour. Hopefully she'll have some interesting things to say. Don't worry. I won't try to speak with Margaret directly."

"Why not?"

"Detective Mills told me not to when he came to see me yesterday. In fact, he came specifically to tell me to back off."

There was a long silence then she said, "Right."

"I did have one question to ask you, though," Peter ventured.

"Go ahead," Patton said.

Nicole Kimberling

"About Margaret's dispatcher friend—"

"The one who thinks I'm making the whole thing up to get ahead?" The tone that Peter heard in Patton's voice wasn't exactly rancor, but it came close.

"That's the one. Do you know who that is?"

"I have an idea. And before you ask, I'm not going to share that idea," Patton said.

"Listen, there has been one interesting bit of information uncovered."

"Yeah?"

"Traces of the cooked death camus were found inside the Spunky the Squirrel getup," Patton said.

"So whoever put the camus on Roger's plate that night concealed it inside the suit?"

"Exactly."

"Who was wearing the suit when dinner was served?" Peter asked.

"Well, there is some disagreement about that. About six different people wore that suit on Friday night and Saturday. They took shifts, apparently."

"Do you want me to see if I can figure out exactly who wore it at what time?"

"I think that we can handle establishing the timeline," Patton said. Peter heard a hint of amusement in her voice as she continued, "We do know that Roger himself was in the thing for a while on Friday evening as was Jenn Jones, Skuter Reynolds and Jackie Chambers. Thomas Linderman wore it the next day."

"So that's the list of suspects?" Peter said. "You can go ahead and cross Tommy off right away. He didn't have any reason to kill Roger. He didn't even really know the guy."

"And yet he has no one who can confirm his whereabouts at the exact time of Roger's death," Patton countered.

"I just don't think—"

"Relax Mr. Fontaine. I doubt your friend has much to do with it, but I also don't like to rule out any options. Just keep

82

me in the loop on—" Patton's voice cut off abruptly. Peter heard the screen door opening again and a female voice informing Patton that she had better get into the kitchen since they were about to cut the cake. In tones so soft and respectful that Peter barely recognized the speaker, Patton assured her companion that she'd be right in. Then, to Peter, she said, "Sorry about that. Gotta go. Kid's birthday party."

Peter ended the call and went to gather his muck boots for his Sunday drive in the country. He invited Nick along but the other man demurred, saying he'd already gone on a great number of recreational tours, including one of Margaret's agricultural holdings when he'd been with his now deceased first lover, Walter de Kamp.

"Remember to bring your camera," Nick said. "You'll want to take some pictures."

"Right, it might help the investigation."

Nick shrugged and said, "That and her property is stunningly gorgeous."

Peter suddenly felt like a cretin for not even bothering to consider beauty as a reason one might want to photograph a location. He pressed a kiss onto Nick's cheek, "As gorgeous as our property?"

"Not when you're in it," Nick countered, causing Peter to blush.

They'd been sickeningly lovey-dovey like this for days, but neither of them seemed to be able to stop. Not-quite-wedding residue, Peter supposed.

Nick continued, "But otherwise, yeah, once you get to the farm, you'll want to snap a few pics."

True to Nick's word, Margaret's property in Everson was beautiful. It sat right on the edge of town, alongside the Nooksack River. Eagles soared above the neat rows of vegetables and wheeled over the ranks of greenhouses that sheltered the less cold-tolerant crops.

Green Goddess Farm was only one of several small-scale operations that rented land from Margaret. Some of them grew food exclusively for sale at farmer's markets and roadside stalls, while others had gotten into wholesaling.

Jenn Jones met them near a farm stand out front. She was dressed in the standard Carhartts-and-unisex-rubber-boots combo that seemed to be the dress code among Whatcom County farmers. Behind her Peter could see a stocky, handsome man in overalls fixing an elderly tractor. That would be Skuter Reynolds, the man Jenn had been conversing with at Roger's memorial service. He wondered if their connection was strictly business or if it spilled over into the personal. There were two separate poisonings, after all. That meant that there could have been two separate poisoners.

"We've recently started working with the hospital, providing fresh vegetables to their kitchen." Jenn was clearly giving him the standard promotional line; he was a member of the press. "You said before that you might be interested in a CSA? It's not too late to get the preseason discount."

"Absolutely." Peter had only discovered the existence of the CSA the previous day as he made his rounds through the market. For a fee, one could basically subscribe to receive fresh vegetables from a farm. Every week for twenty weeks, he could pick up a blue tote full of whatever the farm was harvesting right then. The sample list seemed to include more cruciferous vegetables and roots than Peter normally included in his diet.

Having been a huge fan of neither vegetables nor cooking, Peter's interest in the CSA was lukewarm, but he feigned like a champ.

"Do you ever include any of the local food in the CSA?"

Jenn cocked her head in confusion. "It's all local food."

"I mean the kind of food that was served at that Local Eats dinner. You know, salmon and camus and berries."

Jenn let out a loud laugh. "Sometimes we include things like strawberries or blueberries but we try not to put in too many weird vegetables that people don't know how to cook. Were you at the dinner?"

"No, but my friend Evangeline was. She said it was a lot of fun. I hear you got to wear the Spunky Suit."

"Not for long, thank God," Jenn said, rolling her eyes. "The inside of that suit stank so bad. I only got in it because it was making Roger sneeze so much. We've got to get that thing dry cleaned before next year."

"Or buy a new one," Peter suggested.

Jenn shook her head. "Those things cost more than a thousand dollars. The market committee would never agree to fork that much money out."

They walked a few more rows of mysterious vegetables. Peter sensed Jenn's patience wavering, so he asked more about CSA prices, suggesting that he'd use the information in an article.

"Do you mind if I take a few photographs?" Peter asked. "Just to have something to break up the blocks of text."

"Go right ahead," Jenn said. "This land is so beautiful. Margaret's a good landlord too. This farm's been in her family for about a hundred years."

"Really." Peter pointed his camera down a row of budding plants. Cabbages? He really had no idea. They were pretty though, so he snapped a picture. Refocused his viewfinder, snapped again. Apart from the newly tilled rows and tender shoots, greenhouses dotted the landscape. There was a big farmhouse too, and a smaller, much more modest house. The smaller house seemed to be surrounded by a variety of junk. A small cross, fashioned out of a couple of repurposed fence pickets sat behind it. Somebody's beloved cat, most likely.

Jenn noted the direction of his focus. "That little house was the original building Margaret's great-grandfather built."

"Looks like it's mostly used for storage now," Peter commented. He zoomed in. On the south side of the building a line of white, rectangular boxes came into focus.

"No, that's just Jackie's overflow. She lives in the small house now," Jenn said. She gave a nervous laugh. "I'd appreciate it if you wouldn't print any pictures of that, if you wouldn't mind. We're in a little bit of a fight with the county about that right now, but it's going to be resolved."

"Sure thing." Peter snapped the picture anyway. "What are you in a fight about, if you don't mind my asking."

"Well, Jackie's a little bit of a pack rat."

"A pack rat?"

"I guess the technical term is compulsive hoarder. You should see the inside of the house. It's floor-to-ceiling in there. Roger and I had a big fight about Jackie right before he died," Jenn said. "It tears me up that I didn't really get a chance to make up with him now."

"Why were the two of you fighting about Jackie?"

"Last year the neighbors started to complain about the junk on the property around her house. They said it was a haven for rats and other vermin. The county came out and threatened to fine Margaret if she didn't get the place cleaned up. All of us out here got together to try and help Jackie get the house back into shape."

"And it didn't go too well?"

"She just wouldn't let us throw anything away. After that Margaret wanted to evict Jackie and sent Roger over to talk to her," Jenn said. "Roger went over and gave Jackie this completely unhelpful ultimatum. I mean, Jackie's sick and she's ruining that house, but she's been here for fifteen years. She's part of this farm. I was hoping to get her some psychological help instead."

"Why didn't you?" Peter snapped another picture.

"No money. Jackie doesn't have health insurance. I was calling around to sliding-scale clinics but didn't have a lot of luck. I even phoned that TV show, *Clutter Cops*. They sent someone out to scout the place for one of next season's episodes."

"But it didn't work out?"

"No, they actually agreed. They thought she'd make great TV, I guess," Jenn said. "It's worked out for all of us. We're going to get the property cleaned up and Jackie will get some aftercare money which I think she really needs. She's been really depressed since her dog died. She was sick for so long."

"Jackie?"

"Celestia, the dog," Jenn corrected.

Peter nodded. Probably Celestia was the one buried beneath that cross. "But if the problem of cleaning up the property was going to be solved, why were you and Roger still fighting?"

Jenn seemed reluctant to answer. Peter said, "It's okay. You don't have to tell me. Just reporter's instinct—asking questions."

"No, it's all right. Margaret had decided to draw up a will that would split this land between Roger and me fifty-fifty. I've been farming out here for seven years. I understand the people out here. Roger shows up and suddenly thinks he's got any right to give orders. He knows fuck-all about farming. I guess the fight about Jackie was more of a fight about how things are going to get done around here after Margaret passes away. Before Roger moved in, we had a pretty good system, and I didn't want it wrecked by some know-nothing artist." Jenn seemed to suddenly remember who Peter was and then realize her blunder. "No offense to your boyfriend."

"None taken," Peter said. "Art school isn't famous for preparing someone for a career as an agrarian landlord."

"Truer words were never spoken, " Jenn said. "But I felt bad about it. I shouldn't have said the things I said. I called him a freeloader and that wasn't true. He made Margaret really happy. That's something money can't buy. He earned his keep just by doing that, I think."

Chapter Nine

Monday morning in the *Hamster* office was never good, but this morning Peter felt serious frustration.

He had spent an entire week talking to everyone he could think of about Roger and at the end of it he still had nothing. Everything about Roger's death was disconnected, like a pocket full of disparate puzzle pieces that refused to assemble themselves into any larger picture. Of the people he'd spoken with over the last week only one person had any real motivation for killing: Jenn. But his conversation with her the previous day had left him with no suspicion.

Yes, she'd killed her brother-in-law. Information on that had been easy to find.

She'd shot him in a hunting accident. And yes, the brother-in-law had been arrested twice in domestic disputes with Jenn's sister, but police could produce no evidence that the shooting had been anything but a genuine hunting accident.

And it didn't add up. A woman who shoots her brother-in-law, presuming that Jenn truly had premeditated that crime, does not then go on to solve another personal problem by poisoning.

According to all his research, poisoners generally stuck to poison if they committed successive murders. They often practiced on an unrelated person before taking out their actual target. Though poisoners utterly lacked empathy, they were not confrontational people.

Shooting a guy, as Jenn had allegedly done, was about as confrontational as it got.

No, it had to be someone else.

Most likely a person who had poisoned at least one other person for practice. The poisoner would have had to practice, especially considering how esoteric these particular poisons had been. Honey and lily bulbs weren't the kinds of toxins that assured a fatality at just any dosage. But no one else had been poisoned in the city—not that they knew at least. And with such a unique combination of poisons Peter couldn't help but think it would have been noticed.

According to his research, neither the death camus nor the honey would be enough by themselves to kill a healthy guy like Roger. And because of the medical report, they knew that Roger had ingested the camus on Friday night and the honey on Saturday morning. The person or people who poisoned him would have had to have opportunity on both Friday night and Saturday morning. That should have narrowed the suspects down, but because of the Local Eats dinner, the same vast cast of characters had been present at both events.

Peter spent the morning drawing graphs, Venn diagrams, and charts that ultimately didn't do anything but rearrange the information that he already knew in different unhelpful shapes. Finally at noon, Doug rose, stretched and began to amble his way.

Peter pretended to be very busy in hopes of avoiding an invitation to lunch. Not that he disliked lunching with Doug, but the conversation would invariably turn to what Peter had been working on all week. An inquiry about word count would follow that.

Peter needed at all costs to avoid any discussion of word counts.

He heard Doug's footsteps approach and then stop. Peter glanced up in time to see a set of worn russet corduroy trousers perch themselves on the edge of his desk. The trousers gave way to a tattersall dress shirt decorated with a brown and burgundy paisley tie. Above the collar of this, Doug's face floated in a halo of thinning white hair.

He wore a detached, kindly expression that frightened Peter. For a man as cantankerous as Doug, deliberate calm could only mean that he anticipated some sort of confrontation.

"How's your week been?" Doug asked.

"Pretty good. Busy with the Roger Hager thing." Peter looked pointedly to his screen, wearing an expression of intense interest as though no mere momentary interruption should be allowed to disrupt his creative flow.

"I heard you and Nick got registered as domestic partners," Doug said, disapproval obvious in his tone. If he hadn't known Doug well, he would have assumed homophobia motivated him. But Doug's beef was the government itself. Any government regulating anything about the personal lives of adults irritated him.

"Yeah, we did," Peter said. "I know what you're going to say—"

"No you don't." Doug bristled.

"Yes I do, you wrote a whole screed on it when the domestic partnership law was passed in 2007. You think it's just another way for the state to get fees out of people without providing any services. You think marriage itself is an outmoded institution that you want no part of." Peter could tell Doug wanted to issue a rebuttal, but Peter wouldn't stop talking long enough to let him. "But what you don't understand is that getting that piece of paper is meaningful to me, regardless of what you think. Not only is it an important step for Nick and I eventually gaining all the civil rights that you are free to not use, deride and discard at your leisure, but domestic partnership is what I can get right now and so I'm going to take it."

Peter stopped. He realized that he'd raised his voice and now the whole office was looking at him.

"I'm sorry to yell like that," he said. "It's like that old saying: one man's trash is another man's treasure."

Doug took a deep breath, then clamped a hand on Peter's shoulder and said, "I didn't think you read my articles. I'm touched."

"I always read your articles," Peter said.

"Well, I didn't mean anything about you personally. I'm glad you're happy... Congratulations."

"Thank you."

Doug glanced around the office and the rest of the staff suddenly all found a wide variety of ways to be busy. "Have you spoken to the cops about Hager again?"

"It's just the one cop," Peter answered, then had to amend. "Okay, I talked to two cops."

"And how many inches is the article going to be, do you think?"

"Well, I don't know if I'm that well-placed to break the story about Roger's murderer yet. Legally—"

Peter's explanation was cut short by Doug's hand slamming down on the desk. "I knew you didn't have anything to turn in." Doug stood, stuck his hands in his pockets. "You haven't written a word, have you?"

"Investigative reporting requires investigating," Peter said sourly. He'd had this argument with Doug so many times that it had become almost a formality between them.

"I require a full, three thousand word article of some sort by two o'clock this afternoon."

"I really don't know who killed him yet," Peter pleaded.

"Then write about something else." Doug rocked back on his heels. "What else have you got?"

"Nothing, I mean, I found out that Roger was an art forger, but that's it. I have two of the fake vases at my house."

Doug sucked in his breath sharply. He regarded Peter with an expression of complete bafflement. He said, "And you don't think you have a story?"

"Well, I don't know that the *Hamster* readers care about art enough—"

"Just write about the goddamn counterfeit vases."

"Forgeries," Peter corrected.

"Whatever they're called. Write about them. We've got to give the people a reason to advertise with us." Doug turned grandly on his heel. "At two o'clock there better be something in my inbox."

Rebuked and slightly humiliated, Peter got to work. He turned the article in at one fifty eight and then took the excuse of lunch to get out of the office.

He headed down Chuckanut Drive toward the Castle feeling grimy and worn down.

When he got home, Nick was, as always, painting. Gigi, his constant companion lounged among crumpled tubes and bottles of acrylic. She looked up blinking as Peter entered.

"How was the office?" Nick asked.

"Boring. Frustrating. How was painting?" He wiggled his fingers at Gigi, and she went over to receive her due ration of affectionate back scratches.

Really, Peter thought, this cat was the most spoiled creature he'd ever met.

"Also sort of frustrating." Nick rinsed his brush in the large tub of water.

Attracted by the noise and motion, Gigi walked over, watching the motion of the water as though nothing could be more interesting. And weirdly enough, Nick was also watching her—with suspicion. He poked a long finger at Gigi and said, "Don't even think about it."

"Are you two fighting?" Peter inquired.

Nick sighed. "Only because she keeps trying to kill herself."

"Did she chew through your headphone cord again?" The cat had a bad habit of attempting to electrocute herself by gnawing through thin electrical cords. No cable of light gauge was safe from her.

"No, she just keeps trying to drink my rinse water. What is it about cats that they can't get enough dirty old paint water?"

"Maybe it tastes good," Peter offered. "Puts the *yum* in cadmium."

"How good can heavy metals taste?" Just as Nick asked, Gigi made a dive for it, managing to dip her tongue twice before Nick shooed her away and covered the tub with a paint-smeared glass palette. "Seriously, cat, stop drinking this. It's poison."

Foiled in her unwittingly self-destructive plan, Gigi let out a frustrated yowl.

Peter, on the other hand, found that he was, for the first time today, relieved of the burden of frustration.

Because, all at once, he thought he knew who killed Roger.

And he even knew how to prove it—or thought he did.

And he almost said so out loud before he thought better of it. The evidence would have to be acquired in a way that he was certain Nick would disapprove of. As casually as he could he said, "Well, I just came by to say I've got to head back out to the farm in Everson."

"Oh?"

"Yeah, I won't be long. I've just got to get some information to finish the article before Doug replaces me with someone who's better at puff pieces."

"Will you be back for dinner? I found a couple of recipes for garlic scapes that look interesting."

"Sure," Peter said. "I'll only be a couple of hours."

Alive with excitement, Peter slid through the front door and into the cracked bucket seat of his car.

Everything had come together.

Jackie's dog. Her sickly, ailing dog that had taken a long time to die.

Maybe the killer couldn't afford the attention of poisoning two people with such an unusual combination of toxins, but the authorities were much less likely to notice the death of a dog. If Peter was right, then all he had to do was wait till dark, go to the farm, dig up the dog, and bring it into town to be autopsied.

The tangle of broken and rusted farm equipment would shield the dog's grave from view from both the big farmhouse and Jackie's falling-down shack.

Briefly, he considered telling Patton about his plan but decided on the whole that it would be a bad idea. He was about to trespass at the very least. Plus he didn't think she'd buy his dog theory. And he obviously couldn't offer sufficient evidence for her to acquire a warrant.

He couldn't tell Nick for reasons very similar to the ones that got Patton crossed off the need-to-know list: illegal, borderline unethical even for a reporter, disgusting, and possibly dangerous.

He chose not to enlighten Evangeline as to the specifics of his plan simply because he knew that she'd probably want to dress up in disguises or want to document the whole thing for some future art installation.

But he needed her to be on the lookout.

So Peter picked her up in town and waited until they'd stopped at the gas station in Everson—he needed new batteries for his flashlight—before saying, "I lied about needing your help to interview the people at the farm."

"I figured," Evangeline said. "Are you and Nick in a fight? They say that relationships change after you get married."

"Fight? No, I just need your help to dig up a dead dog."

Evangeline sat still for a long moment and then said, "Is this for your work?"

"Yes. It has to do with Roger Hager's murder."

Evangeline nodded slowly. "Okay then."

Her surprisingly copasetic attitude pleased him so much that he bought her a king-size candy bar while he was picking up the batteries. They drove the half mile to the farm. As he turned down the winding ruts that led toward Jackie's house, Peter switched off his headlights and thanked the Great Reporter in the Sky for the full moon.

Evangeline said, "You don't have permission to do this, do you?"

"Not technically," Peter replied sheepishly.

No more words passed between them as Peter maneuvered the car over the rutted road and at last came to a stop. He killed the ignition and took a moment to make sure that he'd switched

off the interior car light so that it wouldn't automatically illu-
minate them when they opened the doors. Then he turned to
Evangeline. "Don't slam the door when you get out, okay?"

"Right."

"Actually, don't close the door. We might have to run for it.
And don't turn on the flashlight unless I say so."

Evangeline gave him a hard look before whispering, "You
are going to owe me so big for this."

"That's fair."

Peter eased the door opened, got the shovel out of the
back seat and handed Evangeline the flashlight. Together they
crept across the uneven terrain to the white cross stuck into the
ground.

Jackie had hung a wreath of plastic flowers over it. Red and
blue roses.

Momentary doubt passed through Peter. But it was too late
to turn back. He had to know if he was right. He started digging.
The ground was damp and heavy.

"Somehow this seems cruel," Evangeline whispered.

"It's not like we're waking him up," Peter countered. "And
it's not illegal to dig up a dead dog."

"I'm pretty sure it's illegal to be here at all, though," Evangeline whispered.

"You two stop that right now!"

The voice made Peter's blood run cold. He heard the un-
mistakable click of a rifle being cocked. Very slowly he put up
his hands.

"You're trespassing on my property."

Jackie stood with her .22 aimed right at him.

"Technically it's only illegal if you have a sign posted," Peter
said. "Or if you ask me to leave and I don't. But I can see you'd
like my friend and me to go, so we'll just be on our way."

Peter backed up a step. Evangeline was white as a sheet and
staring down the barrel of the rifle. She wasn't following his
lead.

She was rooted to the spot with fear. And seeing that fear, Jackie advanced.

"Don't you move!" Jackie hissed. Peter could see the gun barrel shaking in her grip. It would only take one twitch to kill Evangeline.

Peter did not take one more step.

A strange silence ensued. Bats flew overhead calling to one another. Peter realized that Jackie was thinking up a plan. Or rather he realized she hadn't had a plan when she'd picked up her rifle.

Conversationally, he said, "If you're not going to let us leave, what are you planning to do with us?"

"Shut up! I haven't decided yet," Jackie said. "I have to think."

The doubt that Peter so longed to hear in her voice was not there. The only thing keeping them alive, apparently, was Jackie's indecision about how to do away with them.

"Look, I'm sorry we were trespassing, but is it really worth it to shoot us?" Peter glanced to Evangeline, who actually managed to peel her eyes off the gun long enough to stare at him in WTF?-level confusion. Peter continued, "We'll just go."

"Don't patronize me," Jackie said. "I know what you're trying to do."

"Okay, you're right. I was trying to steal your dog. I wanted the bones for an art project. I'm willing to call the police and turn myself in and take the punishment. I have a phone in my pocket." Peter moved his hand very gently down.

Immediately Jackie whipped the gun around on him. He froze. "Or you could use your own phone. Whichever you choose."

Far across the field, Peter spied a set of headlights moving along the road.

Please, please turn and see us.

The driver kept going. No salvation of headlights flashed across them. The car drove by and they stood, an unseen tableau in the darkness. Again the silence fell. He could scream, he thought, maybe get the attention of someone from the farmhouse. But screaming might startle Jackie, and Evangeline might end up dead.

Why is Nick always right about me and the night and the lunatics? Why does he have to be right all the time? Can't I be right sometimes?

Then his phone went off. It played the little tune Peter had programmed it to play when Nick called.

Nick was calling him right now. Probably to ask him when he planned to be back for dinner. And here he was, going behind Nick's back, digging up corpses, getting his BFF held at gunpoint. No wonder it was hard to get Nick to say what it was he loved about him.

Nick was definitely a better boyfriend than him. If he got to see Nick again, he would certainly tell him so immediately.

The tune emitted by Peter's phone seemed to mobilize Jackie.

"You two come with me to the house," she said. Peter had been down this road before. Moving to a more secluded location with a person holding a gun was not a good idea. He was not going to go inside and let Jackie shoot him in the privacy of her own home. He'd have to make his stand right here.

But Evangeline started walking. She took one shaky step after another toward Jackie's dubious abode.

He could run now. Maybe if Jackie shot at him, Evangeline could make a break. One look at his friend's face told him that was not going to happen. She was too scared to run. And he couldn't leave her behind, so he followed her across the muddy ground to the wicker-cluttered, sagging porch of Jackie's house.

Evangeline opened the door, and the stench hit them like a wall. Peter began to choke then cough. Evangeline balked.

"I said go inside right now." Jackie shoved his shoulder with the butt of the rifle.

Peter went forward.

Jackie came last, flipping on the lights as she crossed the threshold.

What Peter could see of Jackie's kitchen was filthy. Peeling black and white linoleum tiles curled up from the warped subflooring. Here and there puddles of standing water sheeted across them so their sharp corners broke the surface like islands in a fetid sea.

He couldn't really see much of the rest of the room because it was piled, floor to ceiling with garbage. Stacks of papers, black plastic bags, and moldering corrugated boxes took up every surface. The dinette set had been completely engulfed, chairs and all. He assumed there must be a stove and sink, but he couldn't see where they were.

Beyond the kitchen, Peter spied flashing light. He guessed there was a television on in that room, but it looked just as full as this one.

"See that jar of honey?" Jackie gestured to where Peter thought the counter stood.

"No," Peter said, honestly. He couldn't see anything in the jumble.

"The one with the red label."

"Yes." Peter located the patch of red. The word *vintage* came to mind as well as the word *antique*. The discolored, peeling label looked like it had been submerged in water and then fished out and left to dry. From the look of the floor, that seemed to be exactly what had happened. As he pulled it out, his motion dislodged a laundry-basket-size pile of papers—mostly junk mail—that slid down to the wet floor.

"Be careful!" Jackie shouted. "I need those coupons!"

"I'm sorry," Peter said immediately. "I'll pick them up."

"Never mind. You've already ruined them. Just open up the honey and eat it," Jackie said. Keeping the gun trained on them, she sidled over to a drawer, opened it, pulled out two sporks, and tossed them to him. Peter caught them in a startled fumbling way. He'd never been so afraid of cutlery falling on the floor in his life.

Though small, the sporks seemed sturdy. A tiny, bas-relief bust of Colonel Sanders adorned each white plastic handle.

Peter wrenched the lid of the honey jar open. As he did so, most of the label ripped away.

The honey was old. Very old. Crystals had formed a crust over the top. Peter took comfort in the fact that if two-thousand-year-old Egyptian tomb honey had failed to kill the archeologists who ate it, food poisoning alone would not do in him and Evangeline.

And his research on rhododendron honey showed that if he could avoid eating too much, it probably wouldn't kill him either.

A skittering sound came from overhead, and a fine shower of dust and paper scraps rained down on them. Something had run across the top of the listing tower. A squirrel? A rat? He couldn't imagine even a rat staying in this place on purpose.

Simply sitting in this house might kill him and Evangeline both. It seemed entirely possible to be flattened if any of these teetering mountains of garbage fell on them. He felt his chest constricting. He hated confined spaces like this—*hated* them. He felt his cheeks flushing hot.

If he could just get Jackie to step out of the doorway, he realized there was a chance that he could use her house against her. Toppling any one of these piles of crap couldn't be that hard. The trick would be to not bury himself or Evangeline in the process.

"Can I just ask you something?" Peter inquired.

Jackie stared at him levelly. Since she didn't respond he continued. "Why did you have to kill Roger?"

"What makes you think I killed him?" Jackie asked.

Peter thought this was pretty rich, since she was currently attempting to kill them in exactly the same way. Somehow Jackie's cluelessness made him feel slightly better, made the walls of garbage seem to pull back. Made him feel more in control.

He swallowed and found his voice. "I heard that Roger was cruel to you. That he was trying to have you evicted."

"He didn't respect my possessions. He called them trash. This is not trash," Jackie said.

"Of course not." This surprisingly, from Evangeline. "I'm a found-object artist you know. This place looks like a treasure trove."

"I have lots of ideas for art projects. I have a collection of silver spoons that I think could be made into bracelets," Jackie said.

"I saw a vendor at an art market in Portland selling those once." Evangeline dipped her Colonel Sanders spork into the honey.

"He got that idea from me," Jackie said quickly. "I was too busy with my bees to do it right away. But I told him that he could do it. I have the silver right here someplace."

Outside, Peter saw a faint motion. A man's figure moving.

It occurred to him that his assumption that Jackie had worked alone was baseless. Or this man could be just a passer-by. Or a guy taking a leak on the junk pile outside because the bathroom at the big house was occupied.

Peter's eyes met Evangeline's. She was still scared, but somehow she'd recovered some of her moxie. Peter took the spork from her hand and nibbled from the tip of it.

"This tastes pretty good," he said. Again, outside he saw a shape move. This was not a random passerby, he realized. And if it were Jackie's accomplice, he'd have come in by now.

Maybe, just maybe, somebody inside the big house had seen them being forced into Jackie's place at gunpoint and called the cops. The idea of cops so close by emboldened him. He pointed to a plastic bag that appeared to be full of McDonalds Big Mac Styrofoam clamshells, circa 1980, and said, "You sure saved a lot of those."

"They can be reused," Jackie said. "There are a lot of useful things that other people just throw away. She turned fully away, the rifle drooping. "I have more over there—"

The moment she turned away, a big man blasted through the door. He bypassed Peter and Evangeline and threw himself against Jackie.

Peter's heart leaped. He'd know that sweater anywhere. Nick clamped his hand firmly over Jackie's, around the rifle.

As Nick yanked the weapon up, Jackie let out a surprised yelp and pulled the trigger. A gunshot exploded through the night. Peter felt nothing except anger. He rushed forward. Nick had already twisted the rifle from Jackie's grip. She clawed at him, screaming. Nick released her, keeping the rifle.

Lights flashed on in the big house.

Peter slammed his arm around Jackie's throat and hauled her back. Her shrieks were instantly reduced to one strangled squawk. She rammed her head into his jaw. Stars exploded through his vision, and he fell backward but didn't let go. He squeezed harder, willing the crazy bitch to go limp.

More screams erupted from behind him, but this time it was Evangeline yelling out the front door for help.

Through the pounding rush of blood in his ears he heard Nick saying, "Don't. Peter, stop choking her. It's dangerous."

"What the fuck do I care?" Peter gritted out. Still he let Nick pull his hands away. Jackie scrambled up. Nick hooked her foot and she went down again. Instantly, he was on her, easily twisting her arms back and pinning her to the floor.

Jackie's sobbed, pleading, "You're hurting me. Please stop."

"I'm not hurting you," Nick said evenly. "Stop crying and calm down."

Jackie did neither.

Peter glanced over to Nick, who still leaned on Jackie, seeming almost bored.

Almost.

"What do we do now," Peter asked.

"Wait for the police."

"Shouldn't we tie her up?" Peter surveyed the ground around him. "I'm sure there's something we could use here."

"The Everson police station is three blocks away. It can't take them that long to get here."

Sure enough, at that moment he heard sirens. And through the open door he could see the flashing lights of the Everson Police riding to the rescue.

About an hour, and a hundred questions later, Everson police released the three of them, warning them not to leave the county. Peter promised to do no such thing and started moving through the now well-lit junk pile to his beat-up old car. Nick was standing there with Evangeline. Neither of them seemed overwhelmed with joy to see him.

He supposed he deserved that, but decided to play it cool anyway. He walked up to Nick, smiled a little and said, "How did you know where we were?"

"I called your phone and followed the sound of the ringtone." Nick spoke as if this were the only sensible thing to do.

"But how did you know to come out here at all?" Peter asked.

"Apparently Evangeline phoned Tommy from a gas station to tell him that she was out here helping you dig up a dead dog." Nick paused to give him a pointed look. "And so Tommy called me to ask if I knew what she was talking about. Not surprisingly I didn't, so I thought I should drive out and see why you were doing that. It seemed like a situation that could end up...exactly like it did."

Peter turned a recriminating glance on Evangeline, who simply shrugged and said, "I was going to be late. I always call when I'm going to be late."

"You could learn something from her," Nick remarked.

Peter knew he owed Nick a wide variety of apologies, or maybe just one encompassing apology for being his own asinine self. Instead he babbled, "You're the best boyfriend ever. I was thinking I should tell you that before when I thought I was going to die. So, there you go. Best ever."

Peter grinned, then winced. His mouth was bruised from violent contact with Jackie's skull.

Nick turned away and stared off into the night for what seemed like forever. Then he sighed and said, "No, I'm not your boyfriend anymore."

"But—"

"I'm the best everything-but-husband ever. Don't forget it."

Chapter Ten

Patton didn't return his calls for a while.

At first Peter thought she was mad at him for the attempted exhumation of Celestia the dog. Then Patton informed him via e-mail that she had a lot of work to do and would contact him when she could. Jackie Chambers confessed to the murder after Everson police found her dog.

It hadn't been buried at all. It was wrapped in a plastic shower curtain and shoved in the freezer. Apparently, she had the idea that she was going to take Celestia to a taxidermist and have her stuffed and mounted. She just hadn't gotten around to it yet.

She'd put the marker outside because she didn't want people to know she was storing a dead dog in her freezer.

Then one morning a few weeks later, Patton appeared at the *Hamster* office. She wasn't wearing a uniform. She wore an oxblood suit with a boring beige overcoat.

"I guess congratulations are in order," Peter said.

"How's that?"

"You made detective right?" Peter grinned. "I could tell 'cause you're wearing street clothes."

"Yeah," Patton—Detective Patton—said. "They finally decided to let me have a shot at it."

"Is your wife happy about it?"

Patton gave him a long, indecipherable look, then said, "She's proud of me, yeah. She doesn't like the hours, but she's proud."

"You knew that Jackie did it right from the beginning, didn't you?" Peter asked.

"You get a certain intuition about things like this after a while. I didn't have any proof though," Patton said. "Fortunately, your escapade into grave-robbing gave us a reason to search the house—not that that wasn't an ordeal."

"I'll bet." Peter shuddered at the idea of having to go through that massive heap of decaying treasure. He didn't envy the forensics team at all. "How did you get her to confess?"

Patton shrugged. "It's easy to get narcissists to brag about what they've done if they think it will get them more attention."

"But why did she do it?" Peter couldn't help but feel a little disappointed by this one. Though he'd figured out exactly what had happened, he still didn't know why.

"Basically Chambers felt she'd been railroaded into appearing on this TV show, and she thought that if she killed Roger Hager, Jenn Jones wouldn't make her go through with it."

"So she murdered a guy so she wouldn't have to clean her house?" That made no sense at all, but to be fair, neither did the massively hoarded house.

"It's slightly more complicated than that, but yeah, in a nutshell. She didn't perceive the garbage in her house as garbage but as precious treasure and having someone force her to throw it away felt like being robbed. So she retaliated. She tried out the death camus and honey plan on the dog, just as you thought. There was a notebook where she kept track of the doses—did all the math."

Peter nodded, swallowing back his disgust. Somehow, poisoning her own dog as a dress rehearsal for murder seemed almost as heinous as the murder itself. Aloud he said, "What a shitty pet owner."

"She was a shittier mother. I'll never be able to prove it, but I know she's guilty of that death too. Whether through intention or negligence, Jackie Chambers let that kid drown. She never paid for that, but at least she'll be out of the general population now."

"For how long?" Peter asked. "What if she convinces the doctors that she's all sane and can be let out? She's very manipulative."

Detective Patton smiled, though grimly. "The difference between going to prison and going to the state hospital is that prison sentences end. Parole exists. There are ways to get out of prison that just don't exist once you're in the state hospital. That woman is never going to convince any doctor she's not a danger to the public. No way. I'll make sure of that myself."

Peter stashed that lesson away. *Note to self: never get involuntarily committed and never get on the bad side of a cop with a long memory.*

Aloud he said, "Well, thanks for giving me the scoop. Anytime you need me to ask some questions, just call."

Patton pulled a crooked smile.

"Mr. Fontaine, though I appreciate your help this time, I'm sorry to say that you turned out to be a little too impulsive for me to ever do that again," Patton said.

"Impulsive?" Peter cried with mock affront. "*Moi?* What could you possibly mean?"

"For starters, going to Chambers's place wasn't very bright," she said.

"I know. I just wanted to get the evidence myself." Peter felt like an idiot admitting this now, but there seemed to be no reason in concealing it from Patton. "I guess I got carried away."

"You are very, very lucky that Mr. Olson came when he did," she said.

"I'm lucky he puts up with me at all," Peter said.

Patton smirked. "You try and stay out of trouble, Mr. Fontaine."

With that, she departed the *Hamster* office in a rustle of beige overcoat. Peter realized there was still one thing he didn't understand and rushed after her, cutting her off before she could egress.

"Can I just ask you one more thing?" Peter prefaced and then went on to make his inquiry before she could refuse his permission. "Who was the dispatcher?"

"The dispatcher?" Patton looked genuinely confused. Then understanding dawned across her face. "Oh, you mean the one that told Margaret Bear I was inventing a murder to get ahead?"

"Right," Peter said. "Who was it? Why would they say such a thing?"

Patton gazed at him levelly, obviously weighing her decision. Finally she said, "Wife's ex-girlfriend."

Really, Peter thought, that just explained it all.

Epilogue

February 14, 2012

Because of the lag in print time, Margaret didn't live long enough to see the big exposé in *Artworld* about Roger's naughty behavior. But when the magazine arrived in the Castle's mailbox, Peter clipped the article and slid it inside the counterfeit Fulper that now sat in a place of honor on their mantel.

Margaret also didn't live long enough to see Washington become the seventh state to allow same-sex marriage.

Peter was, himself, shocked that he had.

When he and Nick had signed their registered domestic partner papers the year before, he'd thought that was as good as it would get. Sure, maybe in twenty years they'd have the chance to get married. But now, less than a year after he'd sat in front of a notary legally entangling himself with Nick Olson, the holy grail of genuine matrimony shimmered on the horizon.

He realized that he needed to act, and act fast, before Nick could steal his moment of glory. He needed to ask Nick to marry him before Nick found a way to slip it into conversation. Filled with conviction, he stalked through the house toward the studio where Nick was just finishing one of his larger canvases.

Peter stood—posed, really—in the doorway, hoping he looked good. Nick glanced up at him and said, "Yes?"

"I just wanted to know—" Peter choked. His throat went abruptly dry, and his palms turned clammy.

Again, Nick said, "Yes?"

Peter suddenly realized that the radio was on, tuned to a talk radio station. The announcers discussed the political implications of the Washington decision.

"Do you keep saying *yes* because you know I'm trying to ask you to marry me? I mean, switch over our domestic partnership or… however that's going to work…?"

Peter trailed off, realizing that he didn't actually know the procedure. He should have done some research before embarking on this rash wedding-proposal plan.

"You won't know until you do ask, will you?" Nick rinsed his brush and dried the bristles with a paint-spattered towel.

"Will you…" Peter began but then thought better. "How would you like to be the best husband ever?"

The corner of Nick's mouth curled into that handsome, smug smile of his. He said, "There's nothing I could want more."

BIRDS
OF A
FEATHER

Chapter One

From the personal planner of Peter Fontaine:
Scout photo location
Call florist
Call caterer (gluten-free vegan option?)
Research vows.
CALL YOUR MOTHER!!!

Peter frowned down at the all-caps order. He'd been frazzled lately, but he felt sure that these last three words had not been included in the note he'd initially written to himself regarding his plans for the day.

He would not, for example, have used three exclamation points in any text not intended for his best friend, Evangeline. Also, he did not normally print in capital letters or use a mechanical pencil. But the clincher certainly had to be the fact that these fourteen letters (or nineteen characters, counting the exclamation points and spaces) instructed him to do exactly opposite of his own personal intention and sense of self-preservation.

Still frowning down at the planner, he ambled through the stone, wood, and metal decor of his kitchen. The pedal clips on his cycling shoes scraped the tiles as he progressed, but went silent as he stepped into the plushly carpeted living room and down the hall. There he paused in the doorway of his boyfriend, Nick's, home studio.

Nick stood on the third rung of a paint-spattered wooden ladder facing a canvas that stretched floor-to-ceiling.

He wore his usual uniform, consisting of old jeans and a ratty, stained, cream-colored cable-knit sweater that Peter felt might be at least three decades old. Certainly the fact that the sweater's left arm had fallen off in the laundry the previous week testified to its elderly infirmity. Hoping to preserve his lover's image as a handsome and stylish painter, Peter had thrown both the arm and the remaining sweater parts into the laundry room garbage.

In an apparent exercise in sentimentality, Nick had retrieved and repaired the sweater with a length of cotton kitchen twine.

Now instead of looking like a big blond Viking-descended forty-something whose rugged good looks just improved with time and stubble, Nick looked like a bum.

Granted, he looked like a sexy bum who had just been to the charity center laundry room for fresh underpants, a shower, and a hot meal. But both his shaggy hair and ragged clothes told the story of a man who had not considered his personal appearance for at least three months.

Which by a staggering coincidence was exactly the length of time he'd been working on his new canvas.

Next time he got control of the sweater, Peter thought, he should throw it over the edge of the cliff.

Or maybe buy a little rowboat and give the heroic garment a tiny Viking funeral on the emerald-green waters of Puget Sound.

As he considered his toy boat purchasing options, Peter noticed a small, furry shape slinking along the floor near the bottom of the canvas. Ink-black against the gesso white, the cat-shape paused, blinked, and lashed its tail violently.

Then, propelled by some inner feline impulse, the shape rushed up the ladder and launched herself onto Nick's leg.

Nick froze, bracing against the impact.

Gigi—for the cat-shape had a name—began her ascent. Like a nimble college undergraduate with too much time on her hands, she free-climbed the sheer verticals and overhangs of Nick's garments to reach the summit of his shoulder.

There she sat, shoved her muzzle directly into his ear, and meowed. Loudly.

"Wow, Gigi, I had no idea you were here," Nick remarked. Then, catching sight of Peter, he gave a faint smile that barely creased his cheek, before directing his attention back to his canvas. He lifted his brush—an implement with short square bristles that Peter had recently learned was called a bright—and smoothed a long stroke of eggshell-colored paint onto the canvas.

Watching Nick, Peter began to imagine a scene. Soon he was writing a story in his head:

Dear ManHump Magazine,

I would have never believed it would happen to me.

It was just like any other day on my bike courier route. Nothing special. Just pedaling hard and getting sweaty so guys in suits don't have to. But today there was something new in my pouch. An envelope for reclusive artist Rick Molsen. So I cycled up to his big house on Wildcat Cove. It sat on the edge of a cliff, just like a house in a movie.

I expected the guy to be shriveled and old, but when he opened the door I saw this six-foot blond Viking. He wasn't wearing a shirt, just skintight jeans. All I could think was how much I wanted to go down on my knees right there and start sucking his meaty cock in front of God and everybody, but I didn't.

Unfortunately, bike shorts are really revealing, and I was sure that with one glance he'd be able to see my dick getting hard just thinking about him. I held my courier pouch in front of my crotch while he signed for his package. I was almost in the clear, waiting to pedal away into the woods and jack off in the trees, 'cause no way could I ride with a chub that big, when he asked me if I'd ever modeled. I said no, and he said that my body was perfect for a painting he was doing.

He said he'd pay me a hundred bucks for just an hour. How could I refuse?

When we got to the studio, he told me to take off my clothes. No way to hide my boner then, but he didn't seem to mind. He was staring at it, turning his head back and forth, looking at it like it was just some bowl of fruit or something. I was getting pretty embarrassed now, but somehow that made my dick even harder.

In the middle of the room, there was a raised platform covered up with a sheet. He told me to lie down on it, and I went to lie on my back, but he flipped me over onto my stomach and pulled my ass right up in the air. Then I felt his tongue on the back of my balls, licking all the way up to my asshole. I couldn't believe how amazing it felt. I'd never felt that before. Not from another guy, or anybody—

"Are you telling yourself some kind of story right now?" Nick's words interrupted Peter's train of thought.

"Maybe. How could you tell?"

Without turning back toward Peter, Nick said, "You get this faraway look when you're doing it. Does this fantasy of yours contain toast or coffee?"

"Not yet, but I have both of them in the kitchen, if you want," Peter replied. "If you think you can tear yourself away from this thing long enough to have breakfast with me."

"I think I have to move this ladder anyway." Nick pulled his hand back from the canvas. "What time is it?"

"Just after eight," Peter said.

"No wonder I'm so hungry."

"When did you get up?"

"About four thirty." Nick daubed more paint on his canvas. "The light coming through the window was exactly what I'm trying to capture in this piece."

"What light is that?" Peter inquired. After having lived with an artist for years, he'd become accustomed to having conversations about things like line weight and various kinds of light. Also he had, by osmosis, absorbed the names of a dizzying array of brushes, paints, mediums, canvases, and obscure modern artists.

Not that all artists weren't, in a way, obscure. Nick's work had been featured in a dozen major exhibitions during the last few years, and he was still in no danger of being recognized as a rising artist by any casual bystander.

"Cool morning light before the sun has risen over the mountains. There's a grayness that's close to predawn, but brighter." Nick scooped Gigi off his shoulder and started down. "I think I'm close to getting it right. Especially in this area."

Nick gestured over the expanse of his canvas.

Peter gave a brief nod in response. He studied the massive strokes of sand and eggshell-colored paint.

Nope. He could not figure out what this painting was supposed to be.

Nick was an abstract painter who normally specialized in landscapes. For example, one recent piece had been a depiction of the wave shapes that they saw from their kitchen window. Peter had deciphered that one pretty easily, going by the very specific color of the sea in the Puget Sound area.

But this one…what the hell was it?

At first he thought it represented a shoreline cliff face as if seen from a boat floating on the water. Certainly the lower third of the canvas appeared to be taken up with a triangle-shaped blue-gray surface with brushstrokes that could have represented water. And the middle third was a series of shapes that resembled weather-worn boulders.

But the top third did not in any way resemble a sky—not even in an abstract way.

Rather than having depth—as a sky of any sort would in one of Nick's paintings—this looked flat, almost like a wooden slab.

Nick sidled up beside him, holding Gigi over his shoulder as if she were a baby, which she never allowed Peter to do without violent retribution.

"You look—what's that word you like to use to describe the cat?"

"Vexed," Peter supplied. "I *am* vexed."

"Is it because of my note about your mother?"

"No, it's about this painting. I'm starting to get a little jealous that you spend more time with it than you do with me." Peter recognized his statement as being childish and deliberately misleading. But he absolutely did not want to admit that he couldn't figure out what the damn image was supposed to be, so he took the out Nick offered.

And that was why he was so chagrined when Nick leaned close to him, nuzzled against his neck, and whispered, "You don't know what this is a painting of, do you?"

Peter felt his cheeks flush. "It's not that."

"I can tell that it's driving you crazy," Nick went on. "You found seven different ways to ask me what the title is last week. You're hoping that will tell you what you're looking at." Nick pressed a kiss against his throat, sending a tingle of sensation across Peter's skin. "And it would, if I were to tell you what the title is."

"I just want to know what to call this painting when I brag about you to Evangeline," Peter said, somewhat primly, then added, "What is the title, anyway?"

"I'm not going to tell you," Nick whispered, lips brushing against Peter's ear. "You're going to have to figure it out."

Peter pushed him away. "You are being such a dick about this. Do you know how many early-morning blowjobs I've missed because you had a date with this thing?"

"A lot?" Irritatingly, this question seemed to elevate Nick's amusement to the point that there was an actual twinkle in his eye.

"At least a dozen, by my count. You owe me a dozen blowjobs for putting up with this painting," Peter said, trying to enter into full tirade, but finding himself unable to.

"Do you want one right now?"

"I don't—" Peter began to refuse, then reconsidered. He glanced at his watch. He had forty minutes till he had to be at work. It took him thirty minutes to cycle into town from their house. "Can you give me and my bike a ride into town?"

"Sure thing," Nick said.

"You have to take off the sweater," Peter said peevishly. Nick complied without comment. He tossed the garment over the ladder, and then with great gentleness, he lifted the cat, dropped her in the hallway, and closed the door.

Arousal zinged through Peter as he realized that they were going to have sex in Nick's studio.

During the three years that they had lived together, they had never once had sex in either Nick's home studio or in the one he kept at the Vitamilk Building downtown.

In a way, Peter could see why. Artist studios were generally dusty spaces filled with paint-spattered drop cloths and randomly placed sharp objects. They were workspaces—meditative places, even.

But from the moment that Peter started dating Nick, he had entertained two secret fantasies. First that Nick would make a painting of him that would become so famous that it would be immortalized throughout all time and studied by art students in perpetuity as a classic of adoration and love. And, second, that he would get to have sex in an artist studio.

Since Nick was a landscape painter, Peter could count on the first fantasy never being realized.

But the second? It seemed to be happening right this minute. Giddy delight flashed through him in anticipation. Already Nick knelt before him, pulling down the waistband of the cycling pants he wore. Peter leaned back against the ladder, laying his head back against the horrible sweater.

The smell of an oil painter's studio was much like the smell of the sea in that it's not actually pleasant, but over time becomes so by association. Nick's studio smelled of linseed oil and turpentine. Overhead ventilation fans whirred, exhausting the highly flammable and harmful vapors of those same two substances. When he tilted his head back, he had to squint against the glare of the color-correct floodlights blazing down on him.

And yet, feeling the head of his cock disappear into Nick's mouth, Peter felt like he was in a scene from a movie. His legs tensed, and the slippery metal clamps on the bottoms of his shoes slid against the polished wood floor.

"I think you should lie down before you fall down," Nick said.

"I think you're right." Peter crumpled down to his knees and let Nick nudge him over onto his back, pull his tight cycling shorts completely off, and push his knees wide apart.

Nick gazed down at him for what seemed like forever, then said, "What a view."

"This isn't really going to be a blowjob, is it?" Not that Peter minded, but logistics had to be considered. "I'm going to have to call in late."

In response, Nick wrapped his hand around Peter's shaft and worked it gently, saying, "Don't worry. You'll get your rocks off and be on time too."

"It's just that I can't get too messy. I don't have time to shower," Peter said. Even he found the tone of his protest unconvincing as his arched into Nick's palm.

Nick bent forward, nuzzling his face against Peter's groin. His mouth closed around Peter again, sending delicious, thought-annihilating waves of pleasure through him.

Nick had loosened his own belt and was working himself with his free hand.

The sensation was so delicious that Peter forgot everything but the feeling of Nick's tongue on delicate skin. Then Nick's mouth was around the head of his cock again, and orgasm was rocking through him, shooting long silky strings onto the bright lycra of his cycling shirt. As he lay there gasping, Nick shoved the shirt up, moved over him, and thrust his hard dick against the hot, slick skin of Peter's abdomen. After only a few strokes, Nick, too, befouled the cycling shirt with spunk before collapsing forward onto Peter. Peter wrapped his arms around Nick's shoulders and pulled him into a humid kiss.

Nick rolled off him and stared up at the ceiling. "So what's the time?"

Peter lifted his arm to look at his watch. "Eight twenty-five. We better get going."

Peter changed quickly, opting for immediate work drag and tucking a new set of cycling gear into his messenger bag for the ride home. He loaded his bike into Nick's Audi, and they started down the wooded private drive toward the main road.

As they neared the entrance, Peter caught a flash of color in the corner of his eye.

Dyed green hair.

"Alec!" Automatically his arm flew toward the emergency brake. But Nick had already pulled the car to a skidding halt just as Alec, their reckless teenage neighbor, flew in front of their car on his mountain bike. Alec wore no helmet, didn't seem to have any brakes or sense of self-preservation, and as far as Peter could tell, didn't own a single shirt.

Logically, Peter knew this had to be false. All children in this scenic and wealthy neighborhood owned clothes. But so far he hadn't seen much evidence of Alec having access to any garment except one pair of tight cutoff jeans that he held up with a dirty knotted shoestring.

His attention was diverted from Alec by the sight of an unfamiliar car turning onto their private drive. The foreign sedan was silver, luxurious, and contained one man who Peter did not like and a woman he did not know but didn't like the look of.

The man was Bradley de Kamp, the eldest son of Nick's much older, now deceased ex-lover Walter.

A successful Manhattan painter, Walter had first engaged Nick as a model and muse. Not content to be just another pretty body, Nick had started teaching himself to paint. During the years that Nick and Walter had been together, Nick had become indispensable to the older man. Nick started off with heavy lifting and ended by assisting in the creation of many of Walter's most famous paintings.

Being quasi-closeted, Walter had remained married to his estranged society wife until his death. He'd been generous with Nick, though. He'd bought the house Peter and Nick now shared and put Nick in charge of his artistic estate.

Because of a stipulation in Walter's will, proceeds from the sale of any of Walter's paintings had to be split three ways between Nick and Walter's two adult sons. That meant that Peter had the misfortune of seeing Bradley every couple of years now.

Apart from being a pompous old yacht-club blazer-wearing prick, Bradley was perpetually broke.

Bradley's frequent insolvency meant that he practically made a career of finding ways to sell off his father's collection.

While Peter felt that this was a lousy way for a grown man to make his living, he had resolutely determined to stay out of these negotiations. Nick's relationship with Walter's sons was none of his business. He had regarded it as a family matter—which is to say the private matters of a family he didn't belong to. But his opinion on this had recently changed.

On February 14, 2012, Washington State legalized same-sex marriage. The legislation had been challenged via a citizen petition demanding that the matter be put to a popular vote. Election day rolled around, and Referendum 74 passed, and Washington joined Maine and Maryland as the newest places to get gay-married.

On November 7th, 2012, at 7:01 a.m., Peter's mother had phoned him to ask when his wedding would be. During that brief and groggy conversation, Peter had assured her that the wedding would take place "sometime" and hung up. Five minutes after that, his best friend, Evangeline, had phoned to ask him the same question. He'd given the same answer.

While Peter lay in the 100 percent organic linen sheets that Nick had paid too much money for, trying to wake up enough to ponder the daunting task of planning a wedding, the landline had rung.

"It's for you," Nick had muttered into the pillow.

"It could be for you," Peter said.

"I very much doubt that." Nick had reached to the nightstand and handed him the receiver without looking at it.

But it wasn't for Peter after all. It was Bradley, calling to demand that Nick have a prenuptial agreement drawn up before he married Peter.

In hindsight, that had been the moment when Peter had really started to hate Bradley. Before he'd pitied the old loser.

Bradley's gay father had cheated on his mom with a man who was a decade younger than Bradley himself. Then the father had gone so far as to leave half of his property and custodianship of his entire artistic estate to the interloper. He could see why Bradley would hate Nick. But seeing the complete fiasco Bradley had made of his own financial affairs, he could also sympathize with Walter's point of view. Appointing Nick as custodian would ensure that some responsible person would govern the sale of his legacy.

Certainly, only Nick's sense of fairness ensured that Bradley's younger brother, Troy, got a fair shake. Not that Troy needed a fair shake, having made his own fortune as an investment banker. But it was the principle of the thing.

Seeing Bradley on their property always put Peter into a bad mood. Today Bradley's presence underscored the fact that this piece of land was not really Peter's property, but Nick's. That made him feel even crummier.

"Did you see that?" Peter asked.

"Yes, I did." Nick's blissful after-sex glow dimmed somewhat.

"Were you expecting Bradley to show up?"

"I was."

"Shouldn't you turn around then?" Peter craned his head around and saw that the silver sedan had stopped short of the house, as if waiting for them to reverse.

"It won't kill him to wait a few minutes."

They rounded the corner and came up against the bane of neighborhood traffic flow—the cargo train. Peter glanced to the north and to the south. He couldn't see either end. Because of a recent community kerfuffle involving shipping coal through the area, Peter happened to know quite a bit about the local trains. This southbound exercise in transmodalism was most likely between two and three thousand meters long. While significantly shorter than the monsters that carried materials from the oil sands in Alberta, it was a long train. Nick glared at the passing boxcars as though they had personally betrayed him.

Glancing over his shoulder, Peter noted that the silver sedan had not moved.

"I think they're waiting for us," Peter remarked. Then when Nick didn't answer he went on. "Why don't you just turn around? I'll phone work to say I'll be late."

"It's not necessary."

"Did he say why he wanted to see you?"

"What does he always want?" Nick returned with a bitter smile. "We don't both need to be there to listen to his latest sob story."

That Nick wanted to leave him out of this interaction was obvious to Peter.

"You're not going to give him any money, are you?" Peter asked.

"I don't know."

"Is he here about the prenup?"

"I don't know."

"You don't know much this morning, do you?" Peter's words came out sharper than he intended.

Nick's hands clenched around the steering wheel. He watched the train cars roll past. Peter thought he might be counting them. Or maybe just counting to ten before speaking. Nick would go to extraordinary lengths to avoid an argument, especially if Peter was trying to start one.

After an extended silence Peter asked, "Why do you think that Bradley's here? Don't say you don't know again."

Nick turned to face him, then shrugged. "I'm not going to make something up just because you don't believe me."

"That's not what I'm saying," Peter said. "You don't want me there when you talk to him, do you?"

"No, I don't," Nick finally said. "If you stay, you're just going to get mad and start a fight."

"You can't know that."

Nick let out a short, sharp laugh. "Baby, you're already doing it. Just the sight of this guy makes you see red."

While this was undeniably true, the sheer veracity of it further infuriated Peter.

"You've got a lot of fucking nerve telling me—"

The remainder of Peter's vitriolic screed was cut short as the driver's side window suddenly broke with a sharp pop. The safety glass window didn't shatter. The only evidence that the glass had sustained an impact was a small round hole surrounded by a fine spiderweb of cracks.

In a fraction of a second, Peter's anger had gone. His hands shook as he stared at the obvious bullet hole. Turning, he saw that the passenger-side window had a similar mark. The bullet had gone right through the car, inches in front of his face.

Chapter Two

"I think most likely it was a stray bullet," Detective Patton, Peter's favorite lesbian police officer, said. "It happens out here sometimes. People get drunk and discharge their weapons."

Peter nodded. He pulled Nick's jacket closer around his shoulders. Not that he was cold. The June sun beat down on him and the sturdy Patton with unusual force. But having a bullet whiz through their car had rattled him, and somehow putting on Nick's clothes made him feel better.

The smell probably—calming pheromones or something.

He should look that up when he finally got to work, he thought. Maybe write an article about the comforting smell of a strong man. Maybe he could write a little historical romance on the side...

Even before Young Peter knew he was shaking, Lord Nicolas had draped his splendid silken frockcoat over the scholar's slim shoulders. "That arrow came too close for comfort," he whispered.

"Mr. Fontaine, are you feeling okay? You're looking a little foggy," Patton said.

Sunlight glinted off her mirror shades and lit auburn highlights in her brunette mullet.

"I just look that way sometimes," Peter murmured. He should try to avoid spacing out now that people where taking shots at him. At least this time he'd informed the police immediately.

Except that he hadn't. Patton had just showed up.

"Wait—how did you know to come here?"

"I was out here on a different call when about twenty old-timers and three stay-at-home moms called it in. Around here you can't pick your nose without somebody seeing you flick the booger," Patton said.

"Tell me about it." After three years, Peter well knew the pitfalls of living in the close-knit neighborhood. Most of the waterfront properties had been purchased cheap after World War Two. Many octogenarian owners now spent their days monitoring the neighborhood dogs and watching passing boats with binoculars.

The neighborhood association had its own phone directory, which Peter had never used. His name had been listed there for the first time this year as an official resident of the Castle. He knew this because local residents began calling him to attend various meetings. Mainly, they opposed things. The range of oppositional stances ran from being against the annexation of the neighborhood by the city of Bellingham to fighting development of forested areas to defeating the opposition to the development of forested areas.

Because Nick was the owner of the largest property in the neighborhood, everyone tried to get him on their side of any battle. But Nick had little time and no stamina for dull yet also contentious meetings at the local firehouse. Whereas Peter's tenure at the *Hamster* had led him to develop mad skills in soldiering through boredom.

"Just to be on the safe side, though, have you made any new enemies recently?" Patton inquired in a mild tone.

"Not that I know of," Peter said.

"I only ask because you have a history of aggravating violence-prone individuals." She pushed her hands in her pockets. "Been doing any investigating around here?"

"Not at all."

"Do you know of anyone here who might have a grudge against you? Have you done anything to wreck one of your neighbors' million-dollar views, for example?"

"I haven't built anything, investigated anything, or even talked to anybody here for months," Peter said. "All I've been doing is planning my wedding."

"Yes," Patton gave a slight cough. "I got your invitation."

"You didn't RSVP." He tried not to sound hurt. He didn't want to come off like some gay Groomzilla. Still, he had to get some hard numbers to the caterer soon.

"I'm not sure I'll be able to attend." Patton's expression didn't change, but he detected a minor alteration in her tone. Then she was back to business. "What about your fiancé? Anyone ticked off at him?"

"Are you serious?"

"I wouldn't ask if I wasn't."

"Nick has barely left the house since he started his new painting."

"And as a couple, do you feel fairly welcome in this neighborhood?" Patton scanned the surrounding houses. Most facades were partially obscured by trees.

Though the properties themselves were worth millions of dollars each, many of the structures were modest, even small, having been originally conceived as vacation homes.

"We've never had any trouble with anyone," Peter said.

"So you have no reason at all to believe that this bullet was intended for you?" Patton tapped the glass.

"None."

"That wraps it up for me, then." Patton closed her notebook. As she turned to get into her unmarked vehicle, Alec whizzed by on his bike again. "Do you know if that kid's supposed to be in school?"

"He was expelled a while ago for disruptive behavior," Peter said. "Basically he's just hyperactive and unmedicated."

"Next time you see him, tell him to wear his helmet."

With that, she departed.

Peter opened the driver door of the Audi, preparing to drive it back to the house. Nick was waiting there, entertaining Bradley and the mystery woman while he spoke with Patton.

As Peter studied the car's broken window, he felt a residual chill from his brush with death. Prior to this, Peter had several near misses with the Grim Reaper, but those had been the result of intrepid reporting, not random drunken gun firing. The idea that he could be killed accidentally was somehow far more sobering than death by misadventure. As he studied the cracks in the glass, he heard the crunch of bike tires skidding to a halt behind him.

It was Alec.

"Hey, Peter."

"Hey, Alec." Peter leaned back against the car. "That cop said to tell you to wear a helmet."

He shrugged. "Helmets are gay."

"How can helmets be gay?"

"You wear one, don't you?"

Peter smirked. He'd walked right into that one.

"Nice zinger, Slick. But seriously, you should wear a helmet if you don't want to end up brain-dead from a head wound. Is your mom too poor to buy you one? I'll give you the money if you mow my lawn." Peter gestured grandly at the acre of grass. "I've got a nice push mower."

"Yeah, right, like I'm working for you." Alec glanced over at the lawn. Peter thought for a moment that he was actually considering it. Come to think of it, he'd never seen either of Alec's parents. Maybe the kid did need money. Peter watched as he scratched his wiry arm, then said without looking at him, "So you're a reporter, right?"

"That's right."

"I think I know who shot your car."

This was the last thing that Peter expected to hear. "And?"

"I've got something to show you." Alec's eyes darted sideways, scanning the surrounding trees.

"What is it?" Peter followed Alec's gaze but saw nothing.

"I just want to show you something."

Was this some kind of trap? Lure the fag into the woods so that you and your buddies can ambush him and beat the shit out of him? Neither Alec nor his tribe of shirt-impaired friends seemed to be the type for that. "Look, kid, I've got to go to work. Just tell me who shot the car."

Alec leaned close and whispered, "The eagle poachers. Come with me, and I'll prove it. I've got evidence."

"What's that?"

"A dead eagle. It's right up there next to the train tracks by the park. It will take five minutes, tops."

Peter cast a glance at the house. More than likely, Bradley and Nick's conversation was nearly over, as Nick preferred to disengage from Bradley as soon as possible.

He might have time to at least find out what Alec was talking about.

"Are you sure it's an eagle?"

Alec gave Peter a look of scorn. "I know what an eagle looks like."

Again Peter regarded the exterior of his own house. Now that he really thought about it, he didn't want to go in there. Nick was right. Listening to Bradley would just make him angry. And if Alec was telling the truth, he might be able to write a story that didn't involve the search for the perfect boutonniere. "Okay, so how far away is this carcass?"

"It's right inside the state park." Alec pointed ahead. Peter could just see the fretted sandstone cliffs surrounding the Larrabee State Park's tiny, pebbled public beach and boat launch. If he'd been in his kitchen, he'd have had a clear view of those cliffs, which went straight down to the jade-colored water. But on the ground, trees and foliage obscured his vision.

"Do you want me to drive?"

"Nah, we'll just take the tracks." Alec started walking, and Peter followed. Their feet crunched along the gravel between the ties. On either side of them stood a ten-foot chain-link fence. The fence separated the thin strip of property owned by the railroad from the state park on either side. Beyond that, thick walls of cedar forest rose up. Peter noticed several kid-sized holes cut in the fence. He supposed if he'd been lucky enough to grow up out here, he'd have felt moved to modify the accessibility of this easy thoroughfare too.

After a few minutes, Peter was looking down at what was undeniably a dead bald eagle. Even minus its head and feet, the majestic bird would have been hard to misidentify.

"When did you find this?" He crouched down and used the tip of his pen to lift one of the eagle's heavy wings. Even disheveled, the feathers were glossy black-brown and beautiful.

"This morning. I was coming back to get you to tell you about it when that bullet went through your car." Alec dropped his voice to a whisper. "I think he was shooting at me and accidentally hit your car."

Peter gently laid the eagle wing back on the gray rock. He gave Alec a long, appraising look. At fourteen, he couldn't be considered a little kid, exactly, but the story he told sounded like something a child would concoct to get attention.

"So, let me get this straight. You were walking along doing what?"

"I was looking at the incline," Alec said. "My buddies and I are thinking of building a new bike trail right along that ridge." He pointed at the line of mountains.

"Isn't that inside the park?"

"Is it?" Alec's feigned ignorance lacked the strength to convince Peter.

"Okay, so you were walking along, planning to build an illegal trail, when you find this eagle. Then what?"

"I came to get you," Alec said, as though contacting a reporter would be the next logical step for a person who had discovered a crime. "Then as I was riding up, I saw your car stopped. I tried to flag you down, but you weren't paying attention to me."

"I was having a discussion," Peter said.

"It seemed more like a fight to me," Alec commented. "And it was just then that the guy took a shot."

"Did you see this guy?"

"Not exactly," Alec said. "But I did see a weird truck parked in the neighborhood."

"What made it weird?" Peter asked, eager to discover what Alec would find odd.

"It didn't belong here. Plus it had a handicapped parking permit."

"Okay, assuming that the guy and the truck were connected, why do you think the guy with the weird truck was shooting at you?"

"Because the bullet hit the ground about six inches from my foot." Alec reached into this pocket and pulled out a bullet. The tip was slightly mushroomed, meaning that it had been fired at some time. Other than that, Peter had no idea what sort of bullet it might be. "I dug it out so I'd have evidence to show you."

Peter considered explaining to Alec that pulling a dusty bullet out of one's pocket did not constitute evidence of anything but having once put the same bullet into one's pocket in the first place. He didn't bother. Different questions troubled him.

"I assume you were standing here the whole time Detective Patton was talking to me," Peter said.

"That's right. I was hanging back till she was gone."

"Who do you think I would give this evidence to?" Peter held the bullet up. "Why didn't you come forward with it yourself?"

"I just don't like talking to cops." Alec shifted nervously. "They're even worse than park rangers. But somebody should do something about that eagle."

"Hence you came to me." Peter resisted the urge to sigh.

"I thought maybe you could pretend to be the one that found the eagle," Alec suggested.

"What about the bullet? How am I supposed to have found that?"

"I can show you where I dug it up." Alec jerked his thumb over his shoulder. "It's right near the top of that embankment."

"I don't think I can plausibly pretend to have found a bullet that shot through my car. I'm going to have to tell them I talked to you."

"No, you can't! Besides, you're a reporter. Can't you say I'm an anonymous source?"

"I could do that, yes. But it would be easier if you did it yourself."

"I really can't do that, man." Alec shook his head slowly. "If you tell them I told you this, I'll deny it."

Peter forced himself to back off. It was normal for teenagers to be afraid of speaking to authority figures, but he wondered if Alec might have extra reasons to be cautious about police coming to his house—his parents, for example. "What do you think would happen to you if you went to the police?"

"I don't know, and I don't want to find out." Alec gave him a pleading look. "Come on, I thought you were cool."

Peter sighed heavily. "Okay, Alec, I will keep your name out of it."

Alec broke into a huge grin. He mounted his tiny BMX bike. "Thanks, man, I hope you catch whoever is shooting those eagles."

"Wait, aren't you still worried about getting shot?"

"Nah, I figure that guy's long gone by now. When I looked for the truck, it wasn't there."

"Right." Peter tried to cast his memory back to a time when his thoughts had made so little logical sense. If the shooter truly had been aiming for Alec, the green-haired boy was not only highly identifiable, but an easy target. He should go find a reason to speak with Alec's parents, he decided. Just to see what his situation was like. Then again, Peter didn't know that he should take any part of Alec's story at face value.

Then his phone rang. It was Nick.

"Hey, handsome," Peter said. Alec gave him a salute and pedaled away.

"Where are you?" Nick didn't sound surly, but an edge of annoyance tinged his tone.

"I'm just finishing up talking with that kid Alec. He just told me the craziest story—"

"Right. Well, if you could cut that short, I'd appreciate it. We're all waiting on you."

"Who is we?" Peter began to walk briskly up the drive. How long had he been talking to Alec? Ten minutes? Twenty? Nick would be...well, not pissed, but certainly not happy by this point.

"Bradley and his friend." Nick delivered his words in a clipped tone.

Peter abandoned the idea of driving and broke into a jog. The private lane was about three hundred yards from the Castle's multicar garage.

"Who is the friend?" Peter rounded the final corner. He spied Nick standing on the patio, looking down at him.

"Some realtor," Nick replied. "I'm going in." He rang off without saying good-bye.

Peter paused a moment to get his breath, cursing Bradley afresh. Then he put on his best reporter smile and opened the front door.

Compared to the cramped apartment living rooms of his youth, Peter's two-story great room in the Castle was a soaring space of hotel-like proportions. When Peter had moved in, Nick's former lover's massive abstract paintings had adorned the walls. Since they redecorated, one wall had remained conspicuously bare.

Nick had said he was saving it for something special. Peter thought that might be the intended location for the painting currently occupying the home studio.

Which only made Peter's inability to divine the painting's subject matter more frustrating.

Bradley's realtor friend didn't seem to care about the huge blank wall. She was standing with Nick at one of the floor-to-ceiling glass windows, staring out at the ocean view with a look of sheer delight. Her manicured fingers wrapped around her cell phone as if they were itching to list this property for sale right this instant.

Bradley himself slumped on the sofa in the primary seating area, next to the television. Although the screen was off, he still stared at it as if hoping to turn it on by force of will.

"I'm sorry to have kept you." Peter introduced himself and shook hands with the realtor, who turned out to be named Roberta. He would have shaken Bradley's hand, if they hadn't been jammed into Bradley's pockets. He offered beverages, which they both declined; then he said, "What can we do for you?"

"I represent a client who is interested in acquiring land in this area, and I just wanted to meet with you, Mr. Olson, to see if you would be interested in selling—"

"Not at this time," Nick cut in before Roberta had even finished. He turned to Bradley. "And I suppose you are the client?"

"Me?" Bradley looked at Nick as though he'd gone crazy. "Why in God's name would I want to live here?"

"Then why are you riding around with a realtor?" Peter felt it was a valid question.

"Roberta is a school friend of my daughter's."

"I'm afraid I heard Mr. De Kamp was coming to town, and I offered to drive him here. I admit I was hoping that he'd introduce us," Roberta said. She gave what looked like a practiced sheepish smile. "It's very hard to reach Mr. Olson on the phone."

"I don't find it that difficult," Peter commented.

"That's because when you call, I answer," Nick remarked, then to Roberta, "I don't mean to be rude, but we do have some business to discuss now, so if you wouldn't mind…"

"Sure, I'll wait for Mr. De Kamp in the car. But would you mind if I leave my card, just in case?" Roberta asked. Nick gave a noncommittal shrug. Roberta left it on the granite slab that served as the breakfast bar and departed. "Now what was it that you wanted to discuss?" Nick asked Bradley.

"I was hoping that this conversation would be private." Bradley shot Peter a meaningful glance.

"Anything you'd like to tell me, you can say in front of Peter."

"He'll just tell me later anyway, so we might as well save time and shorten the loop." Peter tried to keep the loathing from his voice. He ended up sounding snarky.

That was all right. He could live with snarky.

"Very well, I had hoped that you wouldn't be present. I don't wish to hurt your feelings." Bradley took on a sanctimonious air that made Peter want to throw one of the many objets d'art at him. "This has to do with the property belonging to my late father."

"So you want to talk about the prenup you want Nick to sign?" Peter filled in the blank, hoping to hurry Bradley along.

"Yes, I simply do not think that his legacy—his artistic works—should pass to you in the event of Mr. Olson's death. I think they should rightfully go to my family."

"So you can liquidate the inventory and finance your early retirement?" Nick said.

Interestingly, Bradley did not appear to take any offense at this blatant shot across the bow. "I did not say they should go to me. My father has five grandchildren who could all benefit greatly from his legacy. It would be a deeply unselfish act, Mr. Fontaine, if you would consider entering into an agreement of this nature. As long as you insist on inserting yourself into my family negotiations, I would personally ask you to consider making sure that my father's works go to their rightful owner if Mr. Olson should die. I don't think that is an unreasonable request."

This approach was not the one Peter expected. For one thing he hadn't thought Bradley had the balls to appeal to him directly. If anything, he would have thought that Bradley would take the "greedy gold digger" argument.

Well, two can play at this game.

"I don't have any objection to signing a prenup if Nick asks me," Peter said sweetly. "But he hasn't asked me."

"And I won't," Nick pronounced.

Bradley's reasonable visage cracked. "You have no right to give my father's paintings to a complete stranger."

"First, Peter isn't a stranger, and second, I have every right." Nick's voice raised, unnerving Peter, who had never heard him shout at anyone who wasn't holding a loaded weapon. "I own those paintings. They are 100 percent, completely mine. Now get out."

"I'm going to hire a lawyer—"

"I said get out." Nick took three rapid steps forward, bringing his face inches from Bradley's. "Leave now before I lose my temper."

Bradley cast a last, pleading, look at Peter, who only shrugged and gave a fatuous and campy wave good-bye. Bradley retreated without another word. Nick spun on his heel and stalked into his studio. Peter lingered in the living room, unsure of how to proceed.

He had honestly never seen Nick so angry. Even when they argued, Nick maintained a certain detachment, as though fighting with him was an unpleasant but necessary process that must be completed in order for their relationship to continue.

Even when Peter goaded him, Nick never took the bait. Obviously, he'd been using the wrong tactic. He should have been trying to piss Nick off by talking about art. And the worst part of it was, Peter found himself siding with Bradley, which was insane. He hated that man. But regardless, Bradley had a point. Walter's paintings should stay in Walter's family. It wasn't as though Bradley was asking Nick to exclude Peter from inheriting the Castle and its multimillion-dollar view.

Maybe he should talk to Nick about it.

Or maybe he should leave Nick the hell alone.

One thing he knew he should do was go to work, or at least call work. Since that offered a brief distraction, Peter did. On an impulse, he explained that he was following a lead on potential eagle poaching. His editor responded with enthusiasm and told him to check in this afternoon.

Five minutes had passed. It didn't seem like enough time for Nick to have recovered his cool, but now that Peter had excused his own lateness with what appeared to be a juicy story, he knew he should go at least report the dead bird to the ranger station at Larrabee.

And that meant saying good-bye.

The studio door was closed, so Peter knocked. Resisting the urge to knock tentatively, he overdid it and ended up pounding on the oak door. Nick opened the door and said, "Something wrong?"

"I was just coming to say that I'm going to work now."

"Want me to drive you? I promise we won't get shot at again."

Peter gave a relieved chuckle. "I'm just riding over to Larrabee to report a dead eagle."

Nick raised his eyebrows quizzically, and Peter explained about Alec.

"That scenario sounds highly unlikely," Nick remarked when he got to the part about the poachers shooting at Alec.

"I know, but there really is a dead eagle out there," Peter said. "I can be back for lunch if you want to have PB and J's with me."

Nick gave a slight smile and said, "Sure."

As Nick turned back to his painting, Peter found his courage and said, "You know I really don't want Walter's paintings."

Nick stopped so suddenly that Peter thought he'd miscalculated. Then he lifted a paintbrush and studied it. Without meeting Peter's eyes he said, "I know you might have a hard time believing this, but this isn't about what you want."

Peter blinked. He thought for one moment that Nick might finally be picking a fight with him. If he was, Peter wasn't up for battle. He merely said, "It isn't?"

"It's about what I want. It's probably hard for you to under-stand, but these last paintings are the works created during the last few years Walter and I lived together. They have a special value for me." Nick put down the paintbrush and chose another. He ran his fingers along the bristles. "If I were to die, I do not want Bradley to have them. He didn't have anything to do with them or with Walter, for that matter, by that time. It might be unfair of me to ask you to take care of them if I die, but that's what I'd like you to do. Are you willing to do it?"

Insofar as Peter could remember, Nick had never said that many words in sequence before. Without hesitation he said, "I will."

"Good. Thank you." Nick finally met his eyes. "Do you really think there's an eagle poacher out there?"

"At this point I don't know."

"Well, be careful anyway. I'm counting on you to outlive me."

Chapter Three

When Peter located the ranger on duty at Larrabee State Park, she was in the playground area men's room, plunging the toilet. She was a petite blonde woman, fit and—as one would imagine—aggravated.

Peter leaned slightly through the door. The smell of damp concrete and summer-camp latrine rolled over him. "Hello?"

"What can I do for you?" she asked. She scowled, but Peter couldn't tell if that was because of him or the toilet.

"I came to report a dead eagle."

"Okay." Her scowl remained fixed in disgust. Peter did not naturally pursue drama, but her lack of response was somewhat anticlimactic. After all, his entire childhood had been filled with public service announcements about the importance of saving the United States national bird. He'd first understood the concept of an endangered species because of it.

"A bald eagle," he clarified, childishly hoping to elicit some further reaction.

"Where did you find it?" At last she put her plunger aside. Her name tag read *Svedin.*

Peter explained about the eagle on the tracks. Svedin's expression remained bland until he explained about the head and feet.

Then she cocked her head sideways. "Just the head and feet were missing?"

"Right." Now, Peter thought, they were getting somewhere.

"But the wings and tail feathers were still intact?"

"Exactly."

"Let's go up there and have a look," she said.

They headed for Svedin's SUV, but to Peter's amusement, they did not drive it. Rather she crawled through one of the holes in the fence and walked the ten yards to the carcass. "Saves time and gas," she explained. "And there aren't any kids around to see us right now."

"Do you get a lot of trouble with kids in the park?" He wondered if she knew Alec by name.

"All the time," Svedin said. "The local kids think the park's their backyard. They're always building structures."

"Like bike trails?"

"Bike trails, tree houses, driftwood forts. You name it. Some of them are pretty good, actually. But we've still got to take them down." When they reached the eagle, she took a long look at it. "This bird has been deceased for less than a day, I think. We should get off the tracks before the next train comes by." She glanced at her watch. "In six minutes."

Svedin worked quickly and headed back to the park. She thanked him for reporting the incident and took his contact information.

"Just one thing," Peter said. "Why did you ask about the wings and tail?"

"Individuals who traffic eagle parts usually only leave a torso," she replied. "The only thing we know for sure is that this eagle didn't just fall out of the sky."

"Why is that?"

"Well," she said gently, "because it has a gunshot wound."

Armed with an official statement from the Washington Department of Fish andGame and a couple of photographs that he knew were too grisly to ever be printed in the *Hamster*, Peter returned to the Castle. It was shortly before one in the afternoon. As he pedaled up the private drive, he passed Alec again. As usual, the boy zoomed at breakneck speed down the steep gradient. A look of maniacal glee lit his eye. He nearly turned to follow the boy down and let him know about the eagle when a glimmer of unfamiliar auto paint caught his eye. There, in his driveway, was an RV. It was beige and black and looked like more like a souped-up camper top than a rock-star tour bus.

An attached car trailer carried a tiny two-door beige hatchback. The brake lights were on, and exhaust still chugged from the tailpipe.

As Peter pedaled onward, the driver switched off the ignition and stepped down from the vehicle.

The driver was Nick.

But not Nick.

The driver was…old Nick. Old Nick wearing a baby-blue striped polo shirt and a trucker cap that advertised Cruel Jack's Restaurant in Rock Springs, Wyoming. He also sported khakis and a mustache and white tennis shoes.

This could not possibly be anyone but Nick's father, Erik. But why he was in the driveway nine full days before the wedding, Peter did not know.

For a cowardly moment, Peter considered just hightailing it back down the lane. But Erik had already seen him. It would be too obvious. Theirs was the only house on the road. Plus Nick's mother, Ingrid, had also disembarked. She was stout and wore her gray hair cropped so short that if he hadn't known she was Nick's mother, Peter would have thought she was a lesbian. She wore nurse shoes, but he supposed that followed, since she was a retired nurse. She padded, with short, orthopedic steps around the front of the RV to join her husband.

When Peter had fantasized about meeting his in-laws, he had imagined himself well-groomed, well-rested, and with at least one cocktail under his belt, for confidence.

Now here he was, sweaty and hungry and filled with dread.

Summoning his courage, he rolled up to Erik and braked. "Hi, I'm Peter Fontaine. You must be Erik and Ingrid."

Chest filled with dread, he offered his hand to his future father-in-law.

Knowing Erik had been career military, Peter expected his fingers to be summarily crushed. Instead he received a normal handshake.

Erik said, "You know what happened with that car at the end of the road? Looks like it has a couple of bullet holes in it."

Peter blinked. It was not the question he'd been expecting.

Ingrid rolled her eyes, which is to say she made a minute motion that indicated eye rolling, in a subdued way.

She said, "That car isn't your business, Erik."

"A fellow can be curious." A smile tugged at the corner of Erik's mouth.

"Actually, the car is our car," Peter admitted. "Well, Nick's car. So I guess you could argue that it's at least partly your business." Even before he was finished speaking, Peter realized his misstep. Siding with one in-law over the other before he'd really met them was flat-out unintelligent.

"Nick's car was shot at?" Ingrid's face did not show concern. Rather, it hardened. "What happened?"

"Nothing to worry about at all. It was a stray bullet. People get stupid and fire off guns out here sometimes," Peter explained in a rush. He glanced to Erik, who wore an expression of skeptical concern. "Do you want to see Nick? I think he's still in his studio."

The Olsons agreed and followed him into the Castle. In his nervousness, Peter mistook himself for a tour guide and began relating the amenities of the house. "And here's the kitchen. The countertop is made of solid granite. Apparently, it took a crane to move it into place when the house was being built."

"You don't say?" Erik glanced around the kitchen with the air of a police officer memorizing details of a crime scene. Peter wondered what branch of the military Erik had been in, exactly, and what he'd done while enlisted.

"Anyway, I'll get Nick. Help yourself to whatever is in the fridge." As he walked to the studio, he felt a brief irrational fear that there was something terrible in the fridge.

Then he realized that the icebox contained nothing but sliced bread and condiments. Well, he thought there might be a bottle of vodka in the freezer. Hopefully, the Olsons weren't judgmental teetotalers. All he knew about them was that they were retirees who spent most of their time traveling the country in their RV. Nick spoke to them on birthdays and holidays. Peter guessed that they were conservative.

When he leaned into Nick's studio to inform him that his parents had arrived, Nick said, "That's early."

"Should I make up a room for them?" Peter had reserved rooms for both sets of parents at a swank B and B in Bellingham's historic Fairhaven neighborhood, but those rooms wouldn't be open for four days.

"They'll probably want to hook up their RV at the campground and sleep there. Mom likes her own space."

Back in the kitchen, Ingrid was in the middle of making lunch, though Peter could have sworn they didn't have any stuff to make lunch with. As it turned out, they didn't.

Ingrid had brought her own food from the RV. She produced a loaf of high-fiber date-nut bread, some salt-free sliced turkey that looked dry enough to strike matches on, and one thick ring of yellow onion. As Peter watched, Ingrid assembled these three items into sandwich form. She then opened a can of Healthy Life low-salt hearty tomato bisque, diluted it with water, heated it up, and divided it into four mugs. From this action, Peter guessed that she was cooking for all of them.

She did this all without speaking.

"Those sandwiches sure look great," Peter finally commented.

"The bread has twenty-five grams of fiber," Ingrid replied, nodding. "And fifteen grams of protein."

Peter had no idea where to go with that, so he glanced around for Erik and saw that he was outside, backing the hatchback off the trailer.

By that time, Nick had emerged from his studio, given his mother a stiff but sincere embrace, and seated himself at the dining room table. Erik returned and lunch was served—one mug of soup and one half sandwich each. While Peter could never claim to be a culinary genius, he was pretty sure that sandwiches normally contained some sort of lubricant. Mayonnaise, for example, or butter. Sometimes jam. Ingrid's sandwich could have benefited from all three condiments, plus a gallon of water to wash the bread down. Nick and Erik didn't seem to mind. Both wore expressions of resignation, as if this sandwich was their unavoidable fate.

Occupied with chewing, Peter was at least saved from trying to make conversation. When he ate with his own family, words flew in thick fast torrents that he sometimes had to duck to avoid. Even his calm and rational father had the capacity to release a stream of supremely well-reasoned syllables that could carry the conversation aloft or deal it a devastating blow. Eating, though not a secondary task, could be forgotten entirely at these moments. Peter had once paused while holding a fork of mashed potatoes so long it went from piping hot to stone cold.

The Olsons appeared to see no correlation between speaking words and ingesting grams of nutrients. These were separate activities with different goals. Erik made a few remarks about the weather, but that was all.

Uncomfortable, and still hungry, Peter excused himself to work in his study. He needed to get some information on eagles.

His first move was to phone the local Indian college and ask to speak to someone who might have information on the illegal eagle parts trade. The receptionist reacted to his inquiry with frigid disdain. She said that though she knew nothing about eagle poaching, she'd pass his message along to someone who might and disconnected.

Peter had no great hope of hearing from her again. His first theory shot down, he resorted to actual research.

Conventional wisdom said that eagles didn't just fall out of the sky. But over the next couple of hours, Peter discovered that they often did. He would have thought that poaching was the single greatest threat to eagle-kind.

Not so. As it turned out, trauma from hitting vehicles or telephone poles, or from scrapping with other raptors, accounted for the majority of eagle deaths.

Electrocution also loomed large on the list of ways an eagle's ticket could get punched. This was because the wide wingspan of the birds allowed them to touch two wires simultaneously in flight, complete the circuit, and get fried.

Some birds did die of gunshot wounds. Peter was surprised to discover, though, that most eagles were not shot to fuel the trade in illicit animal parts, but because they constituted a threat to livestock.

A brief survey of arrest records showed that free-range poultry farmers appeared to be the main perpetrators of violence against eagles in the modern day. As apex predators, eagles dined on most available sources of protein from scavenging dead whales to snatching spawning salmon straight from the water to descending, like the angel of death, upon unfortunate, inattentive rabbits.

If he were an eagle, Peter imagined that the sight of a bunch of hapless chickens and ducks in a green pasture might look a lot like an all-you-can-eat buffet. Regardless of the bird's capacity for majesty, no chicken farmer liked to watch his hard-earned money get nabbed by winged freeloaders.

And chickens were big money.

In 2009, the average American eater ingested nearly eighty-four pounds of her favorite protein. While only a quarter of those poultry purchases came from buyers of organic or free-range birds, that segment still amounted to billions of dollars. Factor in dramatic increases in consumer demand for free-range chickens, turkeys, and ducks, and conflict between hungry raptors and struggling farmers became inevitable. Especially in Whatcom County—a place well supplied with both.

Firing a gun in the air was an ineffective, yet common, way to attempt to scare off mooching raptors.

That got Peter thinking. What if, in attempting to scare a bird, a farmer had accidentally killed one? Not only did eagle killing carry a fine and possible jail time, the social stigma of capping a protected animal would be devastating in uber-environmentally aware Whatcom County. If a farmer had killed an eagle, he or she would want to dump the body somewhere fast.

Peter changed his search to a list of all poultry growers in the area.

"Trying to figure out what to have for dinner?"

Peter nearly jumped out of his skin. Erik stood inches behind him, reading over his shoulder.

Peter cleared his throat and said, "I'm doing research for an article."

"What about?" Erik did not cease his perusal of Peter's desktop. Rather, he blatantly eyed Peter's handwritten notes. "Something to do with eagles killing chickens, I guess."

In as calm a tone as he could manage, given his pulse still hammering in his throat, Peter explained what it all had to do with. He omitted the theory that the stray bullet that had damaged Nick's car had been the work of poachers trying to ice Alec. It seemed too far-fetched.

As Peter finished explaining his morning's activities, Erik's expression changed to one of outrage.

"Someone did that to our national symbol? That's a damn disgrace. We've got to figure out who it was."

"That's what I'm trying to do." Peter then realized that Erik had used the word *we*, as though he and Erik had morphed into some kind of Hardy Boys-style sleuthing team.

While Peter had nothing against comparing himself to a Hardy Boy, he'd always imagined his partner to be a hot guy—not an old dude who wore both a cop mustache and Aqua Velva.

If Erik had similar reservations about being paired with him, he did not show them. His eyes practically gleamed with excitement. Was this the same man who, just a couple of hours before, had been stonily discussing the weather between bites of nearly inedible high-fiber sandwich?

"How far have you gotten in the search?" Erik asked.

Peter glanced down at his notes. "I've just come up with the Chicken Grower Theory."

"What other theories have you got?" Erik dragged Peter's spare chair over beside the desk.

"Only the Eagle Poacher Theory."

"Because the head and feet were cut off," Erik said, nodding. "Just for a second, though, maybe we should think of a couple other scenarios, just to see what shakes out."

A couple other scenarios? Did Erik think they were on the *A-Team*? Come to think of it, Erik did look a little like George Peppard.

"Have you got one?"

"Jealous Vengeful Canadians," Erik pronounced.

"Are you serious, because I don't think the Canadians envy our freedom," Peter remarked.

"The way I see it, the Canadians have the beaver for their national animal, right? A beaver. Now along comes this eagle soaring like a symbol of hope for democracy for all."

"The Canadians have democracy." Honestly, was the guy winding him up on purpose? Was he just loony? In many ways this entire conversation shocked him more than anything. Wasn't this Nick's father? Stolid, taciturn, tight-lipped Nick? He would have thought Nick had been adopted if they weren't physically identical.

"They have parliament with a constitutional monarchy. It's not the same." Erik grinned broadly at him. "So these Jealous Vengeful Canadians shoot the eagle and take its head and claws back to Ottawa to send to Queen Elizabeth as a symbol of British dominance over the US of A. What do you think?"

"I think that's baseless speculation my editor would find unfit to print."

"Okay, then here's another scenario: Drunken Yokels. A couple of hicks get a case of—what's the cheap beer around here?"

"Rainier," Peter supplied.

"Rainier, right. These dimwits get themselves liquored up, shoot an eagle, and take its head and feet as trophies."

"To send to Queen Elizabeth?" Peter asked.

"To keep to try and pick up women."

"That works on women?"

"Like I said, they're dimwits," Erik said.

Peter almost asked if Erik was making fun of him, then thought that would make him sound too girly. Instead he said, "The Drunken Yokel scenario seems like the most plausible, in the circumstances. Unfortunately, there's not a lot of story in that. What headline would I be pitching to my editor? 'Yokels Fire Guns'? That's not news."

"I'm not saying the Chicken Grower Theory is bad, but it doesn't explain the head and feet being cut off."

"Maybe drunken yokels came by and cut them off in order to seduce women?" Peter offered. "Kind of the recycled-roadkill approach?"

Erik leaned in close. "Or maybe the chicken rancher was trying to throw us off the scent by trying to make the killing look like the work of poachers, but didn't know anything about them."

"And also couldn't use the Internet to find out?"

"Not everyone is online. Even if the perpetrator could have looked up what poachers take, maybe he or she didn't have time. Or was too scared. Shooting an eagle is a federal crime."

"So, what did you do in the military?" Peter fully expected him to say something like Navy SEAL military detective.

"Aviation mechanic. I've always been good with my hands. Nick inherited that from me. We used to build model planes together when he was little. What did you think I did?"

"I didn't know. Your cop talk sounded pretty authentic, though," Peter said, shrugging.

"I read a lot of books when I was at sea. Mainly crime stories, but sometimes a guy would have a whodunit laying around and I'd read that," Erik said. "But back to our problem. What's our next move in solving this eagle thing?"

"Since the ranger didn't lead me anywhere, I"—Peter put great emphasis on the I—"was going to drive up to Lynden and talk to a few farmers."

"Great. Let's go." Erik hopped up to his feet, spry and eager. "I'd love to see you on the job. I've read your articles."

"You have?" For some reason, though his articles were freely available to even the slightest random Googler, Peter had never imagined either of Nick's parents had read them.

"Sure, I read them right away when I found out you were with Nick. Read them again when Ingrid told me he was going to marry you. I wanted to check you out."

"Did you like them?" Peter couldn't help but ask.

"They were interesting. And you didn't seem like a candy-ass or a creep."

"I try my best to avoid going to candy-ass-creep territory."

"I have to tell you, when I saw that green-haired kid riding his bike, I just about shit myself, thinking he might be you. You know when you go to those gay Web sites, none of the guys are ever wearing shirts. But you seem like a good guy. Taller than I expected too."

Peter had no idea how to react to even one of the things Erik was saying, much less all of them at once. So he said, "You're a pretty straight shooter, aren't you?"

"Always have been. Always will be." Erik glanced at his watch. "We should get going pretty soon. Ingrid's taking a nap. If we hightail it, we can go and come back before she even knows we're gone."

Suddenly it all came together, like a blurry, confusing film sharpening into focus. When he'd seen Erik, he thought, because he looked like Nick, he would act like Nick. But if lunch had demonstrated anything, it was that Nick took after his mother, personality-wise.

He'd long heard it said that people chose spouses who resembled one of their parents in temperament. Nick's calm demeanor reminded Peter of his psychologist father's insuperable ease. Insofar as Peter had considered this theory applied to Nick's parents, he'd imagined Ingrid would be chatty and fanciful—perhaps even crafty, like his best friend, Evangeline. What he'd never suspected, in a million years, was that his *father-in-law* might be like him— an unrepentant busybody and snoop.

His heart filled with a kind of angelic joy. The old military guy might not secretly hate him. They might be able to be friends.

"I don't want to disappoint you, but most farmers will have already packed it in for the day," Peter said.

"I suppose they do get up early," Erik said. He looked disappointed. "What about tomorrow?"

"I've got appointments on Friday. The next day is my bachelor party." Peter pulled out his phone and paged through the calendar screens. "I can do it on Sunday. How about that?"

"You think you'll be okay to do that after your bachelor party? I couldn't see straight for two days after mine."

"I think I'll be all right."

Chapter Four

When Peter showed up at his job the following day, his editor greeted him with suspicious enthusiasm—even for a Friday morning. Not that his editor was dour. Far from it. As Bellingham's leading conspiracy theorist, Doug was prone to long rants, either written down or delivered verbally in person. But his secondary position as the city's foremost marijuana advocate generally meant that his mood and subsequent rants remained somewhat low-key.

Not today.

"So, how did it go with the eagle thing?" he inquired.

Years of dealing with Doug told Peter two things. First he knew that Doug cared somewhat about the eagle story and wanted it written by the end of the day. Second he knew that Doug had an ulterior agenda.

"I can report that an eagle was shot, but apart from that I don't have anything for you yet."

As Doug nodded, his gaze roved around the room. It was then that Peter noticed how his coworkers were watching him. Expectation lit their expressions. What the hell? They hadn't looked like this since Doug bought the ad rep a strip-o-gram for his fiftieth birthday.

Peter's attention zinged toward the door, but no hot guy stood there holding an iPod and a set of portable speakers. He didn't know whether to be disappointed or relieved. He felt a little of both.

"Evangeline came by," Doug said. "She invited us to your bachelor party."

"Right, it's tomorrow," Peter said. "At the gay bar."

"Cheap drinks there," Doug went on, undeterred.

"I guess." Peter swiveled in his chair. Glancing around the room, he realized that no one seemed worried about going to the gay bar. Some of them seemed downright excited, and not because they were gay. With a sense of impending dread, he realized that for at least a few of them, Bellingham's gay bar was some exotic and taboo location that Peter's bachelor party offered them a good reason to enter.

They were going to be seriously disappointed. It looked just like any other bar, but with hotter bouncers. He supposed they would learn.

"Well, I'm going to get on writing that eagle piece," Peter said.

"Good, and what about that bullet that went through your car? Any connection?" Doug seemed to have recovered his editorial imperative toward getting words on paper.

"None. Just a stray bullet."

"Can you make that into an essay? I've got a page to fill."

"How about a piece on organic chicken production in Whatcom County?" Peter offered.

Doug's eyes lit. "Have you been doing a little muckraking? Unsafe labor practices? Health department violations?"

"None of the above. We have a lot of good outfits that deserve some media attention. That's all."

Doug shook his head. "I'm not going to subsidize the advertising budget of agri-business with free press. Not unless there's a drumstick in there for me."

"What about giving it a 'Consumer Beware' angle? You know, 'Corporate Chicken Kills, Buy Local'—that sort of thing."

"Only if you've got nothing else. In terms of dead birds, I'd rather go with the eagle."

Peter sighed. "You're the boss."

He bent to his work, trying to stretch five words, "I found a dead bird," into three inches of column space.

When his phone rang, he answered it without looking to see who it was. That, as it turned out, was a mistake.

"Are you avoiding me?" His mother's voice blasted out of the earpiece. "Because if you are, I just want to know what I could have done to cause you problems from five states away."

Claudia Fontaine was sixty years old and did not like to be ducked, ditched, or ignored. It was from her that Peter had acquired his dogged tenacity and slight flair for the dramatic. Peter thought fast. He could not claim to not have received her calls, texts, and e-mails. Such was the curse of living in the modern era—to know exactly when you are being shuffled into the *To Read Later* folder. So Peter went with his only available option—a play for pity.

"I'm just a little frazzled, Mom. Nick's parents arrived yesterday and I've been working on this story about eagles—" He let an edge of childlike whine creep into his voice.

"Nick's parents are already there?" Claudia cut him off. "How come they get to come early?"

"They just got here faster than they thought they would, I guess."

"Why can't I come?"

"Don't you have to work?"

"The school year ended last week," she said. "Is there some reason you don't want me there?"

"No, it's not that. I'd love to have you here to help, but—"

"Good. I'll change the date of my flight," Claudia pronounced. "I have a lot of frequent flyer miles to use up anyway. So have you thought at all about those living sedum boutonnières I was talking about before? They can be shipped anywhere, but the florist needs a week's notice, so I need to get back into contact with her today."

Just like that, the subject was settled and changed. Peter felt slightly dizzy. How had it happened?

"I haven't had a chance." Peter's fingers flew across his keyboard, opening his mother's e-mail and clicking on the link she'd sent. The living sedum boutonniere looked like a tiny star-shaped cousin of the aloe vera plant. Peter had to admit that he liked it, in terms of a masculine flower substitute. The small succulents could apparently be planted after the wedding so that memories of your special day (as his mother had called it) would linger on so long as the plant shall live.

That was a sticky point right there. If lack of attention didn't kill the thing, certainly his cat, Gigi, who had a special aversion to indoor plants, would dig it up and carry if off where it would never be seen again. But his mother wanted him to get it, and he didn't have the spirit to resist just for the sake of it.

"Yeah, go ahead and order two, please," he told her.

No response came, save for the sound of fingers clicking on a keyboard.

"Mom? Were you ordering them already?"

"No, I was changing my ticket to Bellingham."

"What about Dad?"

"He has appointments, so he'll come later. I'll be there on the midnight flight. You don't have to worry about coming to get me. I'll just take a taxi out to your place. If you just leave the key under the mat, I can let myself in. I'll be no trouble at all. See you then."

"You don't have to take a taxi—" Peter stopped speaking as he realized that his mother had disconnected. He rolled his eyes and flopped back in his chair. His melodramatic posturing attracted Doug's attention.

Peter said, "My mother is so annoying."

Doug smirked. "See, this is why I said you gays should have fought for your right to *not* get married. You had it all backward. Too late now, though."

Peter struggled through his day, managing to stretch the dead-eagle story into an environmental commentary piece that filled the space Doug needed. Though comprised mostly of assertions that led nowhere, Peter still felt his essay sent the laudable, if somewhat obvious, message that shooting eagles was bad.

To shore up his plans for the wedding, he spoke to the florist and confirmed the number of pavilions needed with the equipment rental company, then headed over to Evangeline's place for vegetarian barbecue. Nick had been invited but declined in favor of spending some quality time with his mother.

Better him than me, Peter thought grimly. He had the notion that Ingrid hated him—or if not him, the concept of him. If she'd have been around earlier in the day, he might have suspected her of firing the stray bullet.

Hell, if Bradley hadn't been in a car behind them, he would have thought Bradley had tried to take him out. But that was far-fetched. Just because a person had been shot at once, didn't mean every bullet that zinged through the car was intended for him. As Patton pointed out, he wasn't working on any story.

More plausible was that some idiot out target shooting chose a bad direction to aim in.

He should not succumb to paranoia, especially since he knew his anxiety was fueled by his agitation over his mother coming into town early.

It wasn't even that he didn't like his mother. He loved, respected, and admired her as any son should. But the moment they came within a mile of each other, she had a habit of attempting to indirectly control his movements by constantly inquiring about his plans. A natural roamer, Peter balked at all this accountability. His entire childhood he'd been treated as a curious kitten who kept trying to explore the underside of the couch, only to feel big kind teeth on the back of his neck, hauling him back to safety.

Bathed in the scatterbrained love and secondhand smoke of his BFF and her stoner boyfriend, Tommy, Peter nearly forgot his mother's imminent arrival. He relaxed and enjoyed adult conversation, completely forgetting he'd ever been somebody else's baby.

Only his mother's persistent text messages kept him apprised of her northward progress via three connecting flights, which was all she could book at the last minute.

By the time midnight rolled around and he stood outside the Bellingham Airport baggage claim, Peter had regressed fifteen years. He slouched against a wall, jacket collar pulled snugly against his skin, and watched for the sight of his mother and her purple flower-print rolling luggage.

She rounded the corner in the midst of the deplaning herd. She blinked around her, peering through puffy eyelids. Her glasses were pushed atop her head. It hadn't been that long since Peter had last seen her, but it struck him now that she looked old and even a little vulnerable standing there.

Then again, she was old now. Sixty. Six zero.

He wondered what it would be like for him when he was as old as her. He'd be just as tired getting off a plane at midnight, but he'd have no strong young son—or daughter—to meet him.

His momentary melancholia receded with the dawning knowledge that if he had no children, he'd have no reason to be getting off planes so late in the first place.

In his moment of observant reverie, Peter paused too long, and his mother bee-lined it for one of the taxis waiting curbside. Peter legged it toward her and intercepted her just as the driver was opening up the passenger door.

"I told you I'd be here," he said, panting.

"Well, I didn't see you, so I thought something might have happened, and I didn't want to miss all the cabs," she said. She stepped aside to allow another weary traveler to steal her ride.

"You didn't even look for me."

"All right, I forgot you said you were coming. Don't give me a hard time. I just woke up," she muttered.

Peter got her and her luggage into his car and pointed his car toward home. To him the summer night was warm, but having just come from Texas, his mother was cold, so he left the windows rolled up. The scent of his mother's perfume filled the cabin.

"So what do you think of Nick's parents?" she asked.

"Erik and Ingrid?" Peter supplied the names. "Erik is friendly. Ingrid takes a while to warm up to people. Or so everybody tells me."

"She probably feels awkward," his mother said.

"Because I'm a guy."

"Because you're going to marry her son, and she's only just met you." His mother gave him a look of reproach unlike any he'd received since middle school. "You could be anybody. How's she supposed to know if you're going to be a good son-in-law or not?"

"A good son-in-law?" Insofar as Peter had thought of Erik and Ingrid at all, he thought of them as being attached to Nick. But he supposed that once he and Nick were married, he would be a son-in-law. What did that even mean? Were there special obligations? He had no idea. "It's not like I'm going to steal all of Nick's money or try to cut them out of his life. I wouldn't need to anyway. They're barely connected as it is."

"Then she probably feels even worse," his mother said. "If I were you, I would have tried to meet her sooner. But there's nothing you can do about it now. We'll just have to make the best of it and try to make everybody comfortable."

"When you say *we*, who do you mean?"

"All of us." His mother yawned and closed her eyes. "How much longer is it to your house?"

"Twenty minutes."

"Well, wake me up and lead me to the couch when we get there."

"We have a guest room," Peter said.

"Even better," she mumbled into her shoulder. Ten seconds later she was snoring.

Chapter Five

Saturday morning dawned bright and full of promise. After making a breakfast of scrambled eggs and toast and saying hello to Nick, Peter's mother took herself—and Peter's car—to the Olson's RV for coffee and to get acquainted. She wanted to meet them alone, which baffled Peter, but he accepted it. He had at least a dozen calls to make before he attended his bachelor party that evening at Bellingham's best—and only—gay bar.

Nick's own party would also take place this evening, here at the Castle. They'd decided on concurrent yet separate parties as a way to economize on time lost to non-simultaneous hangovers. Plus there was no real overlap in their close friends. Peter had his work cronies, and Nick had his art and army crew. While Peter did wonder how the social mix at Nick's party would pan out, he could tell from the care with which Nick cleared out the fire pit that he was looking forward to the evening.

But there was still a lot of day and a lot of work left for Peter to do before he could have his own little blowout bash. He spent the morning making a series of successful calls.

First he arranged the farm tour that he and Erik would be taking the following day. Even as he did this, he questioned his own decision to do anything important the day after his bachelor party. He couldn't cancel, though, without disappointing Erik.

And the trip with Erik gave him a good excuse not to drink too much. Though usually an enthusiastic imbiber, Peter felt strangely nervous about the prospect of his bachelor party. He knew it was traditionally a time to cut loose for one last hurrah. But he felt like a hurrah of any sort might be the last thing he needed right now. He had the distinct feeling that Doug would do or try to get him to do something really embarrassing. It disinclined Peter to loosen his own inhibitions.

More than that, Peter suspected that if he loosened the reins on any part of this event, whether they be practical or social, the whole thing might careen into catastrophe.

The florist and rental agency were both on target for the event. Even the DJ picked up when Peter called. Then Peter called the caterer, and all forward motion stopped.

"Yes," the unctuous-sounding man said, "we have you down for July thirteenth."

"It's June fifteenth," Peter said. "A week from today."

"I don't think so." The caterer's tone had an air of finality that sent knives of alarm skipping through Peter's stomach.

"I think I know when my own wedding is," Peter remarked. He tried to play it off as a joke, but it didn't come out that way.

"We have Fontaine-Olson scheduled for the thirteenth of July," the man replied.

"But that's wrong. The wedding is next weekend. I paid the 50 percent down already. There must have been some mix-up."

"I'm sorry, but there isn't. We have three events for next weekend, but yours isn't one of them. I made this schedule myself."

For a moment, Peter stood speechless. Of all the things he thought might go wrong with his big party, he had not imagined that this would be one of them.

"So what are you saying?" Peter finally managed to ask.

"I'm afraid our company won't be able to cater your event. I'm sorry."

"Can I speak with the owner?"

"I *am* the owner."

Of course you are, Peter thought grimly. What would they do without a caterer? Put out bowls of chips and dip? Nick's agent was flying in from New York and had mentioned bringing some art writer who would cover the event. And what about the rest of the guests? What was he supposed to do? Tell them to pack a lunch?

"I suppose I will be receiving a refund for the down payment then?" Peter said.

"Our contract states that the deposit is non-refundable," the man went on primly. "I'm very sorry about the mix-up, Mr. Fontaine, but you were there when I scheduled the date. You signed off on it."

Had he? He could barely remember talking to some skinny hipster mustache prick.

"I can give you a list of other vendors who might be able to help you," the caterer went on.

"Like who?" Peter demanded. "Who is going to be available at short notice?"

"There's always the supermarket. They do party trays—"

Peter hung up on him. He stared down at the ocean, hands shaking. He resisted the urge to hurl the phone down onto the rocks below. It was, after all, his phone.

Still, he wanted to hurl something.

Or maybe just to hurl.

Behind him he heard a car approaching on the drive. He prayed it wasn't his mother. He did not want to reveal that he had somehow been too incompetent to know the day of his own wedding. Glancing around the corner of the house, he saw a small SUV pulling up the drive. He didn't recognize the driver, but Nick did. These must be the army friends—the last people who Peter wanted to meet right now. Not that he was against the military or Nick having friends, but there was an inevitable comparison of masculinity that occurred when veterans met civilians that he didn't feel up to enduring. Especially not in light of his recent fail.

But it was unavoidable. He must go down. He took a few minutes to look at the sea below.

He searched inside himself for a calm place—some center from which to draw strength, compose himself, and be his own charming self. And as usual, he found himself writing a scene in his own head:

Young Peter of Fontaine stood on the parapet of the Castle at Wildcat Cove, staring at the unfeeling sea. Nay, the sea was worse than unfeeling. It mocked him with its summer placidity.

He had hoped the brackish waves below would at least have the sympathy to conform with the turmoil he felt in his heart. The sea should have been surging with frothing waves that crashed against the rocks like the hooves of white stallions.

With the arrival of Lord Nicolas's brothers in arms, Peter felt the dreary undertow of inadequacy.

Not that Lord Nicolas had ever suggested that because Peter did not don armor and join in the thick of dread battle that he was less a man—far from it. His beloved Nicolas would never make such a suggestion, for though he was a man of war, he was a man of art as well.

But who were these brave soldiers soon to arrive at their castle gate? What would they make of him, a man who fought with syllables rather than steel? And what would they make of Nicolas for choosing him?

And what of the great feast that Peter had planned? It lay in ruins. Lord Nicolas would be humiliated before these warriors as well as his vassals. Heralds would ride through the land, telling of the Fiasco of the Foodless Feast.

Behind him he heard the noise of a carriage door closing.

Lord Nicolas's fellows in arms emerged from the vehicle, happy to be well-met. Two men and, oddly, a woman. All embraced Nicolas heartily, though Peter thought one cleaved to Nicolas for too long. When the man favored Nicolas with a kiss, Peter felt the jade-green flame of jealous fury rise within him...

Peter snapped out of his imaginary romance novel, hardly believing what he was seeing.

Yes, that guy—the lanky brunet in the rugby jersey—had just grabbed Nick by the head and laid a smackeroo right on his lips. Then the guy slid his hand around Nick and deftly palmed his ass before withdrawing.

Nick scrubbed at his mouth with an expression of good-natured chagrin.

The other two, a fit Black woman in yellow basketball shorts and a stocky balding guy wearing flannel, made no attempts to steal smoochies. They confined their greetings to manly side hugs free of all feel copping.

What the fucking hell? Could this day get any worse?

He wanted to charge down the stairs and demand that the guy get his hands off Nick—to throw down a glove and challenge him to a duel, but he recognized that as residual fantasy intruding on reality.

No, he would enter their abode with quiet dignity and greet these people as though he were the lord of the Castle at Wildcat Cove. Because he was. He'd just have to ask Nick about the ass thing later. More than likely it was some old joke that the two of them had from way back in the day. The explanation would doubtless be amusing and harmless.

Maybe the rugby guy was actually Italian. Or perhaps he had been the victim of a gas attack that now caused him to suffer from a condition that magnetically attracted his palms to other men's asses. Who knew?

The only way to find out was to go in and meet them in the living room and offer hospitable company and soothing refreshment.

The thought of refreshments brought him circling back to the catering fail, but Peter decided that that problem was not one that could be solved at four o'clock on a Saturday afternoon in the thick of the wedding season. Everyone would be out making other people's events happy.

Catering would have to wait until Monday.

Peter walked back into the kitchen just as Nick was bringing his friends inside. Greetings were exchanged. The stocky guy was named Dale. He had calloused hands and a soft Southern accent.

The black woman was Shantee, who Peter remembered was still in the army, working mainly as a recruiting officer now. She gave him a once-over fitting of any high-school senior interested in a career in the military, but she had a wide, friendly smile.

"You're even prettier than Nick said you were," she commented.

"And he's smart too," Nick added. He draped an arm across Peter's shoulders, which was strange. Nick didn't normally go in for public displays of affection. But Peter thought maybe the gesture was slightly more possessive than sentimental.

The ass grabber's name was Shamus. He shook Peter's hand with gusto, using the hand-sandwich method, which made Peter think that maybe he was just a touchy-feely sort after all.

Peter offered drinks—they'd laid in an embarrassing quantity of liquor in anticipation of all the company. Dale and Shamus opted for PBR tallboys while Shantee requested rum and Coke.

Peter played bartender while Nick gave his friends the three-level tour. He caught up with them in Nick's studio, where all four of them stood before the mystery painting. Shantee, Shamus, and Nick observed the big canvas, while Dale seemed more interested in the window fixtures.

Shantee accepted her drink with a nod of thanks. "Who buys a painting that big anyway, Olson?"

"Corporate clients, mostly," Nick replied.

"I can't see this one going in a bank lobby," Shamus said, snickering, though Peter did not know why. He thought the painting looked exactly like any number of bank lobby abstracts he'd seen.

"This one's more of a personal piece." Nick cracked the beer that Peter gave him and took a long swig.

"I'll say." Shamus turned to Peter. "So you're a reporter, right?"

"That's right."

"Working on any juicy stories?"

Peter considered launching into an explanation of the eagle investigation, but decided it was too dull. Give them a little action, he thought.

"This and that," he said, shrugging. "I was thinking of writing an editorial piece on gun safety, though."

"Oh yeah?" Shamus asked. "Why?"

All eyes turned to him and he realized he'd strayed into dangerous territory. Nick's friends' faces went suddenly still while they waited for him to reveal himself as a gun-control nut.

"Peter and I were almost killed by a stray bullet the other day," Nick said.

"The hell you say?" Dale stopped his investigation of the window latch.

"It's true. You can still see the bullet hole," Peter said. Then to Nick, "We really ought to get that fixed, you know."

"I think you should keep it," Shantee said. "Nothing says *classy* like a bullet hole."

"You'd think that living out here you'd be safe from that kind of thing," Dale remarked.

"You'd think," Nick said. "But I guess there are idiots everywhere."

"True that." Shamus clunked his beer can against Nick's.

"Just as long as you're sure it was an accident," Shantee said.

"Well, it's not like I haven't been shot at before, but the cops are pretty sure this one wasn't on purpose," Peter said.

Again all eyes rested gently on him, waiting for him to explain. "As it turns out, sometimes people don't like reporters. Especially ones who ask a lot of questions." Nick's tone was slightly sardonic.

"You can't stop a story there," Shamus said.

Nick steered the group to the living room, where Peter spent the next hour recounting his hairier adventures in investigative journalism.

"So what you're saying," Shantee said, "is that you've been on the wrong end of some crazy guy's gun three times now?"

"Twice," Peter corrected. "One time it was a crazy woman."

"I think you might have a curse on you," she said.

"It's not a curse so much as a predilection," Nick said.

"And I thought *my* wife got up to trouble," Dale commented with a laugh.

"Can I give you some advice, Peter?" Shamus leaned forward, resting his elbows on his knees.

"Go ahead." Genuine curiosity brought Peter's attention fully around.

"Next time you go into a situation like that, bring a weapon."

Peter allowed himself a wide self-satisfied smile. "What do I need a weapon for when I've got Nick?"

Shamus gazed at him for a long, silent moment, then raised his beer can. "Cheers to that, buddy. Cheers to that."

Peter excused himself from the gathering shortly after that, with the excuse of needing to check in on his mother. Despite his resolve to let the catering problem rest until Monday, the thought of failure gnawed at him. His mother, though demanding, had always been a problem solver—nay, a problem slayer. Maybe she had some magical fix that he hadn't considered.

When she answered, though, it was clear she wasn't in the mood to talk.

"Don't worry about me tonight," she announced cheerfully. "Ingrid and Erik and I went on a hike. Then I read for a while. Ingrid got us a nice bottle of wine and some turkey dogs from the grocery store. Now we're having a cookout."

"Sounds great." Turkey dogs did not sound great, but they did sound exactly like something Ingrid would buy.

"I was just calling to tell you that Nick's having some friends over."

"I know. The Olsons told me. I'm going to stay here so you kids can have fun."

"You're staying in the RV?"

"There's an extra bed above the cab," she said, as though this was information that everyone should know.

Peter tried to imagine his mother clambering up into some bunk bed. "Are you sure you're going to be all right?"

"Sure I'm sure. There's a bathroom in the RV, so I'm set. We're all so old, we'll be asleep by dark anyway," she said. From the background came the sound of Erik talking above the strains of music from a radio. "Oh, Erik wants to know when you'll be ready to go on your little investigation tomorrow."

"One o'clock."

"He says he'll see you then. Toodle-oo."

"Yeah, toodle-oo." Peter disconnected, feeling both relieved and confused—and a tiny bit hurt. He had thought that his mother had come early because she wanted to help with the wedding. Now he understood that her sudden change of plans hadn't been about him at all. It had been about meeting Erik and Ingrid. He supposed it was natural that she would want to get to know them, but somewhere deep inside his selfish child's heart, he'd imagined that she'd spend her time doting on him. He'd preemptively rebelled against her predicted attention, thinking of her as an annoyance.

But deep down he'd wanted that.

He had called her for reassurance because he was having a problem, even though he'd spent his entire adult life proving to her that he didn't need her to solve his problems. What was this now? Some sort of stress-induced regression, no doubt. One caterer cancels, and another guy feels up his fiancé, and suddenly he needed to call his mommy?

No, it was good that she was having fun making friends with Nick's parents. He'd been wrong to even think of burdening her with his many trials and tribulations. He must soldier on alone now.

As he thought those words, Nick rounded the corner to the kitchen and opened the refrigerator. "How's your mom?"

"She's fine. She's staying with your parents tonight. They're having turkey dogs."

Nick pulled a sour face. "Poor Claudia."

"I think she's fine with it." Peter watched Nick fish two more beers from the fridge. "I think I'm going to change and head out."

"Great. We're just about to start the fire." Nick opened a cupboard and scanned the interior. He selected a bag of tortilla chips, which Peter hadn't perceived the existence of. Nick must have gone shopping while he'd been at work.

"Can I just ask you one question, before I go?" Peter said.

"Go ahead." Nick opened another cupboard and selected the large bowl normally used to hold snack food items. He seemed to contemplate it briefly before putting it back and pulling the bag open.

"Is Shamus from Europe? Or the Middle East?"

Nick broke into an uncharacteristically wide smile. "Where do you get these ideas?"

"I couldn't figure out any other reason he'd kiss you on the mouth," Peter said. "Though I don't know of any country that combines that with an ass grab."

"He was just doing that to wind you up." Nick glanced up as someone outside bellowed his name. He grabbed a second bag from the cupboard. This one contained barbecue potato chips. "Don't worry about it, baby. Have fun at your party

Chapter Six

Being a liberal midsized city, Bellingham had a gay bar. Or rather at it had a bar that had at one time been gay, but had since morphed into what could be more accurately described as a mixed dance club. Secrets Cabaret occupied a big airy building on the same block as the Farmer's Market.

Warm summer wind rolled off the bay. Overhead stars twinkled in the mostly clear sky. Peter thought that it might not rain on Nick's bachelor party, which was good. As he slid his keys into his pocket, he heard Evangeline shout his name. She wore a dress entirely covered with pink sequins and heels so high and so spindly that Peter wondered how they held her up. It warmed the cockles of his ancient and cynical heart to see how she'd gone all-out for him.

He sauntered toward her, dodging clots of restless, indecisive college students and wending his way through parked cars.

Evangeline caught him in an enthusiastic hug. "You look sexy."

"Right back at you," Peter replied.

"Did I just see you get out of Nick's car?"

"That's right."

"You aren't seriously going to drive back to the Castle tonight, are you?"

"That's the plan," Peter said. "It's my motivation to stay sober."

"But everybody's going to want to buy you shots," she complained. "The whole staff of the *Hamster* is coming. The guys want to do a round of Peruvian goat fuckers."

"You'll just have to take mine for me," Peter said.

Evangeline rolled her eyes. "Okay, but don't fight me later

when you get drunk and I have to take your keys. Anyway before everybody gets here, I wanted to show you. I finally have your present."

"Thanks." Peter held out his hands.

She shrank away from him. "I've been working all night to finish it."

"That's a lot of work."

"Yeah." She clutched the present to her chest.

"Can I have it?" Peter asked.

"The thing is, when I started I thought the idea was really cool and hip and ironic. And then I started working on it and working on it, and now I'm worried that it's really ugly."

Peter rolled his eyes. "That's how you feel about everything you've ever made."

"But Nick is a fine artist. And I think he might hate this."

"Beauty is in the eye of the beholder," he said. Then at her expression added, "We look through the eyes of love."

"I think that even I might hate this, and I made it."

Peter sighed. "Just hand over the present and let me decide for myself, okay?"

"Okay, but I won't be mad if you want to throw it away." She handed him the box.

Nestled inside shredded paper packaging were two three-inch fimo grooms. Great care had been made to create the grooms in his and Nick's likeness. The hair color and height-weight proportions were well rendered. The faces, however, were ugly. Really ugly. *Phantom of the Opera*-level unpleasantness.

"Oh God, Nick's head's on crooked. He looks like a hunch-back." She reached out and tried to tweak the figurine. The head fell off in her hand. She gazed up at Peter, an expression of abject apology on her face. "I'd say I could fix it, but it might not be worth it."

"It's okay," Peter said. "I appreciate the thought. Right now it doesn't look like I have a cake to put them on anyway."

"What do you mean?"

Peter detailed his depressing conversation with the caterer, watching as Evangeline grew more and more indignant.

"What a dick."

"I know," Peter agreed.

"That's it. I'm gonna cater your wedding. That will be my gift."

Peter greeted this proclamation with pragmatic skepticism. "There are two hundred guests."

"I fed five hundred people at last year's Bite-O-The-Ham."

While this was true, Peter felt he had to point out the flaw in this argument, since he'd been there serving tiny gyoza with her.

"That was one gyoza each. This was supposed to be a sit-down dinner."

Evangeline screwed up her face in contemplation. "You're right. We'll definitely have to change it to a buffet. We'll have curry rub for the chicken option and alder-smoked salmon. Tommy can do that. He loves smoking things. Vegetarians can eat falafel."

"What about the gluten-free vegans?" he challenged.

"Also falafel, but without the tzatziki sauce." Evangeline waved his words aside as though they were a cloud of gnats. "There is a question of the banquet permit. Are you going to have a cash bar?"

"No, everybody's getting drunk on us."

"That's excellent news." Evangeline seized his arm. "You don't need anything but me and a couple of other guys to grill shit and pour beer. You're my BFF. I will make this *happen* for you."

Gratitude such as he'd rarely felt before welled up in Peter's heart. He threw his arms around Evangeline and whispered, "Thank you."

"You're welcome." She squeezed him back.

Glancing over her shoulder, Peter saw a large crew of people walking down the street. The men and women of the *Hamster* had arrived. After many embraces—some more awkward than others—the party of thirteen middle-aged people entered the dark, quasi-gay meat market.

Peter got himself a Rainier tallboy and decided that it would be his sole libation of the night. A few of his coworkers were cagey at first. Some seemed to be scanning dark corners for danger. But Secrets was no magical land of Oz. It was a bar much like any other with air hockey and pool tables and neon beer signs. The only difference between it and any other bar was a couple of rainbow flags and a higher than average per-capita allotment of masculine hair product. After the first round they moved onto the dance floor, which was mostly empty at ten thirty.

As one dance mix dissolved into another, the dance floor grew more crowded and hot. Bodies brushed against him on all sides. Bass thundered through his chest while lights flashed overhead. Peter danced with anyone who came near him. His coworkers peeled off one by one until at midnight only he and Evangeline remained.

True to her word, she had gamely taken every shot that Peter should have and so was in an advanced state of inebriation. Her eyes were heavily lidded, and she smiled constantly as she gyrated. She watched the DJ and swayed.

The tempo picked up, and she started to spin. She lost her balance slightly and lurched into another dancer who wore a black mesh catsuit with a black bra underneath and tiny latex skirt on top. That's when it got ugly.

To Peter it looked like the girls were struggling. He rushed to his friend's aid and discovered one of Evangeline's sequins was tangled up in the mesh catsuit, holding them together in an accidental dance-floor boob Velcro. Neither lady was coordinated enough to disentangle themselves, so Peter stepped in. He bent between them, trying to unloop the mesh thread. All the sudden he felt himself jerked back by a strong hand.

Turning, he saw a large, angry college boy. He wore a white hat that glowed beneath the black light.

"What the fuck are you doing?"

Peter drew a breath to answer, but the guy wasn't in a listening mood. He shoved Peter away, grabbed the mesh girl's arm, and started dragging her out. This, in turn, dragged Evangeline, who was still trying to separate her clubwear from Catsuit's.

Peter stepped in front of him. "Listen, the girls' dresses are—"

"Fucking asshole," Angry Guy retorted and shoved Peter back.

Like magicians manifesting from the mist, Secrets' security men materialized around them. One grabbed Angry Guy by the arm, and the other grabbed Peter.

"Time for you two to go," he said calmly. "No fighting."

"I wasn't fighting, I—" Peter gazed back behind the bouncer's shoulder.

Evangeline and Catsuit had managed to disengage from each other and were both staring drunkenly around the dance floor. Peter waved. Evangeline caught sight of him and followed.

Outside on the sidewalk, Peter attempted to plead his case, but the bouncer remained impassive. Evangeline stumbled out, looked at her watch, and said, "Well, damn it. It's only midnight. I was going to get another drink."

Privately, Peter thought she probably didn't need one, but didn't say it out loud. "I'll drive you home," he said.

"No, no." Glee lit Evangeline's expression. "You know what we should do? We should crash the other party."

"Nick's party?"

"Right. I'm sure there's nothing going on there anyway. Nick's such a stick in the mud, and his cousin Kjell's no party bringer either. I bet they're all just sitting around the fire pit drinking beer and wishing we would come save them. You could actually have a drink, since you'll already be home."

"It does sound tempting." And it did, if only so that he could keep an eye on that handsy Shamus.

"It's too tempting to pass up. Now come on. Let's go crash that other party."

As Peter turned the car onto the private drive of the Castle, two thoughts occurred to him. One was that there were a lot more parked cars than he expected, and the second was that this was not a quiet campfire-gazing event.

Upward of twenty individuals milled about on his lawn, and he saw even more shapes moving inside.

Evangeline seemed to come to the same conclusion. "I can't believe Nick's party is better than yours."

"It's not..." Peter couldn't even finish the sentence. This party defined the word *better*. The campfire, which in his imagination had seemed tedious and borderline depressing was, in reality, the party's central focus. And there was music. A woman near the campfire played guitar.

Nick's cousin Kjell stood to one side, chatting with a woman in a shiny red jacket.

As Nick's best man—and the wedding officiant—this party had been his responsibility.

Well done, Kjell, Peter thought.

Kjell was only a couple of years older than Nick, but his beard gave him an air of authority. Though he was a carpenter by trade, his true passion lay in plein air painting. He and his easel could be found in locations all throughout greater Whatcom County capturing the essence of the natural light as it fell upon trees, rocks, broken-down silos, and whatever else Kjell chose to plant his box easel in front of.

"I can't believe that we spent all night at Secrets when we could have been here," Evangeline said. "Look at all these cool people. And they set up tents!"

"I'm not sure I know any of these people." Peter surveyed the far end of the lawn where Evangeline pointed. A dozen or so camp tents were set up, presumably by or for those who declined to drive home. That would be like Kjell—to want to make the whole thing a campout.

"They're mostly artists. A lot of them are from Seattle." Evangeline pointed out a few individuals who he knew by name and reputation and had met once or twice before at art events. He tended to skip about half the regional gallery openings that Nick attended on the grounds that there were only so many cheese cubes that one man could eat before exploding. Nick hadn't seemed close with this many of the artists he'd met. Then again, Nick probably didn't seem close with him either, to an outsider, so who knew?

"Do you see Nick?" Peter felt it only sporting to tell Nick he'd arrived, just in case he was engaged in anything tacky. He didn't think Kjell would be the type to hire a battalion of strippers, but it was best to be safe.

"I don't. Oh my God, it's Luna from the Vitamilk Building!" Evangeline suddenly started jumping up and down and waving. Another woman, who seemed equally drunk, rushed across the lawn to hug her. Tipsy lady catching up ensued, beginning with compliments on hair. Peter slunk away to search for Nick.

Deep in his subconscious he knew that he also searched for Shamus—or rather that irrational jealousy kept him alert to the presence of Shamus.

When he could find neither man, a knot of worry began to form in his stomach.

He spotted Shantee and Dale by the fire pit and went to them. Shantee sat in a lawn chair talking with a burly humpty-dumpty-shaped man who Peter thought might be a glass artist. Dale had stretched out on the ground and appeared to be asleep, though he still held a beer can upright in one hand.

"Have you seen Nick around?"

"Here you are," she said, then to the sculptor, "This is him—Peter."

"Good to meet you." The guy shook his hand. "I think I saw Nick down by the garage."

"He's showing Shamus something or other," Shantee added. "Some fancy tool."

He'd better not be showing him *his* tool, Peter thought, grimly stalking toward the house.

The garage occupied the lower level of the house and faced toward the ocean, rather than the drive. This, Nick had informed him, gave the house a more pleasant facade on approach. It also hid the garage from most of the people at the party. Peter picked up the pace.

He rounded the corner of the house to see exactly what he did not want to see: Shamus and Nick embracing.

They stood near the edge of the drive, where the pavement ended with a decorative railing along the sheer cliff face.

Something about Nick seemed strange—apart from the fact that he was in another man's arms. He seemed loose as a ragdoll and weirdly tractable. Peter had never seen him shattered drunk before.

"Hey, you two," Peter said, just to announce his presence. "What's going on?"

Nick's head came up, swiveled toward him. His stare was a thousand miles long.

"Peter, hey baby, when did you get here?"

"Nick's a little toasted." Shamus didn't let go of Nick, but shifted around so he was not fully embracing him anymore. "I thought he was going to fall off the cliff."

"I was just going to take a leak." Nick blinked at him. "But I forgot where the bathroom was, so I went for the cliff. We were going to piss off it together, right, Shamus?"

"I don't remember that plan, buddy, but sure," Shamus said. Then, to Peter, "You want to grab his other arm?"

Peter ducked beneath Nick's free limb, and together they maneuvered him back toward the garage.

"I love you, baby," Nick mumbled in his ear. "Have you got any gum?"

Peter's annoyance turned to amusement. "You are trashed."

Nick nodded, nuzzling against Peter's head as he did so. Then he flopped his head back to Shamus and said, "Hey can you clear out, buddy? I need some privacy."

"Sure thing," Shamus said. "Have you got this, Peter? I could help you carry him in."

"We'll be fine," Peter assured him.

Shamus clapped Nick on the shoulder and departed. As soon as he was gone, Nick slid his hand down to Peter's crotch and said, "Okay he's gone. Let's fuck. Right here."

Peter nearly burst out laughing, both at the abruptness of the proposition as well as its uncharacteristic coarseness. Even if Nick could have had sex—which Peter sincerely doubted based on his lax muscle tone and wobbly legs—the idea that he wanted to have it here and now was borderline hilarious.

He could not wait to tease Nick about this tomorrow morning. In the meantime, though, he peeled Nick's warm, clumsy hand from his fly and said, "I don't know if that's a good idea. There are still a lot of people out on the lawn."

"Right, but that turns you on." Nick sounded almost reasonable. "We could go inside the garage."

"Okay, let's do that." Peter led him inside the garage. Once inside, Nick forgot why they were there, so it was easy to lead him upstairs to the bedroom and get him into bed.

"Are you coming?" Nick asked.

"I'll be right there." Peter went into the bathroom, counted to ten, and stepped back out. Nick was snoring. It was just past one.

Peter turned him on his side and tucked a few pillows and blankets around him. He considered slipping into bed, but there was still a party going on, and he'd only had one drink all night. Plus, he should tell Kjell that the man of honor was out for the night.

As he made his way across the lawn, he noted that the party was breaking up. People were ambling toward the tents or toward their cars. Six or seven people remained fixed around the campfire. One of them was Evangeline. Somewhere she had gotten hold of some yarn and knitting needles. She was attempting to teach the sadly uncoordinated Shamus to knit.

Now that he saw Shamus there, his idea of having a drink with them vanished.

Yes, Shamus might have saved Nick's life, but that didn't mean Peter had recovered from seeing the two of them in each other's arms. He couldn't stay and listen to him tell Evangeline about weird guys he'd met in the woods while camping or whatever the hell he was saying.

Peter thanked Kjell and went to join Nick in bed. He had a date with Erik in the afternoon.

Chapter Seven

Snuggled into the upper left-hand corner of the continental United States, Whatcom County enjoyed a great diversity of terrain. Mount Baker, the resident dormant volcano, presided over great tracts of rolling hills that had been divided by white settlers into small farms. Because of the northerly climate, berries dominated the commercial produce industry. Dairy farms took up more of the patchwork of parcels divided by the crazy quilt of curving roads and rivers.

It was on these roads that Peter and Erik made their journey into chicken grower country. The day was sunny, and so followed the two men's dispositions. Having abstained at his own bachelor party, Peter was well rested and ready to win the heart of his future father-in-law. Erik appeared to be just happy to be in the passenger seat, riding with the windows rolled down, the balmy Pacific Northwest air rippling through his mustache.

The modern crop of farmers—mostly young women, as far as Peter could discern—had taken up the organic produce mantle. Growing mainly for farmer's markets, restaurants, and specialty stores, these young women represented the most hard-core true believers in sustainable agriculture.

So it did not surprise Peter when both proprietors of Sweet Caroline Farm turned out to be thirty-something women in matching rubber boots.

Though he was surprised that neither of them was named Caroline.

"Caroline was the name of our first goat," Sunshine, the taller of the two women explained. Sunshine was rail-thin and had a face as brown and weathered as any prospector. Her hair was maybe an inch long and had clearly been cut in the bathroom using an electric clipper.

"We get that question a lot," her partner, Margot, put in, with a gentle laugh. She was shorter, with a plump face surrounded by mounds of curling chestnut locks wound through with gray. "If we ever decide to have a kid, we'll probably name her Caroline, though."

"Looks like you've already got quite a few kids." Erik gestured to a paddock containing at least two dozen goats.

Peter groaned internally at this terrible old-man joke, but Margot seemed to think it was funny.

"So you'd like the media tour?" Sunshine asked.

"If that's all right with you," Peter said. "I'd like to get a few pictures as well."

Sunshine nodded, then glanced down at Peter's shoes. "You didn't happen to bring any boots, did you?"

"I'm afraid I didn't."

"I think I've got a spare pair that would fit you," she said. She turned her attention to Erik.

"I'm fine just as I am." Erik displayed his battered white tennis shoes. "These will wash."

They entered the mudroom. While Peter switched out his pointy-toed leather loafers for a set of boots, Erik took the opportunity to look at the walls, which were covered with framed pictures. Various ribbons and trophies adorned a shelf. Mainly they seemed to have been won at the fair. Tiny golden goats and gilded hens adorned big blue and red rosettes.

Erik turned back to Sunshine and said, "Were you in the military, miss?"

"Sure was," she said. "Seven years in the army."

"I'm a navy man myself," Erik said, grinning.

The two of them spoke briefly about military service. Peter tried not to feel alienated. Not that being out-machoed by a lesbian was anything new for him. His personal involvement with even quasi-military organizations had ended when he'd been booted out of the cub scouts for snooping through their den leader's tent during his first Webelo overnight trip. He still recalled the look of amusement on his father's face when he explained he'd just been curious about the older guy's stuff.

The car ride home from Webelo camp had been enlivened by a long lecture about personal boundaries and why Peter needed to control his impulses better.

Thoughts of the bond between soldiers and impulse control converged and brought him straight back to Shamus. What the hell had that asshole being trying on with Nick? Chumminess could not explain his actions. Erik and Sunshine's conversation was chummy. Shamus's demeanor the previous evening had been nothing but suspicious.

"Peter's going to be my son-in-law," Erik was saying. "The wedding's next weekend."

"Congratulations to you both," Sunshine said.

"I'm not sure you should be congratulating him, so much as sending him a sympathy card. My son Nick is as hard to get along with as his mother." Erik said this as a throwaway line, but it had the desired effect. Sunshine warmed to them even further.

They started through the pasture toward a long hoop house from which emanated a cacophony of clucks and squawks.

To Erik, Sunshine said, "Your son can't be as bad as all that." She winked at Peter, who gave a noncommittal shrug.

"Oh sure he can," Erik said. "Him and his mother are both stubborn as mules. And tight-lipped! You'd think they needed top secret clearance to tell me what was for dinner. I remember once I came home from a six-week cruise, and they'd had an argument. I knew because neither one of them said a word for the entire day. I thought I was going to have to break out a can opener just to get a *good night* out of them." Erik paused in front of the hoop house listening to the noise of dozens of pullets within. "These girls don't have any trouble talking, do they?"

"No, they like to cluck. And preen and socialize. Part of the reason that we decided to grow chickens was that Margot really loves eggs. But she was too picky to buy from the supermarket and too poor to pay retail prices for pasture raised. At first we had six hens. Then we started trading the spare eggs for produce. After that we started vending at the farmer's market. Do you go there much?"

"I actually worked there all last season helping my friend at Go-Go Gyoza," Peter said. "But you know how it is when you're working. You don't leave your table much."

Sunshine gave him a piercing look. "Then you were the reporter who solved Roger's murder, weren't you?"

"That's right." Peter couldn't help but straighten with pride when she mentioned it.

"You aren't investigating something right now, are you?" Her expression cooled as she spoke, becoming aloof. Whereas before he could easily imagine her accidentally starting a business to enrich her wife's breakfast choices, Peter now spotted the hardness within Sunshine. This was a woman who routinely cut the heads off of chickens, after all.

"The only thing we're investigating is what to have for breakfast," Erik cut in. "I want bacon and eggs, but Ingrid— that's my wife—hardly lets me get a whiff."

"Well, you can tell her that pasture-raised eggs contain thirty-four percent less cholesterol than those tasteless little white things you get from the big factory farms."

Sunshine's professional demeanor returned.

"What I'm really trying to do is continue to profile small farms in the area." Peter found his angle. "After spending so much time at the farmer's market, I began to really understand the real cost of big agribusiness."

It was as if he'd said Open Sesame, and a magical cave of wonderful chicken minutiae opened before him.

From the hoop house they tromped through a sodden pasture thick with goat droppings. There Peter spied what looked like a horse trailer with openable sides.

"That's the chicken caravan," Sunshine said. "We drive the girls out to whatever part of the pasture we want them in and open her up. The trailer provides roosts, so we can collect the eggs, and our hens can shelter from wind and rain. And it's shady on sunny days."

Erik and he walked around the caravan, dodging skittish chickens while Sunshine explained the inner workings of the caravan.

"So these chickens have their own RV?" Erik said.

"Something like that," Sunshine said. "We bring them in at night. They need protection from predators."

"Such as?" Peter asked.

"Possums, raccoons, rats. Then there are foxes and coyotes. Everything loves to eat chickens."

"What about eagles?" Erik asked.

"They mostly come during the day, but yeah. The raptors tend to view pasture-raised chickens as easy prey."

"What do you do to keep them away?" Peter snapped a picture of the chicken caravan.

"There's not much you can do," Sunshine admitted. "You can keep them completely enclosed in portable cages, but then they're not really pasture raised anymore."

"Can't you put up—what's that called? Flash tape?" Erik asked.

Sunshine laughed out loud. "Eagles aren't scared of flash tape. They're not even scared of guns being fired in the air. About the only thing you can do to scare them is run at them waving your arms like a lunatic. I view the pullets I lose to eagles as my personal contribution to raptor conservation in the Pacific Northwest."

"But not the opossums?"

"They're not endangered," Sunshine pronounced.

"I don't think she's the one," Erik said when they got back in the car.

"Me neither. Actually, I think we might be on a wild-goose chase." Peter put the car in reverse and began to back down the drive. "I think I might have better luck going back to the Indian College. Or just start interviewing random drunken yokels."

"No, you know that's all wrong." Erik put the two fresh broilers they'd bought from Sunshine in the backseat and picked up Peter's sheaf of printouts detailing the other local farms. He leafed through them. "Not the yokels—the Indian College thing. What about trophy hunters?"

"What about them?"

"Say there's a secret society of trophy hunters who have vowed to kill a national animal from every country in the world," Erik began.

"And having bagged their beavers just across the border, they're now cutting a swath through Washington State's eagle population? So what we really need to do is cross-reference all incidences of beaver taxidermy in the state with hunters who have traveled extensively?" Peter broke into a grin. "You have even worse ideas than me."

"What's so bad about the Trophy Hunters idea?"

"Too many eagles, for one thing. There's the Mexican eagle, the German eagle. Austria and Egypt as well. Probably more. Also, there's the problem with the UK."

"What's that?" Erik continued to peruse the papers.

"I'm pretty sure their national animal is the bulldog. Who's going to safari hunt, kill, and mount a bulldog?"

Erik put aside the papers to engage his phone. "Wrong, kiddo. England's symbol is the lion. But there are about six others listed, including the unicorn of Scotland."

"Good old Scotland, keeping it realistic."

"Okay, let's forget the trophy hunters. How do you feel about Mennonites?"

"I feel nothing for them," Peter said.

"I mean as our culprits. There's a chicken farm out here that's Mennonite owned."

Erik flicked the paper with his finger. "Except we can't go there today."

"Because it's Sunday?"

"Exactly. Their farm is closed to the public Sunday and Monday. We'll have to swing by there on Tuesday. But that's all right. We've got to get these fine broilers back home anyway. Does Claudia—your mom know how to fry chicken?"

"I think so. If not, we can always look it up. Nick's good at following instructions."

When they returned to the Castle, they discovered that Nick was not available to follow instructions because he was still in bed.

"He's too sick to be just hungover. I think he got roofied," Ingrid said. She sat with Evangeline and Peter's mother, at the kitchen table, poring over pieces of notepaper.

"Who would roofie Nick at his own bachelor party?" Evangeline asked.

"You never know who's a predator," Ingrid said. "I saw a lot of things when I worked in the emergency room. You'd never believe some of these people had committed the crimes they had."

"Ingrid's suspicious of everybody equally." Erik laid his hands on the back of Ingrid's chair. "She's nice and fair that way."

"It's true that you never really know anybody," Claudia put in. "But it's hard to imagine anybody seeing Nick as an easy target."

"That's why they'd need the roofies," Ingrid said sagely.

"As a person who was actually at the party, I can say that nobody there acted creepy," Evangeline said. "Plus they were all old and mostly guys. Peter and I were probably the youngest people there."

"What's that got to do with it?" Erik asked.

"I just can't see a bunch of old guys deciding to roofie each other, I guess." Even Evangeline seemed unsure of her logic. "It seems like a younger kind of drug."

"I told Nick we should do a urine test, but he wouldn't listen." Ingrid shuffled the paper in front of her.

"That's his prerogative," Erik said. He winked at Peter. "What are you girls up to? Making us dinner?"

"We were hoping you would make us dinner," Claudia said.

"We've got a lot of wedding menu planning to do," Evangeline added.

"And all of these recipes need more fiber," Ingrid finished.

"I guess me and Peter will have to figure out these chickens alone," Erik said. He rubbed his hands together in anticipation. Cutting apart a rubbery freshly dead bird was not an activity Peter relished. Nor did he possess the necessary skills. Mostly he watched Erik, who despite claiming to have no knowledge of avian carcass disassembly, seemed to know exactly what he was doing.

Halfway through the breading process, Shamus showed up. Peter met him in the driveway. He didn't need or want to introduce him to the family. Shamus had dark circles under his eyes, and his skin was ashy and gray.

"Just coming by to see how Nick's doing," he said.

"He's still asleep, but he'll be all right." Peter couldn't keep the coolness from his voice.

Shamus seemed to sense this, because he said, "About last night—I wanted to apologize to you. Walking up on me and Nick... It would have been easy to assume the worst."

"I didn't notice."

"Like hell you didn't," Shamus said, though his expression remained sheepish. "I thought you were going to strike me dead with your eyes. I understand, though. Given Nick and I's history."

"What do you understand, exactly?"

"That you'd be worried, but you don't need to be. All that is ancient history now. We were just new recruits. Neither of us even knew we were gay till it happened. Then I think we both chalked it up to the booze. So there wasn't any relationship other than that. I really was just trying to keep him from killing himself at his bachelor party. You get that, right?"

"Sure." Peter kept his voice calm, though he seethed bitter acid internally. "I understand."

As he watched Shamus go, Peter's pulse pounded in his throat. An image formed in his head. This was not like his fanciful internal writing, which calmed and amused him.

This image was of him grabbing the shovel that sat beside the door, rushing after Shamus, and slamming it into the back of his head. Watching Shamus saunter away, all Peter wanted to do was hit him over and over again so that he stayed down. Never in his life had he wanted so badly to attack someone. Not even when he'd been slandered as a fag in high school had he come so close to acting out a murderous vision of revenge.

This was exactly how crimes of passion happened, he realized. One guy pissed another guy off too much, and all at once homicide seemed like the next logical step. He was better than that. He'd honed his impulse-control skills.

Three deep breaths calmed him somewhat. Then Shamus's words replayed through his skull and sent his pulse racing again.

How dare he?

How dare he come to this house and tell an obviously premeditated story about how he and Nick had—what?—lost their virginity to each other? What was Shamus trying to prove? Nick, this house, all of it was Peter's territory. Why did these assholes—Shamus and even Bradley—think they could come here and taunt and insult him?

But that's what petty losers do, he told himself. And winners don't shovel kill their fiancés' ex-boyfriends. Especially not in broad daylight and when the necessity of hiding the body would cause them to miss a chicken dinner.

The words going through his head sounded so much like something his father would have told him during those dark, tumultuous days when he endured the high school locker room that he almost laughed.

When Peter glanced back down the drive, Shamus had disappeared from view.

Nick didn't come down for dinner, saying that the eggs Evangeline had made him while Peter was gone was enough food.

He sat at the dinner table with his family, which included Evangeline for all intents and purposes, and ate Erik's fried chicken and discussed both the menu and strategy for the food. Then Tommy called Evangeline home, and Erik and Ingrid got sleepy. His mother went to take a bath and read, and Peter was left alone with his thoughts.

He needed to write an article, and he forced himself through an uninspired piece on Sweet Caroline Farm. Reading it through, he was dismayed—or perhaps chagrined?—to realize that his uninspired pieces sounded almost exactly like his works of great passion.

He supposed that was what being a professional was all about.

He sent the article to Doug and went to the bedroom. Nick was awake and reading a book. Gigi, their black cat, lay on Nick's back, looking like she had achieved all goals in life and could now die content.

Without asking, Peter realized that Nick had been awake most of the day. He just hadn't felt stable enough to interact. That was fair.

"How's the book?"

"All right. There are some interesting historical paint recipes in it." Nick closed the book. "How was dinner?"

"Good. Erik can really cook meat." Peter smoothed his hand over Nick's hair. For a moment he wondered if he should ask Nick about his relationship with Shamus but decided against it.

The truth was, he didn't really want to know. Especially if Nick had loved Shamus once. He could barely take the jealousy of seeing another man's hands on Nick. If Nick had once imagined spending the rest of his days with Shamus, Peter knew he wouldn't be able to treat Shamus with the generosity required of him as a host.

And he didn't want to be that jealous bitchy guy.

He kept stroking Nick's hair.

"If you keep that up, I'm going to fall asleep."

"That's all right. I'm coming to bed now." Peter extinguished the lights, stripped down to his boxers, and slid beneath the covers. Gigi mewed in groggy annoyance as he moved the bedding beneath her, then settled back in again.

What would it be like for them to be together as long as Sunshine and her wife? Long enough to grow a whole farm together?

As he shifted toward Nick beneath the blankets, Peter heard himself say, "Do you think we'll ever have kids?"

Nick went still, not moving a muscle in the soft darkness. Then, with the extreme caution of a man who was suddenly engaged in deactivating a bomb, he said, "Why? Do you want them?"

"I never have before," Peter admitted.

"Do you want them now?"

"Not really."

"Good. I don't either. The cat's enough responsibility for both of us, I think."

Chapter Eight

Monday brought more trouble with eagles—the trouble being that his eagle story was going nowhere. Doug rejected the farm profile as being a virtual clone of his previous article and told him he needed to either get a new angle or a new topic. The adjunct professor from the local Indian College finally replied to his phone message.

Her tone was somewhat cool. She informed him that although she was a Native American, she personally knew no poachers and therefore couldn't be of much use to him. She did include several links in her e-mail to articles about trade in eagle parts and to government Web sites that gave the particulars of the Migratory Birds Act.

Need a reporter to be culturally insensitive? Call Peter Fontaine! he thought grimly.

He should just give up on this. Do something else. Maybe write that gun-safety article after all.

Thinking of the bullet that ripped through their car brought Peter's mind circling back around to the rest of last Thursday morning.

What if Patton had been wrong and Alec had been right? Alec claimed he saw a weird truck. What if there really had been gunman deliberately targeting the kid? But that brought the inevitable question of why? He should talk to Alec again.

Thinking he should talk to Alec and actually finding Alec to be talked to turned out to be two entirely separate things. A visit to Alec's bland middle-class home revealed that he'd gone out somewhere building a trail and had failed to take his phone along. His mother didn't seem overly concerned by his absence or by his being incommunicado. He would come home when it got dark, she told him.

Unfortunately, Peter had other plans for after dark. His own father was flying in, and Nick and he would host their first family dinner. Peter picked him up at the airport just past four.

Peter's father, Raymond, was sixty years old and slim with salt-and-pepper hair. He wore a permanent expression of benevolent interest on his lightly lined face. He'd been a clinical psychologist since the late seventies, and his professional demeanor had more or less become constant whether he was in the consulting room or not. His general bearing was calm, though he could be deceptively dogged and relentless if engaged in an argument with the highly emotional Claudia. It had been his idea to move from the Catholic to the Unitarian Church—a decision that Peter's mother disagreed with, preferring to forgo worship altogether. Still, Peter thought his father must have been impressed with priests from an early age, because he acted almost exactly like one. All he needed was the collar, and he could have easily played a priest on any telenovela.

Upon Raymond's arrival at the Castle, greetings were exchanged and hands shaken. Peter poured drinks while Claudia filled Raymond in on the fun she'd been having with Ingrid and Erik. Nick remained in the kitchen cooking steaks, pulling the husks from fresh sweet corn, and chopping salad.

Overall, Peter and Nick stayed out of the conversation. Claudia had already made tremendous inroads with the Olsons so had an array of topics—from RVs to retirement—ready to put into play. If Nick felt any awkwardness about their parents meeting, he didn't show it. He accepted Claudia's teases about the epic hangover of the previous day with embarrassed good humor. As the moderate portions of wine flowed, the conversation became more genial, with Claudia and Erik swapping stories about Peter and Nick as children. Peter's father told the Webelo camp story, and Ingrid countered with a stilted yet proud retelling of how Nick became an Eagle Scout.

If it had been anybody but Ingrid, Peter would have thought she was taking a dig at him. But over the past few days, he'd realized that Nick's mother was just socially awkward. As was his own mother—just in a different way—which she proved when she decided to say, "You know, Ingrid. I've just remembered who Nick reminds me of."

"Who is that?"

"When Peter was in seventh grade, he had a picture that he'd cut out of a magazine. It was one of those black-and-white underwear ads that were so popular for a while. Peter kept this picture folded up in an envelope between his mattress and box spring. Nick is the spitting image of that model."

Peter stared at his mother. Could she have possibly chosen any other time to divulge this information? Or how about keeping it to herself? He felt his cheeks redden as gentle chuckles drifted round the table.

"Sons never think about who does their laundry, do they?" Ingrid commented.

"That's when we were certain Peter was special," his mother continued. "Though he didn't tell us for quite a while."

"We found out about Nick from the Internet," Erik said. "I sleuthed it."

"You confirmed it," Ingrid corrected him. Then to Claudia, "Of course we already knew. No one stays a bachelor for that long."

"Some serial killers do," Erik countered. "And what about James Bond?"

"Well, apart from being fictional, James Bond *did* have a wife," Nick said. "Tracy Bond." He went back to eating his potatoes as though no one had implied that they had once suspected him of being psychotic.

Peter's embarrassment dissolved in the face of confusion. Did that mean that Nick had never come out to his parents? Never? He'd have to ask him about it when they weren't having the world's most awkward dinner conversation.

The opportunity never arose. By the time his mother and father drove to their hotel in town and Erik and Ingrid returned to the RV, he and Nick were too spent to do anything but fall into bed together—too spent even to fuck.

When Peter woke Tuesday morning, Nick had already risen. More than likely he was in his studio going at the mystery painting again. Peter glanced at the clock. Five a.m.? He pulled the covers over his face.

As he drifted, trying to go back to sleep, he caught a warm delicious scent.

Someone, somewhere was frying bacon.

The thought brought Peter up to consciousness. There wasn't another house within three hundred yards of them. If bacon was being cooked, that meant it was being cooked in this very building.

He lurched from bed, and after taking his morning wood for a brief visit to the toilet, he ambled down the stairs and across the plush living room carpeting toward the kitchen.

Erik stood in front of the stove, turning bacon strips with a fork. He smiled at Peter and said, "As soon as I get these sandwiches made, we'll be ready to go."

"Go where?" Peter seated himself on a stool. He wondered if he should go find a shirt, in order to subvert the shirtless-gay-guy cliché. He decided against it. A man should be able to be shirtless in his own kitchen at five in the morning, regardless of what future father-in-law might have decided to let himself in.

"To flush out the Mennonite chicken rancher."

"Chicken farmer," Peter said. "Is that coffee?"

"Sure is." Erik poured him a cup. "I already took one to Nick. He just kind of grunted when I set it down. Does he treat you like that? You bring him something nice, and he grunts like a deaf-mute?"

"I'm not usually awake before Nick," Peter replied. In truth, Nick did communicate quite frequently with affirmative-or negative-sounding vocalizations. It didn't usually bother Peter, though. Peter took a swig of the coffee. Erik made it weak.

But then, he'd found that most people who weren't from the

Pacific Northwest made their coffee too watery for his taste. Peter thanked him anyway and then said, "I appreciate you coming by, but I've decided to give up on the eagle story."

"Why would you do that?" Erik froze, fork in hand.

"Because it's looking pointless, and I need to turn in a story," Peter said. "I was just going to write up something about knowing your poultry from my notes before. I'll make it a consumer interest piece."

"Well, the women do love those shopping articles."

Peter was about to quip that he didn't care what women loved when Nick emerged from his studio, holding a coffee mug. He drifted toward the kitchen, sniffing.

Ah, Peter thought, the scent of bacon. Like a siren's song luring men to their salty, crispy early deaths.

Nick took the place beside Peter and watched his father cook. Erik glanced over at him. "Making my famous bacon sandwiches."

"I can see that."

"After that Peter and I were going out on an investigation, but he's chickened out." Erik fished a couple of slices of bread out of a yellow plastic bag.

Nick's eyebrows lifted slightly. "I find that hard to imagine."

"I would have thought so too, but there he is, saying he's going to write some damn smart shopper column instead of finding the eagle murderer." Erik applied mayonnaise to the bread with the same fork he used on the bacon. Apparently, he was a utensil conservationist.

"Are you worried about your safety?" Nick turned to Peter. For some reason Peter found the concern on Nick's face embarrassing.

"The only thing I'm worried about dying of is boredom talking to another chicken farmer," Peter said.

Erik put four pieces of bacon between the two slices of bread, laid the sandwich on a paper towel, and handed it to

Nicole Kimberling

Nick. He then repeated the process until he'd assembled one for Peter as well. Then, mysteriously, he stopped before making a third, though four more strips of bacon remained in the pan.

"Aren't you going to have one?" Peter inquired.

"Nope, can't go back to Ingrid with bacon on my breath," Erik said. "If I was going to be driving around for a couple hours, the smell would have worn off, but now…"

Peter sighed. "Okay, fine. We'll go harass the Mennonite. Have your bacon sandwich."

"Hot damn!" Erik grinned as he began to slap together a third sandwich.

After Erik disappeared his contraband sandwich, Nick returned to his studio, and Peter went to get dressed. He wore jeans, a blue hoodie, and a printed T-shirt advertising Go-Go-Gyoza, Evangeline's food stand.

The auto-glass repair guy had replaced the windows of Nick's Audi, so Peter and Erik drove it instead of Peter's messy breakdown-prone compact. They had barely hit the public asphalt when Erik started asking questions about Peter's career and life.

Peter saw no reason to not answer them. He grew comfortable telling the old codger about how he and Nick met—minus the pornographic parts—and how Nick had saved his life on more than one occasion. Erik seemed proud.

"That's how it should be. Two people the same age helping each other. You know I never approved of Nick dating that old fart," Erik said. "Walter. That was his name, wasn't it?"

"Uh, yeah. Walter. Maybe that's why he didn't tell you about it. I guess now that I've met you, I'm not surprised that you found out anyway."

"When you've got a kid like Nick, you've got to be proactive about information gathering." Erik leaned back in the seat. "I took Ingrid to visit Nick when he lived in the city. Right away I knew that Walter was a fruit."

194

"Fruit?" Peter gave Erik as long and disapproving a look as he could without crashing the car. Erik recognized his misstep.

"Gay person," Erik amended. "I'm just telling you what I thought at the time, you understand."

"Right, so you saw that Nick was living with some old fruit," Peter prompted.

"And I was worried. From what I could see, the guy was using Nick for free labor. It bothered me. If I had known then that Nick was homosexually inclined and being taken advantage of, I'd have knocked that Walter out. It's wrong—going after someone so much younger. Sure, you can get an eyeful of some young thing and like it, but that's where it should stop. Nick was younger than Walter's children." Erik shuddered as if a slug had slithered through his soul.

Looking at Erik, Peter didn't doubt that he could and would have done exactly as he said.

"I think Nick originally had an apprenticeship with Walter. I guess that sort of arrangement is pretty common in the art world."

"That may be, but it isn't how you'd like to see your son living. Once I got home and started thinking about it, I couldn't stop worrying. Like I said, I didn't know about Nick, so I got real concerned that Walter would indoctrinate him into some weird, fruity art cult and use him like a slave to manufacture those giant paintings of nothing that he sold. I was ready to go back down to the city and call the old guy out, but Ingrid stole my car keys and wallet and told me she'd divorce me if I embarrassed her like that."

Though Erik's delivery was coarse, Peter found it touching that Erik would intercede on behalf of his son, however misguided that intervention might have been.

"It all turned out all right in the end."

"I suppose. I just wish Nick had told me about himself. I guess he was afraid I'd react like his mother did," Erik said.

"How was that?"

"Poorly." Erik shook his head. "Being in the navy I'd known sailors who were that way, so I had an easier time with it. Ingrid wanted grandchildren to show off to her nurse friends and a daughter-in-law to boss around."

"Being gay doesn't preclude being a father." Peter felt he should point this out, even if it did in his case.

"That's what I said. Just this morning I was telling her that if you took one of your sister's eggs and shook 'em up with Nick's sperm, that would be a pretty good-looking baby. Grandchildren problem solved."

"We don't have any plans to have children right now," Peter said. Erik's glazed expression was starting to scare him. "But if Ingrid wants to try and boss me around, she can. I don't know how tractable I'll be, though."

"So far you're not too bad," Erik said. "Here's our turn. Applegrove Farm."

"Think they have any apples?"

"Oh, I imagine so," Erik said.

Applegrove Farm was prettier than Sweet Caroline. There was a green pasture and a white fence and plenty of dark green cedar trees. A small grove of trellised apple trees lined the drive on one side. The other was more securely fenced and held dozens of chickens. Three girls of perfectly descending size—teenage to preschool—walked among the birds, tending them. The girls wore the typical head cover favored by their sect as well as matching calico dresses that gave them the appearance of a set of unnested *matryoshka*.

But it was the tree line that ran alongside the property that caught Peter's attention. He spied a number of large nests in the tall trees there. Maybe this was the place after all. He continued down the lane, with greater enthusiasm than he'd previously possessed.

A pickup truck so old that it probably hailed from the great depression sat in front of a plain white but beautifully proportioned house. Peter pulled in alongside this.

"So, how are we going to play this?" Erik asked.

"I don't want to say we're profiling his farm, because there's no way I'm going to get Doug to let me write that article," Peter said. "Plus I don't want to go on another farm tour right this minute."

"Agreed. So we cut right to the chase. Got it." Erik got out of the car.

The farmer was already coming to meet them. He was a red-haired man in his late forties or early fifties. He had a barrel chest and big, warm hands. He introduced himself as Clifford Funk.

"I'm Peter Fontaine, and this is Erik Olson. I'm here investigating a story for a paper in Bellingham."

"Oh yes?" Clifford stuck his hands in his pockets.

"We've been looking into a case of alleged poaching," Erik blurted out.

"That's right." Peter picked it up again before Erik could keep winging it. "A number of eagles have been found mutilated around this area. I can't help but notice that there are several nests along that tree line. Have you had any trouble with people coming onto your property recently? Maybe trying to get too close to the birds?"

Clifford's response was immediate and enlightening. He flushed red right up to the roots of his hair.

"A number of eagles?" he asked, confusion ringing through his voice. "More than one?"

Peter glanced to Erik, who practically danced with barely restrained glee.

"Do you know anything about this?" Asking a question to get out of answering a question was cheap, but Peter thought they might, against all odds, have this one in the bag.

"I—" Clifford broke off, staring at the girls wading among the chickens. "I've heard sometimes people shoot them on accident."

"Is that what happened with you?" Peter asked.

Clifford nodded, his face a mask of misery. "I should have reported it to the police, but the fine is so much. It was dishonest."

"What did you do with the wings and head?" Erik asked. "Did you figure you might as well sell them since the bird was dead anyway?"

"No! I tossed them in the river," Clifford said. "I didn't sell anything. I was only trying to make it look like the bird had been shot by poachers."

"I've heard of people trying to make crimes look like accidents, but you're the first one I've come across who tried to make an accident look like a crime," Peter said.

"No one has been arrested, have they?" Clifford looked between them.

"Not yet." Peter didn't feel it was necessary to reveal the fact that as far as he knew, no one was even investigating it. He was too busy basking in the triumph of the moment.

Erik, too, looked like he might burst from happiness.

Clifford said, "I suppose you're going to tell the police. I deserve it. I have sinned."

Peter was ready to give a spiel about the story when something gave him pause. It took him a while to figure it out, but eventually he realized it was his conscience.

Looking at the farm, the ancient truck, the little girls, he suddenly felt like writing a story that would result in these people getting slapped with a huge fine might be heartless.

"I just wanted to find out the truth about what happened," Peter said.

Clifford told the tale exactly as Peter would have expected him to. In an effort to scare off hungry raptors, Clifford had fired his gun in the air and brought a bird down. Panicked, he'd cut the wings and head off, but then he'd needed somewhere to dump the torso. But being devout, he'd been racked with guilt. He'd been afraid that someone had seen him when he'd left the eagle's body and confided that he hadn't slept well since that day.

"I'm relieved to have confessed," Clifford finished. "I want to do what's right."

"I think I'm going to leave that up to you," Peter said.

"What do you mean?" Erik asked.

"I'm feeling benevolent this week," Peter said. "I'll find something else to write about."

Chapter Nine

"You won't believe it!" Peter burst in to Nick's studio. Rather than working on the giant, mysterious painting, Nick sat at his drawing table writing on a large square sketchpad. Several books sat beside him—a dictionary, a thesaurus, a book of quotes.

Nick glanced up. "What is that?"

"Erik and I found the eagle shooter. It was the Mennonite after all."

As he approached, Nick flipped his sketchpad closed. It was a strange reaction, considering that Nick was usually comfortable with sharing his drawings with anyone who cared to look at them. Peter had lost count of the number of times some cute waiter (or waitress) had used Nick's ever-present napkin doodles to form an opening line for some come-on.

"Why so shy?"

"I'm trying to write my vows," Nick admitted.

"I guess that would explain the book of quotations." Peter hefted the tome in one hand. It had the approximate dimensions and weight of a cement patio paver. "What have you got so far?"

"I don't want to show it to you yet."

"That's fair, I guess." Peter leafed through the book, wondering what sort of quote would attract Nick as a vows writer. Love? Marriage? He flipped through the index for quotes about homosexuality. There weren't any. He snapped the book closed. "I don't know if you'd necessarily use a quote in your vows, which are supposed to be your own words. Assuming that you're writing your own vows, which you are."

"You are too," Nick pointed out. "How long are yours?"

"Mine?" Peter felt his own gaze growing shifty. Unlike Nick, every thought and emotion generally showed on his face.

"They're still pretty rough."

"You haven't started them yet, have you?"

"Well, I've started thinking about them. Usually I have to get the shape of something in my mind before I start writing." Peter raised his chin in the aloof fashion that had gotten him though many college challenges to his creative prowess.

"What *shapes* have you considered?" Nick's tone was light, and Peter knew he was in trouble. Why had he thought he could bullshit Nick?

"Okay, you're right, I haven't started yet. But it's just one page. How hard could it be? It'll take me twenty minutes—tops."

"I find it pretty hard, actually." Nick moved two muscles in his face. He used these to narrow his eyes.

"But I'm a writer." Peter backpedaled. "I use words all the time."

"I guess I would have hoped you'd think they were important enough to give more than twenty minutes of thought." Nick picked up his sketchpad and stood. "I told my mother I'd go down and watch a movie with her. I guess I might as well take care of that."

"Okay," Peter said. With another man he might have bothered to argue. But if Nick had decided that he needed to go for a walk, he probably did.

Peter hung his head as Nick walked away. He'd hurt his man's feelings—obviously. And that meant he needed to come up with some vows quick.

He walked out onto the patio.

The problem with coming up with vows when he felt like a low-down dog was that the vows ended up sounding like a preemptive apology for crimes one might commit in the future.

Rather than dwell on that, he chose to get on his bike and look for Alec. He should tell the kid that he'd solved the eagle case and that the shooting was unrelated.

By following the sound of whooping, he was able to locate Alec within a few minutes. He and his friends had set up some jumps in the middle of the road and were doing BMX tricks off them.

Peter recognized the other kids from the neighborhood. A round of brief nods and handshakes took place. After that, Peter explained about the Mennonite farmer. It took a while, since he had to also explain what a Mennonite was. Eventually Alec understood.

"And he was the guy with the weird truck?" Alec asked.

"No, the only truck we saw there must have predated WWII. And it didn't have a

handicapped permit. Why?"

"We saw it again yesterday. Asshole almost ran over us," Alec said indignantly.

"You are in the middle of the road." Peter felt it was fair to point this out.

"We are here at the same time every single day. People know to go around."

"So he must not live in the neighborhood," Peter said.

"Then why is he driving around here? Fuck him and his yacht-club jacket." Alec stuck his jaw out defiantly. Behind him, his friends concurred. They exchanged high fives.

Yacht-club jacket?

It had to be Bradley.

Returning home, Peter found Nick had moved to the living room sofa. "I was just talking to Alec," Peter said. "Bradley's been hanging around here."

"Yes, he's been texting me about the prenup. I've seen him out on the road twice."

Slight tension showed in Nick's jaw—evidence of reflexive hostility toward Bradley subsumed beneath practiced stoicism. Briefly, Peter wondered when he'd become such an expert on deciphering Nick's microexpressions. Then again, he supposed he'd had a lot of motivation to learn to read the face of a man who generally used only one of his forty-three facial muscles at a time. "I told him that if he comes onto my property again, I'll have him trespassed."

"Why didn't you tell me he was harassing you?"

"It's over now."

Peter stood awkwardly by, watching Nick's face for any indication of what Nick might be thinking. None came. His face might have been made out of stone for all it moved.

Finally Nick said, "What is it?"

"I know you're angry with me."

"More like frustrated with you," Nick corrected.

"It's not like I'm not frustrated with you too," Peter said.

Nick arched a brow. "Why?"

"You just…" Peter didn't know how to phrase it. "You're not exactly the most demonstrative guy, but since your parents have been here, you haven't even kissed me."

"That's not…" Nick paused, as though reviewing archival footage of his actions for the last few days. Grudgingly he continued, "I guess I haven't."

"And it's not like they're here in the building. They're a quarter mile away at a campground. To hear us they'd have to have a directional microphone and no sense of propriety, which, I grant, Erik probably doesn't have, but Ingrid—"

"If you're trying to get me to make love with you, bringing up my mother is a definite misstep."

"I'm only bringing them up because they seem to be the reason that you won't fuck me." The crassness of Peter's own words startled him, but he went on anyway. "Unless it's because you've just decided you want to take a trip down memory lane with Shamus."

Nick's face was a textbook example of blankness. "I don't know what you're talking about."

"Shamus told me all about how you and him took each other's gay virginity, way back in the day. Before you say anything, I know why you didn't tell me. I wouldn't tell you if I invited my first ex-boyfriend to our wedding either."

"That's not the way I think of Shamus," Nick said. "And virginity is virginity, gay or not."

"It's like you're trying to piss me off," Peter said.

"So what was his name?" Nick asked.

"Whose name?"

"Since you now know Shamus was my first, I'm just curious if yours is going to be making an appearance as well. There must have been a first. What was his name?"

"Julian…or Jordy, or Jesse, maybe? Okay, I don't remember," Peter said.

"How can you not remember?"

"There's this thing called vodka. You may have heard of it."

"*Водка? Да, я знаю ее,*" Nick said.

"What?"

"Vodka? Yes, I know her," Nick clarified in a heavy Russian accent. "So chances of your first guy being on the guest list are slim?"

"Practically nonexistent," Peter said.

Nick caught Peter's hand and pulled him down next to him on the couch, sliding his arm around Peter's shoulders as he did. Peter leaned into him, enjoying the silent moment alone.

In the past week, they hadn't had much time to be alone, either with each other or with themselves. A naturally outgoing and gregarious person, Peter wouldn't have thought being in constant company would be so draining for him. But it had been. And now that he was alone with Nick, he perceived a certain equilibrium returning to his mood. He nuzzled his face into Nick's shoulder and was rewarded with a more attentive hug. Nick stroked his hair in a gentle, almost nonsexual way. Almost.

Peter felt the undercurrent of arousal that underlay Nick's motion. It was always the way with them. Any touch would resonate through them both. Even if it didn't end in sex, each of their bodies were attuned to the touch of the other and responsive in small ways. He felt Nick's muscles relax as his own did. They fitted themselves together almost automatically.

It couldn't have been easy for Nick either, he realized. The perpetual interruption of his internal thought process would be hard for Nick to bear. Painting, Nick's first devotion, would be slow, difficult, and frustrating.

Peter himself was having trouble freeing his mind from the details of his social life long enough even to imagine a single sentence, let alone deliver the articles he was supposed to be writing. Even his curiosity seemed to have been subsumed beneath the enormous weight of expectations.

The worst thing was that they were expectations he was placing on himself. Sure, he wanted his wedding to be fun and enjoyable, but at some point the event had morphed into what seemed like a public relations event, rather than a ceremony during which he promised himself to one man for the rest of his life. He could imagine the tagline on the publicity kit: *Nick Olson and Peter Fontaine Prove Same-Sex Weddings Are A-OK! Have Yours Today!*

While he understood that weddings were in essence about community and taking one's place in society, he'd selfishly wanted the event to be a little more about him and Nick and a little less about every other human being he knew.

He hadn't even written his vows yet.

He knew what the gluten-free vegan dining option would be, but he didn't know what he was going to say to Nick. Talk about losing the center. Talk about missing the point.

But the day after tomorrow, it would be over. If they could just hold out long enough, they would be married. Then all the guests could go back to their regularly scheduled lives.

Peter began to drift, trying to allow himself to relax enough that the words he needed to say to Nick would come to him authentically and naturally. Words and pieces of phrases whispered through his mind, leaving vague impressions, but none stuck. He wondered if he should try reading a book of love poetry, just to have something to riff on for the final text.

"Maybe I'm nervous about kissing in general right now," Nick murmured so quietly that Peter almost missed it, lost as he was in a jumbled haze of disconnected vocabulary.

Normally a long period of unbroken silence was antithetical to Peter's personality. Because of this, Peter broke most lulls in conversation. Nick introducing a subject was quite unique.

Or maybe it wasn't. Maybe if Peter had been able to keep mum long enough for Nick to initiate a subject, he'd be sharing his thoughts all the time.

In any case, he appeared to be communicating now, so Peter felt he might as well go with it. He said, "Do you have a toothache?"

"A toothache?" Nick pulled back slightly to look him in the eye. "Where did that come from?"

"You said you were nervous about kissing."

"No, baby, I mean at the wedding. I've never kissed a man in front of my mother before. Really the first time I kissed in public was when we got registered as domestic partners last year. I feel…awkward about it knowing that she will be there. And it doesn't help that she hates my new painting."

"I still don't know what that painting is of," Peter remarked.

A fractional smile creased Nick's cheek. "Keep trying. You'll figure it out."

Peter laid his head back down on Nick's shoulder, partially to keep from having to make eye contact while he sorted out Nick's message.

"We don't have to kiss," Peter said.

"Yes, we do. It's important. It's part of the ceremony."

"But we don't have to make out like teenagers on ecstasy. We can just kiss like adults and move on to the champagne toasts."

"Would that disappoint you?" Nick asked.

"No." Peter felt he sounded convincing, but apparently he did not.

"Yes, it would. You have an exhibitionist streak a mile wide."

"You forget that my own mother will be there," Peter returned. "Like you, I do not feel the tremendous horny in the presence of the maternal unit. I'm slightly kinky, not totally sick. And besides, my mildly racy fantasies only involve being caught by strangers, not by everybody I've ever met in my life. You had it right when you were trying to get me to blow you in the driveway."

"When I what?"

"The night of your bachelor party, when you were trying to get me to suck your dick 'cause I was into that kind of thing."

"I have no memory of that," Nick said.

"You were pretty drunk," Peter said, laughing.

"I still don't have any idea how I got that drunk," Nick remarked. "I used to be able to drink vodka shots all day when I was in the army. I couldn't have had more than three or four. I guess old age is just catching up with me."

"Because you're such an old man." Peter slid his hand beneath Nick's crappy sweater. The muscles beneath were heavy and firm. Sure, he was hairier than a twenty-one-year-old gym bunny—way hairier than Peter himself, but Peter liked that. He supposed that it meant he'd gotten old himself—that smooth guys who looked like teenage kids no longer interested him. Sure, they were great to look at in cologne ads, but he'd stopped wanting to fuck them when he'd stopped being one of them.

Once Peter got his hand beneath the sweater, the sensation of skin on skin removed his ability to focus on anything but the physicality of Nick.

To Peter's disappointment, Nick caught hold of Peter's hand and removed it from beneath his clothes. He stood, and Peter thought he would return to his studio, but he said, "Come to bed?"

"At eight thirty?" Peter replied, just to be difficult.

"I'm really tired," Nick said.

"Is the sweater coming too?"

Nick chuckled. He turned toward the bedroom, hauling the sweater off as he walked.

Peter bounced to his feet. Though inherent competitiveness would normally compel him to race Nick up the stairs to their bedroom, he lagged behind, just watching the broad expanse of Nick's back as it tapered down from his broad shoulders to what he knew to be muscular buttocks, even though they were now hidden beneath baggy work jeans.

Nick sure looked good walking away.

Once Nick had his hand on the bedroom door, Peter couldn't help himself. He whipped off his shirt and bounded up the stairs, managing to squeak through the doorway just ahead of Nick.

Not content to win the race to the mattress, Peter threw himself onto the wide duvet and wriggled out of his jeans. He lay bare against the slate-gray fabric before Nick even started to untie the laces on his work boots. Peter stretched, wriggled, and ran his hands down his own stomach and the tops of his thighs. Nick took his time. He removed his watch and set it aside—took the time to fold his jeans.

"You lost on purpose," Peter said. What was Nick's game here?

"Maybe I just like to let you win." The bed dipped as Nick knelt on it. He ran his hands up Peter's legs, pushing them steadily apart as he did. Peter kept his hands clenched around the duvet as Nick moved him into a more exposed and vulnerable position.

Of course Peter was getting hard. How could he not with Nick watching him so intently?

Nick paused for a long time, just looking at him, then ran his thumb gently up the length of Peter's now rigid shaft. Peter wanted nothing more than to work his own dick, but knew that was almost certainly not what Nick wanted right now, regardless of the previous exhibitionist comment.

So he waited, nerves on fire in anticipation of the next touch.

Nick ran his fingertips along the insides of Peter's thighs, just tracing the delicate skin, then leaned forward and brushed his mouth across Peter's. He worked down Peter's throat to the tender tips of his nipples before returning to claim a deeper, hotter kiss.

Peter moved against him, in tiny thrusts that scraped their shafts against each other.

That brief friction ignited the latent passion between them, like a match flaming to life. Peter curled his legs around Nick, hooking his heels on Nick's heavy thighs, locking them closer together while they explored each other's mouths. Then Nick gathered him in his arms and rolled onto his back so Peter sat astride him. He curled his big hand around their shafts.

Looking down at the two bulbous heads slipping and nudging against each other, Peter wondered at how awkward they looked, yet how wonderful the sensation. Nick's expression was leisurely, as if he'd been having a quiet wank and somehow found an extra cock had slid into his hand.

Peter closed his fingers around Nick's, urging him faster.

The corner of Nick's mouth curled up, and he withdrew his own hand. For a moment, Peter thought he'd made a misstep.

Nick said, "Okay, show me what you've got, Fontaine." He laced his fingers behind his head, smiling smugly up at him.

Never one to shy from a challenge, Peter reached for the lube. He slicked his hands and slid them round their cocks. While most men had years of practice at masturbation, Peter liked to consider himself an expert at the mutual jackoff. Not only was it a display of manual dexterity, but a chance at a performance. He looked straight at Nick, flaunting his own ecstasy. He added flourishes to his motions, playing himself up like a lap dancer working for a big tip, before the wave of mounting pleasure began to build inside him.

He knew how much Nick loved this—watching Peter bring them to climax with feverish intensity. But this time he wanted to do something to shock that smug smile into pleasure. Moving quickly, he reached over to the bedside and grabbed a condom.

He ripped open the package with his teeth and rolled the latex over Nick's shaft just as Nick realized he was doing something different.

"Wait, what are you..." Nick's words silenced as Peter lowered himself onto Nick's cock. It had been a long time since he'd been fucked in this position, and it took a bit of adjustment to get the angle right.

As he'd hoped, Nick's expression immediately went slack, then glazed over with arousal. Nick's fingers trembled a little as they gripped Peter's hips and urged him into a rhythm. Peter started slow, getting the feel of him, using his thighs to regulate the pace. It felt so good to be filled this way, with Nick below him, inside him, holding him, and his only regret was that he couldn't lean down and kiss Nick while impaled as he was.

Nick seemed to understand his wish, however, and sat up, stomach tightening as he pulled Peter to him. Their fucking stopped, but Peter didn't mind. Nick kissed him with messy abandon, and when Peter rose up and plunged himself deeply down again, Nick fell back, groaning in pleasure.

Nick deftly gripped Peter's slick cock and began to stroke him in time with each plunge. They came almost at the same moment, the rush of his own cum spilling over Nick's fingers triggering Nick's release deep inside him.

Peter slumped off to the side, slowly pulling himself free. Nick immediately rolled over and embraced him, pressing his belly against Peter's, which was warm and slick with sweat and semen.

"How was that?" Peter asked, a little breathless.

Nick kissed Peter's damp brow. "Well done. A masterpiece."

"Will you tell me what that painting is now?" Peter asked.

"Your cock."

Peter caught his breath, confused. "Come again?"

"I don't think I can. You wore me out," Nick said, smirking.

"Did you say that painting is of my *cock*?"

"And your balls. Your inner thighs. It's the view I have when I'm about to suck you."

"It's twenty feet long."

"It's not *that* long," Nick said. "Not to say that it's small."

"I mean the painting. It's huge."

"I wanted to share the sense of grandeur that I feel observing the landscape of your body."

Peter did not know what to say. Of course he'd always wanted Nick to paint a picture of him. Didn't everybody whose lover was an artist want that? But to do a twenty-foot painting of his junk, even in abstract, felt weird.

"Don't you like it?"

Did he like it? He didn't know. How the hell was he supposed to go to Nick's next gallery opening if that painting was looming there? Everybody would know... Or at least all the other artists.

No wonder Ingrid had asked him if he was embarrassed. Remembering the rebuke in her expression, Peter reversed his feelings.

He loved Nick, and he loved Nick's paintings. So what if it was his junk made huge? He'd own that painting and everything about it. He and Nick were a team now.

He said, "I love it."

Chapter Ten

The morning of the day before the wedding, the Castle was a flurry of activity. Trucks arrived bearing white tents and strapping young men to set them up. Evangeline and Tommy had all their equipment present and set up for the barbecue that would follow the rehearsal.

Peter still had not written his vows. He hadn't meant to admit this, but after the run-through, Nick inquired.

"I'll have time tonight," Peter had replied. "But in the meantime what do you think of the set up? Pretty nice, huh?"

Nick's expression darkened. "You still have no vows?"

"No, but I'll do it tonight. Now what do you think about the way the flowers should be arranged on the tables?"

"They're fine. I'm going to my studio to paint until the rehearsal."

"I really want your input on this," Peter said. Out of the corner of his eye, he saw his mother approaching. The expression on her face revealed her to be full of questions.

Nick's patience ended. "I truly do not care what happens at this point, so long as we end up married. I have no opinion about anything." He turned to Claudia. "Except that the boutonnieres are lovely. Thank you so much for finding them for us. But now I'm going. Come get me when the food is ready."

He stalked away just as Claudia arrived. "Is he mad?" she asked.

"I think he's tired."

"It's probably just jitters. We're all a little tired. Baking those cakes was tough." She leaned close to add, "I'm not sure that Ingrid knows what goes in cake, but I put her to work creaming butter, and it all worked out in the end."

"I'm sure they'll be great." In an excess of emotion, he kissed her cheek. "Thank you for taking care of this stuff for me."

"It's what I'm here for," she said, smiling. "Now I'm just going to have a word with Evangeline. You just do what you have to do."

Peter nodded. What he had to do was write his vows. It was clear now. He went to the kitchen and found some paper.

He stared at it for a long while. How was he supposed to sum up everything he felt about Nick and wanted to share in just a few short sentences? Every word that came into his head seemed trite and inadequate.

An hour later, Erik found him there, scratching out the few measly lines he'd managed to scrawl down.

"Working hard?" he asked.

"Failing hard," Peter commented.

"I've got something to cheer you up, then—wedding present." Erik held out a plastic grocery bag. "In case anybody gets rowdy at the reception tomorrow."

"What is it?"

Erik shook the bag at him. "A cop Taser. Don't tell Ingrid. I got it from a buddy of mine."

"A Taser? What am I supposed to do with a Taser? I mean tase somebody, obviously, but I don't think I really need anything like this—"

"It's a wedding present." Erik waved his protest aside.

"But aren't wedding presents supposed to be for both people getting married? What's Nick going to do with a Taser?"

"The gift to Nick will be the feeling of safety he gets knowing that you've got a Taser," Erik said. "Don't you like it?"

"Sure, I guess." Peter carefully opened the box and started reading the instructions. Erik loomed over his shoulder, pointing out salient features with his thick fingers. He remembered his own father showing him things like this, but that had been mostly when he was a little kid who hadn't mastered the art of tying shoelaces yet. It felt comfortable and also weird.

"We should take it out for target practice after dinner," Erik said. "I got two extra cartridges. It'll help you blow off some steam."

"We'll do that. Thank you," Peter said.

"Speaking of dinner, I think your friend is looking for you."

"Which one?"

"The one with the dreadlocks who's cooking."

Peter sighed. He supposed he had to deal with these immediate concerns first. After they ate, after Taser practice, maybe he'd be able to find the words that would express his devotion.

When he found Evangeline, she was setting up plates for the small buffet.

"You needed me?" he asked.

"I was just going to tell you to round everybody up. We're just about ready to eat," she said. "By the way, did you ever figure out that eagle thing?"

"Yeah, I did. It was the religious red-haired chicken farmer." Peter sampled a piece of pulled pork. It was good. Salty and not too spicy.

"Oh, then it really was the same guy," she said.

"Same guy?"

"Yeah, at the bachelor party, Nick's friend—Shane or Dan."

"Shamus," Peter supplied.

"Right, that guy. He said he saw some redheaded dude in an old-timey truck looking sketchy walking down the railroad tracks with a strange bundle. A few minutes later the dude came back without it. You'd think that he would have gone to the check it out, but I guess he's not used to solving mysteries."

"I guess not." Peter took another bite of the pork. He was hungrier than he'd realized. He was about to fix himself a plate when the sound of a horn blasted across the lawn. Looking up he saw Alec skidding to a halt just before getting creamed by the last rental truck as it made its way out.

Peter jogged down to see if he was okay and to belatedly invite him to the reception. The kid was standing on the side of the road with his bike, dusting himself off.

"Truck drivers are dicks," he said, by way of greeting.

"I don't think they're used to watching for speeding teens."

"They're still dicks." Alec brushed the last of the gravel off his leg. "I was just coming by to tell you I figured out who owns the weird truck. It's some guy who's coming to your wedding."

"Yeah, I figured out who owns it too. His name is Bradley. He's not coming to the wedding."

"Crazy," Alec remarked.

"Why crazy?"

"Well, I saw the skinny guy who's camping with the black lady get out of it, and they're both here for your wedding."

"Wait. What?" Why would Bradley be driving Dale and Shantee around? Alec had to be talking about Shamus.

"Anyway, the skinny guy was looking all black-ops. And that yacht-club-jacket fucker gave him a big envelope with some serious cash in it. I saw him counting it. I bet he was buying eagle parts off the dude."

"When did you see this?" Peter's shoulders tensed. But it had to be wrong. No way could Bradley be paying off one of Nick's buddies—could he?

"No, last week sometime... The day I found the eagle." Alec scratched his belly. "I don't want to tell you what to do, but I wouldn't let those guys come to your wedding. They are sketchy."

Peter just stood there for a moment as pieces of information fell together in his mind. Maybe there was a perfectly innocent explanation, but Peter couldn't imagine one.

"I have to go," he told Alec. Then he rushed back to find Evangeline. She was just putting the last of the utensils on the buffet table. Tommy stood close by at the barbecue, monitoring the progress of his coals with an expression of zen serenity on his face.

"But when will they be ready?" she asked. "We need to get those eggplants going."

"When they are ready, baby," Tommy replied. "You can't rush the magic. Isn't that right, Peter?"

"Sure," he said. "Listen, what you said about Nick's friend seeing some old-timey guy on the railroad tracks. Who said that, exactly?"

"What do you mean? Me and Nick's friends. You were putting Nick to bed because he was drunk."

"Not at the party, I mean, who saw the guy with the bundle? Was it Shamus or Dale or both of them?"

"I don't know." Evangeline cocked her head, thinking. "Shamus. It was Shamus. He didn't say anyone else was with him, but he didn't say they weren't with him either. But I think they must have been, because earlier Shantee had been talking about how they'd all taken different flights to Seattle on the same day so they could carpool up here."

"That doesn't make any sense," Peter said.

"Why not?"

"I found and reported the eagle on Thursday. Nick's buddies supposedly did not arrive until Friday. How could Shamus have seen the eagle?"

"He came early?" Evangeline's expression betrayed her confusion. "Does it matter?"

"Yes, it matters. Where's Shamus? Did he go back to the campground?"

"I think I saw him over there." Tommy pointed his tongs toward the driveway.

"How long ago?"

"A while?" Tommy gazed at Peter. "Are you sure you don't want to take a toke? You seem stressed."

"I do not want a fucking toke. I want to find Shamus."

"Okay, take it down a notch, Groomzilla." Tommy held up his hands. "I think I saw him there about five minutes ago."

Peter headed for the driveway, his thoughts in sick turmoil. If Alec was telling the truth about Bradley giving Shamus money, then what? Why would Bradley be paying Shamus off? Did he hope that first-boyfriend Shamus would come and seduce

Nick into calling off the wedding? How could anyone think that plan would work?

And yet Bradley had paid Shamus to do something.

Apart from the fact that he'd been Nick's first gay encounter and secret army boyfriend, what did he know about Shamus? Almost nothing, he realized. Shamus had finished his tour and then met back up with Nick in New York. But Nick had already been with Walter by that time, so they'd gone their separate ways.

So what?

One thing was certain: he had to find Shamus and ask him about the money. If Nick found out that his friend was taking cash from Bradley, he would not be welcome at the ceremony tomorrow. Peter continued to scan the grounds for signs of the lanky man but couldn't see him. The bustle of deliverymen setting up giant tents obscured his view of the grounds.

He didn't want to believe that Bradley would sink so low as to hire a guy to bust up Peter's marriage, but what else could he have been paying Shamus to do? Kill him? Shamus had had plenty of opportunity when they'd been out on the cliff in the middle of the night.

Peter's blood ran suddenly cold. What had Shamus been doing out there with Nick in the first place? He didn't want to think it, and yet there was another option.

Bradley could have hired Shamus to kill Nick.

His pace quickened as the pieces fell into place. If Shamus had been present on Thursday—the day that Alec had found the eagle—he could have been the person who shot at their car.

And what if Ingrid had been right about Nick being roofied? What if that had been a second attempt on Nick's life? Peter had thought Shamus was upset because he'd come home early and interrupted his attempted bird-dogging. What if he'd screwed up Shamus's murder plans instead?

Peter forced himself to calm down. This, he told himself, is just a case of your own overactive imagination getting the better of you. Shamus hit on your boyfriend, and you're jealous and want to think he is a murderer instead of a wannabe home wrecker.

But what if he was wrong?

Finally he caught sight of Shamus. He walked up the drive toward the house just ahead of him.

Okay, the murder thing was nonsense, but the money? He had to ask about the money. If only to give Shamus a counteroffer to go away and leave them alone.

Shamus got to the house and slipped in the garage door. Probably heading for Nick's studio for one last go at seducing his fiancé.

Peter broke into a run, weaving through the antlike stream of rental guys carrying tables, chairs, and lighting equipment.

As soon as he made it into the house, he heard the noise. A crash sounded from Nick's studio.

He rushed down the hall and found Shamus with his arm locked around Nick's throat. Nick's face had gone purple. Rage flashed through Peter's body as he launched himself at Shamus, screaming, "Get your hands off him!"

Shamus's eyes flashed fractionally. He pivoted around, sending Nick's body flailing. Peter tripped over one of the long legs. Shamus took the opportunity to slam his hand into Peter's face. Pain exploded through Peter's eye.

The relaxed grip gave Nick the chance he needed to break Shamus's chokehold. He lurched away and stood staring in disbelief and rage.

"What the fuck are you doing?" Nick croaked.

Shamus didn't answer. He lunged again. Nick met him, and they went down grappling. Peter scanned the room for a weapon.

Then he realized he had one. He tore through the house to the kitchen and grabbed the Taser from his messenger bag and pelted back to the studio.

Shamus had Nick down again, pounding punch after punch into his kidneys.

Hands shaking, Peter flipped the safety. He had one chance at this. And if he got the wrong man, Nick and he might both be dead. He stepped up and fired.

The electrodes spewed out, contacting Shamus's back. The instant they hit, he convulsed in mute agony. Nick slid out from under him, careful to avoid the wires. He got to his feet, breathing hard, staring at Peter first in total confusion. Then in a raspy voice he said, "You have to take your finger off the trigger."

"What if he gets back up?"

"He's not getting back up for a while."

Swallowing hard, Peter eased up on the trigger. Shamus stayed down, rolling mutely to one side. Tears streamed down his cheeks. Whether they were of pain or anger or remorse, Peter could not say.

He wanted to walk over and kick him, but restrained himself. Nick took a few short steps to his worktable and dialed three digits. To Peter he said, "Could you close that door?"

Peter did so, watching Shamus warily. But the other man didn't try to get up again. He lay gazing up at the ceiling, drawing in deep, trembling breaths.

Nick finished speaking to the police and disconnected. "The cops are on their way," he announced to both of them.

For a couple of minutes, the three of them just watched one another, saying nothing, Peter with his back to the studio door, Nick at his worktable, Shamus on the floor.

Finally Nick said, "Why did you attack me?"

"I just lost my cool," Shamus said. He didn't look at Nick. "I'll go. Just let me get a head start on the cops. I've been having a hard time. My head's not clear."

Nick sat on his stool. He seemed more relaxed, though Peter noted that he kept out of arm's reach of Shamus.

Shamus dragged his hand across his face to clear the tears. "Things have been rough for me. I guess I didn't want to see you marry somebody else."

Nick gazed at Shamus with unwarranted pity. But of course he would. Nick didn't know what he did about Shamus.

"This is bullshit." Peter didn't realize he'd spoken aloud until he heard his own voice. "You are a lying sack of shit, Shamus."

"Fuck you, Peter."

"Let's just calm down," Nick began, only to be cut off by Peter.

"I don't want to calm down. This asshole agreed to kill you for money. Alec saw Bradley meeting with him in the campground parking lot. Shamus's the one that took the shot at us in the car. How did a marksman like you miss that shot, anyway? Aren't you supposed to be some expert sniper?"

Shamus looked to Nick. "I don't want to tell you your business, buddy, but I think you might want to throw this one back. He's crazy. I wasn't even here when you got shot at."

"He's never been crazy before," Nick said. "And I'd be willing to bet he has proof."

"Other than the eyewitness who saw Bradley meeting with him?" Peter said, smirking. "How about the bullet I dug out of the embankment? I bet that would match one of his many firearms."

"I told you I wasn't even in town then," Shamus insisted.

"Then how did you see the eagle?"

"What fucking eagle?"

"You told Evangeline that you saw a guy dumping an eagle on the train tracks. Well, he saw you too. And I'd be willing to bet he could identify you. He's a very religious man and wouldn't want to lie," Peter said.

"Is this really true, Shamus?" Nick gazed down at his friend, his expression hovering between disbelief and betrayal.

"Yes, it's true," Peter answered on Shamus's behalf. "And when that didn't work, he roofied you and tried to shove you off a cliff." Peter turned his attention on Shamus again. "Or were you trying to fuck him and then send him over the edge? I haven't figured that one out yet."

"I guess I felt like it was going to be one or the other," Shamus snarled. He started to rise.

Nick stepped toward him. "Stay down. I'm warning you."

"Let me go, Nick," Shamus pleaded.

"Have you really been trying to kill me?"

"I just needed some money and Bradley had some to offer. That's all. He wanted me to try and kill you, but I couldn't take the shot. In the end I couldn't do it—not with everything that's been between us," Shamus said.

"Spare me," Peter growled.

"You don't know shit, you bike-commuting twink." Shamus turned his attention back to Nick. "I realized that if I left, he'd just find somebody else to try and do my job, but if I could get you to call off the wedding, Bradley would be satisfied."

"So you're saying that you've been trying to save Nick's life through home wrecking?" Peter could not hide his scorn nor temper his incredulity. He wished he had a second shot on his Taser.

"Why didn't you just tell me what was going on?" Nick asked.

"I wouldn't have gotten paid. I need the money." Shamus hung his head.

"And attacking me just now? What was that all about?" Nick's voice was remarkably calm.

"I told you. I got frustrated and lost my cool. I wasn't trying to kill you."

Desperation sounded through Shamus's voice now. Peter wondered how far out the police were. They couldn't be long now. Faintly, he thought he could hear the wail of a siren.

Nick took a deep breath then said, "I'm not an idiot, Shamus. I know you wanted to hurt me. Maybe not consciously, but in the back of your mind, you wanted to get back at me for letting you down."

"That's not true," Shamus said.

"It is. You wanted us to be together after we were both discharged. You blamed me for leaving you behind when I moved on with my life. Then I got rich, and you got poor, and that made it worse," Nick said.

"I swear it was just for the money," Shamus said. "I still love you, buddy. You've got to believe that I would never have done it. I had plenty of chances."

Nick just shook his head. The sirens sounded clear now. Peter thought the cops must be coming up the drive.

When the knock of authority came, Shamus looked up at Nick and said, "I'm sorry."

"Me too," Nick replied.

After the cops loaded Shamus into the patrol car, after their statements were taken, after Peter surrendered the bullet Alec had given him, Peter and Nick sat alone in the kitchen, two hours late for their own rehearsal dinner.

They merely looked at each other, communicating by observation until Peter reached up and ran his fingers gently over the red marks on Nick's throat.

"That was close," he said.

Nick nodded. "You're going to have a shiner."

"I guess so," Peter said, smiling.

"We should probably get out there." Nick jerked his chin toward the white tents on the lawn.

"Yeah, people are probably getting hungry."

"That sounds like a good idea," Nick said. "Can I just ask you one thing?"

"Sure."

"Where in hell did you get that Taser?"

Peter grinned sheepishly. "Your dad gave it to me as a wedding present."

Nick nodded again. "Good thing you opened it early."

Epilogue

The first and only person who made a comment on Peter's black eye was the wedding photographer. She observed his profile, smiled, and said, "Don't worry. We can retouch that."

Peter glanced to Nick, who draped an arm over his shoulder and said, "No, we'll leave it. We're going for natural images."

The photographer nodded to Nick, then leaned in to Peter and whispered, "I'll try and shoot you from the right."

"Thank you."

She stepped out onto the lawn, and they were left alone in their living room. Peter reached up and straightened Nick's collar. He was more excited than he thought he'd be to finally see Nick's suit. He wouldn't have thought Nick would go for cream linen, but he looked great in it. When he reached up to slide the living sedum boutonniere into Nick's buttonhole, Peter realized his hands were shaking. His attempts to fasten the non-flower with a long pearl-top pin only resulted in bending the thin silver stem.

"I'm a little nervous," Peter admitted.

Nick took the bent fastener from Peter's fingers, righted it, and threaded it through his own lapel. He then fixed Peter's boutonniere in place. He seemed supremely calm for a man who'd openly fretted about kissing another man in front of his mother the day before yesterday. With a slight smile he asked, "Did you ever write any vows?"

Peter's eyes popped open. "Oh God, I forgot."

Nick leaned forward and kissed his cheek with serenity that made Peter wonder if he'd been roofied again. "You'll think of something. Just be yourself."

Evangeline ducked into the doorway. "Are you two ready? They want to cue the music."

All of the sudden Peter wanted to run. He wanted to say that he wasn't ready, that he had a black eye, no vows written, his best man was doubling as the caterer, and the whole day would end in a humiliating fiasco. But he didn't. He slid his hand into Nick's and walked out through the door.

Evangeline walked down the aisle ahead of them. Peter focused on putting one foot in front of the other, just making it to the front of the crowd, where Nick's cousin Kjell waited to perform the short ceremony.

Warm June sunlight shone down on them. A gentle breeze whipped up from the sea to wind its way through the artistically dressed crowd. Peter could barely feel it and remained only aware enough of Kjell's address to the guests to listen for when it stopped.

How the hell could he have forgotten to write vows? He wrote constantly. He wrote whole imaginary scenes in his mind every day. Now he'd failed to scratch down those few words that might be the most important he'd ever say to Nick.

In the midst of his internal rant, he realized that Kjell had stopped speaking and that Nick was reaching into his pocket and unfolding a scrap of some kind of expensive art paper. Peter could see at least a paragraph of text there. Even reading upside down he could make out adverbs like *faithfully* and *eternally* nuzzling up against verbs like *cherish* and *honor*. Nick glanced at the paper, then folded it away again. He took Peter's hands and said, "Peter Fontaine, I promise to love you exactly as you are, forever."

Without thinking Peter replied, "Right back atcha."

Gentle laughter rippled through the crowd, then stilled. Kjell glanced back and forth between them, then said, "I should get on with finishing it then." He asked Peter if he would take Nick and Nick if he would take Peter. They both agreed. Evangeline produced their rings, and after some confusion and fumbling, they managed to get them onto each other. Then Kjell said, "By the power granted to me by the Internet, I pronounce you married. You may now kiss."

Peter moved forward, prepared for a single dry, shy peck. And that is exactly what he got...the first time. Then Nick clamped his hands around Peter's shoulders, and he pulled Peter into a lip-lock worthy of a victory parade. He kissed as though he was attempting to create in one action a work of art that would save the damned, cure cancer, and prove that true love could and would forever triumph in a world of darkness and/or post-apocalyptic zombies. He kissed better than Batman, Superman, and King Elessar Telcontar combined.

In short, Nick kissed well. And from the whoops and whistles coming from the rowdier guests, it looked as good as it felt. When he finally broke for air, Peter couldn't stop grinning. He'd just been married in front of his family, friends, neighbors, and a handful of guys who he'd never met before but seemed okay. It made no difference. He felt profoundly happy. No matter what happened after this, the memory of today would always be with him.

Out of the corner of his eye, he saw the photographer sidling around to his right side, as she'd promised to do. Without warning he turned his head and winked at her, giving her a full view of the shiner. There should be at least one picture of it, he thought. It was part of the perfection of the moment—the *wabi-sabi* element of his otherwise faultless day.

That got him thinking of the catering, and for a moment an edge of anxiety touched him. He should see what she was doing. Then his friends, released from their seats, gathered round, and Peter was lost in a tsunami of well-wishing that abated only slightly when the bartender opened the free bar.

Late into the evening, when the sun had sunk low on the horizon and the lights strung over the scattered tables had been switched on, Detective Patton arrived. She drove an unmarked car and appeared to be on duty. She held a small parcel wrapped in white and silver paper. Peter rose to greet her. She handed him the package.

"It's a copy of Brenda Starr," she announced before Peter even had a chance to shake it. "I figured you'd like it."

"What did you get for Nick?"

"A bottle of antacid," she replied drily. Then she smiled. "Just kidding. I got him the pleasure of not having to worry about you being cited for possession of an illegal weapon."

"I'm glad you noticed that on the wedding registry." Peter gave a cocky grin. The residue of many champagne toasts marched through his loose muscles. "Did you find Bradley?"

"Not yet, but your pal Shamus did a lot of talking. When he does surface, we'll get him."

"What I don't understand is how Bradley even knew about Shamus," Peter said.

"I normally don't talk about cases, especially not to reporters, but as it's your wedding day, I'll make an exception—strictly off the record."

"Of course."

"Shamus worked security at the company where Bradley was last employed. They got to talking one day and discovered they had a mutual acquaintance."

"Mutual enemy is more like it," Peter murmured.

"I don't think Shamus ever thought of Mr. Olson as an enemy. He felt betrayed," Patton said. "When Bradley needed someone to off Mr. Olson, Shamus came to mind. By that time Shamus was in debt and had a taste for Oxycontin. He claims he'd changed his mind about killing Mr. Olson, but junkies aren't known for being very reliable."

"I want to be the kind of person who is good enough to say I feel sorry for him, but I'm not," Peter said. "He tried to kill my husband."

"Love can make people do crazy things." Patton's gaze roved over the wedding proceedings. "I should get back to work now."

"Thank you for coming by. And thanks for the present."

"No problem." Patton opened up her car door, then paused. "And Mr. Fontaine?"

"Yes?" Peter perked up. He half expected some gem of sentimental wisdom about marriage to be drawn unwilling from her cop lips. He waited.

"Tell that green-haired kid to stop drinking out of the keg."

"Yes, ma'am."

Pentimento
Blues

Chapter One

Though it might seem paradoxical, for the normal inhabitant of the Pacific Northwest the only thing worse than months of gray cloud-cover and endless light drizzle is month after month of blue skies and relentless sunshine. Peter Fontaine, small-town reporter and big-time busybody, was no exception to this rule.

A sunny day, he felt, should be a rare and beautiful event when one rushed, squinting, into the brightness to revel and luxuriate in warmth and vitamin D production. It should be, itself, cause for celebration. But this year? This year the sun had shown up like an unwanted houseguest in mid-April and hung around for four months, endlessly staring down on Bellingham as if to ask, "So, what are we up to today, bro?"

Because of the predisposition to rush outdoors immediately on the first hint of sunlight, the relentlessly pleasant weather had been exhausting for most of the population. Even die-hard outdoor enthusiasts found themselves praying for rain, if only to have a reason to stay in and watch TV all day without feeling guilty.

As Peter cycled the winding road to work that morning, he'd noticed there had been another brush fire on the verge—another side effect of unending summer sun. The acrid tang of charred reed grass still hung in the air. The record-breaking heat wave this summer had left his beloved Evergreen State tinder-dry, yellow, and intermittently bursting into flames.

The haze of smoke from numerous forest fires now hung over Bellingham, the City of Subdued Excitement, coloring the sunset electric tangerine and impairing the breathing of the town's asthmatics.

The downtown alleys stank of stale piss and sweet garbage.

It had to rain soon.

It just had to.

He ended his journey in downtown Bellingham, dismounting at the *Hamster* offices. He checked his phone and noticed that his editor, Doug, had texted him during his ride, which was suspicious.

As an editor, Doug ranked among the most callous and insensitive, blithely killing his darlings, run-ons, and clever asides without remorse. But as long as Peter met his deadlines, Doug didn't sweat small stuff like tardiness or the occasional unexplained absence. After long association, he expected both from Peter.

So the text must be a warning. Doug wanted him to know something before he entered the *Hamster* office. With great trepidation Peter tapped his phone screen and read the following: *Some guy named Samuel Powers is waiting for you. He dresses like a douche.*

After removing his helmet and mounting the stairs to the second floor, Peter stepped through the door to the large, open-plan office and caught sight of his visitor for himself. The man lounging in Peter's uncomfortable guest chair was slim, dark-haired, and in his late-thirties to early-forties. He plainly hailed from a more cosmopolitan locale.

To Peter, Samuel Powers was an excellent example of how weird New York style looks on people who are not physically in New York at the time. He wore a V-neck tee with a too-small blazer, cropped chinos, and polished brown loafers with no socks. His bare, tanned ankles dared the world to question his well-examined casualness. He would have looked amazing if he'd been walking through Central Park, holding some kind of whey-enriched smoothie. But sitting in the main offices of the *Hamster*, surrounded by mismatched office furniture, he just looked like he'd been beamed there from a cooler future—the victim of a science-fiction transporter accident.

At the same time, he looked vaguely familiar. But that might have been because he looked like every other handsome, stylish guy from New York.

"I'm sorry I kept you waiting." Peter extended his hand, and Sam shook it with exactly the right amount of manly pressure and eye contact familiar enough that Peter felt certain that this couldn't be their first meeting. He considered attempting to fake it—go in for a hug, or air-kiss even, just to take it to the next level—but decided against it. It was far too hot to hug, and he'd never been a kissy guy. "I'm sorry, but have we met before?"

Sam pulled a wide, perfectly toothed smile and said, "I came to your wedding three years ago."

Now it all fell into place. Sam had attended their wedding as Nick's agent, Donna's, date.

The wedding itself had been such a blur—not just because he'd been excited and stressed by the first mingling of his and Nick's respective families but because one of their guests had attempted to murder Nick. Lesser details of the occasion, like the names of their non-murdering guests, had largely slipped through the cracks of Peter's memory.

"I'm so sorry." Peter felt a line of red creeping up the back of his neck. "Please sit down."

"It's all right. I don't think we spoke much beyond the congratulations." Sam seated himself and then leaned in, elbows on Peter's none-too-clean desk. "So the reason I'm here is that I'm working on a book and I was hoping I might convince you to help me. It's about the Werks Collective."

Peter ran down a list of every collective, commune, and co-op he could recall operating in greater Whatcom County, but nothing rang a bell and he said so.

"It's the artists' collective that Walter de Kamp was part of in New York."

At the mention of that name Peter's naturally ebullient heart cooled to a dull simmer.

Of course Sam wanted to talk about Walter de Kamp, Nick's first lover—the ghost who just wouldn't stay down. Every time Peter thought he and Nick had finally broken free of the specter, he rose up to complicate their lives, bringing with him secrets and lies and old history.

"I'm afraid I can't help you," Peter said. "I never met the man. And before you even ask, Nick won't be interviewed about him at all. Ever. Period."

"Oh, I wasn't hoping to interview Mr. Olson." Sam held up his hands as if to show himself innocent of such notions. "I only hoped to have a closer look at a few of the paintings that you two have at your house. I'm specifically interested in the blue landscape in the dining room. It is such an amazing piece. Ever since I saw it three years ago it's been on my mind."

"Haunting you?" Peter asked. He couldn't help it.

"In a way yes," Sam said, apparently in complete seriousness. "I would be so grateful if you would just let me have another look at it."

Peter weighed the request. Although it would annoy Nick to have someone in the house, maybe if Sam could publicize the painting, there might be enough interest in it that Nick would finally auction the thing off. After that last piece of Walter's art had gone, Peter could hire an exorcist, and the spirit of Walter could be laid to rest. He could just picture it: a tall, thin man in a priest's collar standing before his house, the Castle at Wildcat Cove, eyes pressed closed, whispering in Latin… For an instant, Peter nearly succumbed to his long-standing bad habit of writing the scene out in his head, but Sam had already gathered up his things and started for the door.

"Is it all right if we take my car?" he was saying. That took a moment for Peter to process.

Finally, feeling stupid, he said, "You want to go now?"

"If you're free," Sam returned. Peter glanced across the office at Doug, who had been observing the entire exchange.

Doug gave a silent shrug, which Peter interpreted as a go-ahead.

"Let me just take a leak before we head out," Peter said. Sam magnanimously agreed to wait in the car while Peter took the opportunity of the lone stall in the men's room to fact-check Sam's story.

Years ago, before he'd met Nick and taken up amateur sleuthing, Peter would have gotten into Sam's car on the strength of his handshake alone. But experience had made him wary of riding in cars with random strangers, well-dressed or not.

Sam Powers' web page was everything Peter would have wanted for his own. Clear, organized, full of stylish fonts and praise about his writing from the *New York Times* and the *Guardian*. It also contained a full bibliography of Sam's previously published book titles, three of which involved crimes that were related to the art world.

That hurt most of all.

Though Peter had written thousands of articles and even won a national award for journalism, he didn't have even a single book with his name on the spine. He'd started numerous times, attempting to cobble together a concept that would hold his interest long enough to pitch it to an editor, but after a couple of days' research into this or that subject he'd lose interest, get depressed, and eventually degenerate into writing fiction.

Bad fiction.

Peter's narratives brimmed with irrelevant commentary on modern life and lacked in any sort of dramatic tension. He'd even attempted to write pornography, then given up, realizing how hard it was to be shocking in a world where a book about the gay X-rated exploits of were-dinosaurs who strove to control the Freemasons could actually get good reviews.

Now here came Sam Powers, flaunting his ability to stave off boredom by writing incisive long-form prose. Peter had half a mind to crawl out the window but turned instead to Sam's social media pages, where he found, to his delight, that Sam did have some detractors after all.

Several citizen reviewers called him pretentious and unprincipled. Others disliked his tendency toward wild speculation.

In fact, a brief perusal of Sam's bio led Peter to believe that Sam was some kind of alternate version of himself—the self that made different choices. Sam's natal city was the unfortunately named Boring, Oregon—a city whose main claims to fame were having an accidentally funny name and a series of unsolved serial rapes in the late nineties. Whereas in comparison, Peter's hometown of Bellingham had hosted a great number of actual serial killers in addition to a funny unofficial town motto: *City of Subdued Excitement.*

Though they both originated in small towns in the Pacific Northwest, Sam had lit out for the Big Apple immediately, whereas Peter had attended the local state university. Where Peter had traveled on his own and taken a long time to settle into writing, Sam landed a magazine gig straight out of private college.

Last, Sam's Facebook page showed him to be almost relentlessly single up to the point that he started dating Donna, opposite of serial monogamist Peter. Yet the subjects they wrote about and even their writing style seemed eerily similar, like a literary doppelgänger or…evil twin.

So Sam checked out as a legit writer, not a serial killer, hired assassin, or art thief.

And despite the mad jealousy he might feel at Sam's various awesome book deals, the classy thing to do would be to help him out with his research.

So thinking, Peter left the toilet, ready to face the better version of himself and to help that man become even more successful.

Sam's rented hybrid sat on the curb, not idling, but ready to spring into action nonetheless. As Peter approached the car, Sam looked up from his own phone and gave another big smile.

"I was just reading the column you wrote in the *Hamster* this week. I can never get the observational humor stuff quite right, but you nail it. ' *Sunshine has become passé here in the City of Subdued Excitement, and if that's not a sign of the end-times, I don't know what is. If I squint hard enough across the placid waters of Lake Padden, I can see the four horsemen of the apocalypse, mounted on paddleboards, ready to unleash Pestilence, War, Famine, and Death…as soon as they finish their case of Rainier tallboys.* ' Hilarious!"

Peter didn't know whether he found it disconcerting that Sam and he had been mutually cyberstalking each other, or just funny.

He decided, on balance, to go with funny. "I enjoyed the excerpt of *Young and Wilde: In Berlin with the German Avant Garde*. I hadn't realized that Walter had been associated with them."

Peter noticed his own tone faltering as he spoke of Walter and so apparently did Sam because he said, "Do you not like de Kamp's work?"

"It's not that," Peter said too quickly.

"It's that he's your husband's ex?" Sam filled in.

"He's not even Nick's ex," Peter said. "More like my husband's *first*. I used to feel like we lived in the shadow of his tombstone."

"That's a little dark." Sam smoothly pulled away from the curb, coasting on silent electric power. If darkness bothered him, he didn't acknowledge it.

Realizing that he might be giving too much away, Peter quickly added, "But then we switched out the gigantic, looming furniture, and it was all right. So what about you? I'm assuming that you like Walter's work."

"Yes and no," Sam said. He offered Peter a strange, smug smile. "I enjoy everything about that era in art—the Eighties, that is. So much excess and hedonism. It was bound to all come crumbling down, of course, but what a collapse! AIDS, murder, suicide, insanity. The Werks Collective is practically its own gothic novel."

"Sounds more like a telenovela to me," Peter remarked. The glib way Sam spoke of what must have been terrible suffering unnerved him, but he tried not to sound parochial. "How many got possessed by *El maleficio*?"

"None, so far as I know. But I do have a photograph of one of them dressed as the most vulgar Krampus I've ever seen," Sam said. "The Germans do love their leather, you know."

Peter did know but refused to acknowledge it. "Right, but this new book you're working on?"

"It focuses on the New York scene and the kind of lavish excess that took place there during the coke-fueled orgies of the day. Surely Mr. Olson has talked about them."

"If Nick ever attended a coke orgy, I doubt he'd talk about it to anyone—but especially not me," Peter intoned.

In truth he couldn't imagine it. Nick did not like hard drugs or people who took them. Still, he'd been young once. Maybe that's where his aversion originated. There was nothing like familiarity to breed contempt, or so the saying went.

Clearly, though, Sam was fishing—trying to get Peter to let something slip. What Sam couldn't know was that when it came to talking about Walter and his time in New York, Nick was like Batman with a case of amnesia compounded by laryngitis. Taciturn was too weak a word to describe Nick's lack of reminiscing. That suited Peter just fine. He didn't want to hear about the endless crazy-fun times he'd missed out on.

Perhaps sensing Peter's growing irritation, Sam switched gears.

"It's great to be back in my old stomping grounds," he said. "It's so easy to forget the natural beauty here. It's a great place to ride a bike."

Peter thought referring to Bellingham as his "stomping ground" might be a stretch, considering that Sam's hometown was more than two hundred and fifty miles away, but he appreciated the fact that Sam seemed to be able to relent. They spent the rest of the drive discussing bikes, the hazards of riding them in NYC, and hit briefly on who might win the Tour de France before arriving at the cliffside domicile that Peter shared with Nick.

As Sam negotiated his car down the long, winding drive, he returned to the subject of his research, this time disguised as a compliment.

"You can really see that this structure was made to house art," Sam commented as Peter's house came into view. "It's almost like a museum. Do you know who the architect was?"

"No, but I'm guessing you're about to tell me it was Walter."

After all, Peter thought, what couldn't Walter do—apart from come out of the closet in one of the world's safest environments to do so?

"Not at all," Sam said, laughing. "It was Monroe Addison. Another of us PNW boys. He committed suicide after it was revealed that he'd raped a girl. I think this house might have been one of the last buildings he designed before hanging himself."

Listening to Sam speak, Peter wondered for the first time if he sounded as callous when he spoke offhandedly of subjects like rape and suicide. Certainly Nick would have known this Addison guy, right?

Or maybe not. Maybe he was just feeling defensive on Nick's behalf.

"So did any members of the Werks Collective get a happy ending?" Peter asked.

"Nick Olson seems to have." Sam's smooth rejoinder caught Peter off guard, and he found himself smiling stupidly at the flattery. Sam continued, "But then he wasn't ever an official member of the collective. I think most of de Kamp's friends considered him a trophy, which was never the case."

"Oh, I don't know," Peter said, "I consider him a prize."

"That's so sweet, but what I'm saying is that de Kamp's journals clearly state that he took Olson on as a true protégé rather than just some muscular, young paramour," Sam said. "Is there anywhere I should park?"

"Next to the Audi."

Sam followed Peter into the modernist, cliffside dwelling, making light commentary that expressed his further appreciation of the architecture and architectural details, including the twelve-foot double-entry front doors.

"Very practical," he said admiringly.

From the foyer, Peter glanced down the long hallway that led to Nick's studio. The door was completely closed, and their cat, Gigi, lay on the carpet outside. If she'd been evicted, Nick must be working on something delicate and important.

Best not to trouble him.

Or wake the cat.

She had a habit of mauling new visitors, leading more than one person to remark that she must be the eponymous "wildcat" of Wildcat Cove.

Sam walked through the foyer at a brisk pace, then stopped mid-stride as he caught sight of Nick's wedding present to Peter. The huge painting took up most of a two-story wall designed to display a gallery-sized canvas. In hues of sand, linen, and Payne's Gray, Nick had created what looked like a landscape—possibly even the landscape directly below this house. Most visitors saw sandstone cliffs beneath the specific blue-gray of the Pacific Northwest sky.

But a few saw the human figure in the painting. And some, such as Peter's best friend, Evangeline, understood how dirty it was.

Peter hoped against hope that somehow Sam would be one of the naive multitude who didn't see Peter's spread legs and erect penis jutting like a geological extrusion up between them. Not that he was shy—he'd been the one who had hinted heavily that Nick should immortalize him in a painting. But he'd found, during the last couple of years, that he had a thin skin when it came to people's remarks regarding the canvas.

That was strange in itself, since he never took any other sort of criticism to heart and he got plenty for both his choice of subject matter and actual writing.

Somehow, though, because the painting had been a gift made specially for him, Peter wanted everyone to love it as much as he did and therefore couldn't help but be slightly offended if they didn't.

Sam stood, eyes riveted to the massive painting. Finally he said, "I saw this painting when I was here for your wedding. It's a breathtaking work now that it's finished."

"It's a favorite of mine too," Peter said casually, "but didn't you want to look at the blue de Kamp? It's over here near the kitchen."

"Of course," Sam said. He took a few steps and turned back to gaze again at the painting. "Do you mind if I take a picture of this piece?"

"Nick doesn't allow photos of paintings he hasn't shown yet. I'm sorry," Peter said. "You could ask him yourself, though. He's probably in his studio right now." Peter gestured down the long hallway.

"Oh, it's all right. I completely understand. There's no need to trouble him. I just…" Sam trailed off, staring upward in a way that Peter found familiar but couldn't place. After a few seconds he realized that the expression on Sam's face resembled one of the old paintings he'd seen on his honeymoon in Vienna—the rapture of some saint or other. "It's everything I hoped it would be."

"I'm glad you like it." Peter felt an embarrassed flush redden the back of his neck.

Was Sam coming on to him? It didn't seem likely, but then what did he know? "Can I get you something to drink?"

"Anything with caffeine," Sam replied. "I have a lot of work to do tonight."

"I've got pod espresso."

"Sounds fantastic," Sam said. He followed Peter as he made his way toward the kitchen, stopping in front of the only de Kamp painting still on display in the house.

This smaller canvas hung behind their dining-room table, mainly because Peter liked the shade of blue as well as the fragmentary, overlapping planes depicting different dimensions of the same image.

What was that image? Waves, maybe? Or the sky?

Some mythical landscape inside Walter's head?

"So what makes you so interested in the blue painting?" Peter asked as he riffled through the box of coffee pods for one that wasn't decaf. He found one, popped it into the machine, and hit the Start button. The smell of fresh coffee curled through the large kitchen as the espresso began to brew.

"Well, I suppose I like this painting because it's the most classic de Kamp I've ever seen."

"How so?" Peter glanced over his shoulder.

"Every part of it is cold, cubist, and authoritative." Sam straightened from where he had bent close to look at the bottom edge of the canvas. "Here you have an artist who keeps himself under strict self-control, never ceding any power to his subject. As a painter de Kamp restrains his subject matter to his sharp definitions. He even goes so far as to chop it up into these fragments—only showing small glimpses of any one aspect."

Peter considered the painting, which, he hated to admit, he'd previously only seen as a series of pleasing shapes and colors rather than any sort of statement. Finally he said, "I see what you mean, but it makes me like the painting less."

"Don't let my interpretation spoil your enjoyment," Sam said with a laugh. "You could also say that he tries to show you only the best, most beautiful parts of the image, removing the undesirable."

"Isn't that just a nicer way of saying the same thing—that the artist ruthlessly controls his subject matter?" Peter crossed to Sam and handed him the small espresso cup and saucer.

"Right," Sam agreed. "But it *is* a nicer way. And I would argue that understanding that crucial duality is important. That same desire to control what the viewer sees is neither inherently positive nor negative, but completely contextual."

"In art?" Peter crossed his arms and leaned back against the table, gazing with new eyes on the painting.

"In everything. As reporters, you and I seek to discover and publicize the truth, which we find noble, but I'm sure at least one of your subjects had cursed you to hell for spilling some secret."

"A couple of them have even tried to send me there personally." Peter said this offhandedly but still felt rattled by the times—several times—that a fellow human had tried to kill him for uncovering an ugly truth.

"An inquisitive nature itself can be brilliant or inappropriate, depending on the circumstance." Sam finished off his espresso in one gulp. "The classic double-edged sword, this artist. You don't mind if I snap a couple of pics of this one? Since it's already been displayed?"

"Be my guest," Peter said.

He returned to the kitchen to get another coffee while Sam turned this way and that, trying to photograph parts of the painting.

"These older de Kamps are so different from his final works. Don't you find?" Sam asked over his shoulder.

"Honestly, I haven't done a whole-career survey," Peter said. Out of the corner of his eye he saw motion. Nick had emerged from his studio and stood in the hallway, rubbing his shoulder and staring at the back of Sam's head. Even Nick's perennial shoddy outfit of baggy jeans and unraveling sweater could not diminish the man's attractiveness. He stood, tall and broad as a hockey defenseman, full of muscle and aggressive suspicion.

That was unlike him—the suspicion. Normally, Nick took Nordic blond aloofness to the next level of detachment.

Before Peter could greet Nick, or introduce their guest, Sam said, "Well, it seems to me that de Kamp had what one might call a late spring. In the last year of his life he broke from years of formal cubism and started painting the most amazing figurals—painting of the human form."

Peter glanced to Nick, whose expression had deepened to a profound scowl.

Unbeknownst of the storm brewing behind him, Sam continued, "These nudes were so vital and potent that one simply has to acknowledge how much he must have been influenced by his protégé." Sam glanced up, finally seeing Nick across the room. "And speak of the devil. I was just admiring your work." He gestured toward the massive painting Peter had prevented him from photographing earlier.

"Get out," Nick said, by way of greeting. "Now."

"What? Wait, Nick. This is Sam. I told him he could photograph Walter's painting."

Ignoring Peter's protests, Nick stalked toward Sam, who held up his hands in immediate surrender, phone clutched hard in his left fist. "I think there must have been some kind of mistake."

"No mistake." Nick turned to Peter. "Except you letting him in the door."

Peter stood momentarily speechless, too stunned to even feel anger. Nick had never spoken to him like this. Well, he had, once, when he'd thought Peter had been doing research to write a story about him. But that had been years ago.

Also, Peter thought, with a belated but righteous rush of anger, who the hell did Nick think he was?

Aloud he said, "What the fuck, Nick?"

"I'll just let myself out," Sam said as he sidled along the wall. A smug smirk contorted his mouth. Seeing his plain enjoyment at their domestic squabble, Peter lost all sympathy for his new friend. Still, he wasn't going to let Nick get away with such pompous highhandedness.

Nick turned his glower back to the interloper. Seeing that Sam was about to reach the door, he stormed forward to block his exit.

"Give me your phone," Nick said.

Sam's smirk changed to an expression of such disbelieving incredulity that Peter might have laughed if he wasn't already so fucking angry at Nick.

"My phone?" Sam gave a mirthless, nervous laugh. "I don't think so."

Faster than Peter could take a breath, Nick seized Sam's arm and slammed it against the wall. The drywall crumpled, and Sam let go of his grip. The phone clattered to the stone tiles of the foyer. Without saying another word, Nick twisted Sam's arm behind his back and shoved him up against the wall. He said something Peter couldn't hear, but Sam paled.

Then Nick let him go, and Sam fled. Nick slammed the door behind him and stalked back down the hallway to his studio.

Peter stood aghast.

What the fuck had just happened? Had his husband gone totally insane? The billowing anger in Peter's chest warred with a freakish new feeling he'd never felt toward Nick—the feeling of fear. He did not want to go down that hallway to confront Nick, and yet he could not allow this behavior to pass with no remark.

On his way toward the studio, Peter paused to pick up Sam's handset.

Images shone through the cracked screen—not the blue painting—the nude in the living room. The prick had been using the selfie mode to photograph the painting behind him.

A dick move—and one that Peter decided to file away into his own bag of dirty tricks, should he have to use it later—but Nick couldn't have seen what Sam had been photographing from all the way across the room, could he?

He slid Sam's phone into his pocket. Later he'd find Sam's hotel and return the thing—hopefully before Sam called the cops or, God forbid, tweeted about the incident to all of his New York art-scene friends.

Probably lack of a cell phone would delay any of those actions—at least until he reached his hotel room.

As he started down the hallway, Gigi the cat slunk along in his wake. She too seemed upset by Nick's behavior. Though, to be fair, she was probably more annoyed by the closed studio door than anything else, as she considered it to be her personal naptime area.

Peter knocked on the door.

No answer came.

His irritation, which had cooled somewhat when he'd seen Sam's deception, flared again, and he opened the door and entered the studio.

Nick wasn't painting. He stared out the big window through the hazy morning sky onto the green waters below with the expression of an angry thunder god thinking of smiting the barely visible San Juan Islands with his hammer.

"I don't want to talk about this," Nick announced without turning around. "And I'm not going to talk about it now or ever, so you might as well just go back to work."

Possibly no phrase could have ignited a more instantaneous reaction from Peter. Anger and confusion twisted together into a small cyclone of flummoxed rage.

"Why are you acting this way?" He heard his voice shaking. "Why did you beat up my houseguest?"

"I didn't beat him up." Scorn rang through Nick's voice. "He'll be fine."

"You assaulted and robbed him."

"Quit exaggerating."

"It's not an exaggeration!" Peter heard the stridency increasing in his voice. "It's literally what you did just now."

Nick finally turned around. His jaw and fists were both clenched hard. "Listen, Peter, I don't need this drama right now."

"You think this is drama?" Peter lost all control of both his volume and tone. His own hands shook. "You think this is something I'm just blowing out of proportion?"

"I think you like to instigate conflict," Nick said. Maddeningly, he seemed to relax a little. He walked straight up and laid his hands on Peter's shoulders. "And you like to pry into every-thing that isn't your business."

"How—" Peter had to pause to keep himself from shoving Nick's hands away. "How can you think that what you just did to my houseguest isn't my business?"

"Sam isn't a guest. He's a slimy sack of shit. I know you didn't know that, and I shouldn't have snapped at you." Nick looked straight at Peter for several seconds and then said, "I have to go."

And just like that, he released Peter and made his way down the hallway. Peter followed on his heels, finally catching Nick by the arm as he picked up his car keys.

"Where are you going?" Peter demanded.

"I'm going to fix this." He gently pulled his arm free. "We'll talk when I get back."

Chapter Two

"Oh my God!" Evangeline's eyes popped out of her head. "Has Nick finally gone crazy?"

"What do you mean *finally*?" Peter slumped back into the passenger seat of Evangeline's car. After Nick had left, stranding Peter at the house with no vehicle and a boss who expected him back at work, he'd called his best friend for a ride.

And a sympathetic ear that would understand his outrage.

Evangeline did not disappoint. She arrived in her newest saved-from-the-junkyard vehicle—a blue Geo Spectrum with a massive dent on the driver's side.

Evangeline had an unerring sense for fitting in with PNW hipster fashion and sensibility. Hence this summer her wardrobe had blossomed with all things nautical. Her dense curly hair had been pulled back into a retro bun, and she wore eyeliner so dark and exact Peter sometimes wondered if she drew it on with a Sharpie.

"Do you think Nick could be going through man-o-pause?" Evangeline asked as they chugged down the drive. "He is getting pretty old. Can he still get a boner?"

One additional thing Evangeline could be counted on for was to say something so completely sideways that Peter would be jolted out of whatever mood afflicted him.

"Yes, he had a boner as recently as this morning," Peter said with a relieved laugh.

"But was it a good boner or one of those soft ones?" Evangeline persisted. "I think a man like Nick would have a hard time dealing with soft boners. He's stoic like that."

"I'm absolutely sure this isn't a boner thing," Peter said. "This has to do with that Sam guy."

"Oh my God, do you think he's another one of Nick's bitter exes who is trying to kill him?"

"I think the odds of that happening again are astronomical," Peter replied.

"True, but maybe Nick's just the kind of guy who attracts stalkers. I mean, he's married to you."

"I'm not a stalker. I'm an investigative journalist."

"So what does that mean? That you just stalk on a professional level, that's what."

Evangeline turned onto Chuckanut Drive, the road that would take them back into town. "But this Sam guy is a reporter too, right? Maybe he found out Nick is really a crack secret agent who has retired to become a painter, and now he's here in Bellingham to shake him down for hush money."

Peter paused to consider this. In his opinion, Nick did have many secret-agent-type qualities. But he hadn't been in the army long enough to achieve any meaningful rank.

"I like where you're going with this scenario, but Nick was dishonorably discharged way before he could have been trained to be a super-spy," Peter said.

"Maybe that's the cover story his handlers want you to believe. Of course it could be something entirely different. Is Sam young enough to be Nick's long-lost son?"

"That's the least plausible idea you've come up with yet."

"Not really," Evangeline countered. "Look what happened with Tommy. It took me half a year to find out he had a daughter. And Nick is way more tight-lipped."

Peter had to concede this point. Ever restless and entrepreneurial, Evangeline had attempted to level up her once-weekly Farmer's Market food stall, Go-Go Gyoza, to a full-time business by purchasing a secondhand food truck. When she'd gone to get financing she'd discovered her newly-married husband, Tommy, had withdrawn several large cash advances without telling her.

Distraught and enraged, she'd called Peter, who had been there within the hour, pouring over the bank records and very slowly convincing her to just ask Tommy what he needed all that money for. Eventually she'd calmed down enough to reasonably inquire. Tommy had broken down. He explained that he'd been approached by an ex-girlfriend who revealed that she'd had his baby almost ten years before and never told him. She'd come forward now to ask Tommy for help with tuition to a special-needs school.

At Peter's urging, Evangeline had requested a paternity test, which confirmed the mother's claim. Now Evangeline was the stepmother to a nine-year-old named Anya, who had Down syndrome. When questioned about why he'd taken six months to mention this to Evangeline, Tommy had confessed to being scared she'd leave him.

"Having a child suddenly enter your life is a huge adjustment," Evangeline was saying. "And Nick's gay, but he's still a man. He could have gotten anybody pregnant."

"Mainly the women, I think," Peter said.

"You know what I mean," Evangeline said. "But this Sam guy is too old to be Nick's secret love child, huh?"

"Way too old. He's around my age actually."

"So he's not a long-lost kid but could still be a psycho ex."

"I get the feeling he's not either," Peter said. "Nick and I's wedding was the first time we'd all met."

"I think you'll probably just have to make Nick tell you," Evangeline said. "After he's less mad."

"No shit." Peter rubbed his eyes. "It freaked me out—the expression on his face. I've never seen him so angry. I felt like I didn't know him."

"Are you worried he'd hurt you?" The pitch of Evangeline's voice rose, very slightly, betraying her concern. "You could come stay with us tonight."

"No, I'm not worried about my physical safety," Peter said quickly. "It's hard to explain—I didn't think he could ever seem like a stranger to me."

"People have hidden sides," Evangeline said with a shrug. "And sometimes also hidden offspring."

As Evangeline pulled the car alongside the curb to let Peter out at Samish Brewing, she eyed the food truck parked in front of them with both sadness and avarice that tugged at Peter's heart. His bestie worked harder than any person he'd ever met in his life, and it seemed like she could not get a break. Her whole life just fell too far outside the norm for people like loan officers to trust or understand her.

"You know," he ventured cautiously, "Nick and I could go in with you on the truck. Or at least cosign on a loan for you if you don't want us as silent partners."

Evangeline shook her head. "Thanks, but right now Tommy and I need to get this thing with his daughter figured out before taking on any other responsibilities."

"Okay, but when you get that solved, don't be shy."

Evangeline gave him a smile so big he could see her three gold molars and said, "I'm never shy."

After Peter watched Evangeline drive away, he resigned himself to drinking a beer at lunchtime.

Not that Peter disliked beer.

Normally the opportunity—nay, *obligation* to go a-visiting at the town's many taprooms would fill Peter with adolescent glee. But the fight with Nick had removed Peter's capacity for interest in happiness.

Still, he had a story to write. Bellingham had recently been named the snobbiest beer city in the nation by some hipster data-crawling firm, and Doug (and the board of tourism) had naturally latched on to the story.

Samish Brewing was located in a converted feed-and-seed store that even after three years in operation as a brewery still had a whiff of alfalfa about it. The exposed wooden beams lent a feel of the Old West. The old plow hung on the wall alongside antique traps and harpoons amplified the feeling of yesteryear. The pioneer motif carried through to their brand design.

It was interesting, Peter thought, the different approaches microbreweries took. Some liked the super-modern look, trying to create a stainless-steel retro-future vibe. Others went homey, trying to be everyman's hipster living room.

Peter sat at the bar, and the owner and brewmaster, Travis, immediately came over to shake his hand and, without asking, plunked a cold, foamy pint down in front of him.

"Six-Gun Sour," he proclaimed. "Our new release for summer. I love this stuff." Travis grinned at him through his full, black beard. That was another thing about brewers that Peter had noticed—beards. He'd never seen a brewer without one. It was as if proximity to hops encouraged follicle growth. Between his clear tenor voice, the flannel shirt, and thick, stocky build, Travis could have easily played the part of a young, spry lumberjack in any Fifties' musical. Though Peter knew him to be a family man of forty-two.

The full-sized beer presented a quandary. It would be impolite to refuse it. And Peter would need something to write about anyway. So he took a sip.

Sour described it perfectly. And yet, how could it be so perfectly sour in the best possible way? A sharp note of acid rang through the round, soft taste of malt and sizzle of carbonation.

"This. Is. Amazing," he said, mentally punctuating every single word. "I have never, ever tasted a beer like this."

"It's crazy, right?" Travis sat down next to him, grinning. "Refreshing, crisp. Perfect for summer. You could drink it all day."

Now there was an idea. Peter took a long, cold gulp and felt the alcohol begin to move through him immediately. He really should have something to eat, he thought, glancing at the food truck parked in the taproom's parking lot. A Korean taco sounded fantastic right now.

But no, he had to be responsible—get at least one thing done before lunch. He took out his phone and set his voice-recorder app.

"What do you think about Bellingham being named snobbiest beer town?"

"It doesn't surprise me," he said. "People here love beer and love local. But personally I'm not a beer snob. I'm a beer nerd. I like all kinds of beer, cheap, rare, weird, foreign—everything. I once accidentally bought a can of French malt liquor while I was traveling in Europe. Worst beer I've ever tasted. But I finished it all, just in case I changed my mind by the end."

"Very egalitarian of you," Peter commented. He took another big, thirsty swallow of the Six-Gun Sour. "So can you tell me a little bit about yourself and the brewery?"

"We started three years ago with the intention of making beers we wanted to drink." Travis then began a well-rehearsed spiel of the kind that all entrepreneurs mastered within the first year of business. But they both knew that in these promotional words pulsed the lifeblood of commerce—especially commerce in the advertising section of the free weekly paper. "I first came to Bellingham when I was eighteen and fell in love with the place. Back then if I wanted to drink beer, I had to brew it myself, right? 'Cause I wasn't twenty-one."

Peter smiled and nodded. "I think most guys who didn't have older brothers tried making beer around that age for that very reason. Mine exploded in my closet and ruined my lambskin jacket."

"My first beer wasn't all that great either, but the process itself just fascinated me. So I kept trying. I spent a while in Portland, working the breweries there and getting the hang of the industrial production."

"Did they let you experiment there?" Peter asked.

"Absolutely not," Travis said with a melodic laugh. "I followed the metrics laid out by the brewmaster there to the letter. Just like my guys follow mine when they're here. Ninety percent of being a brewer is cleaning because the yeast is alive, you know. Fermentation is a living process."

Peter finished his beer, and Travis brought him another.

"These sours are really interesting," Peter said.

"A change in production has recently allowed brewers to make sours with *Lactobacillus*, instead of the more traditional *Pediococcus*. This eliminated the need for barrel-aging and reduced the time required to make the beer. What used to take months or years can be done more or less overnight," Travis said.

"So it's the same bacteria that's used to make sauerkraut?" Peter had just finished his second pint on an empty stomach and had begun to feel decidedly drunk.

"Exactly." Travis gave a big bright smile. "I'm not sure too many people other than beer nerds would be interested to know that. Speaking of beer nerds, though, you should come back tonight. We're having a party to welcome the female brewers association. It should be fun."

Peter was about to ask how ladies managed to be brewers without having beards when Travis reached into his pocket and pulled out his phone.

"Speaking of the ladies," Travis said. "I'm sorry, but I need to take this call."

"Please feel free." Peter waved his hand magnanimously.

Travis sidled past the bartender into the backroom where the production facility lay.

Peter glanced around the taproom, wondering if he should stay or go. Though Samish had just opened at noon, plenty of wholesome people already filled the big wooden tables. Some looked like tourists starting an early survey of microbreweries, but locals also populated the venue. Glancing up into the mirror behind the bar, Peter recognized his old boyfriend Nate sitting with his friends. Nate worked as a baker and would have come off an eight-hour shift minutes before.

Using his phone on selfie mode, Peter scrutinized Nate. The other guy had aged well.

Peter considered getting a third beer and joining Nate's party. They'd broken up on amicable terms after they'd both realized they had little in common apart from basic homosexuality.

Actually if he thought about it, the word amicable could have described their entire relationship: smooth sailing in placid waters. His feelings for Nate had never moved away from safe parameters.

Nick, on the other hand... How annoying could that man be?

Who in hell did he think he was? Clint Eastwood? Why couldn't he perform the simple task of making his lips move to make words of explanation?

From the tone of his mental rant, Peter knew he'd managed to get drunker than he thought or intended.

Perhaps it was the Old West decor—or maybe it was the handsomely roguish figure adorning his beer glass, but Peter slipped into composing a scene in his mind.

Peter Fontaine, a.k.a. the Wildcat Kid, slumped against the bar, belligerent and lonesome.

Sure, he'd been wild once, but after being caught and converted by Sheriff Olson, he'd thought his days as an outlaw were behind him.

The sheriff had given him a tin star and deputized him. He'd traded his black hat for white and stopped running around. But apparently the sheriff still didn't trust him.

When old Travis's horses on Six-Gun Ranch went missing, the sheriff had suspected Peter, and that hurt more than he could stand.

Why couldn't the sheriff see the real culprit was that no-good horse thief Sam, who rode into town with his fancy attitude and charm?

Wildcat surveyed the cowboys filling the tables at the saloon. He could have had any one of them—okay, he could have had at least one of them, possibly two. But the main thing was that he'd stayed loyal to the sheriff when the sheriff still kept secrets from him.

Then the sheriff's tall silhouette darkened the doorway. Wildcat decided on the whole it would be best to ignore the man. Coldest Shoulder in the West—that's what he'd be called from now on.

"You're under arrest for stealing Travis's horses, Wildcat," the sheriff mumbled, voice as gritty as the dirt on his cowboy boots.

"It weren't me!" Wildcat cried, standing up to defend his honor. "It was that son-bitch horse thief Sam! You should trust me by now."

Wildcat was taken aback as the sheriff gripped his arm, hard, and twisted him around.

"Don't ask questions," Olson demanded. He led Wildcat in front of him, pushing him up the stairs of the saloon to the second floor.

The sound of sex was everywhere as the hookers got liquored and the cowboys got busy.

The sheriff pushed Wildcat through the door of a small bedroom and shoved him onto the bed.

"You gonna steal horses, you gonna pay. My way," the sheriff said.

"It was never me, I swear it!" Wildcat protested.

Sheriff Olson looked him over. "How can I trust you?"

"I'd be happy to prove my loyalty. Any way you want."

A gleam lit the sheriff's eye. "Take off your clothes, then. All of them. You can leave the hat on."

Wildcat stripped in no time flat. He stood naked before the sheriff and tipped his hat.

Olson unbuckled his gun belt and placed his six-shooters within easy reach on the bedside table. Then he pulled open the front of his leather trousers and out sprang the most enormous cock Wildcat had ever seen. It burst from the hairy base of his pubic hair like a Colt .45, long and curved slightly, leaking cum from the slit.

Wildcat felt his mouth start to water at the sight. Wasn't this what he always wanted anyway?

The sheriff spread himself out on the bed. He still wore his leather vest and tin star.

"Bring that pretty ass over here, Deputy."

Wildcat didn't need to be asked twice. He climbed on the bed and knelt over the sheriff's head, turning his body so he could watch Olson's captivating cock.

The sheriff spread Wildcat's ass cheeks wide with his large hands and lifted his head to lick up the crack. Wildcat shuddered.

"Oh, Sheriff!"

"Hush, Deputy." The sheriff probed Wildcat's ass with his tongue, then started pressing it inside the dark hole. Wildcat felt tingles of ecstasy shooting up from his ass deep into his groin and along his spine, and all he could hear was the slurping of the sheriff's tongue.

The sheriff added a finger alongside his tongue, opening Wildcat up. When he added two, the burn was intense but the pleasure so much greater that Wildcat started to tremble.

"Let me ride you, Sheriff; lemme show you how good I can be," he cried.

Sheriff Olson pulled his fingers out of Wildcat's ass, and before the sheriff could change his mind, Wildcat slid down to that thick, dripping cock. He fisted it tall and straight, and slowly lowered his ass onto the tip. The feel of that thick meat spreading him wide.

Damn, he loved this lawman.

He began his ride slow and deep, taking the burning pleasure inside him, listening to Olson grunt his approval. He couldn't see the lawman—he only saw the man's filthy cowboy boots flexing as his legs tensed. He used his thigh muscles to control his rhythm. He began to bounce up and down on that cock, spearing himself on each thrust. At last he got the right angle, hollered a full-on "yee haw!" and gripped the sheriff's hairy knees.

Sheriff Olson's hands tightened on Wildcat's hips, and he began to thrust up with all his strength, shoving into the core of him.

The door to their bedroom opened just as Wildcat started riding the sheriff in earnest. He saw Sam the horse thief enter, his gun drawn.

The bastard! He clearly thought this was his chance to take Olson down.

Without slowing his pace, Wildcat grabbed the sheriff's pistols from the bedside table and opened fire, shooting the man down while still riding the sheriff's massive cock.

"That's it, Wildcat!" the sheriff cried.

The guns smoked in Wildcat's hands. His thighs shook as he slid up and down the sheriff's pole hard and fast. He held both guns as Sheriff Olson wrapped his big hand around Wildcat's cock and began to stroke it frantically.

"Pump it, Sheriff!" Wildcat shouted.

A persistent buzzing in his pocket jolted Peter out of his Old West inspired mental porno.

Nick's text flashed across his phone screen.

Where are you?

Peter narrowed his eyes at the query. Then smirked as he thought of an appropriate reply. After missing his security code twice, he made it to the reply box.

You'll never take me alive, Sheriff!

Then, with a sense of profound satisfaction, he powered down his phone.

Travis returned, took one look at him, and insisted Peter allow him to comp him an order of tacos with a side of fries.

"The sour is nine percent," he said, chuckling. "Did I not tell you that?"

"Barkeep, you did not," Peter said, still half-immersed in his Old West fantasy, "but I concede that it's having the expected effect on my elocution… And coordination."

Travis clapped a hand on his shoulder. "You're not slurring too bad, if that's what you mean. But yeah, you've more or less had the equivalent of a six-pack of lite beer."

"At a third of the calories!" Peter said, then burst into loud drunken laughter. The small part of his brain that still understood social norms, feeling slight embarrassment at being drunk in public in the middle of the day, suggested that he stop drinking. But the rest of his brain had already started singing the lesser-known lyrics to "Oh My Darling, Clementine," and this sound advice went unheard. *Ruby lips above the water, blowing bubbles soft and fine... How I missed her till I kissed her little sister...*

When Travis went to get the food, Peter ordered another beer and sipped it while eating. Travis excused himself, as he needed to oversee the addition of some dry hops to a batch of IPA, leaving Peter to indulge in increasingly lurid cowboy fantasies as well as fragmentary conversations with the rotating occupants of the seat next to him.

A fourth beer made it to the bar in front of him. He was halfway through this when a new man sat down beside him.

Peter turned to introduce himself and found the living embodiment of his Sheriff Olson staring back at him with an expression of wary tension.

"Well, howdy, Sheriff, how are you?" Peter asked. He thought he might detect a slight slur in his voice but put it down to his excellent cowboy drawl.

Nick took his time to respond, then finally said, "Did you lose your phone?"

"Nope." Peter lifted his pint and eyed it with what he felt passed for incisive scrutiny, then continued, "Turned it off."

"Do you know what time it is?" Nick asked.

Peter glanced at him sidelong, then hazarded a guess. "Dark?"

Nick lapsed into silence while Peter drank more. The friendly, ruddy-faced bartender approached, then seeing Nick's expression, veered sideways.

Sheriff Olson—such a killjoy. Why Wildcat had a mind to turn in his tin star and go back to his old outlaw ways. At least the outlaws knew how to have some fun.

"Now that I've found you and figured out that you are alive, I'm going home," Nick said. "Do you want a ride?"

"I wanted a ride earlier when I had to go to work and you took the car and left me," Peter said. He could definitely hear the slur in his voice now, but he didn't care. "Where the hell did you go?"

"Do you think we could have this conversation at home?" Nick asked.

"Is there more beer at home?" Peter asked, feeling he must be the funniest gunslinger this side of the Cascades.

"I'm pretty sure you don't need more beer."

"You're not the boss of me, Sheriff; I resign," Peter mumbled.

Nick leaned close and whispered, "I get that you're calling me sheriff because you're in some weird drunken fantasy, but if you keep this up, you're going to get 86'd from this bar."

"No I won't. They love me here. Barkeep!" Peter flapped an arm in what he felt to be the manner of a laconic baby-faced gunslinger. The bartender, whose name Peter didn't remember, sauntered over, a look of amusement tinged with pity crossing his face. "You wouldn't kick me out, would you?"

"Nah, but I'm not going to serve you any more today either," he said. "That sour crept up on you, didn't it?"

"You're telling me." Peter leaned toward the bartender. "I really had no idea it was possible to get so drunk off beer."

"I know," the bartender, who Peter remembered was called Shane, agreed. "It happened to all of us the first time Travis brought out the sour. But at least you have your friend to take you home."

"Friend?" Peter asked, frowning. Then he caught sight of Nick's unamused glower. "Oh, Shane, this isn't my friend. This is my *husband*. And he is mad at me. But he has no right to be mad because he was acting like a complete prick. For no reason."

"I think it's time to go." Nick stood and grabbed Peter's bag.

Peter scowled at Nick. Or he tried to. He was having a hard time keeping his balance on the barstool because the floor suddenly seemed to have been transformed into a tilt-a-whirl.

Shane watched Nick with the neutral expression of a man who didn't know whether to be happy that Nick was removing an overserved customer from his bar or worried for Peter's immediate future in the hands of a fit, muscular man who seethed with fury.

"I could always call you a cab, Peter, if you'd rather have a different ride," Shane said. This earned him an immediate death stare from Nick, but Peter warmed to Shane for the show of concern.

"No, it's all right. I just need to settle up." Peter reached into his pocket for his wallet and pulled out his phone instead. For some reason, it had powered down. But once Peter fumbled through the security code he saw that he had thirty-two texts—the majority of them from Nick. When he looked back up, Nick had finished paying his tab and had even slid a sizeable bill directly to Shane.

When he stood up, wooziness set in more suddenly than he expected. He lurched sideways. Nick caught him immediately, and while his initial instinct was to shake him off, some small, still-rational part of him understood that not only was Nick his best chance for getting home, he was the best chance for getting out of the taproom at all, so he let Nick put his arm around him and guide him out through the now full and busy bar.

He wordlessly allowed himself to be poured into the passenger seat of the car and closed his eyes. He should keep his mouth shut, he thought, to avoid saying anything stupid.

Aloud he murmured, "I still need to get my bike from work. I can ride it home."

To which Nick responded, "Okay, I'll get your bike, and you can ride back home, but first you have to take a nap."

Peter's eyelids drooped. A nap did sound good…

Chapter Three

Peter woke lying atop the covers of his own bed in the Castle at Wildcat Cove. His eyes felt like they'd been transformed into two tiny aquariums filled with darting silverfish and hazy, distorted light. His brain... Best not to think about what was happening to his most vital organ right now. Or his liver or kidneys.

He remained fully dressed except for apparently having removed one shoe. The other side of the bed—Nick's side—had not been slept in. Queasy remorse moved through his guts. Or maybe he was just queasy.

He didn't want to stand or walk or move ever again. But thirst drove him to shuffle through the living room toward the kitchen. He found Nick on one of the two facing sofas, asleep and wrapped in a too-small throw.

Gigi the black cat lay curled atop him. As Peter passed, she cracked a green eye; then, finding him not worth the effort of two eyes, she went back to sleep.

Ungrateful feline, he thought ungraciously, I was the one who rescued you. Yet you always take his side...

Again came the remorse; this time Peter felt it might be genuine. He truly had behaved badly the previous day. Not that Nick hadn't as well. But getting falling-down drunk didn't leave Peter on the moral high ground.

He aborted his mission to the kitchen to return to the bedroom to get a better blanket. He laid this over Nick's feet, glancing up at the man's face as he did so, hoping he wouldn't wake, as Peter didn't feel up to sorting out their argument quite yet.

Nick didn't stir, but to Peter's shock, he saw that someone had blackened Nick's right eye. When had that happened? After he'd passed out in Nick's Audi—because he felt sure that was the last time he'd been conscious.

Peter continued his dreadful progress to the kitchen and drank as much of a glass of water as he could manage. The blinding light streaming through their unnecessarily massive windows told him it was early morning. The clock clarified the time: seven a.m.

Accounting for showering and riding into town, that gave him about forty-five extra minutes to complete the mission of returning Sam's phone.

That, he decided, would be the best way to start undoing the catastrophe of yesterday.

Cycling into town gave Peter time to reflect upon his best course of action. The first step he would take was to never, ever get that drunk again. He wasn't twenty-one anymore, and the effects of getting legless seemed both amplified and irresponsible.

Though he couldn't pinpoint the exact moment when being cripplingly hungover had moved from a sign of worldly panache to a stigma (and possible signifier of nascent alcoholism), he guessed it might be somewhere around age thirty.

After biking through a drive-through coffee joint to buy an egg sandwich, Peter reached Sam's motel. He was drenched in sweat but feeling better for the exertion.

The Lodgepole Motor Inn had been constructed during that time when the Pacific Northwest had been mainly known as a camping destination. The three-story U-shaped building had a totem-pole-inspired sign that had historically been the subject of much derision by the local Native American tribal members.

Like many off-ramp motels sporting kitchenettes, the Lodgepole, which had once hosted rosy-cheeked young families on obligatory Fifties' road trips, now mainly accommodated meth addicts who needed a place to cook up a new batch of crystal.

Dirty, haggard men and hollow-looking women loafed on the terraces, smoking cigarettes and eyeing Peter, trying to figure out what a person like him was doing there.

What, for that matter, was a person like Sam doing here?

Surely he could have afforded one of the mid-range business hotels that surrounded Bellingham's small regional airport. Sam could have rented an entire floor of this place for the price of one of his designer shoes. Numerous theories kaleidoscoped through Peter's vivid imagination: Sam the Secret Junkie, Sam the Unspeakable Pervert. Most likely, though, Sam had simply made the mistake too many other people had made in these days of online bidding for cheap reservations and ended up in a shitty motel full of sad hookers and meth.

The indiscreet desk clerk informed him that Sam had not checked out of room twelve yet, and that his car had been there since the previous day. When Peter paused too long in answering, the clerk said, "I don't want any trouble."

"I'm not the police," Peter said. "I'm just a friend of Sam's."

The clerk—a thin, sallow man with a droopy moustache—looked him up and down at that. Then leaned forward and said, "Just so you know, this motel has a no overnight guests policy. I told that to the other guy too."

It took Peter a moment to figure out what the receptionist was talking about, but when he did, he couldn't help but laugh out loud at the idea he would ever have sex in a dump like this, let alone sleep here. "I'll keep it in mind."

The receptionist nodded, then leaned even closer and whispered, "If you're with an escort service, you should know that Anthony doesn't like anybody working this motel. Even if you're a dude. That other guy was big, but you're kind of slim, you know? I'm not judging. I'm just warning you about working here."

"That's good to know. Thank you for looking out for me,"

Peter said. The receptionist gave a proud smile. Peter found the whole notion of himself being a prostitute ludicrous. What kind of hustler showed up sweaty and hungover on a bike at seven thirty in the morning? Then a thought gave him pause: he wondered who the big guy visiting Sam might have been. "But this other guy—what did he look like?"

"I can't really remember," the receptionist replied.

Peter dutifully went into his wallet and offered a neatly folded bill.

"Kinda like Thor in a sweater," the guy said, memory lapses banished. "Except he had short hair."

"Did he have a hammer?" Peter couldn't help but ask.

"No, but he looked mad."

Peter retrieved his phone and pulled up a photograph of Nick. "Is this him?"

The receptionist nodded. "Is he one of your coworkers?"

"No, he works for a different agency," Peter said. "He's the competition. So is the guy I'm going to visit having a lot of... guests?"

"Oh, I don't know..." The receptionist waited while Peter performed the customary handing over of a second bill before continuing, "Yesterday he had the Thor guy and this tall tranny."

Peter winced at the term.

The receptionist mistook his expression of distaste at the language for a general aversion and continued, "I know, right? This guy's got really broad taste. I expect the next escort will be a dwarf chick or Siamese twins or something."

"Thanks for the heads-up," Peter mumbled.

As he walked his bike to the doorway of number twelve, he was aware of twenty sets of beady eyes watching him. He didn't know which belonged to Anthony the Territorial Pimp, but he wasn't keen to make eye contact and find out either. Why the hell were so many of these people awake so early in the morning anyway? Didn't this sort of seedy nightlife mainly happen after dark?

Eyes fixed forward, Peter shifted his thoughts to what he would say when he finally saw Sam.

He'd thought he would open with an apology for Nick, and depending on how Sam reacted, he'd go from there. But the discovery that Nick had already visited Sam put a wrench in the works.

What had happened? Why would Nick go to visit a guy he'd physically thrown out of his house?

And then there was the worrying black eye Nick had acquired.

Over the years he'd come to realize that although Nick was not a naturally violent man, he also had no particular aversion to the use of physical force. Peter put it down to the time Nick spent in the army and then working as a security guard afterward. The previous morning had been the only time he'd ever seen Nick attack a man unprovoked, though.

Or maybe the assault hadn't been completely unprovoked. Maybe Sam had been in contact with Nick for some reason. That followed, since he'd obviously wanted to photograph the paintings in their house. And it would have been like Nick to not tell Peter that he'd refused to allow something having to do with art. Not only did Peter not know that much about the business of the art world, he didn't really find talk of the wheelings and dealings of the world's great art collectors interesting.

So maybe that's what had happened. Sam had been refused by Nick and then pulled an end run by going to Peter instead.

The more Peter considered this, the more he realized it had to be true. Despite his abrupt and somewhat terrifying display of aggression the previous morning, Nick was not a guy who routinely beat up houseguests.

With defense of his husband now firmly in his mind Peter decided not to apologize at all, but, in fact, demand the same from Sam for obviously attempting to use Peter against his own husband.

That felt better than apologizing anyway.

When he reached number twelve, he could see through the crack in the hideously stained avocado drapes that the lights were on.

His first knock failed to rouse any response.

"Sam?" Peter called, knocking again. "It's Peter Fontaine. I have your phone. The screen is cracked, but it seems okay. I'd be happy to write you a check for a new one, though, since it was our fault that yours got broken."

Again, no response.

Maybe Sam had taken a shower? More likely he'd been overcome by residual fumes from meth manufacture.

Peter considered leaving and coming back, but he just wanted this situation to be resolved. And to his great fortune, the Lodgepole sported old-fashioned doorknobs rather than a fancy card-key system. So he tried his luck and turned the knob to find Sam's door unlocked. Cautiously, he poked his face around the edge of the door.

The first thing that hit him was the smell. Rank chemicals and decades of stale cigarette smoke mixed with the pervasive, earthy smell of blood. The smell did not give him a good feeling, but he kept opening the door nonetheless.

"Sam? Are you in here?" He took a step inside and heard the carpet actually crunch beneath the clips of his bike shoes. The stiff-looking bedspread showed no signs of being slept or even sat on. The television was tuned to some morning show. Oddly, Peter could see no suitcase or luggage. "Sam?"

Peter stepped inside the room and rounded the corner to the alcove containing the kitchenette, where he stopped in his tracks. Sam lay slumped against the single, battered cabinet, chin bowed against his chest, skull cracked to reveal brain matter.

A slim fire extinguisher lay beside him on the green-gray linoleum.

All at once the smell choked Peter. He convulsed, ejecting his breakfast with the direction and speed of an irrigation sprinkler. The stream of semi-digested egg sandwich soared out and splashed down into Sam's lap.

Peter staggered back, dragging his hand across his mouth. Instantly he reached into his pocket for his phone. Halfway to dialing 911 he stopped.

The last person he knew to have threatened this man was Nick.

A strange sense of calm washed over him, erasing every-thing—the smell of the room, the sight of the corpse's open skull. He crossed back through the room and closed the motel door. He leaned against it, breathing slowly and steadily.

He knew he didn't have much time to make a decision—there were simply too many onlookers in this place. At least a few of them must be snitches who would tell the cops how long he'd been in the room.

He dialed Nick anyway. The moments between hitting the Call icon and waiting to hear Nick's voice elongated into an ag-ony.

Please, don't let him be so mad at me that he doesn't an-swer, he thought.

"Hi, Peter," Nick said. His voice sounded gravelly from sleep. "How are you feeling?"

"Really bad," Peter said. All at once he didn't know what to say. How did you ask your husband if he killed a guy last night?

"You should have called in to work," Nick said. "We need to talk."

"We sure do." Peter heard his voice crack.

"Are you all right?" Alarm sounded in Nick's voice.

"Not really," Peter admitted. "Listen, I don't have much time. I just wanted to tell you that I went to return Sam's cell phone."

He heard Nick sigh, then give a dull, "Okay."

"I'm in the room with him now," Peter continued, testing the waters.

"What's he told you?" Nick asked.

"Nothing. Nick, he's dead!" Once the words finally emerged Peter couldn't keep the rest of them from spilling out in a fervent whisper. "I just... The motel receptionist told me you came here yesterday."

"Why were you interrogating—" Nick cut himself off, seeming to grasp the silliness of asking a question like that about a person as nosy as Peter. After a deep breath, he continued, "Why, exactly, are you calling me?"

"I just thought you should know before I call the cops. That's all."

"Peter, what are you trying to say?"

"I've got to go. It will seem weird if I'm in here too long without reporting the body." Peter hung up and took a moment to collect himself.

Or at least he tried to collect himself, but he found that between the stench of the room, his nausea, and the tearing feeling ripping through his chest, he could not.

He lurched out of the motel room and heaved again on the sidewalk path. He glanced up to see that most of the audience of smoking men seemed to still be inhabiting the balcony opposite him. One leaned forward and called out, "You okay, buddy?"

Peter nodded and forced himself to stand. Here, he thought, is the proverbial peanut gallery. Several of them would have seen Nick come and go the previous day. Observing their haggard faces, Peter felt sure that when the cops arrived, they'd have a whole slew of witnesses.

Thinking on that, Peter did something he never thought he would ever do. He squinted right up at the burly guy who'd inquired after his health and said, "Hey, you might not care about this, but I just found a dead guy in that room behind me. I'm about to call the cops. Just thought I'd mention it."

These words hung in the air momentarily while all parties considered the information. Then Peter turned and ducked back into the motel room and closed the door. Outside he heard doors slamming and old cantankerous vehicles roar to life as more than three dozen men and women took their leave of the dump.

Then he dialed 911.

As the dispatcher answered he saw even the clerk on duty snatch Peter's own bike and pedal away.

Peter didn't even have the will to chase him down and take it back.

Speaking to police officers about a dead body that one has found oneself associated with had, over the last few years, become one of Peter's specialties. He knew most of the officers in Bellingham as well as many of the sheriff's deputies of greater Whatcom County.

This would be the first time he planned to withhold information from any of them—in fact it was one of the first times in his life he'd tried to conceal anything of serious importance from anyone.

Watching the officers shoulder through the door, Peter considered the ethical problem involvement with the police presented. The corpse in the kitchenette had been murdered, no question about it. But who'd whacked him with the fire extinguisher?

Nick or somebody else?

He didn't want to believe Nick had it in him to crush a guy's skull like that, but you never really knew what any man was truly capable of. And part of him had to admit that he'd been into danger when he'd first met Nick.

Maybe that's why some part of him felt a cheap thrill at the idea that Nick could have done this guy in, while simultaneously being convinced that if Nick had killed Sam, Sam must have really deserved it.

But had he really? Or was that just Peter's vile hangover filling his brain with a fog of loyalty that put fuzzy edges around the notion of justice for dead guys in kitchenettes?

No, loyalty alone didn't convince Peter of Nick's innocence. It was the circumstances. Nick wouldn't have left Sam laying there dead. He would have disposed of the body, somehow. Nick was just practical that way.

Peter wished he had a Scotch and water and maybe a raw egg.

"Peter Fontaine? Are you serious?"

Peter turned toward the sound of a familiar voice.

Detective Patton, Bellingham's finest lesbian police officer, had clearly just arrived and was speaking to another officer on the thin strip of sidewalk outside. Patton stood a couple of inches taller than him and outweighed him by a solid twenty-five pounds or more. Peter hadn't seen much of her for the past couple of years, as he'd not been involved with any violent crimes. They moved in different social circles.

Yet when she stepped into the motel room, Peter could see that she had made no effort to update her haircut. She still sported the vintage Eighties' mullet he'd come to know and respect and still wore pantsuits and cop shoes even though she could have gone for a nicer look now that she was in plainclothes.

Or maybe she'd just taken that plain clothes thing really literally.

In any case, she didn't seem angry to see him, which he found relieving.

"Hello, Detective!" He gave a brief wave. "I was wondering if I could talk to you."

"What a coincidence," Patton said with a smile.

"Could we maybe do it somewhere else?" Peter asked. "The smell in here is crazy-bad."

"Sure thing." Patton led him to her car, opened the door, and gestured to the backseat. "How about here?"

"Thank you." Peter slumped onto the vinyl seat and allowed his head to loll backward for a moment.

"You look like hell," Patton commented.

"It's because that's how I feel," Peter replied.

"They tell me you found the body," Patton said. "Why don't you tell me what happened again. Starting from the reason you came here."

Peter took a deep breath and realized he had to just tell everything he knew. Withholding information was useless, as Patton would find out eventually.

"Yesterday this guy, Sam Powers—"

"The deceased."

"Right. He came to our house, and he and Nick got into an argument, and Nick broke his phone. I was coming here to bring the phone back and to apologize," Peter got the words out in a rush, before he could reconsider them or feel guilty.

He wasn't ratting out Nick, he told himself, because Nick hadn't committed the crime. He couldn't have. He'd just sounded too surprised when Peter had phoned him a few minutes earlier. And not telling Patton everything he knew would just prolong the time when Nick would be a person of interest in the investigation.

Patton was not exactly an easy person to read, but Peter thought he might have caught a micro-expression of surprise at his sudden rush of information.

"Did Nick threaten Mr. Powers?"

"No, but he did throw him out of our house," Peter said.

"Why would Nick do that?"

"I don't know," Peter replied. Then seeing her expression, he continued, "I seriously don't know. He wouldn't tell me. So I left, and then I ended up drinking too much beer at Samish Brewing and passing out."

"So when were you with Mr. Olson yesterday?"

"I didn't see him between about noon and six p.m."

"That's a long time."

"I was really pissed at him. Anyway, I know Nick came here; the receptionist told me." Peter rubbed his eyes, then added, "The receptionist also just stole my bike, so when you find him I'd appreciate it if you could get it back for me."

"It's interesting that you would volunteer that information," Patton remarked.

"About the bike?"

"About Nick coming here," Patton said.

"You're going to find out anyway. It only took me three minutes, and I don't have a badge." Peter gave a shrug. "Besides, I know Nick didn't do it."

"How do you know that?" she asked.

"Because I'm married to him," Peter replied.

Patton didn't seem convinced by this argument. "Is there anything else the receptionist said?"

"He told me that Sam had two visitors: one of them was Nick and the other was some transperson. From the way he was talking, I'm guessing the transperson was female-looking."

Patton nodded and made a couple more notes in her book. "And you still have the phone, I assume?"

"Yes." Peter retrieved it from his pocket and handed it to her. "The code is 6464."

"How do you know that?"

"I watched him put it in," Peter said. "It doesn't work, though. The touch screen is broken and stuck on that image."

"So you don't know why Nick and the deceased argued?" Patton asked again, circling back to the question.

Peter shook his head. "I seriously have no idea. But as soon as Nick saw Sam, he threw him out. The only thing I know for sure is that Sam is Nick's agent's boyfriend. He was at our wedding with her. I hadn't seen him again until he showed up at my office yesterday morning."

"Okay," Patton said. "Can you think of anything else I might need to know?"

"I don't think so," Peter said. "Oh, except that the puke on the body isn't from him. It's from me. I'm not feeling that well, and finding the body came as kind of a shock."

Patton released him a few minutes later, offering a ride in from an officer, which he declined in favor of a cab.

Peter waited until the cab was well away from the motel to text Nick again.

Nothing incriminating—just a quick couple of words to find out whether or not he was home and to tell him the police were most likely going to be there soon. Nick's reply came back immediately.

Am at home. Donna is here with me.

Nick's agent Donna? Sam hadn't mentioned that she'd come to town with him, but then again, maybe he didn't know. He supposed he would find out when he got back home.

Chapter Four

The first time Peter had met Nick's agent, he hadn't believed she was real. First there was her height. A former model, Donna stood solidly six feet tall in bare feet, but always wore four-inch heels in order to tower over the general population. She was so thin that she could have been used to pick a lock. In fact, to Peter, she resembled nothing so much as a human-shaped wire hanger that someone had draped beautiful clothes on and then accessorized with blazing-red lipstick and a blonde chignon so consistently perfect that Peter had always suspected it might be a wig.

She'd originally represented Walter, then picked up Nick as a client once he'd started showing promise. Peter theorized she must be in her late fifties at least, though Botox made it hard for him to pin it down to a specific age past forty-five.

But Peter had found that once he made it past her freakish appearance, he liked her quite a bit. She genuinely loved art, advocated for Nick tirelessly, and drove a hard bargain. She also appeared to have worked with or dated every single significant person in the art industry since 1980. He had never seen her eat, frown, or wear her hair down.

That was why Peter found the sight of her weeping and disheveled on his sofa disturbing to the core, even if it did disprove his theory about her hair being fake. The shoulder-length locks hanging around her face had been processed extensively but were real.

"Tell me it isn't true." She glanced up at him sharply as Peter approached. "Tell me Sam isn't dead."

"I can't," Peter replied. "I've just come from being interviewed by the police at the motel where I found his body."

"That fucking bastard!" Her hands clenched against the leather sofa cushion so hard Peter thought her knife-like manicure might actually achieve penetration of the fine leather.

Anger at a murder victim wasn't exactly the reaction Peter had expected, but didn't fall outside the range of emotions he felt Donna could be capable of. He glanced sidelong at Nick, trying to gauge what the other man might be thinking. But even at the best of times Nick lacked transparency. He had feelings, and they ran deep and strong.

But the exact nature of those feelings was a mystery to Peter most of the time. Nick offered no conversational hints now either. He merely reached out and gently squeezed Donna's shoulder.

"I didn't realize you'd come to town with Sam," Peter said. "Why were you staying at that shitty motel instead of our guestroom?" Even as Peter asked the question he realized that Nick must have refused to have Sam in their house.

"I didn't come to town with him," she said. "I hopped the red-eye last night when I realized he'd come here. I was trying to keep him from badgering Nick."

Nick and Donna shared a look then that Peter felt acutely excluded from. Too tired and too hungover to be polite he said, "Okay, what's the big fucking deal here? What is it that you think Sam would be badgering Nick about?"

When neither of them immediately answered, Peter went on, "Why was Sam trying to photograph that painting?"

"He wanted to document it," Donna said.

Peter felt that this was quite possibly the most meaningless answer he'd ever heard and said so, adding, "What are you two trying to hide from me?"

Again Nick and Donna exchanged a glance, but neither said a word. "Listen, the cops are probably going to be here soon to speak with both of you. I don't know what the deal is, but if you're being as obviously deceptive to them as you're being to me right now, you're probably both going to spend the day in the police station."

Donna crumpled in on herself like a compostable plastic cup dissolving under an onslaught of hot coffee.

At this Nick spoke up, though it was not clear whom he addressed. "We need to talk alone."

"Do you mean you and I?" Peter asked. "Because that's not news, Captain States-The-Obvious."

Nick gave him a look of sour annoyance. "Let's go to my studio. We'll talk in there."

He stood and started for across the living room, pausing to look back when he saw Peter heading for the kitchen instead. "Are you coming?"

"I'm just going to grab a Coke and some aspirin," Peter said. "I'll meet you there."

On his way to the kitchen, Peter passed the dinner table.

There in plain view sat a man's satchel—a courier bag with the corner of a laptop computer sticking out the top. An open manila file folder sat beside it. This appeared to contain some photocopies of newspaper prints.

The last time he'd seen this bag it had been sitting in the backseat of Sam's rented hybrid.

Peter resisted the urge to touch or paw through it. Partially because he didn't care to get his prints all over it, but also because he needed—absolutely needed—to talk with Nick before Detective Patton's imminent arrival.

He retrieved his Coke and made his way back to Nick's studio—bypassing the softly weeping Donna.

Nick had turned on all the lights in the studio and stood in front of his most recent work—a companion piece to the large figural that adorned their living room.

Peter sat down on the stool that had been expressly placed in this room for him to sit on when he felt like chatting to Nick during his long painting sessions.

"Okay," he said. "What is the deal with this Sam guy? Why do you have his stuff sitting on the dinner table?"

"I took it from his motel room," Nick said.

Peter waited a few seconds while that information sunk in; then diplomacy failed him, and he blurted out, "Was he alive when you did that?"

"Yes, of course he was alive." Nick shot him a glare. "You can't seriously think I killed that little shithead for a laptop, do you?"

"I really don't know what to think," Peter admitted.

At this Nick looked hurt, as though the notion that Peter considered him capable of murder was itself an insult.

Peter continued, "I don't think you killed Sam, but I really don't know anything beyond that. You are acting so weird that I would practically be willing to believe that you'd been replaced by an alien replica."

"Alien replica?" Nick shook his head. "Where do you come up with this stuff?"

"From trying to build hypotheses about you, you big weirdo."

Surprisingly, Nick actually smiled; then he said, "Have you ever heard of being an accessory after the fact?"

Peter felt his eyes goggle. "You helped your agent cover up killing her boyfriend?"

"I'm not talking about me, Peter," Nick said. "I'm talking about you."

"I don't follow you."

"I didn't want to tell you about the business with Sam because I didn't want you to become an accessory after the fact." Nick picked up one of his brushes and studied the bristles. "While you were out at the brewery yesterday, did you happen to look up the kind of books Sam writes?"

"I did that before I even got into his car." Peter rolled his eyes. What kind of dummy did Nick think he was, anyway?

"Then you'd have noticed that he writes about scandals in the art world."

"Right," Peter said. Then it dawned on him. "Do you think he was going to write about the fact that you helped Walter end his life?"

"No, that's ancient history. Everybody knows that already. He was going to write about the last twelve de Kamp figurals."

"Right," Peter said. Sam had said as much himself, but the significance of it escaped Peter.

"I painted those, Peter," Nick said.

"I know. You told me before; you assisted Walter after he became weak."

"No, I mean Walter didn't have anything to do with them. Those were my paintings that were sold as Walter's."

"And so?" Peter hated the fact that he had to prompt, but the hangover was really slowing him down.

"That's called fraud," Nick said.

"How can it be fraud if everybody knows you assisted him?"

"There's a difference between assisting an artist with his own design and concept and just signing your name to another artist's canvas," Nick said. "Okay, I'll spell it out for you—"

"Please," Peter said.

"A de Kamp painting sells for a quarter of a million dollars. Mine are a hundred thousand at the very best—"

"Hey, the value is going up every day," Peter cut in. "Your work is way more accessible than Walter's. And you have that German art-book deal."

Nick actually smiled at him. "That's sweet, baby. But if you do the math, that means that when my paintings were sold with Walter's signature on them the value had been inflated by many, many zeros."

"So Sam planned to let the world know that the last twelve de Kamps were actually Olsons?"

"He's already written most of the book. I skimmed it yesterday. It's sensationalist trash but unfortunately accurate on the legal points."

"But you didn't sell all of them," Peter pointed out. He knew. He'd seen them in storage.

"No, we only sold two."

"I get that you and Walter might have committed fraud, but I don't get where the accessory after the fact comes in," Peter said.

"Well, if I told you about it, that's what you might end up being," Nick said. "And in truth, that's what both Donna and I already are."

"What do you mean?"

"During the last few weeks of his life, Walter wasn't doing too well, and I was running ragged trying to deal with everything that needed to be done for him. One day Donna brought a collector through to view Walter's canvases. She had a key and knew we were strapped for cash—end of life care isn't cheap. Even if it's only palliative care."

Peter nodded, then said, "So Donna sees your works but thinks that the canvases are Walter's and shows them to the collector? Am I right?"

"She didn't know I painted at the time," Nick said. "Anyway, the guy loved them. Donna told Walter, and he went ahead and signed them. He was worried that I'd be left with nothing, you know. So he wanted to make sure there was a lot of cash. When I got back, he told me about it."

"Making you an accessory after the fact because you didn't stop the sale."

"Exactly."

"Why didn't you stop it?"

"I didn't think my art would ever be worth anything, so I didn't think I had anything to lose. I didn't expect to have an art career in my own right then." The simplicity of Nick's answer made Peter's heart ache.

"What about Donna?"

"Walter never told her, and we've never spoken about it until now. But I'm pretty sure she figured it out when I refused to sell the other ten paintings. Any person looking at those ten pieces as they compare to my art today would be able to see the very clear resemblance."

"Yeah, I had always wondered why you were so reluctant to sell. I always just figured that you didn't want Walter's shitty sons to get any of the money," Peter said.

Suddenly a lightbulb lit in his tiny pea-brain. "Wait! That *is* why you didn't sell them."

"Right, but it wasn't out of spite. They're shitty, but I would be happy to give them what they were entitled to. I wouldn't have any problem with splitting the proceeds from their father's art. But I don't owe them anything from the sale of mine."

Peter slumped on his stool, rubbing his temples. "This is really complicated."

"I know. I'm sorry."

"I'm just trying to figure out what will happen when this information gets out," Peter said. "Because that's inevitable now."

Nick shrugged and said, "I don't know."

"What if you contacted the buyer of the original two pieces and explained? I mean, it's not like you're a forger. And your work does have value."

"Explained what? That he paid half a million for what should have gone for a hundred thousand dollars at best?"

"I don't suppose you can give him a refund?"

"Do you have that kind of cash lying around someplace?" Nick asked.

"No." Peter racked his brains, refusing to be stymied. "But this all occurred years ago! What about the statute of limitations?"

"In New York State it's six years after the fraud is discovered." Nick's answer came with surprising speed. "And it hasn't been discovered yet, so the clock hasn't even started counting down."

"I guess you probably looked that up at some point," Peter said.

Nick nodded. "And it could ruin Donna's career. Reputation is everything in her business."

A knock at the door interrupted their conversation. Peter shifted from his stool, yanked open the door, and looked up into Donna's terrified eyes.

"There are cop cars in the driveway," she whispered.

"We expected them," Nick said. "They're here for me."

"Please don't tell them that I'm here."

"I'm not going to lie to Detective Patton," Peter said.

"I'm not asking you to lie. I'm just saying don't tell them I'm here if they don't ask. Please, Peter, I just need a few minutes to get myself under control. I know I have to talk to them, but just not right now."

Peter was about to refuse; then the raw anguish and fear in her face moved him.

"Fine," he said. "Just go upstairs."

Donna didn't wait another second. She took the stairs by twos and vanished into the guest bedroom before the doorbell rang.

Detective Patton stepped into Peter's foyer, wearing the expression of bland skepticism that Peter had come to know and respect her for. She gave Nick the once-over, her eyebrows raised slightly as she took in his black eye; then without preamble she said, "Mr. Olson, I was wondering if we could talk at the station."

"Sure," Nick said. "I'll just go get some shoes."

Nick padded up the stairs to the bedroom.

"Why at the station?" Peter blurted out. "Why can't you talk to Nick here?"

"I have one additional question for you, Peter," Patton said, completely failing to acknowledge Peter's question. "How did Mr. Olson get that black eye?"

"I don't know," he said.

"When did he get it?"

"Sometime yesterday. I don't know. I was really drunk. I know he didn't have it at six." Peter shrugged. Then realization lit in his mind. "Is that why you're taking him downtown? Because he has a black eye? He could have gotten that any number of ways. It doesn't make him a bludgeoner."

"Please calm down, sir," Patton's partner said, stepping forward slightly.

"You calm down," Peter returned before rational thought could intervene and tell him to keep his mouth shut.

"Peter, stop it," Nick's voice came close behind him. "They're just doing their job."

Peter spun around to see his lover had donned his paint-spattered boots and seemed ready to be taken to the police station. Peter wanted to rush forward and hug him, but Nick's stance told him not to make a scene.

Why the hell did he have to be so staid and casual? The cops could be marching him straight to a firing squad, and he'd just slide into his crappy old shoes and go bravely to his death.

Nick gave Peter a nod, then turned to Patton and said, "Let's go."

They departed without further conversation, leaving Peter alone in the silent living room, panicking. He needed to call a lawyer, didn't he? To make sure Nick's rights were respected? He recalled that Nick had used a lawyer during an art purchase last year, but for the life of him he couldn't remember the guy's name. Did Nick have an address book?

Peter stopped himself at the stupidity of that idea. Nick's lawyer's number would be on Nick's phone just like every other adult this far into the twenty-first century. His heart hammered. What to do?

Maybe Donna would know the lawyer's name. Peter raced upstairs and found her lying under the covers in the guest bed, pretending to sleep.

The corner of the blanket lifted and he saw one blue eye peeping up at him. "Are they gone?"

"Yes, but they took Nick!" Peter wanted to be able to say it calmly but could not.

What if somehow Nick was actually convicted of Sam's murder? What if some piece of forensic evidence pointed right at his husband?

"Why did they take him?" Donna cautiously peeled back the cream-colored duvet.

"Because he had a black eye, I think. Do you know how he got it?"

"He didn't say."

"Listen, do you know the name of his lawyer? I just think I need to call and get some advice on this."

Donna nodded, then sat up and swung her stick-like legs off the edge of the bed. "I have it in my phone. It's in my purse downstairs."

Donna scuttled down the stairs in a semi-crouch, as though worried the police might still be lurking. After she verified that they were alone she straightened up and smoothed her hair back into a more careful arrangement.

She fished into her purse and began to thumb through her phone. "Do you have a pen and paper?"

"Just a second." Peter dashed back to the studio. After rummaging through the table that served as Nick's desk, he found a scrap of thick watercolor paper and a burnt-sienna-colored pencil. He jogged back to the living room, somehow feeling better for accomplishing a simple mission. The very fact that he felt good about doing this told him his mental state must be dire.

He emerged into the living room in time to see Donna heading out the door. She held her purse in one hand and Sam's brown leather satchel in the other.

"Where are you going?"

"Look, I've got to run. The number for the lawyer is on the table."

Peter shouted, "Wait!" but it was too late. Donna slammed the door on his words. Now more alarmed, he yanked open the door and rushed out onto the gravel drive. Donna had already reached her car and flung her bags inside. Peter made it to the vehicle just as she got the doors locked again.

Furious and afraid, Peter pounded on the window.

"What is wrong with you? Why are you taking that briefcase?"

"I'm sorry!" Donna shouted back, though she didn't look at him. She fired up the engine and pulled forward. Peter slammed his foot into the side of her car, but it didn't do much to stop her progress. She peeled out, leaving him standing in a cloud of dust.

She'd done it, he realized. She must have.

All at once, hurt and rage welled up inside him. How could she have hung Nick out to dry like that?

Still stinging from the insult and full of wrath, he dialed Detective Patton and told her who Donna was, that she'd hidden from the police and subsequently fled. She thanked him for his honesty and then disconnected, leaving Peter standing, phone in hand, with no idea what to do or how to proceed.

He took a deep breath and tried to gather his beyond-scattered thoughts.

The lawyer—he needed to call Nick's lawyer. He turned and stalked back inside, hoping that Donna had at least been kind enough to leave him the number.

She had.

Apparently having no paper, she'd written the lawyer's name and number in searing-red lipstick on the glass-topped coffee table. Just the sight of the lipstick gave Peter a sickening turn. Had she never heard of serial killer William Heirens' famous "catch me before I kill more" scrawled in lipstick on the mirror of his victim?

Or maybe, if you were a killer—and there was now no reason to believe that Donna wasn't one—scrawling things in lipstick just seemed appropriate.

Peter's stomach lurched as the sight of Sam's open cranium reasserted itself in his mind's eye. He didn't think there'd been a message scrawled in lipstick on any surfaces in the dank motel room. But he couldn't be sure. He hadn't looked around much after spewing up on the guy's corpse.

Peter took a steadying breath and punched the digits of Amanda Maclean, attorney-at-law. A tired-sounding receptionist answered and attempted to rebuff him.

Peter managed to get past her by practically beginning to cry.

As he waited in the darkness created by the Hold button, Peter sniffed and tried to think away from his feelings—just to be able to make it through the phone call with his pride intact.

He had to think back to before he'd found Sam's body. What had he been going to do before that?

Well, go to work.

Doug would be expecting him to write a piece for Bellingham Beer Week that highlighted the City of Subdued Excitement's local brews. Unfortunately, he'd been too drunk the previous day to remember to get a single photograph of their newest star brewer.

He would need to phone Travis, he decided. He would call and ask for a short tour to gather some basic brewing information so that he could write his puff piece about how Bellinghamsters loved John Barleycorn.

Once the lawyer—Peter glanced down to the coffee table to recollect that her name was Amanda—had been put on the case, Peter could return to his normally scheduled workday without panicking.

Because there was no reason to panic.

Despite everything that had happened this morning. Everything would work out. Peter felt his breathing coming easier. He felt he might be winning his struggle against dissembling.

Then a cheerful voice said, "Hi, this is Amanda."

And Peter's words all came out in a hideous, confused rush. "The cops took Nick to the station for questioning, but he didn't kill that guy."

"Who is this?" Amanda's voice retained the air of calm that Peter wished his had.

"This is Peter Fontaine. I'm Nick Olson's husband."

"Oh, right!" Amanda's voice brightened. "I met you at the wedding."

"Yes," Peter said. "Now I'm calling you because Nick needs a lawyer."

"Has he been arrested?"

"No." After once more focusing on his breathing, Peter managed to relate the story of his morning, emphasizing the discovery of Sam's body and omitting Nick's inadvertent confession of art fraud.

"I'm so sorry," Amanda said. "It sounds like you've had a hell of a morning."

"I really have," Peter conceded.

"I can't believe Sam is dead," she went on. "I just had dinner with him and Donna last week."

Peter wondered what the odds were of that, but then realized that an attorney specializing in art sales would naturally be dining with an art rep as well as a reporter who also specialized in covering the sale of art for an international journal.

"Did he seem upset about anything?" Peter asked. His old reporter instincts rose up from where they'd been knocked flat by fear and shock. "Or afraid of anyone?"

"Not at all," Amanda said. "If anything, he seemed especially excited about his trip to the Pacific Northwest."

"Did he mention anybody he was going to meet? Apart from me and Nick?" Peter persisted, with a heavy sniff.

"Nick mentioned you were something of an amateur sleuth," Amanda answered with a laugh. Attorney Amanda's question-avoiding instincts had surfaced to counter Peter's reporter nosiness. "I think now I understand what he might have been talking about."

"I try not to disappoint," Peter said.

"Well, listen. It was good of you to call here and get advice in this situation. Unfortunately I'm a transactional lawyer, not a criminal one. Everything's going to be okay though, I promise. While you were talking I emailed a colleague who recommended a guy in Seattle. But right now it sounds like the cops are on a fishing expedition, so I'd expect Nick to be home by tonight." Amanda gave Peter the Seattle lawyer's name and contact information, then said, "So do you feel more comfortable with the situation now?"

"I suppose so," Peter conceded. "But I just don't understand—why did they take him in for questioning?"

"Probably the black eye," Amanda said. "That and cops always try to rattle big guys like Nick by taking them in if they can. Makes them feel like they've got the home-turf advantage, I imagine."

After engaging the services of the Seattle-based law office of Schuller and Schuller and cleaning the lipstick off the coffee table, Peter had little to do but wait for Nick to be released.

Until his phone rang—it was Doug, the editor at the *Hamster* and Peter's boss.

Then he remembered that another thing he might consider doing to pass the time was go to work.

"Hi, Doug, I'm sorry I'm very, very late," Peter began. He felt like it was a good start. Then in the nanosecond it took for Doug to draw a breath, Peter considered what he should say. Initially he thought he might go for the grand slam of all excuses: "*My husband is being questioned for murder.*"

Then he reconsidered.

More than anything else, Doug loved a juicy scandal—exactly like the one Nick was currently involved in. So far Doug had no way of knowing that Peter was sitting right on top of a great news story without doing anything about it. And Peter needed to keep it that way. So he said, "I got really drunk at the brewery yesterday, and I guess I overslept."

There. Now he looked like an idiot and a loser, but at least he wouldn't be betraying his husband to his boss.

"Did you manage to get the article written?"

"No," Peter said. "And I didn't get any pictures either."

Doug was silent, apparently considering his next words carefully. Finally he said, "Well, go back down there, and get the pictures. I need those and your copy by Thursday."

Chapter Five

When Peter walked through the doors of Samish Brewing thirty minutes later, he had to pause a moment to lean against a table, fighting down nausea at the smell of hops, malt, and barley that had so delighted him the previous day.

The same bartender, Shane, was on duty and gave him a sympathetic smile.

"Hair of the dog?" he offered.

"Not for me." Peter held up a hand. "My morning's already been hairy enough as it is. Is Travis around?"

"He's in back," the bartender said. "Feel better."

Peter gave a curt nod and made his way toward the brewery proper.

Through the wide, plate-glass window, he could see the brewers were in full industrial-fermentation mode. Beard nets and safety goggles abounded. He spotted Travis back by the canning line, spraying out a large, wheeled tote. Even beneath the safety gear he looked haggard. Peter waved until the other man caught sight of him and returned his gesture. Travis wove his way through the massive two-story fermentation vats and opened the door that separated the brewing facility from the taproom.

Deafening noise immediately assaulted Peter—noise so grinding that he almost passed out from the fresh stab of pain it sent through his prefrontal cortex—a region of his brain currently experiencing great suffering already.

The racket of the canning line rolling aluminum cans along provided the tempo, accompanying the rumbling base of the massive pumps that moved both water and proto-beer from tank to tank. Booming, distorted classic rock filled the rest of the available space in the air.

Travis stepped through, and the door fell closed. The relative quiet settled over Peter like a comforting cloud.

"Peter, how are you?"

"A little worse for the wear." Peter gave Travis what he felt might be his best sheepish grin. "Yesterday I was too busy enjoying your beer to remember to take photos. Do you think we could do that today?"

Travis winced and rubbed his eye as if the notion pained him. Then he said, "You know, I'm not feeling that well myself."

"The lady brewers kept you up pretty late?"

"Yeah," Travis said, a look of anxious embarrassment crossing his face. "I think I'm in trouble with my wife now."

"Hey, join the club," Peter said.

Travis smiled then and said, "Right. Shane told me your partner came to take you home."

"It's going to be a while before I live this down," Peter said. Though to be honest, the embarrassment he still felt at having been publicly fished out of the bar paled before the shocking fear for Nick that now underlay his conscious thoughts. He pushed the rising bulge of anxiety back down. Patton would not arrest Nick. She couldn't. She had nothing on him because there was nothing to have.

"Trust me—nobody remembers anything from yesterday," Travis said. He smiled but still seemed like he might abruptly eject his stomach contents at any moment.

"Listen, would you mind if we rescheduled? I think I might have to sit down for a while."

"Not at all," Peter replied.

"Thanks, you're a good guy." Travis gave Peter the friendly clap on the shoulder that seemed to be the brewer's traditional cultural gesture.

Well, Peter thought ruefully as he returned to the car, at least somebody had a good time last night.

As Peter wove through the picnic tables outside the brewery, he realized that though his stomach felt like he'd eaten ground glass and live scorpions, he still needed to eat. He stopped by the food truck that was perennially parked outside the brewery and bought himself a fancy hamburger with double bacon.

Like Travis, the tattooed young guy running the food truck seemed to have thoroughly enjoyed himself the day before. He squinted at Peter through puffy eyes, and when he wrote down the order he moved like a malfunctioning robot, apparently not able to remember how to spell the word "burger."

Not wanting to return to work and feeling like he should thank Shane for his kindness the previous day, Peter took his food back into the bar. Again he declined the offer of alcohol but accepted a pint of locally brewed kombucha on the house. The health drink tasted like vinegar soda, but Peter did have to admit it seemed to have a positive effect on his physical state overall. After downing half a pint, the hamburger started going down easier.

As a bartender, rather than a brewer, Shane wore no beard and appeared to be less shattered than the rest of the humans Peter had seen haunting the brewery that day.

"Great party here last night, huh?" Peter asked. "With the lady brewers."

Shane cracked the proud not-quite-able-to-regret-it smile of a man who had a one-night stand with a visiting lady brewer the previous night. "Yeah, it was amazing."

"Did I miss anything good?"

"Yeah, they did the Cotton-Eyed Joe on the bar."

"Wow, that must have been something."

"See for yourself." Shane fished his phone out of his pocket and turned the screen toward Peter. The photo showed a line of ten fit women, all wearing cowboy boots, kicking up their heels. Overall a fantastic photo, perfectly exemplifying what could be great about beer.

"Would you mind sending this to me? I'd love to run it with my article in the *Hamster*."

"I really can't give it to you. The health department and the liquor board don't like stuff like dancing on the bar—not even at private functions. I've got some other pics of happy people drinking in accordance with state regulations. I could send you those."

"I'd appreciate it." Peter handed over a card. "Thank you so much. And thank you for putting up with me yesterday. I was a little obnoxious."

"Oh, no," Shane said. "I'd say it was your finest hour. Especially when you started holding your hands like a little kid pretending he's got a set of guns and calling your husband 'sheriff.'"

Peter slumped down and allowed his head to gently thunk against the bar, overcome with embarrassment. "I thought I was only doing that in my mind."

Shane pulled a huge grin. "Happy trails, cowpoke."

Peter had just finished writing his rundown of the festivities at Samish Brewing and was scrolling through the photographs that Shane had sent him, when Nick called. Detective Patton was through with him, and he was waiting outside the police station, hoping for a ride home.

Overhead the sky retained its gray and orange haze. The wind had shifted, bringing the smoke from massive interior fires to blanket the city in a thick and insulating blanket that kept the summer heat pressing down on all of them. As he drove, Peter wondered at the alien surrealness of both the sky and of Nick's deep involvement in these crimes—art fraud, murder, blackmail... Did the rabbit hole go any further?

Standing on the sidewalk outside Bellingham Police Station, hands in his pockets, Nick looked positively forlorn. He'd put on a pair of aviators, which hid his black eye somewhat, but fatigue showed in his shoulders and the set of his jaw.

The sheen of sweat caused by the punishing heat outside did nothing to change the image of a man who bore the weight of the world.

Peter cranked up the air-conditioning as Nick dropped into the passenger seat.

"What did they say?" Peter asked.

"That I was free to go...for now," Nick said.

"But Patton can't seriously think you did this." Peter pulled out onto the quiet road.

"So long as I don't have an alibi, I don't think she's ruling me out. The good news is that you do." Nick leaned his seat back. Peter could see that he had his eyes closed.

"I have an alibi?"

"You were passed out cold." Nick glanced sideways at him.

"Patton told you that?"

"No, but she asked me to confirm my whereabouts between two and four in the morning, so I just assumed that's when it happened." Nick glanced over at him meaningfully. "Anyone who saw you last night could confirm that you wouldn't have had the strength or the coordination to...get all the way into town and kill a guy."

"That sounds like an accurate description of me yesterday."

"I didn't get a chance to ask you, was it bad—when you found the body?" Nick asked.

"Yes. I threw up," Peter said. "His head was open, and I could see his brains."

"That's terrible. Are you okay?"

"I don't even know. I think I might not be because I can't feel anything." Peter stared out at the sunlight dazzling along the deep green waves of Wildcat Cove. "Except for hungover. I feel like I will die of exhaustion right this second. What about you?"

"Very tired," Nick admitted.

"Want to take a nap?" Peter's initial offer was tentative, but as he saw Nick's mouth curve slightly up he gained hope and, emboldened, reached out and laid a hand on Nick's thigh. "I promise I'll make it worth your while."

"Good idea. I've got just the cure for a hangover," Nick said.

When they entered the house, they wordlessly undressed, then crawled into bed. Peter reached for Nick, and the two fell together with practiced coordination. There was something so relieving, especially after a fight, in knowing they could return to this simple, trusting embrace. Their arms and legs locked around each other in a way that maximized contact and comfort.

Sun blazed through the sheer bedroom curtains, giving the late afternoon lie-in a deliciously luxurious, stolen quality. Nick kissed Peter sloppily with his eyes closed.

Peter had a headache, so he decided to limit his head movements by resting it on a pillow and letting his tongue and lips do all the hard work.

Their cocks hardened as they rubbed against each other, kissing leisurely. Peter's headache faded in direct proportion to the pleasure coming from the friction on his dick.

When the force of their rutting got nearly painful, Peter rolled onto his side and sidled up alongside Nick's large body, pressing his ass against Nick's hard cock.

"I've got a headache," he told Nick. "So you have to do all the hard work."

Nick chuckled. "Lazy," he said, but he obligingly reached behind himself to grab the lube of the bedside table. Peter pressed closer and closed his eyes, listening to the sounds of Nick getting himself slicked up and ready.

Peter lifted his top leg to grant better access to his ass and was rewarded with the blunt width of Nick's cock at his entrance. Peter breathed out shakily. He adored making love this way, the two of them spooning, the languid embrace so much more than simply fucking.

Heat and stretching pressure filled him. Nick took his time to press all the way in.

He worked slowly, but at last his groin was flush with Peter's ass, and Peter felt stuffed full of his husband. He could feel the press of Nick's balls against his ass cheeks. The heavy weight of Nick's cock inside him caught Peter's breath. For a long minute, neither of them moved. They remained held together in their embrace, Nick's leg thrown over Peter's, arm wrapped around Peter's chest, his cock buried deep.

And then Nick began to move. Peter rested his head on the pillow to minimize his headache. But when Nick hit his prostate, the headache became really unimportant.

They fucked in slow motion. Peter wished they could do this for hours, until it got dark—but of course his dick had more urgent plans.

Nick sped up. Pleasure tightened his grip. When Peter groaned aloud, Nick lowered his hand to Peter's cock and pumped him in the rhythm of his thrusts.

Peter was close to bursting. He turned his head. It was an awkward angle to kiss, but he couldn't help it—he wanted to have Nick in his mouth, in his ass, around his cock. Nick kissed him hard and messy, and within moments Peter's orgasm burst forth, spurting over Nick's palm.

Nick fucked him for another minute before his hips stuttered and he thrust deeply, moaning Peter's name as he filled him with cum.

Nick didn't pull out right away, and Peter was grateful, firstly because he was way too tired to put effort in pulling away or cleaning himself up. Secondly, because the idea of falling asleep with Nick still inside him—at least for a little while—sounded sort of romantic.

"Told you a nap was a great idea," Peter said.

Nick chuckled. "I love you," he said groggily. He squeezed Peter close. Peter couldn't see his face, but he reached up to blindly stroke Nick's head. Instead he managed to poke Nick in his good eye.

"Hey now, you have to at least leave me one."

"Sorry." Peter withdrew his wandering hand.

"That's all right. I'll let you make it up to me with more of these newfangled 'naps.'"

Chapter Six

Peter woke early, as the first light of morning penetrated the persistent veil of drifting smoke. *It would be another canta-loupe-colored day. More acres of temperate rainforest burning with no relief in sight.*

The unnatural sky fit with his current feelings about life in general. So thinking, he went to take a shower.

As the water poured down on him, he felt much more human. Being more fully human had its downside, though. Now that the physical misery and fog of overindulgence had lifted from his brain, he felt the full weight of Sam's death.

How was it possible that the death of a man who was nothing more than an acquaintance—and a complete villain—could still affect him? He didn't grieve for Sam.

How could he? But the violence of it shook him.

Some person or persons had decided that Sam needed to die and had taken action to ensure that result. But had there really been no other way to solve whatever problem Sam's murderer had? Or had Sam's death been the result of a fit of rage? Thinking back on the scene the previous day, Peter recalled that the weapon of choice seemed to have been a fire extinguisher, which implied that the murderer had not come to Sam's sleazy motel room with the intention of committing homicide, or he or she would have brought a better weapon, like a knife or shotgun.

And the way Sam's face had been—crumpled and beaten— implied more than one blow.

So there would have been noise, wouldn't there? At least one of the pimps or prostitutes patrolling the Lodgepole Motor Inn balcony in order to eliminate rival panderers would have heard something like that. But probably in a place like that any noise of human suffering would be assumed to be business as usual.

Humans, Peter thought, are ugly.

He left the shower, toweled off, and returned to bed where he snuggled close to Nick. If he could breathe deeply for a few minutes, Peter felt certain that he would be able to think of the murder more clearly. He needed to feel the sensation of Nick's skin on his skin. He couldn't deny that just laying his cheek against Nick's shoulder comforted him in a way that he'd struggled to quantify for their entire relationship.

At first he'd suspected Nick of harboring special hormones or microbes of some kind that produced an especially comforting scent that breezed past the blood-brain barrier on his olfactory nerve and went directly to the medium spiny receptors in his nucleus accumbens core, causing a flood of rewarding dopamine, and that this chemical sensation was the real root of his love of Nick.

In his mind he donned a white lab coat and explained that given the number of times they'd had sex, this love was inevitable—that Nick could be anyone and therefore if Peter lost Nick, he could be replaced, given time.

But Nick was more than a person. He was a life that Peter had chosen, bypassing other lives he could have had but didn't because he didn't want them enough to leave Nick for them. Inertia played no part in their relationship.

He had never considered that being separated from Nick could be anything but his own choice or Nick's untimely death. Even in imagined scenarios where Nick broke up with him, fictitious Peter could always convince notional Nick to change his mind.

The idea that somehow Nick could be convicted of Sam's death and taken away terrified him.

He pressed his face to Nick's shoulder, closing his eyes against the uncertainty of the situation. He allowed himself for a moment to consider the most dreaded possibility.

Nick did completely loathe Sam for good reasons. What if—and he hadn't because that was ridiculous—but what if Nick had really killed him? Would that make a difference?

The humanitarian in Peter wanted to believe that he would do the right thing for society and turn Nick in to the proper authorities, but the selfish, most inner part of him knew that he wouldn't.

Peter glanced up to find Nick looking down at him with an oddly thoughtful expression.

"What is it?" Peter asked.

"You have the weirdest expression on your face," Nick remarked. "Were you having some kind of daydream?"

"No, I was thinking that if you've killed Sam, I wouldn't turn you in."

A shocked expression of surprise crossed Nick's face; then he said, "Lucky for Justice, I didn't."

"So where did you get that black eye, anyway?" Peter tried to ask this casually, as if there were no connection to the conversation they were having.

Nick paused, smirked, and actually laughed out loud. "Are you kidding?"

"No, I'm not."

"I got it from you." Nick shook his head. "You don't remember it?"

"No," Peter said. "No wonder the cops asked me about it."

"No wonder the cops took me in directly afterward," Nick said ruefully.

"I took a swing at you?" Peter knew he'd been drunk and fairly surly, but he'd never been much of a scrapper—not even when completely inebriated.

"No, you kicked me in the face when I was trying to take your shoes off," Nick said.

"That's why I woke up wearing one shoe!" Peter congratulated himself on solving at least one mystery—even if it was more or less a preschool-level one. "Oh jeez, Nick, I'm sorry."

"It's okay." Nick squeezed his shoulder. "I should have known better than to get my face next to your kickin' foot. You were probably having some dream about being a placekicker about to score a field goal and win the Super Bowl."

"My daydreams are never that heroic," Peter replied. "It would be more like, 'the bandits had me by the leg. And I had to kick them off and make it to town before Sheriff Olson got on that train to California.' And then there would be some long, expository thing about how much I—as the Wildcat Kid—had come to love the lawman who had helped me to change my ways. And then maybe the whole thing would degenerate into pornography."

"That's right," Nick said. "You were in some sort of Wild West fantasy when I came to pick you up. I don't know how I ended up as sheriff. In the circumstances you'd think I'd be a guy in a black hat."

Peter considered this, then said, "While it's true that you were behaving badly, you're still more or less a paladin."

"If I were, then you wouldn't be wondering if I'd killed Sam."

"No, that's not true. I would be wondering what incredibly heinous crime Sam had committed to drive you to murder." Peter lay for a while, taking comfort in the solidity of Nick's body, eyes closed.

He imagined he looked as though he'd dozed off, but inside his mind, the wheels had started turning.

Now that he felt safe (and his brain wasn't coursing with acetaldehyde), Peter was able to turn his mind toward the question—if Nick didn't kill Sam, who did? And why with such rage?

As the significant other, Donna would be first on the list of humans who might be enraged enough to beat Sam's brains in. But even if Peter wasn't feeling too charitable toward Donna at the moment, he found it difficult to imagine her having the physical strength to pick up the heavy fire extinguisher. The strength of will and fortitude—sure, she'd been a fashion model for years. He had no doubt she could kill a guy. But her twig-like biceps could barely manage to lift her handbag, let alone an object heavy enough to crush Sam's skull.

Could it have actually been the pimp at the motel? Had he mistaken Sam for a hustler? It seemed far-fetched—Sam's clothes were far too expensive to be a meth-motel-level rent boy's.

And that brought Peter back to the question of why Sam had been in the substandard motel at all, when better rooms had been available all over town.

He shifted to peer up at Nick, who was gazing at the ceiling. Probably he was taking in the weird light as well.

"Nick?"

"Yes?"

"What actually happened yesterday?"

Nick sighed. "I really should have just requested a transcript of Patton's interview with me to bring home to you."

"She wouldn't have given you one anyway."

"Sam called me from the motel, demanding that I meet him. I went there about ten thirty in the morning. I didn't see anyone else there, but it didn't look like Sam was really staying in that room because there was no luggage."

"So you think Sam was using that room for business only?" Peter asked.

"That sounds right," Nick said. "He asked me for money. He wanted ten grand to suppress the information about the fake de Kamps. I told him he could fuck himself and let him know that I planned to press extortion charges against him."

"Would you really have done that?"

"That was my plan," Nick said.

"After taking his briefcase and laptop?"

Nick looked slightly abashed. "I wanted to see what he really knew. And I wanted some evidence to hand over to the police when I went to press charges."

"Did you tell Patton about the briefcase?"

"She didn't ask," Nick murmured.

"But if he stayed there after you left, that must mean he had other business, right? Because why would he have stayed in a dump that shitty if you were his only target? I was only in that room for a few minutes and I thought the meth fumes were going to give me cancer."

"That's a good point." Nick resumed his sturdy inspection of the ceiling. "I can't think of a single person I know here who he would know, though."

"Well, there is everyone who was at our wedding," Peter pointed out. "Sam was an opportunist. I don't think he would confine his extortion to the art world if he stumbled upon a good opportunity. And the desk clerk did say that Sam had at least one other visitor after you. A transwoman."

Nick frowned. "If he did, I didn't see her. And the only transwoman I can remember being at our wedding lives on the East Coast."

"Do you think she could have actually been a prostitute?" Peter asked.

"Maybe. That did seem to be the main activity occurring at the motel," Nick conceded.

"You know, I think we should go find that pimp." Peter pushed himself up onto his elbows. "The guy at motel reception said his name was Anthony. I'm thinking that if he really keeps track of everybody, he might have seen who Sam's guest was."

Nick regarded Peter for a long moment. Then he gently put his hand on Peter's shoulder and said, "Just to be sure, are you suggesting that you and I should go find and attempt to interrogate a violent pimp in a meth motel? And that we should do this when there are perfectly good police who we pay do perform dangerous tasks such as that?"

"When you put it like that it sounds foolhardy." Peter leaned over and kissed Nick's big hand. "But it's not like it's the middle of the night. By the time we'd get there it would be like eight in the morning. And it's really sunny."

"I don't think the weather is relevant. He's a professional criminal, not a vampire," Nick remarked. "Besides, we know that second person is obviously Donna."

"How do we know that?" Peter asked.

"Well, apart from the fact that she is frequently mistaken for being either a transwoman or a man in drag anytime she leaves New York City, she called me when she arrived in Bellingham on the midnight flight. She asked me if I'd spoken to Sam yet, and I told her that I had and where he was."

"Then she could easily have killed him," Peter said.

"She could have," Nick conceded. His expression fell. As much as Peter wanted to find an easy solution in Donna, he could see that Nick dreaded the notion that his agent and friend had committed the murder.

"But in that case, Donna still wouldn't have been the person Sam was waiting for," Peter said. "If he didn't know she'd flown in, there is still a third person."

"Yeah, that does follow," Nick said.

"So we do need to go speak with Anthony after all." Peter popped up to sitting.

Nick immediately pulled him back down into an embrace so much like a headlock that Peter feared he would soon receive a noogie. "No, that means you should tell Detective Patton all this and let her go talk to Anthony," Nick said. "We should be concentrating on figuring out where Donna went."

"I don't suppose she has her Find My Friends app turned on?"

"No such luck." Nick loosened his grip on Peter's head enough for Peter to wriggle free. "I'm going to take a shower. And I'm going to trust you not to sneak out and try to sleuth this Sam thing while I'm in there. People like this Anthony guy—they're the kind of people you don't even want to know your name."

Nick slid out from between the sheets, leaving Peter slightly deflated and stung.

Yes, he had flirted with the idea of sneaking out the moment Nick stepped into the shower, but Nick had obviously put the kibosh on that with only a mere, "I'm trusting you."

Clever bastard, Peter thought.

Much as he hated to give up on an unsolved question, he did concede that he should be phoning Patton. When he picked up his phone, though, he saw that Evangeline had already texted him three times this morning.

He considered texting back, but Evangeline had a tendency to write insanely long texts that took twice as long to tap out as it would to just speak them aloud. So he phoned her.

She picked up immediately. "Hi, Peter, how is it going? Is Nick still crazy?"

"No, he's fine now." Peter considered telling her about the murder and everything that had happened the previous day but decided, on balance, that he was not ready to talk about it at this time. So he just said, "What's up?"

"Well, I wanted your opinion about whether or not to tell Skye she's being a bigot."

Peter blinked and asked, "Who is Skye?"

"The woman who cuts my hair. She works at Transcendence."

"I don't know what that is." Peter could only assume that it was a location, rather than a statement about Skye's interior emotional state.

"The hotel and spa down by the bay. The one with the warm-stone massage. It's on the way to your house."

"Right." Peter closed his eyes and lay back. Normally he would have taken some evasive action to avoid hearing the entire story about Evangeline's hairdresser, but now he welcomed the distraction. "So why do you think Skye's being a bigot?"

"I was down there getting an oil treatment yesterday, and this transperson came into the spa, and Skye got really prickly when she went to use the ladies' room," Evangeline said. "She—Skye—was going to go and stop her, and I was like, 'who cares, let her go,' and Skye was saying it wasn't fair to the other customers, who might feel uncomfortable. But I don't think they would have been. She—the lady—was really convincing."

"Then how did you know she was a transperson?"

"She was just too tall, you know? And wore high heels too. I swear she was, like, seven feet tall and wearing designer clothes. Then after this lady came out of the bathroom, she started asking about the treatments, and Skye got even weirder because normally customers aren't wearing any clothes, right? It's not like Skye doesn't give massages to men and women both. I couldn't figure out what her deal was; then I realized that she must just be really bigoted." Evangeline paused, then took a deep breath and said, "I find this disappointing."

"Yeah, I can see how you would."

"And I'm disappointed in myself because I should have said something to Skye when I was there. What if Skye scared the lady off with her weirdness? I feel like a bad queer ally."

"You're not a bad queer ally," Peter said. "It's not like Skye refused to help her and you didn't intercede, right?"

"I guess not," Evangeline said. "But I think I'm still going to say something to Skye—after I'm not so mad."

"You know, you're the second person in forty-eight hours who has mentioned seeing a non-local transperson. Did you actually see her without her clothes on?"

"No, she was just asking what was available."

"Was her hair blonde?"

"You guessed it. And she was really gorgeous. Like a model. My theory is that Skye was just jealous of her beauty, you know," Evangeline said. "Even though she was in her fifties. I think if she'd been twenty years younger, she could have been a Bond Girl. Do you know that one of them was a transperson too?"

"I think I did know that," Peter mumbled. It couldn't be Donna, could it? Could she really have only fled two miles before pulling into a spa? What kind of disorganized thinking was that? "So did you happen to hear this lady's name?"

"Why?" Bewilderment sounded through Evangeline's voice; then she said, "Oh my God, is this another one of those things where you're trying to solve a murder? Is she a murderer?"

"I don't know yet." How Evangeline made the wild leaps of logic that she did still amazed Peter.

"She's not going to try and kill Nick like the last one, is she?"

"No, I don't think she's a murderer, but I really need to talk to her." Then, as he hung up, he walked straight to the bathroom. "I think I've found Donna. Do you want me to phone the cops, or do you want to go over and talk to her with me?"

After a short silence Nick replied, "Are you actually inviting me to help you interrogate her?"

"I thought you might want to be there," Peter said. Embarrassment crept up on him. "I guess I should call the police."

"No, I'm touched, really," Nick said. "Also, just this once I'd prefer it if we waited to include the cops. Let me get dressed and we'll go together."

Chapter Seven

Transcendence Hotel and Day Spa sat on the edge of a bluff overlooking Bellingham Bay. It was small for a hotel, having only three stories, with the ground level taken up entirely by a restaurant and spa facilities, but Transcendence was by far the most upscale place in Bellingham to have a hot-stone massage followed immediately by a cocktail. The tasteful beige interior, with its sleek modern lines, reminded Peter of the kind of place a science-fiction film hero would go to have his synthetic body refurbished by a combination of lasers and Japanese mysticism.

He'd only visited Transcendence once, to interview a minor local celebrity while she had her pedicure. For that reason he knew his way around the interior of the spa.

As they entered the building, the clerk at the reception desk called out a quiet, "Good afternoon."

Nick started to drift toward the desk, probably to ask if Donna was there. But Peter knew that would never work. He caught Nick's hand firmly and pulled him back toward the entrance to the spa area.

"Right through here, baby," he said, putting on a voice so camp that Nick almost tripped in confusion. "You're going to love it!"

Peter hustled Nick through the doors and was immediately met by another receptionist. This one was younger and wore a not-quite-nurse-like sleeveless coat. She had dreadlocks and a full sleeve of tattoos that appeared to show the entire marine ecosystem of the Pacific Northwest. Here was an otter—there an orca. Various bivalves and anemones clustered around her bicep, on which resided the red tentacles of the giant Pacific octopus.

This woman could be none other than Skye, friend to sea creatures, bathroom vigilante.

"Skye, right?" Peter said before she could rouse herself to say a word. "I'm Evangeline's friend, Peter. I'm looking for my friend—tall woman, blonde hair?"

"Oh, right," Skye said. Panic widened her eyes slightly. "She's in the mud room. Do you want me to tell her you're here?"

"We'll just go in," Peter said.

"But you can't—"

"Is there anyone else in there?"

"No," Skye said. "But you still can't go in. It's private."

"Then I'm sure she won't mind," Peter said, airily waving Skye's protest aside as he headed for the mud room located at the end of the hall. "Come on, Nick."

Peter's plan hinged on one thing—that he could get in the room with Donna before security could get there. Because no way was Skye going to try and physically stop him and Nick, and Donna would not want to cause a ruckus or have the cops called—not now.

Peter glanced back in time to see Skye make a beeline for the front desk.

"Hurry up," he told Nick.

"Are you always this pushy?"

"Only when I'm catching a killer. Or getting a story," Peter said.

"So most of the time?"

"Yeah, I guess so," Peter said. "Here it is." He pushed the door open.

Inside, the room was small, dim, and smelled vaguely of dank seaside and eucalyptus oil. On a raised bed lay a bundle of white sheets that looked like a massive cocoon. From one end a human head emerged. The eyes on that head glared at Peter with shock and fear.

He wasted no time crossing to Donna and kneeling down beside her, Nick close on his heels. Seeing Nick, Donna grew even more agitated but said nothing.

"I'm not going to call the cops yet," Peter whispered. "But you better have a good explanation for running out on me yesterday."

The door burst open, and the front-desk clerk entered in a flounce, her fuchsia silk scarf billowing behind her like a cape. A middle-aged security guard followed behind, wearing a generic gray rent-a-cop uniform. Skye trailed in last, plainly reluctant to engage in any kind of conflict. The security guard pulled in to the lead, making straight for Nick, mistaking him for the architect of this invasion.

"I'm sorry, sir. This area is off-limits." The guard stopped well out of Nick's reach.

"I'm afraid I'm the one who has to apologize," Donna said from her place on the table. "I asked them to come meet me here. We have some business to discuss, and I won't be in this area for long. Thank you so much for coming to check on me, but that will be all I need for now."

The security guard glanced back to the front-desk clerk, clearly the decision-maker for this delegation of employees. She looked to be about fifty years old. Her expertly dyed blonde hair and chunky gold jewelry told Peter she probably worked at the hotel spa for a discount while her husband brought in the real money.

Nonetheless her presence was formidable. The disbelief on her face could have been understood by scientists observing her via a telescope mounted on the International Space Station. However, Peter could also see in her a deeply ingrained streak of customer service. She didn't need to believe that Donna had summoned Nick and Peter—her instinct to please the guest would ensure compliance with Donna's dismissal.

"We usually don't allow guests in the treatment rooms, but since you're traveling, we can make an exception," she said. Then she withdrew, pulling the other two along in her wake.

Peter waited until the door closed completely to turn his attention back to Donna.

The woman looked aged and stricken. Having her face smeared with drying gray mud and her hair wrapped in a severe, turban-like towel didn't help soften her appearance.

"I'm going to get right to the point," Peter said, keeping his voice low. "Did you kill Sam?"

Donna's eyes bugged at the question. "No! Are you crazy?"

"Then why did you run?" Peter asked.

Donna stared at him a long time, chewing at her lip like a child working out a hard math problem. Finally Nick sighed and said, "You thought I did, didn't you?"

"Yes," she finally said. "Yes, I thought you might have. You had a good reason, right? That's why I'm getting this mud wrap."

"So let me get this straight—you suspected Nick might have murdered your boyfriend, so you fled to a spa for a mud wrap?" Peter demanded. "How is that the next logical step?"

"It wasn't the next step," Donna said, rolling her eyes. "I checked into this hotel and looked through Sam's laptop. Then, once I found out Nick hadn't killed him, I came down here for a mud wrap and to try and come up with a plan to get us all out of this mess with our reputations intact. And just so you know, Sam isn't my boyfriend anymore. We broke up two weeks ago. Also I really felt the need to detox after being surrounded by all this stress and forest fires."

Peter looked to Nick, who turned and pulled up the stool.

"There's nothing we can do about the forest fires," Peter said.

Donna turned her head slightly toward Nick. "I'm sorry I suspected you. But you don't know what I've been through in the last two weeks. It's been an absolute nightmare."

"It's okay. I obviously suspected you as well," Nick said with a shrug. "So I'm sorry too."

Peter didn't know that they should all be kissing and making up just yet.

"Why don't you start from when you broke up with Sam," Peter suggested.

"That's when this all started, right?"

"No, it started the day before I broke up with him, when I found out he had blackmailed one of my clients." Donna dropped her voice even lower. "Please believe me when I say I had no idea this was going on at all. I feel like a complete idiot." Tears rolled sideways, down Donna's face.

"How did you find out?" Nick asked gently.

"The estate of a former client contacted me about some commission fees that had been made to me that I didn't know existed," Donna said, sniffing. "That's the thing about blackmail, right? You need a way to launder the money—especially when it's a lot of money. I said that I had never received these payments, but they sent me digital images of the cancelled checks. These checks were going into a joint account that Sam had set up when we started living together two years ago. The reason we'd done it is so we could transfer money easily into this third account for our household expenses, and then set up automatic payments for things like the rent and cable bill so neither of us would have to be nagging the other one for money or spending a lot of time writing checks. I thought it was an excellent idea, and I just paid my portion into the account and let the finance robots handle the details."

Peter had to admit the idea sounded pretty good to him as well, as he constantly forgot to pay every sort of bill and more or less relied on Nick to ensure utilities like gas and electricity continued regularly at their home.

"I'm so stupid," Donna said. "You always hear stories of these women who just sign their name on a bank account and then get cleaned out by some man. I'm so screwed."

"So Sam stole from you as well?" Peter asked.

"No," she said. "What he did was funnel hundreds of thousands of dollars of blackmail payments through an account with my name on it. I don't know what I'm going to tell the IRS."

"Surely they wouldn't make you pay back taxes on your ex-boyfriend's blackmail scheme?" Peter said.

"But that would mean revealing that the blackmail had occurred." Nick rolled to the counter, pulled a tissue out of a container, rolled back to Donna's side, and carefully dabbed away Donna's tears.

"Thanks, Nick," she said, sniffing.

They really should be unwrapping her, Peter thought, but then maybe somehow the wrap really was helping her, hugging her like a swaddled baby. Maybe the mud wrap was the only thing keeping Donna together—while simultaneously working to detox her skin. Unfortunately, there was no Dead Sea mud strong enough to remove the toxic influence of Sam.

"Why would you not want to reveal that Sam was a blackmailer?" Peter asked.

"Because to be blackmailed, a person has to have done something wrong." Nick sounded tired. "And in the art world no one wants to deal with someone who has been involved with anything shady. No pun intended."

"We are talking about my livelihood here. I might never work again," Donna said. "Not to mention that there's a chance Nick and I could end up in prison."

"But if we keep quiet, then Sam just keeps getting to control us all from beyond the grave. That isn't right," Peter protested. "And what about Detective Patton? If no one tells her what Sam was up to, how is she supposed to catch the murderer?"

Glancing between Nick and Donna, Peter could see that his audience didn't much care for finding justice for Sam at this moment and chose to take a different tactic.

"Regardless of Sam's crimes, our society has agreed that bashing a guy's brains out in a motel room is not an authorized method of conflict resolution. At the end of the day, there is still a murderer roaming around town. Who knows who he'll be offended by next?"

This almost got a glimmer of resignation from Donna, but then she shook her head.

Peter decided he had to go in for the kill. "And don't forget that obstruction of justice is also a crime that can result in jail time."

"Oh God!" Donna pressed her eyes closed.

"Sometimes there are no easy options." Nick gently daubed away her tears again. "So we've decided to take the book and the computer to the police?"

Donna took a deep breath and nodded.

"That's good," Nick said.

"Not that we have to do it right this second," Peter put in.

Both Donna and Nick stared at him, Donna stunned and Nick with the quiet resignation of a man who knew Peter too well.

"What do you mean?" Donna asked.

"All I'm saying is that we still have time to do damage control—at least about the accidental art fraud," Peter said. "I think we should call that collector who bought Nick's paintings and start a dialogue. If art is as much about reputation as you both say it is, then it would be better if this guy was in the loop rather than being publicly made to look like a fool."

"I agree," Nick said. "Presuming he's still alive and still in possession of the paintings."

Peter hadn't thought of that. Art was a commodity after all. If the fake de Kamps had changed hands, there would be no way to mitigate the damage to Donna's reputation.

"Well, is he?" Peter asked Donna.

"Yes, very much so," Donna said. "I saw him at an auction last week, actually. His name is Wentworth Simmons-Smythe. British father, Cantonese mother. Everyone calls him Shau. He's a bigwig at HSBC."

Seeing Nick's expression of blank incomprehension, Peter said, "It's a bank."

"Oh, right," Nick said.

"Wentworth lives in Hong Kong now in this fantastic house on the Peak. Sam and I had dinner with him the October after your wedding. That's where Sam saw the misattributed de Kamps and made the connection between Nick's figural style and those paintings." Donna heaved a shuddering, tearful sigh. "Sam had a really fine eye for art."

"If only he had used it for good instead of evil," Peter said.

Donna nodded, then said, "All right. I'm ready to go."

"One more thing," Peter said. "You told us you found out Nick hadn't killed Sam by looking through Sam's laptop."

"Right."

"What made you think that?"

"There weren't any payments from Nick on the account," Donna said.

"But that wouldn't mean anything," Peter countered. "Maybe Sam tried it out and Nick killed him right away rather than making the first payment, then took the check back."

"Whose side are you on?" Nick asked.

"Just sayin'," Peter replied.

"Absolutely not." Donna shook her head with slow certainty. "Nick would never kill in rage. He's just too cold-blooded. He held off asking you to marry him for years just to let you get the man-points of having been the one to propose."

"Really?" Peter looked sharply to Nick, who gave a non-committal shrug. Peter continued, "Wait, does that mean that he gets the man-points retroactively?"

"Are you actually caring about that now?" Donna gave a look sharp enough to pierce his ears. "Anyway, Nick is patient. He'd have found a way to lure Sam to a secluded area and shot him execution-style."

Nick gave a rueful smile and shook his head. "You two make me out to be so much more dramatic than I actually am."

"Well, what did you say when you went to the motel room?" Donna asked.

"I told him I was going to go to the police and accuse him of extortion," Nick replied. "And he said, 'I very much doubt that,' and that was it. What did *you* say to him?"

"First I asked him why he was staying in such a dump, and he said he was using the motel room to conduct some interviews with people who didn't want to be seen with him in public," Donna said.

"How implausible is that?" Peter asked aloud. Both Donna and Nick glared at him. "I mean, the smell was just choking in there."

"I know. I would have thought he was cheating on me, but no self-respecting person would take any of their clothes off in that dump," Donna said. Then, wincing, "How pathetic is it that I still care if he was cheating or not?"

"Do you think he was?" Peter asked in a matter-of-fact way.

"No!" Donna said, then more quietly, "I don't know…do I?"

"Just because Sam was a blackmailer doesn't mean he was also a cheater," Nick put in. He gave Peter a quelling look that Peter felt was accurately preemptive. The chances of Sam being faithful to Donna while conducting a massive blackmail scheme were negligible. But, Peter supposed, it did no good to twist the knife.

"No, he definitely wasn't cheating," Donna said. "He was so surprised when I arrived—but he seemed happy. He said he'd found a way to get the money I would need to pay the IRS back-taxes on the money he'd put through my account. He wanted to get back together."

"I bet he did," Peter mumbled.

"What did you tell him?" Nick asked.

"I said I'd think about it," Donna said. She closed her eyes in misery. "I really liked him."

Peter refrained from pointing out that sociopaths generally presented themselves as likable people, though it hurt him to do so.

Fortunately he was saved from looking at Donna by his phone buzzing to inform him that he had a text from Travis.

Got away from the brewery early today. Do you mind if I drop by to have a look at the photos for the article?

Peter supposed he should, for the sake of his continuing employment, actually make some attempt to deliver his *Hamster* article after all.

Sure. Can you come by my place?

Sounds good.

As Peter typed the address he heard Nick speaking to Donna in soothing tones.

"So I need to go meet Travis from the brewery to get this article I'm writing finished," Peter said. "If I come back to pick you up in an hour, do you think you'll be ready to go to the police?"

"Are you talking to me or Nick?" Donna asked.

"Either," Peter replied.

"Well, I need to get out of this wrap, then shower and—" Donna began, but Nick cut her off.

"We'll be ready," he said firmly. "Swing by and get us on your way back."

Chapter Eight

When Peter made it to the end of the drive, he saw that Travis was already parked in front of the house and waiting for him in the front seat of his big white utility truck. Travis didn't seem to see him at first. He sat staring forward. He didn't even startle when Peter knocked on the side of the truck. He seemed even more tired than the day before, though that hardly seemed possible.

"You doing okay?" Peter asked.

"I was looking at your house. I haven't been here in a long time." Travis stopped, lost in a reverie. Then suddenly he pulled himself out of it. "I didn't recognize the address when you gave it to me. I helped build this place."

Just when you think the City of Subdued Excitement can't get any smaller, Peter thought unceremoniously.

Aloud he said, "Oh, yeah?"

"Yeah. Did you know the girders holding it in place sink forty-five feet into the rock?" he asked.

"I think Nick mentioned it. Was that what you did?"

"Oh, heck no." Travis gave a laugh. "I was only a teenager trying to make some money. So he set me up with this summer job. I stayed with my aunt in town and hauled bags of concrete and lumber and sheetrock for minimum wage—$5.15 per hour. It was the first time I worked with grown-up men. Those guys spent all day smoking cigarettes and talking about cars and women. And sometimes one of them would sneak me a beer— my first one! If that guy only knew he started me on my current career path!"

"Sounds like you had a lot of fun," Peter remarked. His own first job had been as a bagger in a grocery store. He'd been fired within a week for sassing a customer.

"I did," he said. "I never saw it when it was complete. I had to leave to go back home because of a family emergency. It's a beautiful place."

"Well, why don't you come in, and I'll show you what we did with the interior. Hopefully you won't be too disappointed."

Travis followed Peter inside, wiping his feet out of polite habit though the drought had ensured there was nothing but fine dust to track in. Peter offered a cold drink, which Travis declined, so they went directly to Peter's study, where Peter kept his big desktop.

"I only saw the first couple of pictures, so I haven't actually decided on one yet," Peter remarked as they waited for the thing to boot up. "We'll be able to look side by side on this screen, so it should be easy to choose."

Travis nodded. "I just want to make sure the pictures project the right image for our brand."

"And don't include any liquor-board violations?" Peter asked, grinning.

Travis didn't seem amused.

"I know it sounds like a joke, but it's a big deal," he said.

"I really do get that," Peter assured him. "We at the *Hamster* are trying to promote local businesses, not stamp out good times at private functions."

Peter clicked on his mail program and downloaded the photos Shane sent him.

The bartender had sent what he felt were the best ten. The first two showed happy people that Peter did not know, drinking. The third included an attractive woman in the group.

"I think I like this one," Travis said. "Let's go with that."

"It is good, but you can only see a corner of your logo," Peter remarked. "I'd like to get you all the publicity I can."

He clicked on the next image and saw that to spite his best efforts, Shane had included a shot of the lady brewers dancing on the bar after all. He glanced to Travis, who had stiffened the moment the .jpg opened.

"Well, this one's definitely out," Peter remarked.

"Right. Pass on this one," Travis said.

"It's too bad, though. It's a fantastic photo." Peter lingered over the picture. Shane truly showed himself to be a gifted phone-photographer. The framing of the women kicking up their heels—the wonderful way the corner of the bar gave depth of field via use of two-point perspective toward a vanishing point located somewhere in the happy crowd.

Peter was just about to go on to the next picture when he caught sight of Travis's face way down in the lower left corner of the frame. He was about to point it out when some instinct or sixth sense stopped him—or perhaps it was common sense.

Over the years of amateur sleuthing, Peter had come into contact with several murderers and because of that had developed a healthy appreciation of the average killer's reaction to having his innocence called into question. The reaction was never good.

Not that Travis was definitely a killer.

On the contrary, there could be any number of reasons that he'd been sitting at a table with murder victim Sam on the night Sam had died that didn't include being provoked into killing a known blackmailer.

But in Peter's experience, it was better to wait until he was not alone with a man in a secluded cliffside mansion to bring up such delicate and awkward discussions. He quickly clicked on the next picture. This time the girls were out of the frame, but Travis's face was even more obvious in the crowd.

"Nothing much to focus on in this one." Peter kept his voice cool. "And still no whole logo."

"Right," Travis said, also seeming calm. "We should just go with the third picture. A partial logo is fine."

Part of Peter wanted to give in, but another part knew that Travis already knew a photograph of himself with a murder victim existed on this computer as well as on Shane's phone. If Travis really were a murderer, he would be beginning to panic now, and that was not good. Panicking was the sort of reaction that never ended well. He had to get Travis out the door believing that Peter did not suspect him.

"There are five more, though," Peter said. "I bet Shane got at least one good one."

Peter clicked forward. In this photo Travis's face took up a full quarter of the screen and could not be ignored. The picture made it clear that Sam was not sitting next to Travis by accident. Sam was leaning over and smiling while Travis's expression showed revulsion and contempt.

At this point Peter knew he had to make a choice. Travis's face was too obvious not to remark on, but did Travis know Peter even knew Sam? Could he play it off?

"Not the best picture of you." Peter forced himself to glance over at Travis. In that moment he understood two important things: Travis knew Peter knew exactly who Sam was and what Travis had done.

In the weird temporal elongation caused by extreme terror, Peter understood that Travis's hesitation meant that Sam's murder had been a crime of passion and that Travis had most likely never killed anyone before that. He'd never been in the position of having his crime discovered. He didn't know what to do. Travis existed at a crossroads of conscience where he would either step back from the sudden rage-fueled violence that must have been Sam's murder, or he would embrace willful homicide by killing Peter to protect himself.

Peter, on the other hand, had been in this situation several times before and knew his own safety depended on what Travis decided to do next.

He couldn't run for the door—by far the smartest option—because he had to get past Travis to get there.

As casually as he could, he stood up and walked to the window, out of Travis's easy reach. He leaned back against the wall, hooked his thumbs in his belt loops, and said, "So, want to talk about it?"

"What do you mean?" Sweat beaded Travis's brow. His eyes darted around the room.

Probably looking for a fire extinguisher or other blunt object, Peter thought grimly.

"What did Sam Powers say to you?"

"I don't know who you're talking about," Travis said.

"He's the man who is talking to you in the picture on the screen." Peter kept his voice calm and low. "Look, I know he wasn't a good guy. He tried to extort money from my husband, Nick, on the very same day that picture was taken. So if he was talking to you and he looked that happy, it can't have been about anything good."

Travis blinked in confusion. Warring emotions flashed across his face like sudden lightning illuminating the clouds in a summer thunderstorm, showing the turmoil roiling within.

While Travis wrestled with his own conflicting desires, Peter's mind raced ahead.

The next few minutes depended on him getting Travis to see reason, and the best way was to get Travis on his side. So what was the connection between Sam and Travis?

In a flash of insight Peter realized it had to be this house: Travis had worked on this house but had been called away because of a family emergency… All at once Peter knew—or thought he did. He would have preferred to do some research to confirm his theory, but sadly there was no time. He went ahead and spoke anyway.

"Your father was the architect hired to build this place, wasn't he? You're Monroe Addison's son," Peter said.

Instantly, Travis's eyes widened and his breathing quickened—not the reaction Peter had been hoping for.

"He didn't do those things!" Travis shouted. "He was a good man!"

"I believe you," Peter said. "I really do." Once again Peter pondered jumping out the window, but the eighty-foot drop to the ocean would certainly kill him, whereas if he had to fight it out with Travis, he still had a chance of living. Especially if he could find a weapon.

Great, now I'm the one looking for a fire extinguisher.

Though the thought gave him an idea.

"Did Sam attack you?" he asked. "Did he get you to go to the motel with him and then try something?"

"He didn't attack me," Travis said.

Good, at least we're talking now.

"But he said something to you," Peter tried again. "About your father?"

"It's none of your business," Travis said.

"Right. I get that." Peter held up his hands. "I'm just thinking that if he tried to do something to you, like extort money or threaten you, then he would have provoked you by committing a crime against you. That's a plausible argument for manslaughter. If you get a good lawyer and tell everyone what happened, you might only to go to jail for a few years. Or none at all, depending on what happened."

"Nobody is going to believe me," Travis said, standing. His eyes narrowed slightly, so that he looked almost sleepy. Peter felt his heart begin to hammer, his pulse sounding in his ears like a drum.

He had to try to keep Travis from sinking into a void of homicidal paranoia.

"Travis, I will believe you. I swear. And so will Detective Patton. I know her. And I know what a rat Sam Powers was. We have proof of how he blackmailed a lot of other people, so it's not like you'll be alone. Please tell me what he said at the brewery. Did it have to do with your father?"

Travis began to tremble, and Peter's hands shook as well. Here was the moment where he might fight for his life. Then Travis buried his face in his hands.

"He tried to sell it to me."

"Sell what?" Peter could barely remain standing for the relief coursing through him.

"The evidence that proves my father was innocent. Sam had trophy photographs taken by the real rapist, of him assaulting the victim who identified my father. And he had the ski mask the real rapist wore."

"How in hell did he get those? Did Sam commit that crime?"

"No, but he knew where the evidence was hidden." Travis sniffed. "One of the victims was Sam's sister. How sick is that? You see your sister's rapist and know who he is, and then you decide that what you should do is blackmail him? But the real rapist was their uncle, so I guess the family was just fucked up beyond belief."

"Sounds like it," Peter said.

Travis sagged back in the chair. All tension had gone from him. "Sam and I come from the same town in Oregon. During that summer that I was here working on this house, there was a string of assaults against young women, including Janelle Powers, Sam's sister. My father was accused and convicted, and he hanged himself in his cell. That's why I was called back to Oregon."

"But why didn't he fight it?" Even as Peter asked the question, he thought he knew—an accusation like rape stays with you your entire life. Even innocent, Monroe Addison would have been ruined.

"I don't know. It broke him, I guess," Travis said. "Sam's uncle was rich and agreed to pay for Sam to go back east to a college so long as he didn't tell."

"So what changed? Did they have a falling-out?"

"The uncle died this year, so Sam, being the sick, psycho fucker he is, decided he could resell the evidence to me. I told him I wanted to see the pictures, and that's when we went to the motel. He had them all sealed up in plastic bags. All this evidence that should have been at the trial but that he'd kept so he could make an easy buck. In the end I wrote him a check for what he wanted."

"And?"

"And then he said, 'It's a pleasure doing business with you,' and I just kind of snapped." Travis looked stricken, his face contorted in horror. "I didn't know I was going to do it. I didn't plan to, but he looked so happy... It was like I wasn't even inside my own body. After it was over I took the check and the evidence and went home, and that's when I realized it." Travis's eyes brimmed with tears.

"What?"

"That I couldn't show it to anyone. There was blood on the bags, and where was I going to say I got it from? So he won, right? Even from the fucking grave!"

"Not if you tell your side." Peter edged forward, still wary but growing bolder. "Then everyone will know what really happened. The fact is that a guy like Sam's uncle—a serial rapist—will almost certainly have had more victims. This evidence might bring closure to more people than your father."

"I'm scared," Travis whispered, head hanging down. "What will happen to my family—the brewery?"

"You can face those challenges as they come," Peter said. "But if you take that first step, the next ones will be easier."

"I suppose," Travis said. He wiped his eyes, sniffed, and met Peter's gaze again. "Can I trouble you for a drink of water?"

"Sure." Peter left him in the room and walked casually to the kitchen. He didn't know what was going to happen. Would Travis destroy his computer and try to run? Would there be a sudden gunshot as Travis took the same path as his father and ended it all? Peter hoped not.

But he heard neither squealing tires nor any loud bang. As he approached his office, tumbler of water in hand, he heard only the sound of gentle snoring.

"It's not really that unusual for a person to fall asleep after confessing," Detective Patton told Peter an hour later. They stood together on Peter's front porch, watching as Travis walked calmly into custody.

"Killing another human being is incredibly traumatic and stressful," Patton continued. "And then keeping it a secret is even worse. He probably hadn't slept in forty-eight hours."

"What's going to happen to him?" Peter asked. He didn't know Travis well, and he understood that even though Sam had been complete scum, he was still a human being. But he couldn't help hoping that Travis could somehow be absolved of the crime.

"Depending on the plea, he could get as little as two years," she said.

"If only he'd just left," Peter said, "none of this would have happened."

"If only he'd called us instead of going to buy so-called evidence at all," Detective Patton countered. "I'm glad you managed to get through this without an armed confrontation, though. Very unusual for you."

"I know, right?" Peter said, smiling. "It's like I can learn and grow from my previous mistakes."

"Maybe someday you'll become knowledgeable enough to leave investigations to the police entirely," she remarked.

"Maybe," Peter said. "I guess we'll have to wait and see."

Epilogue

Wentworth Simmons-Smythe arrived at the Castle at Wildcat Cove in a bright-orange Lamborghini convertible he'd driven across the border from Vancouver, BC, where he kept a vacation house. Tall, slim, and silver-haired, he reminded Peter of what the character of Sephiroth from *Final Fantasy* might look like if he grew up, got a haircut, and found a new career in investment banking. Though he must have been in his late sixties, he moved nimbly around the property, trailing along as Nick gave the basic tour. Wentworth's cream-colored linen suit sharply contrasted Nick's worn jeans, tight-fitting T-shirt, and boots.

Peter waited in the living room, fidgeting and trying not to fuss over the soft furnishings while he waited for Nick to finally bring Wentworth inside.

Since Sam's death, Donna had retired, and Peter had pitched and sold a book detailing Sam's whole sordid life as a blackmailer to the very same publisher who'd bought Sam's exposé. The advance wasn't massive, but he'd still tendered his notice at the *Hamster*, which his editor, Doug, had not accepted, preferring to call it a sabbatical.

"*You'll come back to me,*" he'd said, puffing away at a fat, legalized blunt. "*You'll get bored sitting in that big house all alone.*"

He'd thought of telling Doug that he wouldn't be alone—that Nick would be here with him, not to mention the cat—but decided not to burst Doug's bubble after all.

Peter gazed out at the far islands, still partially concealed by the now-familiar haze of smoke. On the far horizon he thought he saw some darkening clouds, but he couldn't be too sure. The smoke colored everything in a murky gray.

Donna's last act as Nick's art rep had been to negotiate this meeting between Wentworth and Nick, to try and come to some sort of agreement about compensation for Nick's paintings that had been fraudulently sold as de Kamps. Wentworth had said that in this day of easily-recovered emails and phone messages he preferred to speak with Nick about the paintings in person.

They'd been outside for an hour despite the heat and poor air quality. For all Peter knew, Nick was trading their house for his freedom.

Twenty minutes later, the door opened, and Nick ushered Wentworth in, smiling casually as he said, "And here it is."

Peter stood, puzzled to be referred to as "it," before understanding that Nick had gestured to the massive painting currently presiding over their living room in all its abstract, pornographic splendor. For a fleeting second Peter hoped that Wentworth would fall into the category of people who didn't recognize the naked male form portrayed in its seven-foot glory, then realized he should be hoping for the opposite.

Wentworth gasped, hands to his mouth, then let out a soft chuckle. He observed it for a full minute, his eye moving around the canvas with increasing delight. Finally he turned and, catching sight of Peter, said, "Oh, I'm sorry. It's just magnificent. You must be Peter Fontaine."

His clipped British accent did nothing to dispel Peter's impression that Wentworth might be a reformed supervillain…

Or at least Peter hoped he had been reformed.

He took Wentworth's extended hand, smiled, and said, "And you must be Mr. Simmons-Smythe."

"Please, call me Shau. All my friends do." He gave Peter a wink, which startled Peter considerably both in its conspiratorial nature and sheer charm. He then turned back to the painting, admiring it while Peter wondered what beverage a person offered an ultrarich art collector your husband had accidentally scammed. He decided to leave it open.

"Can I get you anything to drink?" Peter asked.

"I'd love a cola if you have one," Shau replied.

"Coming right up." Peter adjourned to the kitchen to find a tumbler and ice in an attempt to make the canned cola look more classy. He set the drink down on the coffee table and sat back on the sofa.

He shot a glance to Nick, who gave a slight shrug, then took a couple of steps closer to their guest.

"Well," Nick said. "Do you think it will do?"

"Oh yes." Shau glanced back at Peter. "So long as the current owner agrees."

"Agrees…?" Peter glanced between Nick's rueful smile and Shau's kindly but somehow penetrating gaze.

"Nick and I have decided that he'll let me have the remainder of the set of figurals he painted ten years ago as an apology for the signature mix-up," Shau said. "But I'd heard so much about this new painting from the nefarious Sam that I wanted to offer on it too. Nick informs me that it belongs to you."

"It's my wedding present," Peter blurted out, without thinking.

"So you won't part with it?" Shau pulled a slight frown.

"I'd rather not," Peter said.

"Would you consider letting it take a little vacation, then?" Shau asked, seating himself opposite Peter. He took a sip of his Coke. "I'm helping to curate a touring show of homoerotic pieces, and I would love for it to be included. It would help Nick rise to the next level, I think, for people to see this piece. And it has such a charming love story. Prints would sell like mad. I'd certainly have bought one when I was a student."

Peter glanced to Nick, who gave a small, silent nod.

"All right. And when I publish my book? What then?" Peter began cautiously. "Donna said you wanted to discuss that with me."

"Yes, your book." Shau took a thoughtful drink of his cola. "It's absolutely true that I've been pestering Donna for years to broker the sale of the rest of the paintings in that set. So I think it's fair to say that Nick and I were already in negotiations for the sale of his paintings at the time of Sam's unfortunate death. Don't you?"

"Yes." Relief swept through Peter. Shau was going to let it go. He would not press fraud charges so long as Nick gave him the paintings he'd wanted for so long and Peter allowed him to save face. They were going to be okay. Peter gazed out the massive picture windows at the far islands, catching sight of a small blip in his field of vision.

Then came another and another. They were, Peter realized, raindrops slapping against the glass. He hadn't seen them in so long, he'd forgotten what they looked like. But as soon as he thought this, more droplets came in droves, battering the dusty glass.

As Shau rushed outside to put the top up on his car, Nick joined Peter by the window.

"I can't believe it's over," Nick said.

"What? The investigation?"

"The secret about the paintings," Nick clarified.

"Do you feel sleepy?" Peter asked. He couldn't help himself.

"Somewhat," Nick replied in a thoughtful tone. "But also energized. And kind of worried."

"About what?" Peter leaned into him.

"You getting bored," Nick said. His quiet tone conveyed his complete candor. "There's nothing else to discover about me now. No mystery left."

"You're right, I guess," Peter said. Nick glanced at him with sharp worry, as if confirming a suspicion about him. Peter continued, "Unless you count your entire future. Then there's what—fifty years or so of material?"

"Only fifty?" Nick asked.

"Okay, thirty if we're going to go by averages." Peter laced his fingers with Nick's. "But I suppose that will have to do."

About the Author

Nicole Kimberling is a novelist and the senior editor at Blind Eye Books. Her first novel, *Turnskin*, won the Lambda Literary Award. Other works include the Bellingham Mystery Series, set in the Washington town where she resides with her wife of thirty years. She is also the creator and writer of *Lauren Proves Magic Is Real!*, a serial fiction podcast, which explores the day-to-day case files of Special Agent Keith Curry, supernatural food inspector.